Stephen Baxter was born in 1957. Raised in Liverpool, he has a mathematics degree from the University of Cambridge and a Ph.D from Southampton. He sold his first short stories to *Interzone* in 1986 and was a prizewinner in the Writers of the Future contest. His first novel, *Raft*, was published in 1991, to great acclaim. *The Time Ships* is his sixth novel. He is married and lives in Buckinghamshire.

Praise for Stephen Baxter's books:

The Time Ships

'*The Time Ships* is the most outstanding work of imaginative fiction since Stapledon's *Last and First Men*, and it is the best possible contribution to *The Time Machine*'s centennial year. I'm almost tempted to say (I know this is blasphemy) that the sequel is better than the original. After all, it should be, with a hundred years of science and discovery for added inspiration . . . This book is the best evidence for reincarnation I've ever encountered. Welcome back, H.G. . . .'

ARTHUR C. CLARKE

'*The Time Ships* is a ripping yarn. Recommended' *SFX*

Ring

'*Ring* is a rare triumph. The book sends into free-fall the most awesome ideas in science fiction today . . . What makes these ideas assimilable is the prism of people through which they are refracted . . . good SF reveals the mortal host in the machine' *The Times*

'*Ring* recalls the most visionary moments of Wells and Clarke . . . constructs a human-scale drama out of the most far-reaching implications of current cosmological theory . . . makes E. E. Doc Smith look like a minimalist' *Locus*

'In *Ring* Baxter conveys the most up-to-date theories of quantum mechanics and cosmology without losing sight of the ultimate goal, that of telling a story . . . some of the best hard SF I've read this year and probably some of the best I've *ever* read'
Vector

Flux

'Arthur C. Clarke, Poul Anderson . . . Isaac Asimov and Robert Heinlein succeeded in doing it, but very few others. Now Stephen Baxter joins their exclusive ranks – writing science fiction in which the science is right, the author knowledgeable, and the extrapolations a sheer pleasure to read, admire, enjoy. The reaction is that which C.S. Lewis referred to when he described science fiction as the only genuine consciousness-expanding drug . . . Wonderful stuff! It is a rare thing to find such a good read'
HARRY HARRISON, *New Scientist*

'A highly original plot, well written and exciting'
Sunday Telegraph

Timelike Infinity

'*Timelike Infinity* is good science by someone who knows what he is talking about'
Sunday Telegraph

'Baxter fully integrates his concepts in a streamlined, engrossing drama with a nerve-rattling pace. Galaxy-spanning imagination, as outrageously cosmic in scope as any epic by Arthur C. Clarke or Greg Bear, is harnessed to a sleek, turbo-charged narrative pulsing with the urgency of countdown. Baxter is destined to be one of the genre leaders for the Nineties'
Starburst

Raft

'*Raft* polishes its ideas with such realistic brilliance you can see a whole civilization in it'
The Times

'*Raft* is fast paced, strong on suspense, efficiently written, and has moral weight, but it is the creation of a genuinely strange and believable new universe that Baxter excels . . . rigorous, vigorous SF at its enjoyable best'
LISA TUTTLE *Time Out*

'Almost perfect . . . *Raft* is very, very hard SF and it's great fun'
Interzone

Anti-Ice

'There is a breed of romance that nudges the what-is to the what-if. Stephen Baxter's *Anti-Ice* is one of the most compelling of these. A touch of improper amour and impeccable period detail makes all this alarmingly addictive'
The Times

'*Anti-Ice* is outrageous science-fictional entertainment, pulling out all the Vernian stops and playing dice (or is it chess?) with alternative world possibilities'
Vector

Voyager

STEPHEN BAXTER

Time Ships

Illustrated by Les Edwards

HarperCollins*Publishers*

Voyager
An Imprint of HarperCollins*Publishers*
77–85 Fulham Palace Road,
Hammersmith, London W6 8JB

This paperback edition 1995
1 3 5 7 9 8 6 4 2

First published in Great Britain by
HarperCollins*Publishers* 1995

ISBN 0 00 648012 8

Set in Baskerville

Printed in Great Britain by
HarperCollinsManufacturing Glasgow

To my wife Sandra,
and the memory of H.G.

Prologue

On the Friday morning after my return from futurity, I awoke long after dawn, from the deepest of dreamless sleeps.

I got out of bed and threw back the curtains. The sun was making his usual sluggish progress up the sky, and I remembered how, from the accelerated perspective of a Time Traveller, the sun had fair hopped across heaven! But now, it seemed, I was embedded in oozing time once more, like an insect in seeping amber.

The noises of a Richmond morning gathered outside my window: the hoof-steps of horses, the rattle of wheels on cobbles, the banging of doors. A steam tram, spewing out smoke and sparks, made its clumsy way along the Petersham Road, and the gull-like cries of hawkers came floating on the air. I found my thoughts drifting away from my gaudy adventures in time and back to a mundane plane: I considered the contents of the latest *Pall Mall Gazette*, and stock movements, and I entertained an anticipation that the morning's post might bring the latest *American Journal of Science*, which would contain some specula-tions of mine on the findings of A. Michelson and E. Morley on certain peculiarities of light, reported in that journal four years earlier, in 1887 . . .

And so on! The details of the everyday crowded into my head, and by contrast the memory of my

3

adventure in futurity came to seem fantastical – even absurd. As I thought it over now, it seemed to me that the whole experience had had something of a hallucinatory, almost dreamlike quality: there had been that sense of precipitate falling, the haziness of everything about time travel, and at last my plunge into the nightmarish world of A.D. 802,701. The grip of the ordinary on our imaginations is remarkable. Standing there in my pyjamas, something of the uncertainty which had, in the end, assailed me last night returned, and I started to doubt the very existence of the Time Machine itself! – despite my very clear memories of the two years of my life I had expended in the nuts and bolts of its construction, not to mention the two decades previous, during which I had teased out the theory of time travel from anomalies I had observed during my studies of physical optics.

I thought back over my conversation with my companions over dinner the evening before – somehow those few hours were far more vivid, now, than all the days I had spent in that world of futurity – and I remembered their mix of responses to my account: there had been a general enjoyment of a good tale, accompanied by dashes of sympathy or near-derision depending on the temperaments of individuals – and, I recalled, a near-universal scepticism. Only one good friend, who I shall call the Writer in these pages, had seemed to listen to my ramblings with any degree of sympathy and trust.

Standing by the window, I stretched – and my doubts about my memories took a jolt! The ache of my back was real enough, acute and urgent, as were the burning sensations in the muscles of my legs and arms: protests from the muscles of a no-longer-young man forced, against his practice, to exert himself. 'Well, then,' I argued with myself, 'if your trip into

4

the future was truly a dream – all of it, including that bleak night when you fought the Morlocks in the forest – where have these aches and pains come from? Have you been capering around your garden, perhaps, in a moonstruck delirium?'

And there, dumped without ceremony in a corner of my room, I saw a small heap of clothes: they were the garments I had worn to their ruin during my flight to the future, and which now were fit only to be destroyed. I could see grass stains and scorch marks; the pockets were torn, and I remembered how Weena had used those flaps of cloth as impromptu vases, to load up with the etiolated flowers of the future. My shoes were missing, of course – I felt an odd twinge of regret for the comfortable old house-shoes which I had borne unthinking into a hostile future, before abandoning them to an unimaginable fate! – and there, on the carpet, were the filthy, bloodstained remnants of my socks.

Somehow it was those socks – those comical, battered old socks! – whose rude existence convinced me, above anything else, that I was not yet insane: that my flight into the future had not been entirely a dream.

I must return to time, I saw; I must gather evidence that futurity was as real as the Richmond of 1891, to convince my circle of friends and my peers in my scientific endeavours – and to banish the last traces of my own self-doubt.

As I formed this resolve, suddenly I saw the sweet, empty face of Weena, as vivid as if she had been standing there before me. Sadness, and a surge of guilt at my own impetuosity, tore at my heart. Weena, the Eloi child-woman, had followed me to the Palace of Green Porcelain through the depths of the resurgent forest of that distant Thames valley, and had been lost in the confusion of the subsequent fire, and the bleak assaults of the Morlocks. I have always been a man to act first and allow my rational brain to catch up later! In my bachelor life, this tendency had never yet led anyone into serious danger except myself – but now, in my thoughtlessness and headlong rush, I had abandoned poor, trusting Weena to a grisly death in the shadows of that Dark Night of the Morlocks.

I had blood on my hands, and not just the ichor of those foul, degraded sub-men, the Morlocks. I determined I must make recompense – in whatever way I could – for my abominable treatment of poor, trusting Weena.

I was filled with resolve. My adventures, physical and intellectual, were not done yet!

I had Mrs Watchets run me a bath, and I clambered into it. Despite my mood of urgency, I took time to pamper my poor, battered bones; I noted with interest the blistered and scarred state of my feet, and the mild burns I had suffered to my hands.

I dressed quickly. Mrs Watchets prepared me breakfast. I dug into my eggs, mushrooms and tomatoes with vigour – and yet I found the bacon and sausages lying heavy in my mouth; when I bit into the thick meat, its juices, full of salt and oil, filled me with a faint disgust.

I could not help but remember the Morlocks, and the meat I had seen them consume at their foul repasts! My experiences had not dulled my appetite for mutton at dinner the previous evening, I recalled, but then my hunger had been so much greater. Could it be that a certain shock and disquietude, unravelling from my misadventures, were even now working through the layers of my mind?

But a full breakfast is my custom; for I believe that a good dose of peptone in the arteries early in the

day is essential for the efficient operation of the vigorous human machine. And today could become as
demanding a day as I had faced in my life. Therefore
I put aside my qualms and finished my plate, chewing
through my bacon with determination.

Breakfast over, I donned a light but serviceable
summer suit. As I think I mentioned to my companions at dinner the previous evening, it had become
evident to me during my plummeting through time
that winter had been banished from the world of
A.D. 802,701 – whether by natural evolution, geogonic
planning or the re-engineering of the sun himself I
could not say – and so I should have no need of
winter greatcoats and scarves in futurity. I donned a
hat, to keep the future sun from my pale English
brow, and dug out my stoutest pair of walking boots.

I grabbed a small knapsack and proceeded to
throw myself about the house, ransacking cupboards
and drawers for the equipment I thought I would
need for my second journey – much to the alarm of
poor, patient Mrs Watchets, who, I am sure, had long
since resigned my sanity to the mists of mythology! As
is my way, I was in a fever to be off, and yet I was
determined not to be quite so impetuous as the first
time, when I had travelled across eight thousand
centuries with no more protection than a pair of
house-shoes and a single box of matches.

I crammed my knapsack with all the matches I
could find in the house – in fact I dispatched Hillyer
to the tobacconist's to purchase more boxes. I packed
in camphor, and candles, and, on an impulse, a
length of sturdy twine, in case, stranded, I should
need to make new candles of my own. (I had little
conception of how one goes about such manufacture,
incidentally, but in the bright light of that optimistic
morning I did not doubt my ability to improvise.)

I took white spirit, salves, some quinine tabloids,

7

and a roll of bandage. I had no gun – I doubt if I should have taken it, even if I had possessed one, for what use is a gun when its ammunition is exhausted? – but I slipped my clasp-knife into my pocket. I packed up a roll of tools – a screwdriver, several sizes of spanner, a small hacksaw with spare blades – as well as a range of screws and lengths of nickel, brass and quartz bars. I was determined that no trivial accident befalling the Time Machine should strand me in any disjointed future, for want of a bit of brass: despite my transient plan to build a new Time Machine when my original was stolen by the Morlocks in 802,701, I'd seen no evidence in the decayed Upper-world that I should be able to find the materials to repair so much as a sheared screw. Of course the Morlocks had retained some mechanical aptitude, but I did not relish the prospect of being forced to negotiate with those bleached worms for the sake of a couple of bolts.

I found my Kodak, and dug out my flash trough. The camera was new loaded with a roll of a hundred negative frames on a paper-stripping roll. I remembered how damned expensive the thing had seemed when I had bought it – no less than twenty-five dollars, purchased on a trip to New York – but, if I should return with pictures of futurity, each of those two-inch frames would be more valuable than the finest paintings.

Now, I wondered, was I ready? I demanded advice of poor Mrs Watchets, though I would not tell her, of course, where I was intending to travel. That good woman – stolid, square, remarkably plain, and yet with a faithful and imperturbable heart – took a look inside my knapsack, crammed as it was, and she raised one formidable eyebrow. Then she made for my room and returned with spare socks and underwear, and – here I could have kissed her! – my pipe, a set of cleaners, and the jar of tobacco from my mantel.

Thus, with my usual mixture of feverish impatience and superficial intelligence – and with an unending reliance on the good will and common sense of others – I made ready to return into time.

Bearing my knapsack under one arm and my Kodak under the other, I made towards my laboratory, where the Time Machine waited. When I reached the smoking-room, I was startled to find that I had a visitor: one of my guests of the previous evening, and perhaps my closest friend – it was the Writer of whom I have spoken. He stood at the centre of the room in an ill-fitting suit, with his tie knotted about as rough as you could imagine, and with his hands dangling awkward by his side. I recalled again how, of the circle of friends and acquaintances whom I had gathered to serve as the first witnesses to my exploits, it was this earnest young man who had listened with the most intensity, his silence vibrant with sympathy and fascination.

I felt uncommon glad to see him, and grateful that he had come – that he had not shunned me as eccentric, as some might, after my performance of the evening before. I laughed, and, burdened as I was with sack and camera, I held out an elbow; he grasped the joint and shook it solemnly. 'I'm frightfully busy,' I said, 'with that thing in there.'

He studied me; I thought there was a sort of desperation to believe in his pale blue eyes. 'But is it not some hoax? Do you really travel through time?'

'Really and truly I do,' I said, holding his gaze as long as I could, for I wanted him to be convinced.

He was a short, squat man, with a jutting lower lip, a broad forehead, wispy sideboards, and rather ugly ears. He was young – about twenty-five, I believe, two decades younger than myself – yet his lank hair was already receding. His walk had a sort of bounce and he had a certain energy about him – nervous, like a plump bird's – but he always looked sickly: I know he suffered haemorrhages, from time to time, from a soccer-game kicking to the kidneys he had received when working as a teacher in some Godforsaken private school in Wales. And today his blue eyes, though tired, were filled, as ever, with intelligence and a concern for me.

My friend worked as a teacher – at that time, of pupils by correspondence – but he was a dreamer. At our enjoyable Thursday-night dinner parties in Richmond, he would pour out his speculations on the future and the past, and share with us his latest thoughts on the meaning of Darwin's bleak, Godless analysis, and what-not. He dreamed of the perfectibility of the human race – he was just the type, I knew, who would wish with all his heart that my tales of time travel were true!

I call him 'Writer' out of an old kindness, I suppose, for as far as I knew he had only had published various awkward speculations in college journals and the like; but I had no doubt that his lively brain would carve him out a niche in the world of letters of some sort – and, more to the point, *he* had no doubt of it either.

Though I was eager to be off, I paused a moment. Perhaps the Writer could serve as my witness on this new voyage – in fact, I wondered now, it could be that he was already planning to write up my earlier adventures in some gaudy form for publication.

Well, he would have my blessing!

'I only want half an hour,' I said, calculating that I could return to this precise time and place with a mere touch of the levers of my machine, no matter how long I chose to spend in the future or past. 'I know why you came, and it's awfully good of you. There's some magazines here. If you'll stop to lunch I'll prove you this time travelling up to the hilt, specimens and all. If you'll forgive my leaving you now?'

He consented. I nodded to him and, without further ado, I set off down the corridor to my laboratory.

So I took my leave of the world of 1891. I have never been a man of deep attachments, and I am not one for flowery farewells; but had I known I should never see the Writer again – at least, not in the flesh – I fancy I would have made something more of a ceremony of it!

I entered my laboratory. It was laid out something like a milling-shop. There was a steam lathe attached to the ceiling, which powered various metal-turning machines by means of leather bands; and fixed to benches around the floor were smaller lathes, a sheet-metal stamp, presses, acetylene welding sets, vices and the like. Metal parts and drawings lay about on the bench, and abandoned fruits of my labours lay in the dust of the floor, for I am not by nature a tidy man; lying at my feet now, for example, I found the nickel bar which had held me up before my first sojourn into time – that bar which had proved to be exactly one inch short, so that I had had to get it remade.

I had spent much of two decades of my life in this room, I reflected. The place was a converted conservatory, giving onto the garden. It was built on a framework of slender, white-painted wrought iron, and had once given a decent view of the river; but I had long since boarded up the panes, to assure myself of a consistency of light and to deter the curious eyes of my neighbours. My various tools and devices loomed in that oily darkness, and now they reminded me of my half-glimpses of the great machines in the caverns

11

of the Morlocks. I wondered if I myself might not have some morbid streak of the Morlock! When I returned, I resolved, I would kick out the boards and glaze up the room once again, and make it a place of Eloi light rather than Morlock gloom.

Now I walked forward to the Time Machine.

That bulky, askew thing sat against the north-west side of the workshop – where, eight hundred millennia away, the Morlocks had dragged it, in their efforts to entrap me inside the pedestal of the White Sphinx. I hauled the machine back to the south-east corner of the laboratory, where I had built it. That done, I leaned over and, in the gloom, made out the four chronometric dials which counted the passage of the machine through History's static array of days; now, of course, the hands were all set to zero, for the machine had returned to its own time. Beside this row of dials, there were the two levers which drove the beast, one for the future, and one for the past.

I reached out and, on impulse, stroked the lever for futurity. The squat, tangled mass of metal and ivory shuddered like a live thing. I smiled. The machine was reminding me that it was no longer of this earth, of this Space and Time! Alone of all the material objects of the universe, save for those I had carried on my own person, this machine was *eight days older than its world*: for I had spent a week in the era of the Morlocks, but had returned to the day of my departure.

I dropped my pack and camera to the floor of the laboratory, and hung up my hat on the back of the door. Remembering the Morlocks' fiddling with the machine, I settled myself to checking it over. I did not trouble to clean off the various brown spots and bits of grass and moss which still clung to the machine's rails; I have never been one for fussy appearances. But one rail was bent out of shape, and

12

I twisted that back, and I tested the screws, and oiled the quartz bars.

As I worked, I remembered my shameful panic when discovering the machine lost to the Morlocks, and I felt a deep surge of affection for the ugly thing. The machine was an open cage of nickel, brass and quartz, ebony and ivory, quite elaborate – like the workings of a church clock, perhaps – and with a bicycle saddle set incongruous in the middle of it all. Quartz and rock crystal, suffused with Plattnerite, glimmered about the framework, giving the whole a sense of unreality and skewness.

Of course none of it would have been possible without the properties of the strange substance I had labelled 'Plattnerite'. I remembered how, by chance, I had come into possession of a sample of that material: on that night, two decades earlier, when a stranger had walked up to my door and handed me a packet of the stuff. 'Plattner', he had called himself – he was a bulky chap, a good few years older than myself, with an odd, broad, grey-grizzled head, and dressed in peculiar jungle colours. He instructed me to study the potent stuff he handed me, in a glass medicine jar. Well, the stuff had sat uninvestigated on a shelf in the laboratory for over a year, while I progressed with more substantive work. But at last, on a dull Sunday afternoon, I had taken the jar down from its shelf . . .

And what I had found out had, at last, led to – this!

It was Plattnerite, suffused into quartz rods, which fuelled the Time Machine, and made its exploits possible. But I flatter myself to think that it took my own combination of analysis and imagination to realize and exploit the properties of that remarkable substance, where a lesser man may have missed the mark.

I had been reluctant to publicize my work,

13

outlandish as the field was, without experimental verification. I promised myself that direct on my return, with specimens and photographs, I would write up my studies for the *Philosophical Transactions*; it would be a famous addition to the seventeen papers I had already placed there on the physics of light. It would be amusing, I reflected, to call my paper something dry such as 'Some Reflections on the Anomalous Chronologic Properties of the Mineral "Plattnerite"', and to bury within it the thunderous revelation of the existence of time travel!

At last I was done. I set my hat square over my eyes once more, and I picked up my pack and camera and fixed them under the saddle. Then, on an impulse, I went to the fireplace of the laboratory and picked up the poker which stood there. I hefted its substantial mass in my hand – I thought it might be useful! – and I lodged it in the machine's frame.

Then I sat myself in the saddle, and I placed my hand on the white starting levers. The machine shuddered, like the animal of time it had become.

I glanced around at my laboratory, at the earthy reality of it, and was struck how out-of-place we both looked in it now – me in my amateur explorer's garb, and the machine with its other-worldliness and its stains and scuffs from the future – even though we were both, in a way, children of this place. I felt tempted to linger. What harm would it do to expend another day, week, year here, embedded in my own comfortable century? I could gather my energies, and heal my wounds: was I being precipitate once again in this new venture?

I heard a footstep in the corridor from the house, a turn of the door handle. It must be the Writer, coming to the laboratory.

Of a sudden, my mind was set. My courage would not grow any stronger with the passage of any more

14

of this dull, ossified nineteenth-century time; and besides, I had said all the good-byes I cared to make.

I pressed the lever over to its extreme position. I had that odd sense of *spinning* that comes with the first instant of time travel, and then there came that helpless, headlong feel of falling. I think I uttered an exclamation at the return of that uncomfortable sensation. I fancy I heard a tinkle of glass: a skylight pane, perhaps, blown in by the displacement of air. And, for a shredded remnant of a second, I saw him standing there in the doorway: the Writer, a ghostly, indistinct figure, with one hand raised to me – trapped in time!

Then he was gone, swept into invisibility by my flight. The walls of the laboratory grew hazy around me, and once more the huge wings of night and day flapped around my head

BOOK ONE

Dark Night

1

TIME TRAVELLING

There are three Dimensions of Space, through which man may move freely. And time is simply a *Fourth* Dimension: identical in every important characteristic to the others, except for the fact that our consciousness is compelled to travel along it at a steady pace, like the nib of my pen across this page.

If only – I had speculated, in the course of my studies into the peculiar properties of light – if only one could *twist about* the four Dimensions of Space and Time – transposing Length with Duration, say – then one could stroll through the corridors of History as easily as taking a cab into the West End!

The Plattnerite embedded in the substance of the Time Machine was the key to its operation; the Plattnerite enabled the machine to rotate, in an uncommon fashion, into a new configuration in the framework of Space and Time. Thus, spectators who watched the departure of the Time Machine – like my Writer – reported seeing the machine spin giddily, before vanishing from History; and thus the driver – myself – invariably suffered dizziness, induced by centrifugal and Coriolis forces which made it feel as if I were being thrown off the machine.

But for all these effects, the spin induced by the Plattnerite was of a different *quality* from the spinning of a top, or the slow revolution of the earth. The spinning sensations were flatly contradicted, for the driver, by the illusion of sitting quite still in the saddle, as time flickered past the machine – for *it was a rotation out of Time and Space themselves*.

As night flapped after day, the hazy outline of the laboratory fell away from around me, so that I was delivered into the open air. I was once more passing through that future period in which, I guessed, the laboratory had been demolished. The sun shot like a cannonball across the sky, with many days compressed into a minute, illuminating a faint, skeletal sugges- tion of scaffolding around me. The scaffolding soon fell away, leaving me on the open hill-side.

My speed through time increased. The flickering of night and day merged into a deep twilight blue, and I was able to see the moon, spinning through its phases like a child's top. And as I travelled still faster, the cannonball sun merged into an arch of light, spreading across space, an arch which rocked up and down the sky. Around me weather fluttered, with successive flurries of snow-white and spring green marking out the seasons. At last, accelerated, I entered a new, tranquil stillness in which only the annual rhythms of the earth itself – the passage of the sun-belt between its solstice extremes – pumped like a heartbeat over the evolving landscape.

I am not sure if I conveyed, in my first report, the *silence* into which one is suspended when undergoing time travel. The songs of the birds, the distant rattle of traffic over cobbles, the ticks of clocks – even the faint breathing of the fabric of a house itself – all of these things make up a complex, unnoticed tapestry to our lives. But now, plucked from time, I was accompanied only by the sounds of my own breath- ing and by the soft, bicycle-like creaking of the Time Machine under my weight. I had an extraordinary

20

sensation of isolation – it was as if I had been plunged into some new, stark universe, through the walls of which our own world was visible as if through begrimed window panes – but within this new universe I was the only living thing. A deep sense of confusion descended on me, and worked together with the vertiginous plummeting sensation that accompanies a fall into the future, to induce feelings of deep nausea and depression.

But now the silence was broken: by a deep murmur, sourceless, which seemed to fill my ears; it was a low eddying, like the sound of some immense river. I had noticed this during my first flight; I could not be certain of its cause, but it seemed to me it must be some artefact of my unseemly passage through the stately progress of time.

How wrong I was – as so often in my hasty hypo-thesis-making!

I studied my four chronometric dials, tapping the face of each with my fingernail to ensure they were working. Already the hand on the second of the dials, which measured thousands of days, had begun to drift away from its rest position.

These dials – faithful, mute servants – were adapted from steam pressure gauges. They worked by measur-ing a certain shear tension in a quartz bar doped with Plattnerite, a tension induced by the twisting effects of time travel. The dials counted *days* – not years, or months, or leap years, or movable feasts! – and that was by conscious design.

As soon as I began my investigations into the practi-calities of this business of travelling into time, and in particular the need to measure my machine's posi-tion in it, I spent some considerable time trying to build a practical chronometric gauge capable of producing a display in common measured centuries,

21

years, months and days. I soon found I was likely to spend longer on that project than on the rest of the Time Machine put together!

I developed an immense impatience with the peculiarities of our antique calendar system, which has come from a history of inadequate adjustments: of attempts to fix seed-time and midwinter that go back to the beginnings of organized society. Our calendar is a historical absurdity, without even the redeeming feature of accuracy – at least on the cosmological timescales which I intended to challenge.

I wrote furious letters to *The Times*, proposing reforms which would enable us to function accurately and without ambiguity on timescales of genuine value to the modern scientist. To begin with, I said, let us discard all this nonsensical clutter of leap years. The year is close to three hundred and sixty five days and a quarter; and that accidental quarter is the cause of all this ridiculous charade of leap year adjustments. I offered two alternative schemes, both guaranteed to remove this absurdity. We could take the *day* as our base unit, and devise regular months and years based on multiples of days: imagine a three-hundred-day Year made up of ten Months, each of thirty days. Of course the cycle of seasons would soon drift out of synchronization with the structure of the Year, but – in a civilization as advanced as ours – that would surely cause little trouble. The Royal Observatory at Greenwich, for example, could publish diaries each year to show the dates of the various solar positions – the equinoxes and so forth – just as, in 1891, all diaries showed the movable feasts of the Christian churches.

On the other hand, if the *cycle of seasons* is to be regarded as the fundamental unit, then we should devise a New Day as an exact fraction – say a hundredth – of the year. Naturally this would mean that the diurnal round, our periods of dark and light, of sleep and wakefulness, would fall at different times each New Day. But what of that? Already, I argued, many modern cities operated on a twenty-four-hour schedule. And as for the human side of it, simple diary keeping is not a difficult skill to acquire; with the help of proper records one would need plan one's sleeping and wakefulness no more than a few Days in advance.

Finally I proposed we should look ahead to the day when man's consciousness is expanded from its nineteenth-century focus on the here-and-now, and consider how things might be when our thinking must span tens of millennia. I envisaged a new Cosmological Calendar, based on the precession of the equinoxes – that is, the slow dipping of the axis of our planet, under the uneven gravitational influence of sun and moon – a cycle which takes twenty millennia to complete. With some such Great Year, we might measure out our destiny in unambiguous and precise terms, now and for all time to come.

Such rectification, I argued, would have a symbolic significance far beyond its practicality – it would be a fitting way to mark the dawn of the new century – for it would serve as an announcement to all men that a new Age of Scientific Thinking had begun.

Needless to say, my contributions were disregarded, save for a ribald response, which I chose to ignore, in certain sections of the popular press.

At any event, after all this, I abandoned my attempts to build a calendar-based chronometric gauge, and reverted to a simple count of days. I have always had a ready mind with figures, and did not find it hard to convert, mentally, my dials' day-count to years. On my first voyage, I had travelled to Day 292,495,934, which – allowing for leap year adjustments – turned out to be a date in the year A.D.

802,701. Now, I knew, I must travel forwards until my dials showed Day 292,495,940 – the precise day on which I had lost Weena, and much of my self-respect, in the flames of that forest!

My house had been one of a row of terraces, situated on the Petersham Road – that stretch of it below Hill Rise, a little way up from the river. Now, with my house long demolished, I found myself sitting on an open hill-side. The shoulder of Richmond Hill rose up behind me, a mass embedded in geological time. The trees blossomed and shivered into stumps, their century-long lives compressed into a few of my heart-beats. The Thames was a belt of silver light, made smooth by my passage through time, and it was cutting itself a new channel: it appeared to be wrig-gling across the landscape after the manner of a huge, slow worm. New buildings rose like gusts of smoke: some of them even blew up around me, on the site of my old house. These buildings astonished me with their dimensions and grace. The Richmond Bridge of my day was long gone, but I saw a new arch, perhaps a mile long, which laced, unsupported, through the air and across the Thames; and there were towers upthrust into the flickering sky, bearing immense masses at their slender throats. I thought of taking up my Kodak and attempting to photograph these phantasms, but I knew that the spectres would be too light-starved to enable any image to be recorded, diluted by time travel as they were. The architectural technologies I made out here seemed to me as far beyond the capabilities of the nineteenth century as had been the great Gothic cathedrals from the Romans or Greeks. Surely, I mused, in this future era man had gained some freedom from the relentless tugging of gravity; for how else could these great structures have been raised against the sky?

But before long the great Thames arch grew stained with brown and green, the colours of irreverent, destructive life, and – in a twinkling, it seemed to me – the arch crumbled from its centre, collapsing to two bare stumps on the banks. Like all the works of man, I saw, even these great structures were transient chimeras, destined to impermanence compared to the chthonian patience of the land.

I felt an extraordinary detachment from the world, an aloofness brought about by my time travelling. I remembered the curiosity and exhilaration I had felt when I had first soared through these dreams of future architecture; I remembered my brief, feverish speculation as to the accomplishments of these future races of men. Now, I knew different; now I knew that regardless of these great accomplishments, Humanity would inevitably fall backwards, under the inexorable pressure of evolution, into the decadence and degradation of Eloi and Morlock.

I was struck by how ignorant we humans are, or make ourselves, of the passage of time itself. How brief our lives are! – and how meaningless the events which assail our little selves, when seen against the perspective of the great plastic sweep of History. We are less than mayflies, helpless in the face of the unbending forces of geology and evolution – forces which move inexorably, and yet so slowly that, day to day, we are not even aware of their existence!

2

A NEW VISION

I soon passed beyond the Age of Great Buildings. New houses and halls, less ambitious but still huge, shimmered into existence around me, all about the vale of the Thames, and assumed a certain opacity, in the eyes of a Time Traveller, that comes with longevity. The arch of the sun, dipping across the deep blue sky between its solstice extremes, seemed to me to grow brighter, and a green flow spread across Richmond Hill and took possession of the land, banishing the browns and whites of winter. Once more, I had entered that era in which the climate of the earth had been adjusted in favour of Humanity.

I looked out over a landscape reduced by my velocity to the static; only the longest-lived phenomena clung to time long enough to register on my fleeting eye. I saw no people, no animals, not even the passage of a cloud. I was suspended in an eerie stillness. If it had not been for the oscillating sun-band, and the deep, unnatural day-night blue of the sky, I might have been sitting alone in some late summer park.

According to my dials, I was less than a third of the way through my great journey – although a quarter of a million years had already worn away since my own familiar century – and yet, it seemed, the age in which man built upon the earth was already done.

26

The planet had been rendered into that garden within which the folk who would become the Eloi would live out their futile, petty lives; and already, I knew, proto-Morlocks must have been imprisoned beneath the earth, and must even now be tunnelling out their immense, machinery-choked caverns. Little would change over the half-million-year interval I had yet to cross, save for the further degradation of Humanity, and the identity of the victims in the millions of tiny, fearful tragedies which would from now on comprise the condition of man . . .

But – I observed, rousing myself from these morbid speculations – there *was* a change, slowly becoming apparent in the landscape. I felt disturbed, over and above the Time Machine's customary swaying. Something was different – perhaps something about the light.

Sitting in my saddle, I peered about at the ghost-trees, the level meadows about Petersham, the shoulder of the patient Thames.

Then I lifted my face to the time-smoothed heavens, and at last I realized that *the sun-band was stationary in the sky*. The earth was still spinning on its axis rapidly enough to smear the movement of our star across the heavens, and to render the circling stars invisible, but that band of sunlight no longer nodded back and forth between solstices: it was as steady and unchanging as if it were a construction of concrete.

My nausea and vertigo returned with a rush. I was forced to grip hard at the rails of the machine, and I swallowed, fighting for control of my own body.

It is difficult to convey the impact this simple change in my surroundings had on me! First, I was shocked by the sheer audacity of the engineering involved in the removal of the seasonal cycle. The earth's seasons had derived from the tilt of the planet's spin axis compared to the plane of its orbit around the sun. On the earth, it seemed, there would be no more seasons. And that could only mean – I realized it instantly – *that the axial tilt of the planet had been corrected.*

I tried to envisage how this might have been done. What great machines must have been installed at the Poles? What measures had been taken to ensure that the surface of the earth did not shake itself loose in the process? – Perhaps, I speculated, some immense magnetic device had been used, which had manipulated the molten and magnetic core of the planet.

But it was not just the scale of this planetary engineering which disturbed me: more terrifying still was the fact that *I had not observed this regulation of the seasons during my first jaunt into time.* How was it possible that I could have missed such an immense and profound change? I am trained as a scientist, after all; my business is to observe.

I rubbed my face and stared up at the sun-band where it hung in the sky, defying me to believe in its lack of motion. Its brightness stung my eyes; and it seemed to me that the band was growing still brighter. I wondered at first if this was my imagination, or some defect of my eyes. I dropped my face, dazzled, wiping tears against my jacket sleeve and blinking to rid my eyes of stripes of bruised light-spots.

I am no primitive, and no coward – and yet, sitting there in my saddle before the evidence of the immense feats of future men, I felt as if I were a savage with painted nakedness and bones in my hair, cowering before gods in the gaudy sky. I felt a deep fear for my own sanity bubbling from the depths of my consciousness; and yet I clung to the belief that – somehow – I *had* failed to observe this staggering astronomical phenomenon, during my first pass through these years. For the only alternative hypothesis terrified me to the roots of my soul: it was that I had not been mistaken during my first voyage; that the regulation of the earth's axis had *not* taken place there – *that the course of History itself had changed.*

The near-eternal shape of the hill-side was unchanged – the morphology of the ancient land was unaffected by these evolving lights in the sky – but I could see that the tide of greenery which had coated the land had now receded, under the steady glare of the brightened sun.

I became aware now of a remote flickering above my head, and I glanced up with my hand raised. The flickering came from the sun-band in the sky – or what had been the sun-band, for I realized that somehow, once again, I was able to distinguish the cannonball motion of the sun as it shot across the sky on its diurnal round; no longer was its motion too rapid for me to follow, and the passage of night and day was inducing the flickering I saw.

At first I thought my machine must be slowing. But when I glanced down at my dials, I saw that the hands were twisting across the faces with just as much alacrity as before.

The pearl-grey uniformity of the light dissolved, and the flapping alternation of day and night became marked. The sun slid across the sky, slowing with every arcing trajectory, hot and bright and yellow; and I soon realized that the burning star was taking many centuries to complete one revolution around the sky of earth.

At last, the sun came to a halt altogether; it rested on the western horizon, hot and pitiless and unchanging. The earth's rotation had been stilled; now, it rotated with one face turned perpetually to the sun!

The scientists of the nineteenth century had

predicted that at last the tidal influences of sun and moon would cause the earth's rotation to become locked to the sun, just as the moon was forced to keep one face turned to earth. I had witnessed this myself, during my first exploration of futurity: but it was an eventuality that should not come about for many millions of years. And yet here I was, little more than half a million years into the future, finding a stilled earth!

Once again, I realized, I had seen the hand of man at work – ape-descended fingers, reaching across centuries with the grasp of gods. Not content with tilting up his world, man had slowed the spin of the earth itself, banishing at last the ancient cycle of day and night.

I looked around at England's new desert. The land was scoured clean of grass, leaving exposed a dried-out clay. Here and there I saw the flicker of some hardy bush – in shape, a little like an olive – which struggled to survive beneath the unrelenting sun. The mighty Thames, which had migrated across perhaps a mile of its plain, shrank within its banks, until I could no longer see the sparkle of its water. I scarce felt these latest changes had done much to improve the place: at least the world of Morlocks and Eloi had seen the retention of the essential character of the English countryside, with its abundant greenery and water; the effect, looking back on it, had been rather like towing the whole of the British Isles to somewhere in the Tropics.

I pictured the poor planet, one face held in the sunlight forever, the other turned away. On the equator at the centre of the day-side, it must be warm enough to boil the flesh off a man's bones. And air must be fleeing the overheated sunward side to rush, in immense winds, towards the cooler hemisphere, there to freeze out as a snow of oxygen and nitrogen over the ice-bound oceans. If I were to stop the machine now, perhaps I should be knocked off at once by those great winds, the last exhalations of a planet's lungs! The process could stop only when the day-side was parched, airless, quite without life; and the dark side was buried under a thin shell of frozen air.

I realized with mounting horror that I could not return home! – for to turn back I must stop the machine, and if I did so I would be tipped precipitately into a land of vacuum and searing heat, as bleak as the surface of the moon. But dare I carry on, into an unknowable future, and hope that somewhere in the depths of time I would find a world I could inhabit?

Now I was sure that something was badly wrong with my perceptions, or memories, of my time travelling. For it was barely conceivable to me that during my first voyage to the future I might have missed the banishing of the seasons – though I found it hard to believe – but I could not countenance that I had failed to notice the slowing of the earth's spin.

There could be no doubt about it: *I was travelling through events which differed, massively, from those I had witnessed during my first sojourn.*

I am by nature a speculative man, and am in general not short of an inventive hypothesis or two; but at that moment my shock was such that I was bereft of calculation. It was as if my body still plummeted onwards through time, but my brain had been left behind, somewhere in the glutinous past. I think I had had a veneer of courage earlier, a facade that had come from the complacent consideration that, although I was heading into danger, it was at least a danger I had confronted before. Now, I had no idea what awaited me in these corridors of time!

While I was occupied by these morbid thoughts, I

became aware of continuing changes in the heavens – as if the dismantling of the natural order of things had not yet gone far enough! The sun was growing still brighter. And – it was hard to be sure, the glare of it was so strong – it seemed to me that the *shape* of the star was now changing. It was smearing itself across the sky, becoming an elliptical patch of light. I wondered if the sun was somehow being spun more rapidly, so that it had become flattened by rotation . . .

And then – it was quite sudden – the sun exploded.

3

IN OBSCURITY

Plumes of light erupted from the star's poles, like immense flares. Within a handful of heartbeats the sun had surrounded itself with a glowing mantle of light. Heat and light blazed down anew on the battered earth.

I screamed and buried my face in my hands; but I could still see the light of the enhanced sun, leaking even through the flesh of my fingers, and blazing from the nickel and brass of the Time Machine.

Then, as soon as it had begun, the light storm ceased – and a sort of shell closed up around the sun, as if an immense Mouth was swallowing the star – and I was plunged into darkness!

I dropped my hands, and found myself in pitch blackness, quite unable to see, although dazzle-spots still danced in my eyes. I could feel the hard saddle of the Time Machine beneath me, and when I reached out I found the faces of the little dials; and the machine still swayed as it continued to forge through time. I began to wonder – to fear! – if I had lost my sight.

Despair welled up within me, blacker than the external darkness. Was my second great adventure into time to end so soon, so ignobly? I reached out, groping, for the control levers, and my feverish brain began to concoct schemes wherein I broke off the glass of the chronometric dials, and by touch, perhaps, worked my way home.

. . . And then I found I was not blind: I *did* see something.

In some ways this was the queerest aspect of the whole journey so far – so queer, that at first I was quite beyond fear.

First of all I made out a lightening in the darkness. It was a vague, suffused brightening, something like a sun-rise, and so faint that I was unsure if my bruised eyes were not playing some trick on me. I thought I could see stars, all about me; but they were faint, their light tempered as if seen through a murky stained-glass window.

And now, by the dim glow, I began to see that *I was not alone.*

The creature stood a few yards before the Time Machine – or rather, it floated in the air, unsupported. It was a ball of flesh: something like a hovering head, all of four feet across, with two bunches of tentacles which dangled like grotesque fingers towards the ground. Its mouth was a fleshy beak, and it had no nostrils that I could make out. I noticed now that the creature's eyes – two of them, large and dark – were *human.* It seemed to be making a noise – a low, murmuring babble, like a river – and I realized, with a stab of fear, that this was exactly the noise I had heard earlier in the expedition, and even during my first venture into time.

Had this creature – this *Watcher*, I labelled it – accompanied me, unseen, on both my expeditions through time?

Of a sudden, it rushed towards me. It loomed up, no more than a yard from my face!

I was unhinged at last. I screamed and, regardless of the consequences, hauled at my lever.

The Time Machine tipped over – the Watcher vanished – and I was flung into the air!

*

I was left insensible: for how long, I cannot say. I revived slowly, finding my face pressed down against a hard, sandy surface. I fancied I felt a hot breath at my neck – a whisper, a brush of soft hair against my cheek – but when I moaned and made to get up, these sensations vanished.

I was immersed in inky darkness. It felt neither warm nor cold. I was sitting on some hard, sandy surface. There was a scent of staleness in the still air. My head ached from the bump it had received, and I had lost my hat.

I reached out my arms and cast about all around me. To my great relief, I was rewarded almost immediately by a soft collision with a tangle of ivory and brass: it was the Time Machine, pitched like me into this darkened desert. I reached out with both hands and fingered the rails and studs of the machine. It was tipped over, and in the dark I could not tell if it was damaged.

I needed light, of course. I reached for some matches from my pocket – only to find none there; like a blessed fool I had packed my entire supply into the knapsack! A moment of panic assailed me; but I managed to suppress it, and I stood, shaking, and walked to the Time Machine. I investigated it by touch, searching between the bent rails until I found the knapsack, still stowed secure under the saddle. Impatient, I pulled the pack open and rummaged through it. I found two boxes of matches and tucked them into my jacket pockets; then I took out a match and struck it against its box.

. . . *There was a face*, immediately before me, not two feet away, glowing in the match's circle of light: I saw dull white skin, flaxen hair draping down from the skull, and wide, grey-red eyes.

The creature let out a queer, gurgling scream, and

disappeared into the darkness beyond the glow of my light.

It was a Morlock!

The match burned down against my fingers and I dropped it; I scrabbled for another, in my panic almost dropping my precious box.

4

THE DARK NIGHT

The sharp sulphur smell of the matches filled my nostrils, and I backed across the sandy surface until my spine was pressed against the brass rods of the Time Machine. After some minutes of this submission to terror I had the wit to retrieve a candle from my knapsack. I held the candle close to my face and stared into its yellow flame, ignorant of the warm wax which flowed over my fingers.

I gradually began to discern some structure in the world around me. I could see the tangled brass and quartz of the upturned Time Machine, sparkling in the candlelight, and a form – like a large statue, or a building – which loomed, pale and huge, not far from where I stood. The land was not completely without light. The sun might be gone, but in patches above me the stars still shone, though slid about by time from the constellations of my boyhood. There was no sign of our friendly moon.

In one part of the sky, though, no stars shone: in the west, protruding over the black horizon, there was a flattened ellipse, unbroken by stars, spanning fully a quarter of the sky. This was the sun, shrouded in its astonishing shell!

As I came out of my funk, I decided my first action should be to secure my passage home: I must right the Time Machine – but I would not do it in the dark! I knelt down and felt about on the ground. The sand was hard, the grains fine-packed. I dug into it with my thumb, and pushed out a little depression; into this improvised holder I popped my candle, confident that in a few moments sufficient wax would melt to hold it more firmly in place. Now I had a steady light to guide my operations, and my hands were free.

I set my teeth, drew my breath, and grappled with the weight of the machine. I wedged my wrists and knees under its framework, trying to wrestle the thing from the ground – its construction had been intended for solidity, not ease of handling – until, at last, it gave under my onslaught and tipped over. One nickel rod struck my shoulder, quite painfully.

I rested my hand on the saddle, and felt where its leather surface was scuffed by the sand of this new future. In the dark of my own shadow, I reached out and found the chronometric dials with my probing fingertips – one glass had shattered, but the dial itself seemed in working order – and the two white levers with which I could bring myself home. As I touched the levers, the machine shivered like a ghost, reminding me that it – and I – were not of this time: that at any moment now, of my choosing, I only had to board my device to return to the security of 1891, at the risk of nothing more than a little bruised pride.

I lifted the candle from its socket in the sand and held it over my dials. It was, I found, Day 239,354,634: therefore – I estimated – the year was A.D. 657,208. My wild imaginings about the mutability of past and future must be correct; for this darkened hill-side was located in time a hundred and fifty millennia *before* Weena's birth, and I could not envisage a way in which that sunlit garden-world could develop from this rayless obscurity!

In my remote childhood, I remember being entertained by my father with a primitive wonder-toy called a 'Dissolving View'. Crudely coloured pictures were thrown onto a screen by a double-barrelled arrangement of lenses. A picture would be projected first by the right-hand lens of the contraption; then the light would be shifted to the left-hand side, so that the picture cast from the right faded as the other grew in brightness. As a child I was deeply impressed by the way in which a bright reality turned into a phantom, to be replaced by a successor whose form was at first visible only as an outline. There were exhilarating moments when the two images were exactly in balance, and it was hard to determine which details were advancing and which were receding realities, or whether any part of the ensemble of images was truly 'real'.

Thus, as I stood in that darkened landscape, I felt the sturdy description of the world I had constructed for myself growing misty and faint, to be replaced only by the barest bones of a successor, and with more confusion than clarity!

The divergence of the twin Histories I had witnessed – in the first, the building of the Eloi's garden world; in the second, the extinguishing of the sun, and the establishment of this planetary desert – was incomprehensible to me. How could events *be*, and then *not be*?

I remembered the words of Thomas Aquinas: that 'God cannot effect that anything which is past should not have been. It is more impossible than raising the dead . . .' So I had believed, too! I am not much given to philosophical speculation, but I had thought of the future as an extension of the past: fixed and immutable, even for a God – and certainly for the hand of man. Futurity, in my mind, was like a huge room, fixed and static. And into the furniture of the future my Time Machine could take me, exploring.

But now, it seemed, I had learned that the future

might *not* be a fixed thing, but something mutable! If so, I mused, what meaning could be given to the lives of men? It was bad enough to endure the thought that all of one's achievements would be worn away to insignificance by the erosion of time – and I, of all men, knew that well enough! – but, at least, one would always have the feeling that one's monuments, and the things one had loved, *had once been*. But if History were capable of this wholesale erasure and alteration, what possible worth could be ascribed to *any* human activity?

Reflecting on these startling possibilities, I felt as if the solidity of my thought, and the firmness of my apprehension of the world, were melting away. I stared into my candle flame, seeking the outlines of a new understanding.

I was not done yet, I decided; my fear was subsiding, and my mind stayed resilient and strong. I would explore this bizarre world, and take what pictures I could with my Kodak, and then return to 1891. There, better philosophers than I could puzzle over this conundrum of two futurities exclusive of each other.

I reached over the bars of the Time Machine, unscrewed the little levers that would launch me into time, and stored them safe in my pocket. Then I felt about until I found the sturdy form of my poker, still lodged where I had left it in the structure of the machine. I grasped its thick handle and hefted it in my hand. My confidence grew as I imagined cracking a few of the Morlocks' soft skulls with this piece of primitive engineering. I stuck the poker in a loop of my belt. It hung there a little awkward but hugely reassuring, with its weight and solidity, and its resonance of home, and my own fireside.

I raised my candle into the air. The spectral statue, or

building, which I had noticed close by the machine, came into shadowy illumination. It was indeed a monument of some kind – a colossal figure carved of some white stone, its form difficult to discern in the flickering candlelight.

I walked towards the monument. As I did so, on the edge of my vision, I fancied I saw a pair of grey-red eyes widen, and a white back which shivered away across the sandy surface with a shushing of bare feet. I rested my hand on the club of brass tucked in my belt, and continued.

The statue was set on a pedestal which appeared to be of bronze, and decorated with deep-framed, fili-greed panels. The pedestal was stained, as if it had once been attacked by verdigris, now long dried out. The statue itself was of white marble, and from a leonine body great wings were spread, so that they seemed to hover over me. I wondered how those great sheets of stone were supported, for I could see no struts. Perhaps there was some metal frame, I mused – or perhaps some elements of that mastery of gravity, which I had hypothesized in my latest jaunt through the Age of Great Buildings, lingered on in this desolate era. The face of the marble beast was human, and was turned towards me; I felt as if those blank stone eyes were watching me, and there was a smile, sardonic and cruel, on the weather-beaten lips . . .

And with a jolt I recognized this construction; if not for fear of Morlocks I would have whooped with the joy of familiarity! This was the monument I had come to call the White Sphinx – a structure I had become familiar with, in this very spot, during my first flight to the future. It was almost like greeting an old friend!

I paced around the sandy hill-side, back and forth past the machine, remembering how it had been.

41

This spot had been a lawn, surrounded by mauve and purple rhododendrons – bushes which had dropped their blossoms over me in a hail storm on my first arrival. And, looming over it all, indistinct at first in that hail, had been the imposing form of this Sphinx.

Well, here I was again, a hundred and fifty thousand years *before* that date. The bushes and lawn were gone – *and would never come to be,* I suspected. That sunlit garden had been replaced by this bleak, darkened desert, and now existed only in the recesses of my own mind. But the Sphinx was here, solid as life and almost indestructible, it seemed.

I patted the bronze panels of the Sphinx's pedestal with something resembling affection. Somehow the existence of the Sphinx, lingering from my previous visit, reassured me that I was not imagining all of this, that I was not going mad in some dim recess of my house in 1891! All of this was objectively real, and – no doubt, like the rest of Creation – it all conformed to some logical pattern. The White Sphinx was a part of that pattern, and it was only my ignorance and limitation of mind that prevented me from seeing the rest of it. I was bolstered up, and felt filled with a new determination to continue with my explorations.

On impulse, I walked around to the side of the pedestal closest to the Time Machine, and, by candle-light, I inspected the decorated bronze panel there. It was here, I recalled, that the Morlocks – in that other History – had opened up the hollow base of the Sphinx, and dragged the Time Machine inside the pedestal, meaning to trap me. I had come to the Sphinx with a pebble and hammered at this panel – just *here,* I ran over the decorations with my finger-tips. I had flattened out some of the coils of the panel, though to no avail. Well, now I found those coils firm and round under my fingers, as good as

42

new. It was strange to think that the coils would not meet the fury of my stone for millennia yet – or perhaps, *never at all.*

I determined to move away from the machine and proceed with my exploration. But the presence of the Sphinx had reminded me of my horror at losing the Time Machine to the clutches of the Morlocks. I patted my pocket – at least without my little levers the machine could not be operated – but there was no obstacle to those loathsome creatures crawling over my machine as soon as I was gone from it, perhaps dismantling it or stealing it again.

And besides, in this darkened landscape, how should I avoid getting lost? How should I be sure of finding the machine again, once I had gone more than a few yards from it?

I puzzled over this for a few moments, my desire to explore further battling with my apprehension. Then an idea struck me. I opened my knapsack and took out my candles and camphor blocks. With rough haste I shoved these articles into crevices in the Time Machine's complex construction. Then I went around the machine with lighted matches until every one of the blocks and candles was ablaze.

I stood back from my glowing handiwork with some pride. Candle flames glinted from the polished nickel and brass, so that the Time Machine was lit up like some Christmas ornament. In this darkened landscape, and with the machine poised on this denuded hill-side, I would be able to see my beacon from a fair distance. With any luck, the flames would deter any Morlocks – or if they did not, I should see the diminution of the flames immediately and could come running back, to join battle.

I fingered the poker's heavy handle. I think a part of me hoped for just such an outcome; my hands and lower arms tingled as I remembered the queer, soft sensation of my fists driving into Morlock faces!

At any rate, now I was prepared for my expedition. I picked up my Kodak, lit a small oil lamp, and made my way across the hill, pausing after every few paces to be sure the Time Machine rested undisturbed.

5

THE WELL

I raised my lamp, but its glow carried only a few feet. All was silent – there was not a breath of wind, not a trickle of water; and I wondered if the Thames still flowed.

For lack of a definite destination, I decided to make towards the site of the great food hall which I remembered from Weena's day. This lay a little distance to the north-west, further along the hill-side past the White Sphinx, and so this was the path I followed once more – reflecting in Space, if not in Time, my first walk in Weena's world.

When last I made this little journey, I remembered, there had been grass under my feet – untended and uncropped, but growing neat and short and free of weeds. Now, soft, gritty sand pulled at my boots as I tramped across the hill.

My vision was becoming quite adapted to this night of patchy star-light, but, though there were buildings hereabout, silhouetted against the sky, I saw no sign of my hall. I remembered it quite distinctly: it had been a grey edifice, dilapidated and vast, of fretted stone, with a carved, ornate doorway; and as I had walked through its carved arch, the little Eloi, delicate and pretty, had fluttered about me with their pale limbs and soft robes.

Before long I had walked so far that I knew I must have passed the site of the hall. Evidently – unlike the

Sphinx and the Morlocks – the food palace had not survived in this History – *or perhaps had never been built*, I thought with a shiver; perhaps I had walked – slept, even taken a meal! – in a building without existence.

The path took me to a well, a feature which I remembered from my first jaunt. Just as I recalled, the structure was rimmed with bronze and protected from the weather by a small, oddly delicate cupola. There was some vegetation – jet-black in the star-light – clustered around the cupola. I studied all this with some dread, for these great shafts had been the means by which the Morlocks ascended from their hellish caverns to the sunny world of the Eloi.

The mouth of the well was silent. That struck me as odd, for I remembered hearing from those other wells the *thud-thud-thud* of the Morlocks' great engines, deep in their subterranean caverns.

I sat down by the side of the well. The vegetation I had observed appeared to be a kind of lichen; it was soft and dry to the touch, though I did not probe it further, nor attempt to determine its structure. I lifted up the lamp, meaning to hold it over the rim and to see if there might be returned the reflection of water; but the flame flickered, as if in some strong draught, and, in a brief panic at the thought of darkness, I snatched the lamp back.

I ducked my head under the cupola and leaned over the well's rim, and was greeted by a blast of warm, moist air into the face – it was like opening the door to a Turkish bath – quite unexpected in that hot but arid night of the future. I had an impression of great depth, and at the remote base of the well I fancied my dark-adapted eyes made out a red glow. Despite its appearance, this really was quite unlike the wells of the first Morlocks. There was no sign of the protruding metal hooks in the side, intended to

46

support climbers, and I still detected no evidence of the machinery noises I had heard before; and I had the odd, unverifiable impression that this well was far deeper than those Morlocks' cavern-drilling.

On a whim, I raised my Kodak and dug out the flash lamp. I filled up the trough of the lamp with *blitzlichtpulver*, lifted the camera and flooded the well with magnesium light. Its reflections dazzled me, and it was a glow so brilliant that it might not have been seen on earth since the covering of the sun, a hundred thousand years or more earlier. That should have scared away the Morlocks if nothing else! – and I began to concoct protective schemes whereby I could connect the flash to the unattended Time Machine, so that the powder would go off if ever the machine was touched.

I stood up and spent some minutes loading the flash lamp and snapping at random across the hillside around the well. Soon a dense cloud of acrid white smoke from the powder was gathering about me. Perhaps I would be lucky, I reflected, and would capture for the wonderment of Humanity the rump of a fleeing, terrified Morlock!

. . . There was a scratching, soft and insistent, from a little way around the well rim, not three feet from where I stood.

With a cry, I fumbled at my belt for my poker. Had the Morlocks fallen on me, while I daydreamed?

Poker in hand, I stepped forward with care. The rasping noises were coming from the bed of lichen, I realized; there was some form, moving steady through those tiny, dark plants. There was no Morlock here, so I lowered my club, and bent over the lichen bed. I saw a small, crab-like creature, no wider than my hand; the scratching I heard was the rasp of its single, outsize claw against the lichen. The crab's case seemed to me to be jet black, and the creature was quite without eyes, like some blind creature of the ocean depths.

So, I reflected as I watched this little drama, the struggle to survive went on, even in this benighted darkness. It struck me that I had seen no signs of life – save for the glimpses of Morlock – away from this well, in all my visit here. I am no biologist, but it seemed clear that the presence of this fount of warm, moist air would be bound to attract life, here on a world turned to desert, just as it had attracted this blind farmer-crab and his crop of lichen. I speculated that the warmth must come from the compressed interior of the earth, whose volcanic heat, evident in our own day, would not have cooled significantly in the intervening six hundred thousand years. And perhaps the moisture came from aquifers, still extant below the ground.

It may be, I mused, the surface of the planet was studded with such wells and cupolas. But their purpose was not to admit access to the interior world of the Morlocks – as in that other History – but to release the earth's intrinsic resources to warm and moisten this planet deprived of its sun; and such life as had survived the monstrous engineering I had witnessed now clustered around these founts of warmth and moisture.

My confidence was increasing – making sense of things is a powerful tonic for my courage, and after that false alarm with the crab, I had no sense of threat – and I sat again on the lip of the well. I had my pipe and some of my tobacco in my pocket, and I packed the bowl full and lit up. I began to speculate on how this History might have diverged from the first I had witnessed. Evidently there had been some parallels – there had been Morlocks and Eloi here – but their grisly duality had been resolved, in ages past.

I wondered why should such a show-down between the races occur – for the Morlocks, in their foul way, were as dependent on the Eloi as were Eloi on Morlock, and the whole arrangement had a sort of stability.

I saw a way it might have come about. The Morlocks were of debased human stock, after all, and it is not in man's heart to be logical about things. The Morlock must have known that he depended on the Eloi for his very existence; he must have pitied and scorned him – his remote cousin, yet reduced to the status of cattle. *And yet* –

And yet, what a glorious morning made up the brief life of the Eloi! The little people laughed and sang and loved across the surface of the world made into a garden, while your Morlock must toil in the stinking depths of the earth to provide the Eloi with the fabric of their luxurious lives. Granted the Morlock was conditioned for his place in creation, and would no doubt turn in disgust from the Eloi's sunlight and clear water and fruit, even were it offered to him – but still, might he not, in his dim and cunning fashion, have envied the Eloi their *leisure*?

Perhaps the flesh of the Eloi turned sour in the Morlock's rank mouth, even as he bit into it in his dingy cave.

I envisaged, then, the Morlocks – or a faction of them – arising one night from their tunnels under the earth, and falling on the Eloi with their weapons and whip-muscled arms. There would be a great Culling – and this time, not a disciplined harvesting of flesh, but a full-blooded assault with one, unthinking purpose: the final extinction of the Eloi.

How must the lawns and food palaces have run with blood, those ancient stones echoing to the child-ish bleating of the Eloi!

In such a contest there could be only one victor, of course. The fragile people of futurity, with their hectic, consumptive beauty, could never defend themselves against the assaults of organized, murderous Morlocks.

I saw it all – or so I thought! The Morlocks, triumphant at last, had inherited the earth. With no more use for the garden-country of the Eloi, they had allowed it to fall into ruin; they had erupted from the earth and – somehow – brought their own stygian darkness with them to cover the sun! I remembered how Weena's folk had feared the nights of the new moon – she had called them 'The Dark Nights' – now, it seemed to me, the Morlocks had brought about a final Dark Night to cover the earth, forever. The Morlocks had at last murdered the last of earth's true children, and even murdered earth herself.

Such was my first hypothesis, then: wild and gaudy – and wrong, in every particular!

. . . And I became aware, with almost a physical shock, that in the middle of all this historical speculation I had quite forgotten my regular inspections of the abandoned Time Machine.

I got to my feet and glared across the hill-side. I soon picked out the machine's candle-lit glow – but the lights I had built flickered and wavered, as if opaque shapes were moving around the machine.

They could only be Morlocks!

6

MY ENCOUNTER WITH
THE MORLOCKS

With a spurt of fear – and, I have to acknowledge it, a lust for blood which pulsed in my head – I roared, lifted my poker-club, and pounded back along the path. Careless, I dropped my Kodak; behind me I heard a soft tinkle of breaking glass. For all I know, that camera lies there still – if I may use the phrase – abandoned in the darkness.

As I neared the machine, I saw they were Morlocks all right – perhaps a dozen of them, capering around the machine. They seemed alternately attracted and repelled by my lights, exactly like moths around candles. They were the same ape-like creatures I remembered – perhaps a little smaller – with that long, flaxen hair across their heads and backs, their skin a pasty white, arms long as monkeys', and with those haunting red-grey eyes. They whooped and jabbered to each other in their queer language. They hadn't yet touched the Time Machine, I noted with some relief, but I knew it was a matter of moments before those uncanny fingers – ape-like, yet clever as any man's – reached out for the sparkling brass and nickel.

But there would be no time for *that,* for I fell upon these Morlocks like an avenging angel.

I laid about me with my poker and my fist. The Morlocks jabbered and squealed, and tried to flee. I grabbed one of the creatures as it ran past me, and I felt again the worm-pallor cold of Morlock flesh. Hair like spider-web brushed across the back of my hand, and the animal nipped at my fingers with its small teeth, but I did not yield. I wielded my club, and I felt the soft, moist collapse of flesh and bone.

Those grey-red eyes widened, and closed.

I seemed to watch all this from a small, detached part of my brain. I had quite forgotten all my intentions to return proof of the working of time travel, or even to find Weena: I suspected at that moment that *this* was why I had returned into time – for *this* moment of revenge: for Weena, and for the murder of the earth, and my own earlier indignity. I dropped the Morlock – unconscious or dead, it was no more than a bundle of hair and bones – and grabbed for its companions, swinging my poker.

Then I heard a voice – distinctively Morlock, but quite unlike the others in tone and depth – it issued a single, imperative syllable. I turned, my arms soaked in blood up to the elbows of my jacket, and made ready for more fighting.

Before me, now, stood a Morlock who did not run from me. Though he was naked like the rest, his coat of hair seemed to have been brushed and prepared, so that he had something of the effect of a groomed dog, made to stand upright like a man. I took a massive step forward, my club held firm in both hands.

Calmly, the Morlock raised his right hand – something glinted there – and there was a green flash, and I felt the world tip backwards from under me, pitching me down beside my glowing machine; and I knew no more!

7

THE CAGE OF LIGHT

I came to my senses slowly, as if emerging from a deep and untroubled sleep. I was lying on my back, with my eyes closed. I felt so comfortable that for a moment I imagined I must be in my own bed, in my house in Richmond, and that the pink glow showing through my eyelids must be the morning sun seeping around my curtains . . .

But then I became aware that the surface beneath me – though yielding and quite warm – did not have the softness of a mattress. I could feel no sheets beneath me, nor blankets above me.

Then, in a flash, it returned to me: all of it – my second flight through time, the darkening of the sun, and my encounter with the Morlocks.

Fear flooded me, stiffening my muscles and tightening my stomach. I had been taken by the Morlocks! I snapped my eyes open –

And I was instantly dazzled by a brilliant illumination. It came from a remote disc of intense white light, directly above me. I cried out and flung an arm across my blinded eyes; I rolled over, pressing my face against the floor.

I pushed myself up to a crawling position. The floor was warm and giving, like leather. At first my vision was full of dancing images of that blazing disc, but at last I was able to make out my own shadow under me. And then, still on all fours, I noticed the queerest thing yet; that the surface beneath me was clear, as if made of some flexible glass, and – where my shadow shielded out the light – *I could see stars*, quite clearly visible through the floor beneath me. I had been deposited on some transparent platform, then, with this starry diorama below: it was as if I had been brought to some inverted planetarium.

I felt queasy to the stomach, but I was able to stand up. I had to shield my eyes with my hand against the unremitting glare from above; I wished I had not lost the hat I had brought from 1891! I still wore my light suit, although it now bore stains of sand and blood, particularly around the sleeves – though some efforts had been made to clean me up, I noticed with surprise, and my hands and arms were clear of Morlock blood, mucus and ichor. My poker was gone, and I could see no sign of my knapsack. I had been left my watch, which hung on a chain from my waistcoat, but my pockets were empty of matches or candles. My pipe and tobacco were gone, too, and I felt an incongruous stab of regret for that – in the middle of all that mystery and peril!

A thought struck me, and my hands flew to my vest pocket – and they found the Time Machine's twin levers still there. I breathed relief.

I looked around. I was standing on a flat, even Floor of the leather-like, clear substance I have described. I was close to the centre of a splash of light perhaps thirty yards wide, cast on that enigmatic Floor by the source above me. The air was quite dusty, so that it was easy to pick out the rays of light as they flooded down over me. You must imagine me standing there in the light, as if at the bottom of some dusty mine shaft, blinking up at the noonday sun. And indeed it *looked* like sunlight – but I could not understand how the sun could have been uncovered, nor come to be stationary above me. My only hypothesis was that I had been moved, while unconscious, to some point on the Equator.

Fighting a mounting panic, I paced around my circle of light. I was quite alone, and the Floor was bare – save for trays, two of them, bearing containers and cartons, which rested on the Floor perhaps ten feet from where I had been laid. I peered out into the encircling gloom, but could make out nothing, even with my eyes quite shielded. I could see no containing walls to this chamber. I clapped my hands, causing dust motes to dance in the lit-up air. The sound was deadened, and no echo was returned. Either the walls were impossibly remote, or they were lagged with some absorbent substance; either way, I had no clue as to their distance.

There was no sign of the Time Machine.

I felt a deep, peculiar fear, there on that plain of soft glass; I felt naked and exposed, with nowhere to shelter my back, no corner to make into a fastness.

I approached the trays. I peered at the cartons, and lifted their lids: there was one large, empty pail, and a bowl of what looked like clear water, and in the last dish there were fist-sized bricks of what I guessed to be food – but it was food processed into smooth yellow, green or red slabs, so that its origins were quite unrecognizable. I poked at the food with a reluctant fingertip: they were cold and smooth, rather like cheese. I had not eaten since Mrs Watchets's breakfast, many hours of my tangled life ago, and I was aware of a mounting pressure in my bladder: a pressure which, I guessed, the empty pail was intended to help relieve. I could see no reason why the Morlocks, having preserved me this long, should choose to poison me, but nevertheless I was reluctant to accept their hospitality – and even more so to lose my dignity by using the pail!

So I stalked around the tray, and around that circle

of light, sniffing like some animal suspicious of a trap. I even picked up the cartons and trays, to see if I could make some weapon of them – perhaps I could hammer out some kind of blade – but the trays were manufactured of a silvery metal, a little like aluminium, so thin and soft it crumpled in my hands. I could no more stab a Morlock with this than with a sheet of paper.

It struck me that these Morlocks had behaved with remarkable gentleness. It would have been the work of a moment to have finished me off while I lay unconscious, but they had stayed their brutish hands – even, with surprising skill, it seemed, made efforts to clean me up.

I was immediately suspicious, of course. For what purpose had they preserved my life? Did they intend to keep me alive, in order to dig out of me – by whatever foul means – the secret of the Time Machine?

I turned away from the food deliberately, and I stepped out of the ring of light, and into the darkness beyond. My heart was hammering; there was nothing tangible to stop me leaving that illuminated shaft, but my apprehension, and my craving for light, held me in there almost as effectively.

At last I chose a direction at random, and walked into the darkness, my arms held loose at my side, my fists curled and ready. I counted out the paces – *eight, nine, ten* . . . Beneath my feet, more clearly visible now that I was away from the light, I could see the stars, an inverted hemisphere of them; I felt again as if I were standing on the roof of some planetarium. I turned and looked back; there was the dusty light pillar, reaching up to infinity, with the scattering of dishes and food at its base on the bare Floor.

It was all quite incomprehensible to me!

As the unchanging Floor wore away beneath me, I

56

soon gave up counting my steps. The only light was the glow of that central needle-shaft of light and the faint gleam of the stars beneath me, by which I could just make out the profile of my own legs; the only sounds were the scratch of my own breathing, and the soft impacts of my boots on the glassy surface.

After perhaps a hundred yards, I turned through a corner and began to pace out a path around my light-needle. Still I found nothing but darkness, and the stars beneath my feet. I wondered if in all this blackness I should encounter those strange, floating Watchers who had accompanied me on my second voyage through time.

Despair began to sink deep into my soul as I blundered on, and I soon began to wish that I could be transported from this place to Weena's garden-world, or even that night landscape where I had been captured – anywhere with rocks, and plants, and animals, and a recognizable sky, for me to work with! What kind of place was this? Was I in some chamber, buried deep in the hollowed-out earth? What terrible tortures were the Morlocks devising for me? Was I doomed to spend the rest of my life in this alien barrenness?

For a period I was quite unhinged, by my isolation and my awful sense of being stranded. I did not know where I was, nor where the Time Machine was, and I did not expect to see my home again. I was a strange beast, stranded in an alien world. I called out to the dark, alternately issuing threats and entreaties for mercy or release; and I slammed my fists against the bland, unyielding Floor, without result. I sobbed, and ran, and cursed myself for my unmatched folly – having once escaped the clutches of the Morlocks – to have immediately returned myself to the same trap!

In the end I must have bawled like a frustrated

child, and I used up my strength, and I sank in the darkness to the ground, quite exhausted.

I think I dozed a while. When I came to myself, nothing in my condition had changed. I got myself to my feet. My anger and frenzy had burned themselves out and, though I felt as desolate as ever in my life, I made room for my body's simple human needs: hunger and thirst being primary among them.

I returned, tired out, to my light shaft. That pressure in my bladder had continued to build. With a feeling of resignation, I picked up the pail that had been provided for me, carried it off into the dark a little way – for modesty's sake, as I knew Morlocks must be watching – and when I had done I left it there, out of sight.

I surveyed the Morlock food. It was a bleak prospect: it looked no more appetizing than earlier, but I was just as hungry. I picked up the bowl of water – it was the size of a soup bowl – and raised it to my lips. It was not a pleasant drink – tepid and tasteless, as if all the minerals had been distilled out of it – but it was clear and it refreshed my mouth. I held the liquid on my tongue for a few seconds, hesitating at this final hurdle; then, deliberately, I swallowed.

After a few minutes I had suffered no ill effects I could measure, and I took a little more of the water. I also dabbed a corner of my handkerchief on the bowl, and wiped the water across my brow and hands.

I turned to the food itself. I picked up one greenish slab of it. I snapped off a corner: it broke easily, was green all the way through, and crumbled a little like a Cheddar. My teeth slid into the stuff. As to its flavour: if you have ever eaten a green vegetable, say broccoli or sprouts, boiled to within an inch of disintegration, then you have something of its savour;

members of the less well-appointed London clubs will recognize the symptoms! But I bit into my slab until it was half gone. Then I picked up the other slabs to try them; although their colours varied, their texture and flavour differed not a whit.

It did not take many mouthfuls of that stuff to sate me, and I dropped the fragments on their tray and pushed it away.

I sat on the Floor and peered into the dark. I felt an intense gratitude that the Morlocks had at least provided me with this illumination, for I imagined that had I been deposited on this empty, featureless surface in a darkness broken only by the star images beneath me, I might have gone quite mad. And yet I knew, at the same time, that the Morlocks had provided this ring of light for their own purposes, as an effective means to keep me in this place. I was all but helpless, a prisoner of a mere light ray!

A great weariness descended on me. I felt reluctant to lose consciousness once more – to leave myself defenceless – but I could see little prospect of staying awake forever. I stepped out of the ring of light and a little way away into the darkness, so that I felt, at least, some security from its cover of night. I took off my jacket and folded it up into a pillow for my head. The air was quite warm, and the soft Floor also seemed heated, so I should not go cold.

So, with my portly body stretched out over the stars, I slept.

8

A VISITOR

I awoke after an interval I could not measure. I lifted my head and glanced around. I was alone in the dark, and all seemed unchanged. I patted my vest pocket; the Time Machine levers were still safely there.

As I tried to move, stiffness sent pain shooting along my legs and back. I sat up, awkward, and got to my feet feeling every year of my age; I was inordinately grateful that I had not had to leap into action to fend off a tribe of marauding Morlocks! I performed a few rusty physical jerks to loosen up my muscles; then I picked up my jacket, smoothing out its creases, and donned it.

I stepped forward into the light ring.

The trays, with food cartons and toilet pail, had been changed, I found. So they *were* watching me! – well, it was no more than I had suspected. I took the lids off the cartons, only to find the same depressing slabs of anonymous fodder. I made a breakfast of water and some of the greenish stuff. My fear was gone, to be replaced by a numbing sense of tedium: it is remarkable how rapidly the human mind can accommodate the most remarkable of changed circumstances. Was this to be my fate from now on? – boredom, a hard bed, lukewarm water, and a diet of slabs of boiled cabbage? It was like being back at school, I reflected with gloom.

'*Pau.*'

The single syllable, softly spoken, sounded as loud to me in all that silence as a gun shot.

I cried out, scrambled to my feet, and held out my food slabs – it was absurd, but I lacked any other weapon. The sound had come from behind me, and I whirled around, my boots squealing on the Floor.

A Morlock stood there, just beyond the edge of my light circle, half-illuminated. He stood upright – he did not share the crouching, ape-like gait of those creatures I had encountered before – and he wore goggles that made a shield of blue glass which coated his huge eyes, turning them black to my view. '*Tik. Pau,*' this apparition pronounced, his voice a queer gurgle.

I stumbled backwards, stepping on a tray with a clatter. I held up my fists. 'Don't come near me!'

The Morlock took a single pace forward, coming closer to the light shaft; despite his goggles, he flinched a little from the brightness. This was one of that new breed of advanced-looking Morlock, one of which had stunned me, I realized; he seemed naked, but the pale hair which coated his back and head was cut and shaped – deliberately – into a rather severe style, square about the breast bone and shoulders, giving it something of the effect of a uniform. He had a small, chinless face, something like an ugly child's.

A ghost of memory of that sweet sensation of Morlock skull cracking under my club returned to me. I considered rushing this fellow, knocking him to the ground. But what would it avail me? There were uncounted others, no doubt, out there in the dark. I had no weapons, not even my poker, and I recalled how this chap's cousin had raised that queer gun against me, knocking me down without effort.

I decided to bide my time.

And besides – this might seem strange! – I found my anger was dissipating, into an unaccountable feel-

61

ing of humour. This Morlock, despite the standard wormy pallor of his skin, did look comical: imagine an orang-utan, his hair clipped short and dyed pale yellow-white, and then encouraged to stand upright and wear a pair of gaudy spectacles, and you'll have something of the effect of him.

'*Tik. Pau*,' he repeated.

I took a step towards him. 'What are you saying to me, you brute?'

He flinched – I imagined he was reacting to my tone rather than my words – and then he pointed, in turn, to the food slabs in my hands. '*Tik*,' he said. '*Pau*.'

I understood. 'Good heavens,' I said, 'you *are* trying to talk to me, aren't you?' I held up my food slabs in turn. '*Tik. Pau*. One. Two. Do you speak English? *One. Two*...'

The Morlock cocked his head to one side – the way a dog will sometimes – and then he said, not much less clearly than I had, '*One. Two*.'

'That's it! And there's more where that came from – *one, two, three, four*...'

The Morlock strode into my light circle, though I noticed he kept out of my arm's reach. He pointed to my water bowl. '*Agua*.'

'*Agua?*' That had sounded like Latin – though the Classics were never my strong point. 'Water,' I replied.

Again the Morlock listened in silence, his head on a tilt.

So we continued. The Morlock pointed to common things – bits of clothing, or parts of the body like a head or a limb – and would come up with some candidate word. Some of his tries were frankly unrecognizable to me, and some of them sounded like German, or perhaps old English. And I would come back with my modern usage. Once or twice I tried to engage him in a longer conversation – for I could not see how this simple register of nouns was going to get us very far – but he stood there until I fell silent, and then continued with his patient matching game. I tried him with some of what I remembered of Weena's language, that simplified, melodic tongue of two-word sentences; but again the Morlock stood patiently until I gave up.

This went on for several hours. At length, without ceremony, the Morlock took his leave – he walked off into the dark – I did not follow (*not yet!* I told myself again). I ate and slept, and when I awoke he returned, and we resumed our lessons.

As he walked around my light cage, pointing at things and naming them, the Morlock's movements were fluid and graceful enough, and his body seemed expressive; but I came to realize how much one relies, in day to day business, on the interpretation of the movements of one's fellows. I could not *read* this Morlock in that way at all. It was impossible to tell what he was thinking or feeling – was he afraid of me? was he bored? – and I felt greatly disadvantaged as a result.

At the end of our second session of this, the Morlock stepped back from me.

He said: 'That should be sufficient. Do you understand me?'

I stared at him, stunned by this sudden facility with my language! His pronunciation was blurred – that liquid Morlock voice is not designed, it seems, for the harsher consonants and stops of English – but the words were quite comprehensible.

When I did not reply, he repeated, 'Do you understand me?'

'I – yes. I mean: yes, I understand you! But how did you do this – how can you have learned my language

– from so few words?' For I judged we had covered a bare five hundred words, most of those concrete nouns and simple verbs.

'I have access to records of all of the ancient languages of Humanity – as reconstructed – from Nostratic through the Indo-European group and its prototypes. A small number of key words is sufficient for the appropriate variant to be retrieved. You must inform me if anything I say is not intelligible.'

I took a cautious step forward. 'Ancient? And how do you *know* I am ancient?'

Huge lids swept down over those goggled eyes. 'Your physique is archaic. And the contents of your stomach, when analysed' He actually shuddered, evidently at the thought of the remnants of Mrs Watchets's breakfast. I was astonished: I had a fastidious Morlock! He went on, 'You are out of time. We do not yet understand how you came to arrive on the earth. But no doubt we will learn.'

'And in the meantime,' I said with some strength, 'you keep me in this – this *Cage of Light.* As if I were a beast, not a man! You give me a floor to sleep on, and a pail for my toilet -'

The Morlock said nothing; he observed me, impassive.

The frustration and embarrassment which had assailed me since my arrival in this place welled up, now that I was able to express them, and I decided that sufficient pleasantries had been exchanged. I said, 'Now that we can speak to each other, you're going to tell me where on earth I am. And where you've hidden my machine. Do you understand that, fellow, or do I have to *translate* it for you?' And I reached for him, meaning to grab at the hair clumps on his chest.

When I came within two paces of him, he raised his hand. That was all. I remember a queer green flash – I never saw the device he must have held, all the time he was near me – and then I fell to the Floor, quite insensible.

9

REVELATIONS AND REMONSTRANCES

I came to, spread-eagled on the Floor once more, and staring up into that confounded light.

I hoisted myself up onto my elbows, and rubbed my dazzled eyes. My Morlock friend was still there, standing just outside the circle of light. I got to my feet, rueful. These New Morlocks were going to be a handful for me, I realized.

The Morlock stepped into the light, its blue goggles glinting. As if nothing had interrupted our dialogue, he said, 'My name is –' his pronunciation reverted to the usual shapeless Morlock pattern – 'Nebogipfel.'

'*Nebogipfel.* Very well.' In turn, I told him my name; within a few minutes he could repeat it with clarity and precision.

This, I realized, was the first Morlock whose name I had learned – the first who stood out from the masses of them I had encountered, and fought; the first to have the attributes of a distinguishable *person.*

'So, Nebogipfel,' I said. I sat cross-legged beside my trays, and rubbed at the rash of bruises my latest fall had inflicted on my upper arm. 'You have been assigned as my keeper, here in this zoo.'

'*Zoo.*' He stumbled over that word. 'No. I was not *assigned.* I volunteered to work with you.'

'Work with me?'

'I – we – want to understand how you came to be here.'

'Do you, by Jove?' I got to my feet and paced around my Cage of Light. 'What if I told you that I came here in a machine that can carry a man through time?' I held up my hands. 'That *I* built such a machine, with these hands? What then, eh?'

He seemed to think that over. 'Your era, as dated from your speech and physique, is very remote from ours. You are capable of achievements of high technology – witness your machine, whether or not it carries you through time as you claim. And the clothes you wear, the state of your hands, and the wear patterns of your teeth – all of these are indicative of a high state of civilization.'

'I'm flattered,' I said with some heat, 'but if you believe I'm capable of such things – that I am a man, not an ape – why am I caged up in this way?'

'Because,' he said evenly, 'you have already tried to attack me, with every intent of doing me harm. And on the Earth, you did great damage to –'

I felt fury burning anew. I stepped towards him. 'Your monkeys were pawing at my machine,' I shouted. 'What did you expect? I was defending myself. I –'

He said: '*They were children.*'

His words pierced my rage. I tried to cling to the remnants of my self-justifying anger, but they were already receding from me. 'What did you say?'

'*Children.* They were children. Since the completion of the Sphere, the Earth is become a. . . *nursery*, a place for children to roam. They were curious about your machine. That is all. They would not have done you, or it, any conscious harm. Yet you attacked them, with great savagery.'

I stepped back from him. I remembered – now I let myself think about it – that the Morlocks capering

67

ineffectually around my machine had struck me as smaller than those I'd encountered before. And they had made no attempt to hurt me. . . save only the poor creature who I had captured, and who had then nipped my hand – before I clubbed its face!

'The one I struck. Did he – it – survive?'

'The physical injuries were reparable. But –'

'Yes?'

'The inner scars, the scars of the mind – these may never heal.'

I dropped my head. *Could it be true?* Had I been so blinded by my loathing of Morlocks that I had been unable to see those creatures around the machine for what they were: not the rat-like, vicious creatures of Weena's world – but harmless infants? 'I don't suppose you know what I'm talking about – but I feel as if I'm trapped in another one of those "Dissolving Views" . . .'

'You are expressing shame,' Nebogipfel said.

Shame . . . I never thought I should hear, and accept, such remonstrance from a Morlock! I looked at him, defiant. 'Yes. Very well! And does that make me more than a beast, in your view, or less of one?'

He said nothing.

Even while I was confronting this personal horror, some calculating part of my mind was running over something Nebogipfel had said. *Since the completion of the Sphere, the Earth is become a nursery* . . .

'What *Sphere*?'

'You have much to learn of us.'

'Tell me about the Sphere!'

'It is a Sphere around the sun.'

Those seven simple words – startling! – and yet . . . Of course! The solar evolution I had watched in the time-accelerated sky, the exclusion of the sunlight from the Earth – 'I understand,' I said to Nebogipfel. 'I watched the sphere's construction.'

68

The Morlock's eyes seemed to widen, in a very human mannerism, as he considered this unexpected news.

And now, for me, other aspects of my situation were becoming clear.

'You said,' I essayed to Nebogipfel, '"On the Earth, you did great damage –" Something on those lines.' It was an odd thing to say, I thought now – *if I was still on the Earth*. I lifted my face and let the light beat down on me. 'Nebogipfel – beneath my feet. What is visible, through this clear Floor?'

'Stars.'

'Not representations, not some kind of planetarium –'

'Stars.'

I nodded. 'And this light from above –'

'It is sunlight.'

Somehow, I think I had known it. I stood in the light of a sun, which was overhead for twenty-four hours of every day; I stood on a Floor *above* the stars . . .

I felt as if the world were shifting about me; I felt light-headed, and there was a remote ringing in my ears. My adventures had already taken me across the deserts of time, but now – thanks to my capture by these astonishing Morlocks – *I had been lifted across space*. I was no longer on the Earth – I had been transported to the Morlocks' solar Sphere!

10

A DIALOGUE WITH
A MORLOCK

'You say you travelled here on a *Time Machine.*'
I paced across my little disc of light, caged, restless. 'The term is precise. It is a machine which can travel indifferently in any direction in time, and at any relative rate, as the driver determines.'

'So you claim that you have journeyed here, from the remote past, on this machine – the machine found with you on the earth.'

'Precisely,' I snapped. The Morlock seemed content to stand, almost immobile, for long hours, as he developed his interrogation. But I am a man of a modern cut, and our moods did not coincide. 'Confound it, fellow,' I said, 'you have observed yourself that I myself am of an *archaic design.* How else, but through time travel, can you explain my presence, here in the Year A.D. 657,208?'

Those huge curtain-eyelashes blinked slowly. 'There are a number of alternatives: most of them more plausible than time travel.'

'Such as?' I challenged him.

'Genetic resequencing.'

'Genetic?' Nebogipfel explained further, and I got the general drift. 'You're talking of the mechanism by which heredity operates – by which characteristics are transmitted from generation to generation.'

'It is not impossible to generate simulacra of archaic forms by unravelling subsequent mutations.'

70

'So you think I am no more than a *simulacrum* – reconstructed like the fossil skeleton of some Megatherium in a museum? Yes?'

'There are precedents, though not of human forms of your vintage. Yes. It is possible.'

I felt insulted. 'And to what purpose might I have been cobbled together in this way?' I resumed my pacing around the Cage. The most disconcerting aspect of that bleak place was its lack of walls, and my constant, primeval sense that my back was unguarded. I would rather have been hurled in some prison cell of my own era – primitive and squalid, no doubt, but *enclosed*. 'I'll not rise to any such bait. That's a lot of nonsense. I designed and built a Time Machine, and travelled here on it; and let that be an end to it!'

'We will use your explanation as a working hypothesis,' Nebogipfel said. 'Now, please describe to me the machine's operating principles.'

I continued my pacing, caught in a dilemma. As soon as I had realized that Nebogipfel was articulate and intelligent, unlike those Morlocks of my previous acquaintance, I had expected some such interrogation; after all, if a Time Traveller from Ancient Egypt had turned up in nineteenth century London I would have fought to be on the committee which examined him. But should I share the secret of my machine – my only advantage in this world – with these New Morlocks?

After some internal searching, I realized I had little choice. I had no doubt that the information could be forced out of me, if the Morlocks so desired. Besides, the construction of my machine was intrinsically simpler than that of, say, a fine clock. A civilization capable of throwing a shell around the sun would have little trouble reproducing the fruit of my poor lathes and presses! And if I spoke to Nebogipfel,

71

perhaps I could put the fellow off while I sought some advantage from my difficult situation. I still had no idea where the machine was being held, still less how I should reach it and have a prospect of returning home.

But also – and here is the honest truth – the thought of my savagery among the child-Morlocks on the earth still weighed on my mind! I had no desire that Nebogipfel should think of me – nor the phase of Humanity which I, perforce, represented – as brutish. Therefore, like a child eager to impress, I wanted to show Nebogipfel how clever I was, how mechanically and scientifically adept: how far above the apes men of my type had ascended.

Still, for the first time I felt emboldened to make some demands of my own.

'Very well,' I said to Nebogipfel. 'But first . . .'

'Yes?'

'Look here,' I said, 'the conditions under which you're holding me are a little primitive, aren't they? I'm not as young as I was, and I can't do with this standing about all day. How about a chair? Is that so unreasonable a thing to ask for? And what about blankets to sleep under, if I must stay here?'

'*Chair.*' He had taken a second to reply, as if he was looking up the referent in some invisible dictionary.

I went on to other demands. I needed more fresh water, I said, and some equivalent of soap; and I asked – expecting to be refused – for a blade with which to shave my bristles.

For a time, Nebogipfel withdrew. When he returned he brought blankets and a chair; and after my next sleep period I found my two trays of provisions supplemented by a third, which bore more water.

The blankets were of some soft substance, too finely manufactured for me to detect any evidence of weaving. The chair – a simple upright thing – might have been of a light wood from its weight, but its red surface was smooth and seamless, and I could not scratch through its paint work with my fingernails, nor could I detect any evidence of joints, nails, screws or mouldings; it seemed to have been extruded as a complete whole by some unknown process. As to my toilet, the extra water came without soap, and nor would it lather, but the liquid had a smooth feel to it, and I suspected it had been treated with some detergent. By some minor miracle, the water was delivered warm to the touch – and stayed that way, no matter how long I let the bowl stand.

I was brought no blade, though – I was not surprised!

When next Nebogipfel left me alone, I undressed myself by stages and washed away the perspiration of some days, as well as lingering traces of Morlock blood; I also took the opportunity of rinsing through my underwear and shirt.

So my life in the Cage of Light became a little more civilized. If you imagine the contents of a cheap hotel room dumped into the middle of the floor of some vast ball room, you will have the picture of how I was living. When I pulled together the chair, trays and blankets I had something of a cosy nest, and I did not feel quite so exposed; I took to placing my jacket-pillow under the chair, and so sleeping with my head and shoulders under the protection of this little fastness. Most of the time I was able to dismiss the prospect of stars beneath my feet – I told myself that the lights in the Floor were some elaborate illusion – but sometimes my imagination would betray me, and I would feel as if I were suspended over an infinite drop, with only this insubstantial Floor to save me.

All this was quite illogical, of course; but I am

human, and must needs pander to the instinctive needs and fears of my nature!

Nebogipfel observed all this. I could not tell if his reaction was curiosity or confusion, or perhaps something more aloof – as I might have watched the antics of a bird in building a nest, perhaps.

And in these circumstances, the next few days wore away – I think four or five – as I strove to describe to Nebogipfel the workings of my Time Machine – and as well seeking subtly to extract from him some details of this History in which I had landed myself.

I described the researches into physical optics which had led me to my insights into the possibility of time travel.

'It is becoming well known – or was, in my day – that the propagation of light has anomalous properties,' I said. 'The speed of light in a vacuum is extremely high – it travels hundreds of thousands of miles each *second* – but it is finite. And, more important, as demonstrated most clearly by Michelson and Morley a few years before my departure, this speed is *isotropic . . .*'

I took some care to explain this rum business. The essence of it is that light, as it travels through space, does not behave like a material object, such as an express train.

Imagine a ray of light from some distant star overtaking the earth in, say, January, as our planet traverses its orbit around the sun. The speed of the earth in its orbit is some seventy thousand miles per hour. You would imagine – if you were to measure the speed of that passing ray of star-light as seen from the earth – that the result would be *reduced* by that seventy thousand-odd miles per hour.

Conversely, in July, the earth will at the opposite side of its orbit: it will now be heading *into* the path

74

of that faithful star-light beam. Measure the speed of the beam again, and you would expect to find the recorded speed *increased* by the earth's velocity.

Well, if steam trains came to us from the stars, this would no doubt be the case. But Michelson and Morley proved that for star-light, this is *not* so. The speed of the star-light as measured from the earth – whether we are overtaking or heading into the beam – *is exactly the same!*

These observations had correlated with the sort of phenomenon I had noted about Plattnerite for some years previously – though I had not published the results of my experiments – and I had formulated an hypothesis.

'One only needs to loosen the shackles of the imagination – particularly regarding the business of Dimensions – to see what the elements of an explanation might be. How do we measure speed, after all? Only with devices which record intervals in different Dimensions: a distance travelled through Space, measured with a simple yardstick, and an interval in Time, which may be recorded with a clock.

'So, if we take the experimental evidence of Michelson and Morley at face value, then we have to regard the speed of light as the fixed quantity, *and the Dimensions as variable things.* The universe adjusts itself in order to render our light-speed measurements constant.

'I saw that one could express this geometrically, as a *twisting* of the Dimensions.' I held up my hand, with two fingers and thumb held at right angles. 'If we are in a framework of Four Dimensions – well, imagine rotating the whole business around, like this –' I twisted my wrist '– so that Length comes to rest where Breadth used to be, and Breadth where Height was – and, most important, *Duration and a Dimension of Space are interchanged.* Do you see? One would not need a full transposition, of course – just a certain intermingling of the two to explain the Michelson-Morley adjustment.

'I have kept these speculations to myself,' I said. 'I am not well-known as a theoretician. Besides, I have been reluctant to publish without experimental verification. But there are – were – others thinking along the same lines – I know of Fitzgerald in Dublin, Lorentz in Leiden, and Henri Poincaré in France – and it cannot be long before some more complete theory is expounded, dealing with this relativeness of frames of reference . . .

'Well, then, this is the essence of my Time Machine,' I concluded. 'The machine twists Space and Time around itself, thus mutating Time into a Spatial Dimension – and then one may proceed, into past or future, as easy as riding a bicycle!'

I sat back in my chair; given the uncomfortable circumstances of this lecture, I told myself, I had acquitted myself remarkably well.

But my Morlock was not an appreciative audience. He stood there, regarding me through his blue goggles. Then, at length, he said: 'Yes. But *how*, exactly?'

11

OUT OF THE CAGE

This response irritated me intensely!

I got out of my chair and began to pace about my Cage. I came near to Nebogipfel, but I managed to resist the impulse to lapse into threatening simian gestures. I flatly refused to answer any more questions until he showed me something of his Sphere-world.

'Look here,' I said, 'don't you think you're being a little unfair? After all, I've travelled across six hundred thousand years to see something of your world. And all I've had so far is a darkened hill-side in Richmond, and –' I waved a hand at the encircling darkness '– this, and your endless questions!

'Look at it this way, Nebogipfel. I know you will want me to give you a full account of my journey through time, and what I saw of History as it unfolded to your present. How can I tell such a tale if I have no understanding of its conclusion? – let alone of that other History which I witnessed.'

I left my speech there, hoping I had done enough to convince him.

He lifted his hand to his face; his thin, pallid fingers adjusted the goggles resting there, like any gentleman adjusting a pince-nez. 'I will consult about this,' he said at last. 'We will speak again.'

And he departed. I watched him walk away, his bare soles pad-padding across the soft, starry Floor.

After I had slept once more, Nebogipfel returned.

He raised his hand and beckoned; it was a stiff, unnatural gesture, as if he had learned it only recently.

'Come with me,' he said.

With a surge of exhilaration – tinged with not a little fear – I snatched my jacket up from the Floor.

I walked beside Nebogipfel, into the darkness which had encircled me for so many days. My shaft of sunlight receded behind me. I glanced back at the little spot which had been my inhospitable home, with its disordered trays, its heap of blankets, and my chair – perhaps the only chair in the world! I will not say I watched it go with any nostalgia, for I had been miserable and fearful during the whole of my stay in that Cage of Light, but I did wonder whether I would ever see it again.

Beneath our feet, the eternal stars hung like a million Chinese lanterns, borne on the breast of an invisible river.

As we walked, Nebogipfel held out blue goggles, very like the set he wore himself. I took these, but I protested: 'What do I need of these? I am not dazzled, as you are –'

'They are not for light. They are for darkness. Put them on.'

I lifted the goggles to my face. The set was built on two hoops of some pliable substance, which sandwiched the blue glass of the goggles itself; when I lifted the goggles to my face, the hoops slipped easily around my head and gripped there lightly.

I turned my head. I had no impression of *blueness*, despite the tint of my goggles. That shaft of sunlight seemed as bright as ever, and the image of Nebogipfel was as clear as it had been before. 'They don't seem to work,' I said.

For answer, Nebogipfel tipped his head downwards.

I followed his gaze – and my step faltered. For, beneath my feet and through the soft Floor, the stars blazed. Those lights were no longer masked by the sheen of the Floor, or by my eyes' poor dark-adaptation; it was as if I stood poised above some starry night in the mountains of Wales or Scotland! I suffered an intense stab of vertigo, as you might imagine.

I detected a trace of impatience about Nebogipfel now – he seemed anxious to proceed. We walked on in silence.

Within a very few paces, it seemed to me, Nebogipfel slowed, and I saw now, thanks to my goggles, that a wall lay a few feet from us. I reached out and touched its soot-black surface, but it had only the soft, warm texture of the Floor. I could not understand how we had reached the boundaries of this chamber so quickly. I wondered if somehow we had walked along some moving pavement which had assisted our footsteps; but Nebogipfel volunteered no information.

'Tell me what this place is, before we leave it,' I said.

His flaxen-haired head turned towards me. 'An empty chamber.'

'How wide?'

'Approximately two thousand miles.'

I tried to conceal my reaction to this. *Two thousand miles?* Had I been alone, in a prison cell large enough to hold an ocean? 'You have a great deal of room here,' I said evenly.

'The Sphere is *large*,' he said. 'If you are accustomed only to planetary distances, you may find it difficult to appreciate how large. The Sphere fills the orbit of the primal planet you called Venus. It has a surface area corresponding to nearly three hundred million earths –'

'*Three hundred million?*'

My amazement met only with a blank stare from the Morlock, and more of that subtle impatience. I understood his restlessness, and yet I felt resentful – and a little embarrassed. To the Morlock, I was like some irritating man from the Congo come to London, who must ask the purpose and provenance of the simplest items, such as a fork or a pair of trousers!

To me, I reasoned, the Sphere was a startling construction! – but so might the Pyramids have been to some Neandertaler. For this complacent Morlock, the Sphere around the sun was part of the historic furniture of the world, no more to be remarked on than a landscape tamed by a thousand years of agriculture.

A door opened before us – it did not fold back, you understand, but rather it seemed to scissor itself away, much as does the diaphragm of a camera – and we stepped forward.

I gasped, and almost stumbled backwards. Nebogipfel watched me with his usual analytical calm.

From a room the size of a world – a room carpeted with stars – a million Morlock faces swivelled towards me.

12

THE MORLOCKS OF
THE SPHERE

You must imagine that place: a single immense *room*, with a carpet of stars and a complex, engineered ceiling, and all of it going on forever, without walls. It was a place of black and silver, without any other colour. The Floor was marked out by partitions that came up to chest-height, though there were no dividing walls: there were no enclosed areas, nothing resembling our offices or homes, anywhere.

And there were *Morlocks*, a pale scattering of them, all across that transparent Floor; their faces were like grey flakes of snow sprinkled over the starry carpet. The place was filled with their voices: their constant, liquid babbling washed over me, oceanic in itself, and remote from the sounds of the human palate – and removed, too, from the dry voice Nebogipfel had become accustomed to using in my company.

There was a line at infinity, utterly straight and a little blurred by dust and mist, where the Roof met the Floor. And that line showed none of the bowing effect that one sometimes sees as one studies an ocean. It is hard to describe – it may seem that such things are beyond one's intuition until they are experienced – but at that moment, standing there, *I knew I was not on the surface of any planet*. There was no far horizon beyond which rows of Morlocks were hidden, like receding sea-going ships; instead I knew that the earth's tight, compact contours were far away. My heart sank, and I was quite daunted.

Nebogipfel stepped forward to me. He had doffed his goggles, and I had an impression it was with relief. 'Come,' he said gently. 'Are you afraid? This is what you wanted to see. We will walk. And we will talk further.'

With great hesitation – it took me a genuine effort to step forward, away from the wall of my immense prison cell – I came after him.

I caused quite a stir in the population. Their little faces were all around me, huge-eyed and chinless. I shrank away from them as I walked, my dread of their cold flesh renewed. Some of them reached towards me, with their long, hair-covered arms. I could smell something of their bodies, a sweet, musty smell that was all too familiar. Most walked as upright as a man, although some preferred to lope along like an orang-utan, with knuckles grazing the Floor. Many of them had their hair, on scalp and back, coiffed in some style or other, some in a plain and severe fashion, like Nebogipfel, and some in a more flowing, decorative style. But there were one or two whose hair ran as wild and ragged as any Morlock's I had encountered in Weena's world, and at first I suspected that these individuals still ran savage, even here in this city-room; but they behaved as easily as the rest, and I hypothesized that these unkempt manes were simply another form of affectation – much as a man will sometimes allow his beard to grow to great profusion.

I became aware that I was passing by these Morlocks with remarkable speed – much quicker than my pace allowed. I almost stumbled at this realization. I glanced down, but I could see nothing to differentiate the stretch of transparent Floor on which I walked from any other; but I knew I must be on some form of moving pavement.

The crowding, pallid Morlock faces, the absence of colour, the flatness of the horizon, my unnatural speed through this bizarre landscape – and above all, the illusion that I was floating above a bottomless well of stars – combined into the semblance of a dream! – But then some curious Morlock would come too close, and I would get a whiff of his sickly scent, and reality pressed in again.

This was no dream: I was lost, I realized, marooned in this sea of Morlocks, and again I had to struggle to keep walking steadily, to avoid bunching my fists and driving them into the curious faces pressing around me.

I saw how the Morlocks were going about their mysterious business. Some were walking, some conversing, some eating food of the bland, uninteresting type which had been served to me, all as uninhibited as kittens. This observation, combined with the utter lack of any enclosed spaces, led me to understand that the Morlocks of the Sphere had no need of privacy, in the sense we understand it.

Most of the Morlocks seemed to me to be working, though at what I could not fathom. The surfaces of some of their partitions were inlaid with panes of a blue, glowing glass, and the Morlocks touched these panes with their thin, wormlike fingers, or talked earnestly into them. In response, graphs, pictures and text scrolled across the glass slabs. In some places this remarkable machinery was carried a stage further, and I saw elaborate models – representing what I could not say – springing into existence in mid-air. At a Morlock's command, a model would rotate, or split open, displaying its interior – or fly apart, in dwindling arrays of floating cubes of coloured light.

And all of this activity, you must imagine, was immersed in a constant flow of the Morlocks' liquid, guttural tongue.

Now we passed a place where a fresh partition was emerging from the Floor below. It rose up complete and finished like something emerging from a vat of mercury; when its growth was done it had become a thin slab about four feet high featuring three of the omnipresent blue windows. When I crouched down to peer through the transparent Floor, I could see nothing beneath the surface: no box, or uplifting machinery. It was as if the partition had appeared out of nothing. 'Where does it come from?' I asked Nebogipfel.

He said, after some thought – evidently he had to choose his words: 'The Sphere has a *Memory*. It has machines which enable it to store that Memory. And the form of the data blocks –' he meant the partitions '– is held in the Sphere's Memory, to be retrieved in this material form as desired.'

For my entertainment, Nebogipfel caused more extrusions: on one pillar I saw a tray of foodstuffs and water rising out of the floor, as if prepared by some invisible butler!

I was struck by this idea of extrusions from the uniform and featureless Floor. It reminded me of the Platonist theory of thought expounded by some philosophers: that to every object there exists, in some realm, an ideal Form – an essence of Chair, the summation of Table-ness, and so on – and when an object is manufactured in our world, templates stored in the Platonic over-world are consulted.

Well, here I was in a Platonic universe made real: the whole of this mighty, sun-girdling Sphere was suffused by an artificial, god-like Memory – a Memory within whose rooms I walked even as we spoke. And within the Memory was stored the Ideal of every object the heart could desire – or at least, as desired by a Morlock heart.

How very convenient it would be to be able to

manufacture and dissolve equipment and apparatus as one required! My great, draughty house in Richmond could be reduced to a single Room, I realized. In the morning, the bedroom furniture could be commanded to fade back into the carpet, to be replaced by the bathroom suite, and next the kitchen table. Like magic, the various apparatuses of my laboratory could be made to flow from the walls and ceiling, until I was ready to work. And at last, of an evening, I could summon up my dinner table, with its comfortable surrounds of fireplace and wallpaper; and perhaps the table could be manufactured already replete with food!

All our professions of builders, plumbers, carpenters and the like would disappear in a trice, I realized. The householder – the owner of such an Intelligent Room – would need to engage no more than a peripatetic cleaner (though perhaps the Room could take care of that too!), and perhaps there would be occasional boosts to the Room's mechanical memory, to keep pace with the latest vogues . . .

So my fecund imagination ran on, quite out of my control.

I soon began to feel fatigued. Nebogipfel took me to a clear space – though there were Morlocks in the distance, all about me – and he tapped his foot on the Floor. A sort of shelter was extruded; it was perhaps four feet high, and little more than a roof set on four fat pillars: something like a substantial table, perhaps. Within the table there arose a bundle of blankets and a food-stand. I climbed into the hut gratefully – it was the first enclosure I had enjoyed since my arrival on the Sphere – and I acknowledged Nebogipfel's consideration at providing it. I made a meal of water and some of the greenish cheese stuff, and I took off my goggles – I was immersed in the endless darkness of that Morlock world – and was able to sleep, with my head settled on a rolled-up blanket.

This odd little shelter was my home for the next few days, as I continued my tour of the Morlock's city-chamber with Nebogipfel. Each time I arose, Nebogipfel had the Floor absorb the shelter once again, and he evoked it afresh in whatever place we stopped – so we had no luggage to carry! I have noted that the Morlocks did not sleep, and I think my antics in my hut were the source of considerable fascination to the natives of the Sphere – just as those of an orang-utan catch the eye of the civilized man, I suppose – and they would have crowded around me as I tried to sleep, pressing their little round faces in on me, and rest would have been impossible, had not Nebogipfel stayed by me, and deterred such sight-seeing.

13

HOW THE MORLOCKS LIVED

In all the days Nebogipfel led me through that Morlock world, we never encountered a wall, door or other significant barrier. As near as I could make it out, we were restricted – the whole time – to a single chamber: but it was a chamber of a stupendous size. And it was, in its general details, homogenous, for everywhere I found this same carpet of Morlocks pursuing their obscure tasks. The simplest practicalities of such arrangements were startling enough; I considered, for example, the prosaic problems of maintaining a consistent and stable atmosphere, at an even temperature, pressure and humidity, over such scales of length. And yet, Nebogipfel gave me to understand, this was but one chamber in a sort of mosaic of them, that tiled the Sphere from Pole to Pole.

I soon came to understand that there were no *cities* on this Sphere, in the modern sense. The Morlock population was spread over these immense chambers, and there were no fixed sites for any given activity. If the Morlocks wished to assemble a work area – or clear it for some other purpose – the relevant apparatuses could be extruded directly from the Floor, or else absorbed back. Thus, rather than cities, there were to be found nodes of population of higher density – nodes which shifted and migrated, according to purpose.

After one sleep I had clambered out of the shelter and was sitting cross-legged on the Floor, sipping water. Nebogipfel remained standing, seemingly without fatigue. Then I saw approaching us a brace of Morlocks, the sight of which made me swallow a mouthful of water too hastily; I sputtered, and droplets of water sprayed across my jacket and trousers.

I supposed the pair were indeed Morlocks – but they were like no Morlocks I had seen before: whereas Nebogipfel was a little under five feet tall, these were like cartoon caricatures, extended to a height of perhaps twelve feet! One of the long creatures noticed me, and he came loping over, metal splints on his legs clattering as he walked; he stepped *over* the intervening partitions like some huge gazelle.

He bent down and peered at me. His red-grey eyes were the size of dinner-plates, and I quailed away from him. His odour was sharp, like burnt almonds. His limbs were long and fragile-looking, and his skin seemed stretched over that extended skeleton: I was able to see, embedded in one shin and quite visible through drum-tight skin, the profile of a tibia no less than four feet long. Splints of some soft metal were attached to those long leg-bones, evidently to help strengthen them against snapping. This attenuated beast seemed to have no greater number of follicles than your average Morlock, so that his hair was scattered over that stretched-out frame, in a very ugly fashion.

He exchanged a few liquid syllables with Nebogipfel, then rejoined his companion and – with many a backward glance at me – went on his way.

I turned to Nebogipfel, stunned; even *he* seemed an oasis of normality after that vision.

Nebogipfel said, 'They are –' a liquid word I could

not repeat '– from the higher latitudes.' He glanced after our two visitors. 'You can see that they are unsuited to this equatorial region. Splints are required to help them walk, and –'

'I don't see it at all,' I broke in. 'What's so different about the higher latitudes?'

'Gravity,' he said.

Dimly, I began to understand.

The Morlocks' Sphere was, as I have recorded, a titanic construction which filled up the orbit once occupied by Venus. And – Nebogipfel told me now – the whole thing rotated, about an axis. Once, Venus's year had been two hundred and twenty-five days. Now – said Nebogipfel – the great Sphere turned in just seven days and thirteen hours!

'And so the rotation –' Nebogipfel began.

'– induces centrifugal effects, simulating the earth's gravity at the equator. Yes,' I said. 'I see it.'

The spin of the Sphere kept us all plastered to this Floor. But away from the equator, the turning circle of a point on the Sphere about the rotation axis was less, and so the effective gravity was reduced: gravity dwindled to zero, in fact, at the Sphere's rotation poles. And in those extraordinary, broad continents of lower gravity, such remarkable animals as those two loping Morlocks lived, and had adapted to their conditions.

I thumped my forehead with the back of my hand.

'Sometimes I think I am the greatest fool who ever lived!' I exclaimed to the bemused Nebogipfel. For I had never thought to inquire about the source of my 'weight', here on the Sphere. What sort of scientist was it who failed to question – even to observe properly – the 'gravity' which, in the absence of anything so convenient as a *planet*, glued him to the surface of this Sphere? I wondered how many other marvels I was passing by, simply from the fact that it did not occur to me to *ask* about them – and yet to Nebogipfel such features were merely a part of the world, of no more novelty than a sunset, or a butter-fly's wing.

I teased out of Nebogipfel details of how the Morlocks lived. It was difficult, for I scarcely knew how to begin even to phrase my questions. That may seem odd to state – but how was I to ask, for instance, about the machinery which underpinned this trans-forming Floor? It was doubtful if my language contained the concepts required even to frame the query, just as a Neandertaler would lack the linguistic tools to inquire about the workings of a clock. And as to the social and other arrangements which, invisibly, governed the lives of the millions of Morlocks in this immense chamber, I remained as ignorant as might a tribesman arrived in London fresh from Central Africa would have been of social movements, of tele-phone and telegraph wires, of the Parcels Delivery Company, and the like. Even their arrangements for sewage remained a mystery to me!

I asked Nebogipfel how the Morlocks governed themselves.

He explained to me – in a somewhat patronizing manner, I thought – that the Sphere was a large enough place for several 'nations' of Morlocks. These 'nations' were distinguished mainly by the mode of government they chose. Almost all had some form of democratic process in place. In some areas a representative parliament was selected by a Universal Suffrage, much along the lines of our own Westminster Parliament. Elsewhere, suffrage was restricted to an elite sub-group, composed of those considered especially capable, by temperament and training, of governance: I think the nearest models in our philosophy are the classical republics, or perhaps the ideal form of Republic imagined by Plato; and I admit that this approach appealed to my own instincts.

But in most areas, the machinery of the Sphere had made possible a form of *true* Universal Suffrage, in which the inhabitants were kept abreast of current debates by means of the blue windows in their partitions, and then instantly registered their preferences on each issue by similar means. Thus, governance proceeded on a piecemeal basis, with every major decision subject to the collective whim of the populace.

I felt distrustful of such a system. 'But surely there are *some* in the population who cannot be empowered with such authority! What about the insane, or the feeble-minded?'

He considered me with a certain stiffness. 'We have no such weaknesses.'

I felt like challenging this Utopian – even here, in the heart of his Utopia! 'And how do you ensure that?'

He did not answer me immediately. Instead he went on, 'Each member of our adult population is rational, and able to make decisions on behalf of others – and is trusted to do so. In such circumstances, the purest form of democracy is not only possible, it is advisable – for many minds combine to produce decisions superior to those of one.'

I snorted. 'Then what of all these other Parliaments and Senates you have described?'

'Not everyone agrees that the arrangements in this part of the Sphere are ideal,' he said. 'Is that not the essence of freedom? Not all of us are sufficiently interested in the mechanics of governance to wish to participate; and for some, the entrusting of power to another through representation – or even without any representation at all – is preferable. That is a valid choice.'

'Fine. But what happens when such choices conflict?'

'*We have room,*' he said heavily. 'You must not forget that fact; you are still dominated by planet-bound expectations. Any dissenter is free to depart, and to establish a rival system elsewhere . . .'

These 'nations' of the Morlocks were fluid things, with individuals joining and leaving as their preferences evolved. There was no fixed territory or possessions, nor even any fixed boundaries, as far as I could make out; the 'nations' were mere groupings of convenience, clusterings across the Sphere.

There was no war among the Morlocks.

It took me some time to believe this, but at last I was convinced. There were no *causes* for war. Thanks to the mechanisms of the Floor there was no shortage of provision, so no 'nation' could argue for goals of economic acquisition. The Sphere was so huge that the empty land available was almost unlimited, so that territorial conflicts were meaningless. And – most crucially – the Morlocks' heads were free of the canker of *religion*, which has caused so much conflict through the centuries.

'You have no God, then,' I said to Nebogipfel, with something of a thrill: though I have some religious tendencies myself, I imagined shocking the clerics of my own day with an account of this conversation!

'We have no *need* of a God,' Nebogipfel retorted.

The Morlocks regarded a religious set of mind – as opposed to a *rational* state – as a hereditable *trait*, with no more intrinsic meaning than blue eyes or brown hair.

The more Nebogipfel outlined this notion, the more sense it made to me.

What notion of God has survived through all of Humanity's mental evolution? Why, precisely the form it might suit man's vanity to conjure up: a God with immense powers, and yet still absorbed in the petty affairs of man. Who could worship a chilling God, even if omnipotent, if He took no interest whatsoever in the flea-bite struggles of humans?

One might imagine that, in any conflict between *rational* humans and *religious* humans, the rational ought to win. After all, it is rationality that invented gunpowder! And yet – at least up to our nineteenth century – the *religious* tendency has generally won out, and natural selection operated, leaving us with a population of religiously-inclined sheep – it has sometimes seemed to me – capable of being deluded by any smooth-tongued preacher.

The paradox is explained because religion provides a *goal* for men to fight for. The religious man will soak some bit of 'sacred' land with his blood, sacrificing far more than the land's intrinsic economic or other value.

'But we have moved beyond this paradox,' Nebogipfel said to me. 'We have mastered our inheritance: we are no longer governed by the dictates of the past, either as regards our bodies or our minds . . .'

But I did not follow up this intriguing notion – the obvious question to ask was, 'In the absence of a God, then, what is the purpose of all of your lives?' – for I was entranced by the idea of how Mr Darwin, with all his modern critics in the Churches, would have loved to have witnessed this ultimate triumph of his ideas over the Religionists!

In fact – as it turned out – my understanding of the true purpose of the Morlocks' civilization would not come until much later.

I was impressed, though, with all I saw of this artificial world of the Morlocks – I am not sure if my respectful awe has been reflected in my account here. This brand of Morlock had indeed mastered their inherited weaknesses; they had put aside the legacy of the brute – the legacy bequeathed by *us* – and had thereby achieved a stability and capability almost unimaginable to a man of 1891: to a man like me, who had grown up in a world torn apart daily by war, greed and incompetence.

And this mastery of their own nature was all the more striking for its contrast with those *other* Morlocks – Weena's Morlocks – who had, quite obviously, fallen foul of the brute within, despite their mechanical and other aptitudes.

14

CONSTRUCTIONS AND DIVERGENCES

I discussed the construction of the Sphere with Nebogipfel. 'I imagine great engineering schemes which broke up the giant planets – Jupiter and Saturn – and –'

'No,' Nebogipfel said. 'There was no such scheme; the primal planets – from the earth outward – still orbit the sun's heart. There would not have been sufficient material in all the planets combined even to begin the construction of such an entity as this Sphere.'

'Then how –?'

Nebogipfel described how the sun had been encircled by a great fleet of space-faring craft, which bore immense magnets of a design – involving electrical circuits whose resistance was somehow reduced to *zero* – I could not fathom. The craft circled the sun with increasing speed, and a belt of magnetism tightened around the sun's million-mile midriff. And – as if that great star were no more than a soft fruit, held in a crushing fist – great founts of the sun's material, which is itself magnetized, were forced away from the equator to gush from the star's poles.

More fleets of space-craft then manipulated this huge cloud of lifted material, forming it at last into an enclosing shell; and the shell was then compressed, using shaped magnetic fields once more, and transmuted into the solid structures I saw around me.

The enclosed sun still shone, for even the immense detached masses required to construct this great artefact were but an invisible fraction of the sun's total bulk; and within the Sphere, sunlight shone perpetually over giant continents, each of which could have swallowed millions of splayed-out earths.

Nebogipfel said, 'A planet like the earth can intercept only an invisible fraction of the sun's output, with the rest disappearing, wasted, into the sink of space. Now, *all* of the sun's energy is captured by the enclosing Sphere. And that is the central justification for constructing the Sphere: *we have harnessed a star . . .*'

In a million years, Nebogipfel told me, the Sphere would capture enough additional solar material to permit its thickening by one-twenty-fifth of an inch – an invisibly small layer, but covering a stupendous area! The solar material, transformed, was used to further the construction of the Sphere. Meanwhile, some solar energy was harnessed to sustain the Interior of the Sphere and to power the Morlocks' various projects.

With some excitement, I described what I had witnessed during my journey through futurity: the brightening of the sun, and that jetting at the poles – and then how the sun had disappeared into blackness, as the Sphere was thrown around it.

Nebogipfel regarded me, I fancied with some envy. 'So,' he said, 'you did indeed watch the construction of the Sphere. It took ten thousand years . . .'

'But to me on my machine, no more than heartbeats passed.'

'You have told me that this is your second voyage into the future. And that during your first, you saw differences.'

96

'Yes.' Now I confronted that perplexing mystery once more. 'Differences in the unfolding of History . . . Nebogipfel, when I first journeyed to the future, *your Sphere was never built.*'

I summarized to Nebogipfel how I had formerly travelled far beyond this year of A.D. 657,208. During that first voyage, I had watched the colonization of the land by a tide of rich green, as winter was abolished from the earth and the sun grew unaccountably brighter. But – *unlike* my second trip – I saw no signs of the regulation of the earth's axial tilt, nor did I witness anything of the slowing of its rotation. And, most dramatic, without the construction of the sun-shielding Sphere, the earth had remained fair, and had not been banished into the Morlocks' stygian darkness.

'And so,' I told Nebogipfel, 'I arrived in the year A.D. 802,701 – a hundred and fifty thousand years into *your* future – yet I cannot believe, if I had travelled on so far *this* time, that I should find the same world again!'

I summarized to Nebogipfel what I had seen of Weena's world, with its Eloi and degraded Morlocks. Nebogipfel thought this over. 'There has been no such state of affairs in the evolution of Humanity, in all of recorded History – *my* History,' he said. 'And since the Sphere, once constructed, is self-sustaining, it is difficult to imagine that such a descent into barbarism is possible in our future.'

'So there you have it,' I agreed. 'I have journeyed through two, quite exclusive, versions of History. Can History be like unfired clay, able to be remade?'

'Perhaps it can,' Nebogipfel murmured. 'When you returned to your own era – to 1891 – did you bring any evidence of your travels?'

'Not much,' I admitted. 'But I did bring back some flowers, pretty white things like mallows, which

97

Weena – which an Eloi had placed in my pocket. My friends examined them. The flowers were of an order they couldn't recognize, and I remember how they remarked on the gynoecium . . .'

'Friends?' Nebogipfel said sharply. 'You left an account of your journey, before embarking once more?'

'Nothing written. But I did give some friends a full-ish account of the affair, over dinner.' I smiled. 'And if I know one of that circle, the whole thing was no doubt written up in the end in some popularized and sensational form – perhaps presented as fiction . . .'

Nebogipfel approached me. 'Then *there*,' he said to me, his quiet voice queerly dramatic, 'there is your explanation.'

'Explanation?'

'For the Divergence of Histories.'

I faced him, horrified by a dawning comprehension. 'You mean that with my account – my prophecy – *I changed History?*'

'Yes. Armed with that warning, Humanity managed to avoid the degradation and conflict that resulted in the primitive, cruel world of Eloi and Morlock. Instead, we continued to grow; instead, we have harnessed the sun.'

I felt quite unable to face the consequences of this hypothesis – although its truth and clarity struck me immediately. I shouted, 'But some things have stayed the same. Still you Morlocks skulk in the dark!'

'We are not Morlocks,' Nebogipfel said softly. 'Not as you remember them. And as for the dark – what need have we of a flood of light? We *choose* the dark. Our eyes are fine instruments, capable of revealing much beauty. Without the brutal glare of the sun, the full subtlety of the sky can be discerned . . .'

I could find no distraction in goading Nebogipfel, and I had to face the truth. I stared down at my hands – great battered things, scarred with decades of labour. My sole aim, to which I had devoted the efforts of these hands, had been to explore time! – to determine how things would come out on the cosmological scale, beyond my own few mayfly decades of life. But, it seemed, I had succeeded in far more.

My invention was much more powerful than a mere time-travelling machine: it was a History Machine, a destroyer of worlds!

I was a murderer of the future: I had taken on, I realized, more powers than God himself (if Aquinas is to be believed). By my twisting-up of the workings of History, I had wiped over billions of unborn lives – lives that would now never come to be.

I could hardly bear to live with the knowledge of this presumption. I have always been distrustful of *personal power* – for I have met not one man wise enough to be entrusted with it – but now, I had taken to myself more power than any man who had ever lived!

If I should ever recover my Time Machine – I promised myself then – I would return into the past, to make one final, conclusive adjustment to History, and abolish my own invention of the infernal device.

. . . And I realized now that I could *never* retrieve Weena. For, not only had I caused her death – now, it turned out, I had nullified her very existence!

Through all this turmoil of the emotions, the pain of that little loss sounded sweet and clear, like the note of an oboe in the midst of the clamour of some great orchestra.

15

LIFE AND DEATH AMONG THE MORLOCKS

One day, Nebogipfel led me to what was, perhaps, the most disquieting thing I saw in all my time in that city-chamber.

We approached an area, perhaps a half-mile square, where the partitions seemed lower than usual. As we neared, I became aware of a rising level of noise – a babble of liquid throats – and a sharply increased smell of *Morlock*, of their characteristic musty, sickly sweetness. Nebogipfel bade me pause on the edge of this clearing.

Through my goggles I was able to see that the surface of the cleared-out area was alive – it pulsated – with the mewling, wriggling, toddling form of babies. There were thousands of them, these tumbling Morlock infants, their little hands and feet pawing at each other's clumps of untidy hair. They rolled, just like young apes, and poked at junior versions of the informative partitions I have described elsewhere, or crammed food into their dark mouths; here and there, adults walked through the crowd, raising one who had fallen here, untangling a miniature dispute there, soothing a wailing infant beyond.

I gazed out over this sea of infants, bemused. Perhaps such a collection of human children might be found appealing by some – not by me, a confirmed bachelor – *but these were Morlocks. . .* You must remember that the Morlock is not an attractive entity to human sensibilities, even as a child, with his worm-pallor flesh, his coolness to the touch, and that spider-webbing of hair. If you think of a giant table-top covered in wriggling maggots, you will have something of my impression as I stood there!

I turned to Nebogipfel. 'But where are their parents?'

He hesitated, as if searching for the right phrase. 'They have no parents. This is a *birth farm*. When old enough, the infants will be transported from here to a nursery community, either on the Sphere or . . .'

But I had stopped listening. I glanced at Nebogipfel, up and down, but his hair masked the form of his body.

With a jolt of wonder, I saw now another of those facts which had stared me in the eyeball since my arrival here, but which I was too clever by far to perceive: there was no evidence of sexual discrimination – not in Nebogipfel, nor in any of the Morlocks I had come across – not even in those, like my low-gravity visitors, whose bodies were sparsely coated with hair, and so easier to make out. Your average Morlock was built like a child, undifferentiated sexually, with the same lack of emphasis on hips or chest . . . I realized with a shock that I knew nothing of – nor had I thought to question – the Morlocks' processes of love and birth!

Nebogipfel told me something now of the rearing and education of the Morlock young.

The Morlock began his life in these birth farms and nursery communities – the whole of the Earth, to my painful recollection, had been given over to one such – and there, in addition to the rudiments of civilized behaviour, the youngster was taught one essential skill: the ability to *learn*. It is as if a schoolboy of the nineteenth century – instead of having drummed into his poor head a lot of nonsense about Greek and Latin and obscure geometric theorems – had been taught, instead, how to concentrate, and to use libraries, and the mechanisms of how to assimilate knowledge – how, above all, to *think*. After that, the acquisition of any specific knowledge depended on the needs of the task in hand, and the inclination of the individual.

When Nebogipfel summarized this to me, its simplicity of logic struck me with an almost physical force. Of course! – I said to myself – so much for schools! What a contrast to the battleground of Ignorance with Incompetence that made up my own, unlamented schooldays!

I was moved to ask Nebogipfel about his own profession.

He explained to me that once the date of my origin had been fixed, he had made himself into something of an expert in my period and its mores from the records of his people; and he had become aware of several significant differences between the ways of our races.

'Our occupations are not as consuming as yours,' he said. 'I have two loves – two vocations.' His eyes were invisible, making his emotions even more impossible to read. He said: 'Physics, and the training of the young.'

Education, and training of all sorts, continued throughout a Morlock's lifetime, and it was not unusual for an individual to pursue three or four 'careers', as we might call them, in sequence, or even in parallel. The general level of intelligence of the Morlocks was, I got the impression, rather higher than that of the people of my own century.

Still, Nebogipfel's choice of vocations startled me; I had thought that Nebogipfel must specialize solely in the physical sciences, such was his ability to follow my sometimes rambling accounts of the theory of the Time Machine, and the evolution of History.

'Tell me,' I said lightly, 'for which of your talents were you appointed to supervise me? Your expertise in physics – or your nannying skills?'

I thought his black, small-toothed mouth stretched in a grin.

Then the truth struck me – and I felt a certain humiliation burn in me at the thought. I am an eminent man of my day, and yet I had been put in the charge of one more suited to shepherding children!

. . . And yet, I reflected now, what was my blundering about, when I first arrived in the Year 657,208, but the actions of a comparative child?

Now Nebogipfel led me to a corner of the nursery area. This special place was covered by a structure about the size and shape of a small conservatory, done out in the pale, translucent material of the Floor – in fact, this was one of the few parts of that city-chamber to be covered over in any way. Nebogipfel led me inside the structure. The shelter was empty of furniture or apparatus, save for one or two of the partitions with glowing screens which I had noticed elsewhere. And, in the centre of the Floor, there was what looked like a small bundle – of clothing, perhaps – being extruded from the glass.

The Morlocks who attended here had a more serious bent than those who supervised the children, I perceived. Over their pale hair they wore loose smocks – vest-like garments with many pockets – crammed with tools which were mostly quite incomprehensible to me. Some of the tools glowed faintly. This latest class of Morlock had something of the air of the engineer, I thought: it was an odd attribute in this sea of babies; and, although they were distracted by my clumsy presence, the engineers watched the little bundle on the Floor, and passed instruments over it periodically.

My curiosity engaged, I stepped towards that central bundle. Nebogipfel hung back, letting me proceed alone. The thing was only a few inches long, and was still half-embedded in the glass, like a sculpture being hewn from some rocky surface. In fact it did look a little like a statue: here were the buds of two arms, I thought, and there was what might become a face – a disc coated with hair, and split by a thin mouth. The bundle's extrusion seemed slow, and I wondered what was so difficult for the hidden devices about manufacturing this particular artefact. Was it especially complex, perhaps?

And then – it was a moment which will haunt me as long as I live – *that tiny mouth opened.* The lips parted with a soft popping sound, and a mewling, fainter than that of the tiniest kitten, emerged to float on the air; and the miniature face crumpled, as if in some mild distress.

I stumbled backwards, as shocked as if I had been punched.

Nebogipfel seemed to have anticipated something of my distress. He said, 'You must remember that you are dislocated in Time by a half million years: the interval between us is *ten times* the age of your species. . .'

'Nebogipfel – can it be true? That your young – *you yourself* – are extruded from this Floor, *manufactured* with no more majesty than a cup of water?' The Morlocks had indeed 'mastered their genetic inheritance', I thought – for they had abolished gender, and done away with birth.

'Nebogipfel,' I protested, 'this is – *inhuman.*'

He tilted his head; evidently the word meant nothing to him. 'Our policy is designed to optimize the potential of the human form – *for we are human too,*'

104

he said severely. 'That form is dictated by a sequence of a million genes, and so the number of possible human individuals – while large – is finite. And all of these individuals may be –' he hesitated '– *imagined* by the Sphere's intelligence.'

Sepulture, he told me, was also governed by the Sphere, with the abandoned bodies of the dead being passed into the Floor without ceremony or reverence, for the dismantling and reuse of their materials.

'The Sphere assembles the materials required to give the chosen individual life, and –'

'"Chosen"?' I confronted the Morlock, and the anger and violence which I had excluded from my thoughts for so long flooded back into my soul. 'How very *rational*. But what else have you rationalized out, Morlock? What of tenderness? *What of love?*'

'And then–it was a moment which will haunt me as long
as I live–*that tiny mouth opened.*'

16

DECISION AND DEPARTURE

I stumbled out of that grisly birthing-hut and stared around at the huge city-chamber, with its ranks of patient Morlocks pursuing their incomprehensible activities. I longed to shout at them, to shatter their repulsive *perfection*; but I knew, even in that dark moment, that I could not afford to allow their perception of my behaviour to worsen once more.

I wanted to flee even from Nebogipfel. He had shown some kindness and consideration to me, I realized: more than I deserved, perhaps, and more, probably, than men of my own age might have afforded some violent savage from a half-million years before Christ. But still, he had been, I sensed, fascinated and amused by my reactions to the birthing process. Perhaps he had engineered this revelation to provoke just such an extreme of emotion in me! Well, if such was his intention, Nebogipfel had succeeded. But now my humiliation and unreasoning anger were such that I could scarcely bear to look on his ornately-coiffed features.

And yet I had nowhere else to go! Like it or not, I knew, Nebogipfel was my only point of reference in this strange Morlock world: the only individual alive whose name I knew, and – for all I knew of Morlock politics – my only protector.

Perhaps Nebogipfel sensed some of this conflict in me. At any rate, he did not press his company on me;

instead, he turned his back, and once more evoked my small sleeping-hut from the Floor. I ducked into the hut and sat in its darkest corner, with my arms wrapped around me – I cowered like some forest animal brought to New York!

I stayed in there for some hours – perhaps I slept. At last, I felt some resilience of mind returning, and I took some food and performed a perfunctory toilet.

I think – before the incident of the birth farm – I had come to be intrigued by my glimpses of this New Morlock world. I have always thought myself above all a Rational man, and I was fascinated by this vision of how a society of Rational Beings might order things – of how Science and Engineering might be applied to build a better world. I had been impressed by the Morlocks' tolerance of different approaches to politics and governance, for instance. But the sight of that half-formed homunculus had quite unhinged me. Perhaps my reaction demonstrates how deep embedded are the basic values and instincts of our species.

If it was true that the New Morlocks had conquered their genetic inheritance, the taint of the ancient oceans, then, at that moment of inner turmoil, I envied them their equanimity!

I knew now that I must get away from the company of the Morlocks – I might be tolerated, but there was no place for me here, any more than for a gorilla in a Mayfair hotel – and I began to formulate a new resolve.

I emerged from my shelter. Nebogipfel was there, waiting, as if he had never left the vicinity of the hut. With a brush of his hand over a pedestal, he caused the discarded shelter to dissolve back into the Floor.

'Nebogipfel,' I said briskly, 'it must be obvious to

you that I am as out of place here as some zoo animal, escaped in a city.'

He said nothing; his gaze seemed impassive.

'Unless it is your intention to hold me as a prisoner, or as a specimen in some laboratory, I have no desire to stay here. I request that you allow me access to my Time Machine, so that I might return to my own Age.'

'You are not a *prisoner*,' he said. 'The word has no translation in our language. You are a sentient being, and as such you have rights. The only constraints on your behaviour are that you should not further harm others by your actions –'

'Which constraints I accept,' I said stiffly.

'– and,' he went on, 'that you should not depart in your machine.'

'Then so much for my rights,' I snarled at him. 'I *am* a prisoner here – and a prisoner in time!'

'Although the theory of time travel is clear enough – and the mechanical structure of your device is obvious – we do not yet have any understanding of the principles involved,' the Morlock said. I thought this must mean that they did not yet understand the significance of Plattnerite. 'But,' Nebogipfel went on, 'we think this technology could be of great value to our species.'

'I'm sure you do!' I had a sudden vision of these Morlocks, with their magical devices and wondrous weapons, returning on adapted Time Machines to the London of 1891.

The Morlocks would keep my Humanity safe and fed. But, deprived of his soul, and perhaps at last of his children, I foresaw that modern man would survive no more than a few generations!

My horror at this prospect got the blood pumping through my neck – and yet even at that moment, some remote, rational corner of my mind was pointing out to me certain difficulties with this picture. 'Look here,' I told myself, 'if all modern men *were* destroyed in this way – but modern man is nevertheless the ancestor of the Morlock – then the Morlocks could never evolve in the first place, and so never capture my machine and return through time . . . It's a paradox, isn't it? For you can't have it both ways.' You have to remember that in some remote part of my brain the unsolved problem of my second flight through time – with the divergence of Histories I had witnessed – was still fermenting away, and I knew in my heart that my understanding of the philosophy behind this time travelling business was still limited, at best.

But I pushed all that away as I confronted Nebogipfel. '*Never.* I will *never* assist you to acquire time travel.'

Nebogipfel regarded me. 'Then – within the constraints I have set out for you – you are free, to travel anywhere in our worlds.'

'In that case, I ask that you take me to a place – wherever it might be in this engineered solar system – where men like me still exist.'

I think I threw out this challenge, expecting a denial of any such possibility. But, to my surprise, Nebogipfel stepped towards me. 'Not precisely *like* you,' he said. 'But still – come.'

And, with that, he stepped out once more across that immense, populated plain. I thought his final words had been more than ominous, but I could not understand what he meant – and, in any event, I had little choice but to follow him.

We reached a clear area perhaps a quarter-mile across. I had long since lost any sense of direction in that immense city-chamber. Nebogipfel donned his goggles, and I retained mine.

Suddenly – without warning – a beam of light arced down from the roof above and skewered us. I peered up into a warm yellowness, and saw dust-motes cascading about in the air; for a moment I thought I had been returned to my Cage of Light.

For some seconds we waited – I could not see that Nebogipfel had issued any commands to the invisible machines that governed this place – but then the Floor under my feet gave a sharp jolt. I stumbled, for it had felt like a small earthquake, and was quite unexpected; but I recovered quickly.

'What was that?'

Nebogipfel was unperturbed. 'Perhaps I should have warned you. Our ascent has started.'

'*Ascent?*'

A disc of glass, perhaps a quarter-mile wide, was rising up out of the Floor, I saw now, and was bearing me and Nebogipfel aloft. It was as if I stood atop some immense pillar, which thrust out of the ground. Already we had risen through perhaps ten feet, and our pace upwards seemed to be accelerating; I felt a whisper of breeze on my forehead.

I walked a little way towards the lip of the disc and I watched as that immense, complex plain of Morlocks opened up below me. The chamber stretched as far as I could see, utterly flat, evenly populated. The Floor looked like some elaborate map, perhaps of the constellations, done out in silver thread and black velvet – and overlaying the *real* star vista beneath. One or two silvery faces were turned up to us as we ascended, but most of the Morlocks seemed quite indifferent.

'Nebogipfel – where are we going?'

'To the Interior,' he said calmly.

I was aware of a change in the light. It seemed much brighter, and more diffuse – it was no longer

111

restricted to a single ray, as might be seen at the bottom of a well.

I craned up my neck. The disc of light above me was widening, even as I watched, so that I could now make out a ring of sky, around the central disc of sun. That sky was blue, and speckled with high, fluffy clouds; but the sky had an odd texture, a blotchiness of colour which at first I attributed to the goggles I still wore.

Nebogipfel turned from me. He tapped with his foot at the base of our platform, and an object was extruded – at first I could not recognize it – it was a shallow bowl, with a stick protruding from its centre. It was only when Nebogipfel picked it up and held it over his head that I recognized it for what it was: a simple parasol, to keep the sun from his etiolated flesh.

Thus prepared, we rose up into the light – the shaft widened – and my nineteenth-century head ascended into a plain of grass!

17

IN THE INTERIOR

'Welcome to the Interior,' Nebogipfel announced, comical with his parasol.

Our quarter-mile-wide pillar of glass ascended through its last few yards quite soundlessly. I felt as if I were rising like some illusionist's assistant on a stage. I took off my goggles, and shaded my eyes with my hands.

The platform slowed to a halt, and its edge merged with the meadow of short, wiry grass which ringed it, as seamless as if it were some foundation of concrete which had been laid there. My shadow was a sharp dark patch, directly beneath me. It was noon here, of course; everywhere in the Interior, it was noon, all day and every day! The blinding sun beat down on my head and neck – I suspected I should soon get burned – but the pleasurable feel of this captive sunlight was worth the cost, at that moment.

I turned, studying the landscape.

Grass – a featureless plain of it – grass grew everywhere, all the way to the horizon – except that there *was* no horizon, here on this flattened-out world. I looked up, expecting to see the world curve upwards: for I was, after all, no longer glued to the outer surface of a little ball of rock like the earth, but standing on the inside of an immense, hollow shell. But there was no such optical effect; I saw only more grass, and perhaps some clumps of trees or bushes, far in the distance. The sky was a blue-tinged plain of high, light cloud, which merged with the land at a flat seam of mist and dust.

'I feel as if I'm standing on some immense table-top,' I said to Nebogipfel. 'I thought it would be like some huge bowl of landscape. What a paradox it is that I cannot tell if I am inside a great Sphere, or on the outside of a gigantic planet!'

'There *are* ways to tell,' Nebogipfel replied from beneath his parasol. 'Look up.'

I craned my neck backwards. At first I could see only the sky and the sun – it could have been any sky of earth. Then, gradually, I began to make out something *beyond* the clouds. It was that blotchiness of texture about the sky which I had observed as we ascended, and attributed to some defect of the goggles. The blotches were something like a distant water-colouring, done in blue and grey and green, but finely detailed, so that the largest of the patches was dwarfed by the tiniest scrap of cloud. It looked rather like a map – or several maps, jammed up together and viewed from a great distance.

And it was that analogy which led me to the truth.

'*It is the far side of the Sphere, beyond the sun* . . . I suppose the colours I can see are oceans, and continents, and mountain ranges and prairies – perhaps even cities!' It was a remarkable sight – as if the rocky coats of thousands of flayed earths had been hung up like so many rabbit furs. There was no sense of curvature, such was the immense scale of the Sphere. Rather, it was as if I was sandwiched between layers, between this flattened prairie of grass and the lid of textured sky, with the sun suspended like a lantern in between – and with the depths of space a mere mile or two beneath my feet!

'Remember that when you look at the Interior's far side you are looking across the width of the orbit of

Venus,' Nebogipfel cautioned me. 'From such a distance, the earth itself would be reduced to a mere point of light. Many of the topographic features here are built on a much larger scale than the earth itself.'

'There must be oceans that could swallow the earth!' I mused. 'I suppose that the geological forces in a structure like this are –'

'There is *no* geology here,' Nebogipfel cut in. 'The Interior, and its landscapes, is artificial. Everything you see was, in essence, designed to be as it is – and it is maintained that way, quite consciously.' He seemed unusually reflective. 'Much is different in this History, from that other you have described. But some things are constant: this is a world of perpetual day – in contrast to my own world, of night. We have indeed split into species of extremes, of Dark and Light, just as in that other History.'

Nebogipfel led me now to the edge of our glass disc. He stayed on the platform, his parasol cocked over his head; but I stepped boldly out onto the surrounding grass. The ground was hard under my feet, but I was pleased to have the sensation of a different surface beneath me, after days of that bland, yielding Floor. Though short, the grass was tough, wiry stuff, of the kind commonly encountered close to sea shores; and when I reached down and dug my fingers into the ground, I found that the soil was quite sandy and dry. I unearthed one small beetle, there in the row of little pits I had dug with my fingers; it scuttled out of sight, deeper into the sand.

A breeze hissed across the grass. There was no bird song, I noticed; I heard no animal's call.

'The soil's none too rich,' I called back to Nebogipfel.

'No,' he said. 'But the –' a liquid word I could not recognize '– is recovering.'

'What did you say?'

'I mean the complex of plants and insects and animals which function together, interdependent. It is only forty thousand years since the war.'

'What war?'

Now Nebogipfel *shrugged* – his shoulders lurched, causing his body hair to rustle – a gesture he could only have copied from me! 'Who knows? Its causes are forgotten, the combatants – the nations and their children – all dead.'

'You told me there *was* no warfare here,' I accused him.

'Not among the Morlocks,' he said. 'But within the Interior . . . This one was very destructive. Great bombs fell. The land here was destroyed – all life obliterated.'

'But surely the plants, the smaller animals –'

'Everything. You do not understand. *Everything* died, save the grass and the insects, across a million square miles. And it is only now that the land has become safe.'

'Nebogipfel, what kind of people live here? Are they like me?'

He paused. 'Some mimic your archaic variant. But there are even some older forms; I know of a colony of reconstructed Neandertalers, who have reinvented the religions of that vanished folk . . . And there are some who have developed beyond you: who diverge from you as much as I do, though in different ways. *The Sphere is large.* If you wish I will take you to a colony of an approximation of your own kind . . .'

'Oh – I'm not sure what I want!' I said. 'I think I'm overwhelmed by this place, this world of worlds, Nebogipfel. I want to see what I can make of it all, before I choose where I will spend my life. Can you understand that?'

He did not debate the proposal; he seemed eager to get out of the sunlight. 'Very well. When you wish to see me again, return to the platform and call my name.'

And so began my solitary sojourn in the Interior of the Sphere.

In that world of perpetual noon there was no cycle of days and nights to count the passage of time. However I had my pocket watch: the time it displayed was, of course, meaningless, thanks to my transfers across time and space; but it served to map out twenty-four-hour periods.

Nebogipfel had evoked a shelter from the platform – a plain, square hut with one small window and a door of the dilating kind I have described before. He left me a tray of food and water, and showed me how I could obtain more: I would push the tray back into the surface of the platform – this was an odd sensation – and after a few seconds a new tray would rise out of the surface, fully laden. This unnatural process made me queasy, but I had no other source of food, and I mastered my qualms. Nebogipfel also demonstrated how to push objects into the platform to have them cleaned, as he cleansed even his own fingers. I used this feature to clean my clothes and boots – although my trousers were returned without a crease! – but I could never bring myself to insert a part of my body in this way. The thought of pushing a hand or foot – or worse, my face – *into* that bland surface was more than I could bear, and I continued to wash in water.

I was still without shaving equipment, incidentally; my beard had grown long and luxuriant – but it was a depressingly solid mass of iron grey.

Nebogipfel showed me how I could extend the use of my goggles. By touching the surface in a certain way, I could make them magnify the images of remote objects, bringing them as close, and as sharp,

117

as life. I donned the goggles immediately and focused them on a distant shadow which I had thought was a clump of trees; but it turned out to be no more than an outcropping of rock, which looked rather worn away, or melted.

For the first few days, it was enough for me simply to *be* there, in that bruised meadow. I took to going for long walks; I would take my boots off, enjoying the feeling of grass and sand between my toes, and I would often strip to my pants in the hot sunlight. Soon I got as brown as a berry – though the prow of my balding forehead got rather burned – it was like a rest cure in Bognor!

In the evenings I retired to my hut. It was quite cosy in there with the door closed, and I slept well, with my jacket for a pillow and with the warm softness of the platform beneath me.

The bulk of my time was spent in the inspection of the Interior with my magnifying goggles. I would sit at the rim of my platform, or lie in a soft patch of grass with my head propped on my jacket, and gaze around the complex sky.

That part of the Interior opposite my position, beyond the sun, must lie on the Sphere's equator; and so I anticipated that this region would be the most earth-like – where gravity was strongest, and the air was compressed. That central band was comparatively narrow – no more than some tens of millions of miles wide. (I say 'no more' easily enough, but I knew of course that the whole of the earth would be lost, a mere mote, against that Titanic background!) Beyond this central band, the surface appeared a dull grey, difficult to distinguish through the sky's blue filter, and I could make out few details. In one of those high-latitude regions there was a splash of silver-white, with sea-shapes of fine grey embedded in it, that reminded me somewhat of the moon; and

118

in another a vivid patch of orange – quite neatly elliptical – whose nature I could not comprehend at all. I remembered the attenuated Morlocks I had met, who had come from the lower-gravity regions of the outer shells, away from the equator; and I wondered if there were perhaps distorted humans living in those remote, low gravity world-maps of the Interior's higher latitudes.

When I considered that inner, earth-like central belt, much of that, even, appeared to be unpopulated; I could see immense oceans, and deserts that could swallow worlds, shining in the endless sunlight. These wastes of land or water separated *island-worlds*: regions little larger than the earth might have been, if skinned and spread out across that surface, and rich with detail.

Here I saw a world of grass and forest, with cities of sparkling buildings rising above the trees. There I made out a world locked in ice, whose inhabitants must be surviving as my forebears had in Europe's glacial periods: perhaps it was cooled by being mounted on some immense platform, I wondered, to lift it out of the atmosphere. On some of the worlds I saw the mark of industry: a complex texture of cities, the misty smoke of factories, bays threaded by bridges, the plume-like wakes of ships on land-locked seas – and, sometimes, a tracing of vapour across the upper atmosphere which I imagined must be generated by some flying vessel.

So much was familiar enough – but some worlds were quite beyond my comprehension.

I caught glimpses of cities which *floated* in the air, above their own shadows; and immense buildings which must have dwarfed China's Wall, sprawling across engineered landscapes . . . I could not begin to imagine the sort of men which must live in such places.

*

Some days I awoke to comparative darkness. A great sheet of cloud would clamp down on the land, and before long a heavy rain start to fall. It occurred to me that the weather inside that Interior must have been regulated – as, no doubt, were all other aspects of its fabric – for I could readily imagine the immense cyclonic energies which could be generated by that huge world's rapid spin. I would walk about in the weather a bit, relishing the tang of the fresh water. On such days, the place would become much more earth-like, with the Interior's bewildering far side and its dubious horizon hidden by rain and cloud.

After long inspections with the telescopic goggles, I found that the grassy plain around me was just as featureless as it had looked at first sight. One day – it was bright and hot – I decided to try to make for the rocky outcrop I have mentioned, which was the only distinguishable feature within the mist-delineated horizon, even on the clearest day. I bundled up some food and water in a bag I improvised from my long-suffering jacket, and off I set; I got as far as I could before I tired, and then I lay down to attempt to sleep. But I could not settle, not in the open sunlight, and after a few hours I gave up. I walked on a little further, but the rocky outcrop seemed to be getting no nearer, and I began to grow fearful, so far from the platform. What if I were to grow fatigued, or somehow become injured? I should never be able to call Nebogipfel, and I should forfeit any prospect of returning to my own time: in fact, I should die in the grass like some wounded gazelle. And all for a walk to an anonymous clump of rock!

Feeling foolish, I turned and hiked back to my platform.

18

THE NEW ELOI

Some days after this, I emerged from my hut after a sleep, and became aware that the light was a little brighter than usual. I glanced up, and saw that the extra illumination came from a fierce point of light a few degrees of arc from the static sun. I snatched up my goggles and inspected that new star.

It was a burning island-world. As I watched, great explosions shattered the surface, sending up clouds which blossomed like lovely, deadly flowers. Already, I thought, the island-world must be devoid of life, for nothing could live through the conflagration I witnessed, but still the explosions rained across the surface – and all in eerie silence!

The island-world flared brighter than the sun, for several hours, and I knew that I was watching a titanic tragedy, made by man – or descendants of man.

Everywhere in my rocky sky – now I started looking for it – I saw the mark of *War*.

Here was a world in which great strips of land appeared to have been given over to a debilitating and destructive siege warfare: I saw brown lanes of churned-up countryside, immense trenches, hundreds of miles wide, in which, I imagined, men were fighting and dying, for year after year. Here was a city burning, with white vapour arcs scored over it; and I wondered if some aerial weapon was being exploited there. And here

I found a world devastated by the aftermath of war, the continents blackened and barren, with the outlines of cities barely visible through a shifting pile of black cloud.

I wondered how many of these joys had visited my own earth, in the years after my departure!

After some days of this, I took to leaving off my goggles for long periods. I began to find that sky-roof, painted everywhere with warfare, unbearably oppressive.

Some men of my time have argued for war – would have welcomed it, I think, as, for example, a release of the tension between the great Powers. Men thought of war – the next one, at least! – as a great cleansing, as the *last* war that ever need be fought. But it was not so, I could see now: men fought wars because of the legacy of the brute inside them, and any justification was a mere rationalization supplied by our oversized brains.

I imagined how it would be if Great Britain and Germany were projected somewhere here, as two more splashes of colour against the rocky sky. I thought of those two nations which seemed to me now, from my elevated perspective, in a state of aimless economic and moral muddle. And I doubted if there had been a man alive in 1891 in either country who could have told me the benefits of a war, whatever the outcome! – And how ludicrous and futile such a conflict would seem if Britain and Germany were indeed projected up into the Interior of this monstrous Sphere.

All across the Sphere, millions of irreplaceable human lives were being lost to such conflicts – which were as remote and meaningless to me as the paintings on the ceiling of a cathedral – and you would think that men living in that Sphere – and able to see a million island-worlds like their own – would have abandoned their petty little ambitions, and discovered the sort of perspective I now understood. But, it seemed, it was not so; the base parts of human instincts dominated still, even in the Year A.D. 657,208. Here in the Sphere, even the daily education of a thousand, a million wars going on all across the iron sky was not enough, apparently, to make men see the futility and cruelty of it all!

I found my mind turning, for contrast, to Nebogipfel and his people, and their Rational society. I will not pretend that a certain revulsion did not still tinge my mind at the thought of the Morlocks and their unnatural practices, but I understood now that this arose from my own primitive prejudices, and my unfortunate experiences in Weena's world, which were quite irrelevant to an assessment of Nebogipfel.

I was able, given time to contemplate, to work out how the falling-away of Morlock gender differences might have come about. I considered how, among humans, circles of loyalty spread out around an individual. First of all one must fight to preserve oneself and one's direct children. Next, one will fight for siblings – but perhaps with only a reduced intensity, since the common inheritance must be halved. In next priority one would fight for the children of siblings, and more remote relations, in diminishing bands of intensity.

Thus, with depressing reliability, men's actions and loyalties may be predicted; for only with such a hierarchy of allegiance – in a world of shortage and instability – can one's inheritance be preserved for future generations.

But the Morlocks' inheritance *was* secured – and not through an individual child or family, but through the great common resource that was the Sphere. And so the differentiation and specialization

123

of the sexes became irrelevant – even harmful, to the orderly progress of things.

It was a pretty irony, I thought, that it was precisely this diagnosis – of the vanishing of sexes from a world made stable, abundant and peaceful – that I had once applied to the exquisite, and decadent, Eloi; and now here I was coming to see that it was their ugly cousins the Morlocks, who, in this version of things, had actually achieved that remote goal!

All this worked its way through my thinking. And slowly – it took some days – I came to a decision about my future.

I could not remain inside this Interior; after the God-like perspective loaned me by Nebogipfel, I could not bear to immerse my life and energies in any one of the meaningless conflicts sweeping like brush fires across these huge plains. Nor could I remain with Nebogipfel and his Morlocks; for I am not a Morlock, and my essential human needs would make it unbearable to live as Nebogipfel did.

Furthermore – as I have said – I could not live with the knowledge that my Time Machine still existed, an engine so capable of damaging History!

I began to formulate a plan to resolve all this, and I summoned Nebogipfel.

'When the Sphere was constructed,' Nebogipfel said, 'there was a schism. Those who wished to live much as men had always lived came into the Interior. And those who wished to put aside the ancient domination of the gene –'

'– became Morlocks. And so the wars – meaningless and eternal – wash like waves across this unbounded Interior surface.'

'Yes.'

'Nebogipfel, is the purpose of the Sphere to sustain these quasi-humans – these new Eloi – to give

124

them room to wage their wars, without destroying Humanity?'

'No.' He held up his parasol, in a dignified pose I no longer found comical. 'Of course not. The purpose of the Sphere *is for the Morlocks,* as you call us: to make the energies of a star available for the acquisition of knowledge.' He blinked his huge eyes. 'For what goal is there for intelligent creatures, but to gather and store all available information?'

The mechanical Memory of the Sphere, he said, was like an immense Library, which stored the wisdom of the race, accumulated across half a million years; and much of the patient toil of the Morlocks I had seen was devoted to the further gathering of information, or to the classification and reinterpretation of the data already collected.

These New Morlocks were a race of scholars! – and the whole energy of the sun was given over to the patient, coral-like growth of that great Library.

I rubbed my beard. 'I understand that – the motive at least. I suppose it is not so far from the impulses which have dominated my own life. But don't you fear that one day you will finish this quest? What will you do when mathematics is perfected, for instance, and the final Theory of the physical universe is demonstrated?'

He shook his head, in another gesture he had acquired from me. 'That is not possible. A man of your own time – Kurt Gödel – was the first to demonstrate that.'

'Who?'

'Kurt Gödel: a mathematician who was born some ten years after your departure in time . . .'

This Gödel – I was astonished to learn, as Nebogipfel again displayed his deep study of my age – would, in the 1930s, demonstrate that mathematics can never be finished off; instead its logical systems must forever be enriched by incorporating the truth or falsehood of new axioms.

'It makes my head ache to think about it! – I can imagine the reception this poor Gödel got when he brought this news to the world. Why, my old algebra teacher would have thrown him out of the room.'

Nebogipfel said, 'Gödel showed that our quest, to acquire knowledge and understanding, *can never be completed.*'

I understood. 'He has given you an infinite purpose.' The Morlocks were like a world of patient monks, I saw now, working tirelessly to comprehend the workings of our great universe.

At last – at the End of Time – that great Sphere, with its machine Mind and its patient Morlock servants, would become a kind of God, embracing the sun.

I agreed with Nebogipfel that there could be no higher goal for an intelligent species!

I had rehearsed my next words, and spoke them carefully. 'Nebogipfel, I wish to return to the earth. I will work with you on my Time Machine.'

His head dipped. 'I am pleased. The value to our understanding will be immense.'

We debated the proposition further, but it took no more persuasion than that! – for Nebogipfel did not seem suspicious, and did not question me.

And so I made my brief preparations to leave that meaningless prairie. As I worked, I kept my thoughts to myself.

I had known that Nebogipfel – eager as he was to acquire the technology of time travel – would accept my proposal. And it gave me some pain, in the light of my new understanding of the essential dignity of the New Morlocks, that I was now forced to lie to him!

I would indeed return to the earth with Nebogipfel – but I had no intention of remaining there; for as soon as I got my hands on my machine again, I meant to escape with it, into the past.

19

HOW I CROSSED
INTER-PLANETARY SPACE

I was forced to wait three days until Nebogipfel pronounced himself ready to depart; it was, he said, a matter of waiting until the earth and our part of the Sphere entered the proper configuration with each other.

My thoughts turned to the journey ahead with some anticipation – I would not say fear, for I had, after all, already survived one such crossing of inter-planetary space, although insensible at the time – but rather with quickening interest. I speculated on the means by which Nebogipfel's space-yacht might be propelled. I thought of Verne, who had his argumentative Baltimore gun clubbers firing that ludicrous cannon, with its man-bearing shell, across the gap between the earth and moon. But it only took a little mental calculation to show that an acceleration sufficient to launch a projectile beyond the earth's gravity would also have been so strong as to smear my poor flesh, and Nebogipfel's, across the interior of the shell like strawberry jam.

What, then?

It is a commonplace that inter-planetary space is without air; and so we could not fly like birds to the earth, for the birds rely on the ability of their wings to push against the air. No air – no push! Perhaps, I speculated, my space yacht would be driven by some advanced form of firework rocket – for a rocket, which flies by pushing out behind it masses of its own spent propellant, would be able to function in the airlessness of space, if oxygen were carried to sustain its combustion . . .

But these were mundane speculations, grounded in my nineteenth-century understanding. How could I tell what might be possible by the year A.D. 657,208? I imagined yachts tacking against the sun's gravity as if against an invisible wind; or, I thought, there might be some manipulation of magnetic or other fields.

Thus my speculations raged, until Nebogipfel came to summon me, for the last time, from the Interior.

As we dropped into Morlock darkness I stood with my head tipped back, peering up at the receding sunlight; and – just before I donned my goggles – I promised myself that the next time my face felt the warmth of man's star, it would be in my own century!

I think I had been expecting to be transported to some Morlock equivalent of a port, with great ebony space yachts nuzzling against the Sphere like liners against a dock.

Well, there was none of that; instead Nebogipfel escorted me – across a distance of no more than a few miles, via strips of moving Floor – to an area which was kept clear of artefacts and partitions, and Morlocks in general, but was otherwise unremarkable. And in the middle of this area was a small chamber, a clear-walled box a little taller than I was – like a lift compartment – which sat there, squat, on the star-spattered Floor.

At Nebogipfel's gesture, I stepped into the compartment. Nebogipfel followed, and behind us the compartment sealed itself shut with a hiss of its diaphragm door. The compartment was roughly rectangular, its rounded corners and edges giving it something of the look of a lozenge. There was no furniture; there were, however, upright poles fixed at intervals about the cabin.

Nebogipfel wrapped his pale fingers around one of these poles. 'You should prepare yourself. At our launch, the change in effective gravity is sudden.'

I found these calm words disturbing! Nebogipfel's eyes, blackened by the goggles, were on me with their usual disconcerting mixture of curiosity and analysis; and I saw his fingers tighten their grip on the pillar.

And then – it happened faster than I can relate it – *the Floor opened.* The compartment fell out of the Sphere, and I and Nebogipfel with it!

I cried out, and I grabbed at a pole like an infant clinging to its mother's leg.

I looked upwards, and there was the surface of the Sphere, now turned into an immense, black Roof which occluded half the universe from my gaze. At the centre of this ceiling I could see a rectangle of paler darkness which was the door through which we had emerged; even as I watched, that door diminished with our distance, and in any event it was already folding closed against us. The door tracked across my view with magisterial slowness, showing how our compartment-capsule was starting to tumble in space. It was clear to me what had happened: any schoolboy can achieve the same effect by whirling a conker around his head, and then releasing the string. Well, the 'string' which had held us inside the rotating Sphere – the solidity of its Floor – had now vanished; and we had been thrown out into space, without ceremony.

And below me – I could hardly bear to glance down – there was a pit of stars, a floorless cavern into which I, and Nebogipfel, were falling forever!

130

'Nebogipfel – for the love of God – what has happened to us? Has some disaster occurred?'

He regarded me. Disconcertingly, his feet were hovering a few inches above the floor of the capsule – for, while the capsule fell through space, so we, within it, fell too, like peas in a matchbox!

'We have been released from the Sphere. The effects of its spin are –'

'I understand all that,' I said, 'but why? Are we intending to fall all the way to the earth?'

His answer I found quite terrifying.

'Essentially,' he said, 'yes.'

And then I had no further energy for questions, for I became aware that I too was starting to float about that little cabin like a balloon; and with that realization came a fight with nausea which lasted many minutes.

At length I regained some control over my body.

I had Nebogipfel explain the principles of this flight to the earth. And when he had done so, I realized how elegant and economical was the Morlocks' solution to travel between the Sphere and its cordon of surviving planets – so much so that I should have anticipated it, and dismissed all my nonsensical speculations of rockets – and yet, here was another example of the inhuman bias of the Morlock soul! Instead of the grandiose space yacht I had imagined, I would travel from Venus's orbit to the earth in nothing more grand than this lozenge-shaped coffin.

Few men of my century realized quite how much of the universe is vacancy, with a few pockets of warmth and life swimming through it, and what immense speeds are therefore required to traverse inter-planetary distances in a practicable time. But the Morlocks' Sphere was, at its equator, *already* moving at enormous velocities. So the Morlocks had no need of rockets, or guns, to reach inter-planetary speeds. They simply dropped their capsules out of the Sphere, and let the rotation do the rest.

And so they had done with us. At such speeds, the Morlock told me, we should reach the vicinity of the earth in just forty-seven hours.

I looked around the capsule, but I could see no signs of rockets, or any other motive force. I floated in that little cabin, feeling huge and clumsy; my beard drifted before my face in a grey cloud, and my jacket persisted in rucking itself up around my shoulder-blades. 'I understand the principles of the launch,' I said to Nebogipfel. 'But how is this capsule steered?'

He hesitated for some seconds. 'It is not. Have you misunderstood what I have told you? The capsule needs no motive force, for the velocity imparted to it by the Sphere –'

'Yes,' I said anxiously, 'I followed all of that. But what if, now, we were to detect that we were off track, by some mistake of our launch – that we were going to miss the earth?' For I realized that the most minute error at the Sphere, of even a fraction of a degree of arc, could – thanks to the immensity of inter-planetary distances – cause us to miss the earth by millions of miles – and then, presumably, we would go sailing off forever into the void between the stars, allocating blame until our air expired!

He seemed confused. 'There has been no mistake.'

'But still,' I stressed, 'if there *were*, perhaps through some mechanical flaw – then how should we, in this capsule, correct our trajectory?'

He thought for some time before answering. 'Flaws do not occur,' he repeated. 'And so this capsule has no need of corrective propulsion, as you suggest.'

At first I could not quite believe this, and I had to have Nebogipfel repeat it several times before I accepted its truth. But true it was! – after launch, the craft flew between the planets with no more intelligence than a hurled stone: my capsule fell across space as helpless as Verne's lunar cannon-shot.

As I protested the foolishness of this arrangement, I got the impression that the Morlock was becoming shocked – as if I were pressing some debating point of moral dubiety on a vicar of ostensibly open mind – and I gave it up.

The capsule twisted slowly, causing the remote stars and the immense wall that was the Sphere to wheel around us; I think that without that rotation I might have been able to imagine that I was safe and at rest, in some desert night, perhaps; but the tumbling made it impossible to forget that I was in a remote, fragile box, falling without support or attachment or means of direction. I spent the first few of my hours in that capsule in a paralysis of fear! I could not grow accustomed to the clarity of the walls around us, nor to the idea that, now that we were launched, we had no means of altering our trajectory. The journey had the elements of a nightmare – a fall through endless darkness, with no means of adjusting the situation to save myself. And there you have, in a nutshell, the essential difference between the minds of Morlock and human. For what man would trust his life to a ballistic journey, across inter-planetary distances, without any means of altering his course? But such was the New Morlock way: after a half-million years of steadily perfected technology, the Morlock would trust himself unthinkingly to his machines, for his machines *never* failed him.

I, though, was no Morlock!

Gradually, however, my mood softened. Apart from the slow tumble of the capsule, which continued throughout my journey to the earth, the hours passed in a stillness and silence broken only by the whisper-like breathing of my Morlock companion. The craft was tolerably warm, and so I was suspended in complete physical comfort. The walls were made of that extruding Floor-stuff, and, at a touch from Nebogipfel, I was provided with food, drink and other requirements, although the selection was more limited than in the Sphere, which had a larger Memory than our capsule.

So we sailed through the grand cathedral of inter-planetary space with utter ease. I began to feel as if I were disembodied, and a mood of utter detachment and independence settled on me. It was not like a journey, nor even – after those first hours – a nightmare; instead, it took on the qualities of a dream.

20

MY ACCOUNT OF THE
FAR FUTURE

On the second day of our flight, Nebogipfel asked me once again about my first journey into futurity.

'You managed to retrieve your machine from the Morlocks,' he prompted. 'And you went on, further into the future of that History . . .'

'For a long period I simply held onto the machine,' I remembered, 'much as now I am clinging to these poles, uncaring where I went. At last I brought myself to look at my chronometric dials, and I found that the hands were sweeping, with immense rapidity, further into futurity.

'You must recall,' I told him, 'that in this other History the axis of the earth, and its rotation, had not been straightened out. Still day and night flickered like wings over the earth, and still the sun's path dipped between its solstices as the seasons wore away. But gradually I became aware of a change: that, despite my continuing velocity through time, the flickering of night and day returned, and grew more pronounced.'

'The earth's rotation was slowing,' Nebogipfel said.

'Yes. At last the days spread across centuries. The sun had become a dome – huge and angry – glowing with its diminished heat. Occasionally its illumination brightened – spasms which recalled its former brilliancy. But each time it reverted to its sullen crimson.

'I began to slow my plummeting through time . . .'

When I stopped, it was on such a landscape as I had always imagined might prevail on Mars. The huge, motionless sun hung on the horizon; and in the other half of the sky, stars like bones still shone. The rocks strewn across the land were a virulent red, stained an intense green, as if by lichen, on every west-facing plane.

My machine stood on a beach which sloped down to a sea, so still it might have been coated in glass. The air was cold, and quite thin; I felt as if I were suspended atop some remote mountain. Little remained of the familiar topography of the Thames valley; I imagined how the scraping of glaciation, and the slow breathing of the seas, must have obliterated all trace of the landscape I had known – and all trace of Humanity . . .

Nebogipfel and I hovered there, suspended in space in our shining box, and I whispered my tale of far futurity to him; in that calm, I rediscovered details I may not have recounted to my friends in Richmond.

'I saw a thing like a kangaroo,' I recalled. 'It was perhaps three feet tall . . . squat, with heavy limbs and rounded shoulders. It loped across the beach – it looked forlorn, I remember – its coat of grey fur was tangled, and it pawed feebly at the rocks, evidently trying to prise free handfuls of lichen, to make its miserable repast. I got a sense of great degeneration about it. Then, I was surprised to see that the thing had five feeble digits to both its fore- and hind-feet . . . And it had a prominent forehead and forward-looking eyes. Its hints of humanity were most disagreeable!

'But then there was a touch at my ear – like a hair, stroking me – and I turned in my saddle.

'There was a creature just behind the machine. It

was like a centipede, I suppose, but wrought on a huge scale! – three or four feet wide, perhaps thirty feet in length, its body segmented and the chitin of its plates – they were crimson – scraping as it moved. Cilia, each a foot long, waved in the air, moist; and it was one of these which had touched me. Now this beast lifted up its stump of a head, and its mouth gaped wide, with damp mandibles waving before it; it had a hexagonal arrangement of eyes which swivelled about, fixing on me.

'I touched my lever, and slipped through time away from this monster.

'I emerged onto the same dismal beach, but now I saw a swarm of the centipede-things, which clambered heavily over each other, their cases scraping. They had a multitude of feet on which they crawled, looping their bodies as they advanced. And in the middle of this swarm I saw a mound – low and bloody – and I thought of the sad kangaroo-beast I had observed before.

'I could not bear this scene of butchery! I pressed at my levers, and passed on through a million years.

'Still that awful beach persisted. But now, when I turned from the sea, I saw, far up the barren slope behind me, a thing like an immense white butterfly which shimmered, fluttering, across the sky. Its torso might have been the size of a small woman's, and the wings, pale and translucent, were huge. Its voice was dismal – eerily human – and a great desolation settled over my soul.

'Then I noticed a motion across the landscape close to me: a thing like an outcropping of Mars-red rock which shifted across the sand towards me. It was a sort of crab: a thing the size of a sofa, its several legs picking their way over the beach, and with eyes – a greyish red, but human in shape – on stalks, waving towards me. Its mouth, as complex as some bit of machinery, twitched and licked as the thing moved, and its metallic hull was stained with the green of the patient lichen.

'As the butterfly, ugly and fragile, fluttered above me, the crab-thing reached up towards it with its big claws. It missed – but I fancy I saw scraps of some pale flesh embedded in that claw's wide grasp.

'As I have since reflected on that sight,' I told Nebogipfel, 'that sour apprehension has confirmed itself in my mind. For it seems to me that this arrangement of squat predator and fragile prey might be a consequence of the relationship of Eloi and Morlock I had observed earlier.'

'But their forms were so different: the centipedes, and then the crabs –'

'Over such deserts of time,' I insisted, 'evolution-ary pressure is such that the forms of species are quite plastic – so Darwin teaches us – and zoological retrogression is a dynamic force. Remember that you and I – and Eloi and Morlock – are all, if you look at it on a wide enough scale, nothing but cousins within the same antique mudfish family!'

Perhaps, I speculated, the Eloi had taken to the air in that species' desperate attempt to flee the Morlocks; and those predators had emerged from their caves, abandoning at last all simulation of mechanical invention, and now crawled across those cold beaches, waiting for a butterfly-Eloi to tire and fall from the sky. Thus that antique conflict, with its roots in social decay, had been reduced, at last, to its mindless essentials.

'I travelled on,' I told Nebogipfel, 'in strides a millennium long, on into futurity. Still, that crowd of crustaceans crawled among the lichen sheets and the rocks. The sun grew wider and duller.

'My last stop was thirty million years into the future, where the sun had become a dome which obscured a wide arc of sky. Snow fell – a hard, pitiless sleet. I shivered, and was forced to tuck my hands into my armpits. I could see snow on the hill-tops, pale in the star-light, and huge bergs drifted across the eternal sea.

'The crabs were gone, but the vivid green of the lichen mats persisted. On a shoal in the sea, I fancied I saw some black object, which I thought flopped with the appearance of life.

'An eclipse – caused by the passage of some inner planet across the sun's face – now caused a shadow to fall over the earth. Nebogipfel, you may have felt at ease there! – but a great horror fell upon *me*, and I got off the machine to recover. Then, when the first arc of crimson sun returned to the sky, I saw that the thing on the shoal was indeed moving. It was a ball of flesh – like a disembodied head, a yard or more across, with two bunches of tentacles which dangled like fingers across the shoal. Its mouth was a beak, and it was without a nose. Its eyes – two of them, large and dark – seemed human . . .'

And even as I described the thing to the patient Nebogipfel, I recognized the similarity between this vision of futurity, and my odd companion during my most recent trip through time – the floating, green-lit thing I had called *the Watcher*. I fell silent. Could it be, I mused, that my Watcher was no more than a visitation to me, from the end of time itself?

'And so,' I said at last, 'I clambered aboard my machine once more – I had a great dread of lying there, helpless, in that awful cold – and I returned to my own century.'

On I whispered, and the huge eyes of Nebogipfel were fixed on me, and I saw in him remnant flickers of that curiosity and wonder which characterizes humankind.

*

Those few days in space seem to have little relation to the rest of my life; sometimes the period I spent floating in that compartment is like a momentary pause, shorter than a heartbeat in the greater sweep of my life, and at other times I feel as if I spent an eternity in the capsule, drifting between worlds. It was as if I became disentangled from my life, and able to look upon it from without, as if it were an incomplete novel. Here I was as a young man, fiddling with my experiments and contraptions and heaps of Plattnerite, spurning the opportunity to socialize, and to learn of life, and love, and politics, and art – spurning even sleep! – in my quest for an unattainable perfection of understanding. I even supposed I saw myself *after* the completion of this inter-planetary voyage, with my scheme to deceive the Morlocks and escape to my own era. I still had every intention of carrying that plan through – you must understand – but it was as if I watched the actions of some other, littler figure than I was.

At last I had the idea that I was becoming something outside not only the world of my birth – but *all* worlds, and Space and Time as well. What was I to become in my own future but, once again, a mote of consciousness buffeted by the Winds of Time?

It was only as the earth grew perceptibly nearer – a darker shadow against space, with the light of the stars reflected in the ocean's belly – that I felt drawn back to the ordinary concerns of Humanity; that once again the details of my schemes – and my hopes and fears for my future – worked their life-long clock-work in my brain.

I have never forgotten that brief inter-planetary interlude, and sometimes – when I am between waking and sleeping – I imagine I am again adrift between Sphere and the earth, with only a patient Morlock for company.

Nebogipfel contemplated my vision of the far future. 'You said you travelled thirty million years.'

'That or more,' I replied. 'Perhaps I can recall the chronology more precisely, if –'

He waved that away. 'Something is wrong. Your description of the sun's evolution is plausible, but its destruction – our science tells us – should take place over *thousands* of millions of years, not a mere handful of millions.'

I felt defensive. 'I have recounted what I saw, honestly and accurately.'

'I do not doubt you have,' Nebogipfel said. 'But the only conclusion is that in that other History – as in my own – the evolution of the sun did not proceed without intervention.'

'You mean –'

'I mean that some clumsy attempt must have been made to adjust the sun's intensity, or longevity – or perhaps even, as we have, to mine the star for habitable materials.'

Nebogipfel's hypothesis was that perhaps my Eloi and Morlocks were *not* the full story of Humanity, in that sorry, lost History. Perhaps – Nebogipfel speculated – some race of engineers had left the earth and tried to modify the sun, just as had Nebogipfel's own ancestors.

'But the attempt failed,' I said, aghast.

'Yes. The engineers never returned to the earth which was abandoned to the slow tragedy of Eloi and Morlock. And the sun was rendered unbalanced, its lifetime curtailed.'

I was horrified, and I could bear to speak of this no more. I clung to a pole, and my thoughts turned inward.

I thought again of that desolate beach, of those hideous, devolved forms with their echoes of

141

Humanity and their utter absence of mind. The vision had been foul enough when I had considered it a final victory of the inexorable pressures of evolution and retrogression over the human dream of Mind – but now I saw that it might have been Humanity itself, in its overweening ambition, which had unbalanced those opposing forces, and accelerated its own destruction!

Our capture by the earth was elaborate. It was necessary for us to shed some millions of miles per hour of speed, in order to match the earth's progress around the sun.

We skimmed several times, on diminishing loops, around the belly of the planet; Nebogipfel told me that the capsule was being coupled with the planet's gravitational and magnetic fields – a coupling enhanced by certain materials in the hull, and by the manipulation of satellites: artificial moons, which orbited the earth and adjusted its natural effects. In essence, I understood, our velocity was *exchanged* with that of the earth – which, forever after, would travel around the sun a little further out, and a little more rapid.

I hung close to the wall of the capsule, watching the darkened landscape of earth unfold. I could see, here and there, the glow of the Morlocks' larger heating-wells. I noted several huge, slender towers which appeared to protrude above the atmosphere itself. Nebogipfel told me that the towers were used for capsules travelling from the earth to Sphere.

I saw specks of light crawling along the lengths of those towers: they were inter-planetary capsules, bearing Morlocks to be borne off to their Sphere. It was by means of just such a tower, I realized, that I – insensible – had been launched into space, and carried to the Sphere. The towers worked as lifts beyond the atmosphere, and a similar series of coupling manoeuvres to ours – performed in reverse, if you understand me – would hurl each capsule off into space.

The speed acquired by the capsules on launch would not match that imparted by the Sphere's rotation, and the outward journey thereby took longer than the return. But on arrival at the Sphere, magnetic fields would hook the capsules with ease, accelerating them to a seamless rendezvous.

At last we dipped into the atmosphere of the earth. The hull blazed with frictional heat, and the capsule shuddered – it was the first sensation of motion I had endured for days – but Nebogipfel had warned me, and I was ready braced against the supporting poles.

With this meteoric blaze of fire we shed the last of our inter-planetary speed. With some unease I watched the darkened landscape which spread below us as we fell – I thought I could see the broad, meandering ribbon of the Thames – and I began to wonder if, after all this distance, I would, after all, be dashed against the unforgiving rocks of the earth!

But then –

My impressions of the final phase of our shuddering descent are blurred and partial. Suffice it for me to record a memory of a craft, something like an immense bird, which swept down out of the sky and swallowed us in a moment into a kind of stomach-hold. In darkness, I felt a deep jolt as that craft pushed at the air, discarding its velocity; and then our descent continued with extreme gentleness.

When next I could see the stars, there was no sign of the bird-craft. Our capsule was settled on the dried, lifeless soil of Richmond Hill, not a hundred yards from the White Sphinx.

21

ON RICHMOND HILL

Nebogipfel had the capsule dilate open, and I stepped from it, cramming my goggles onto my face. The night-soaked landscape leapt to clarity and detail, and for the first time I was able to make out some detail of this world of A.D. 657,208.

The sky was brilliant with stars and the scar of obscurity made by the Sphere was looming and distinct. There was a rusty smell coming off the ubiquitous sand, and a certain dampness, as of lichen and moss; and everywhere the air was thick with the sweet stink of Morlock.

I was relieved to be out of that lozenge, and to feel firm earth beneath my boots. I strode up the hill to the bronze-plated pedestal of the Sphinx, and stood there, half-way up Richmond Hill, on the site that had once, I knew, been my home. A little further up the Hill there was a new structure, a small, square hut. I could see no Morlocks. It was a sharp contrast to my impressions of my earlier time here, when – as I stumbled in the dark – they had seemed to be everywhere.

Of my Time Machine there was no sign – only grooves dug deep into the sand, and the queer, narrow footprints characteristic of the Morlock. Had the machine been dragged into the base of the Sphinx again? Thus was History repeating itself! – or so I thought. I felt my fists bunching, so rapidly had

144

my elevated inter-planetary mood evaporated; and panic bubbled within me. I calmed myself. Was I a fool, that I could have expected the Time Machine to be waiting for me outside the capsule as it opened? I could not resort to violence – not now! – not when my plan for escape was so ripe. Nebogipfel joined me.

'We appear to be alone here,' I said.

'The children have been moved from this area.'

I felt a renewed access of shame. 'Am I so danger-ous? . . . Tell me where my machine is.'

He had removed his goggles, but I could not read those grey-red eyes. 'It is safe. It has been moved to a more convenient place. If you wish you may inspect it.'

I felt as if a steel cable attached me to my Time Machine, and was drawing me in! I longed to rush to the machine, and leap aboard its saddle – be done with this world of darkness and Morlocks, and make for the past! . . . But I must needs be patient. Struggling to keep my voice even, I replied, 'That isn't necessary.'

Nebogipfel led me up the Hill, to the little building I had noticed earlier. It followed the Morlocks' usual seamless, simple design; it was like a doll's house, with a simple hinged door and a sloping roof. Inside, there was a pallet for a bed, with a blanket on it, and a chair, and a little tray of food and water – all refreshingly solid-looking. My knapsack was on the bed.

I turned to Nebogipfel. 'You have been consider-ate,' I said, sincere.

'We respect your rights.' He walked away from my shelter. When I took my goggles off, he melted into shadow.

I closed the door with some relief. It was a pleasure to return to my own human company for a while. I

145

felt shame that I was planning, so systematically, to deceive him and his people! But my scheme had brought me across hundreds of millions of miles already – to within a few hundred yards of the Time Machine – and I could not bear the thought of failure now.

I knew that if I had to harm Nebogipfel to escape, I would!

By touch I opened the knapsack, and I found and lit a candle. A comforting yellow light and a curl of smoke turned that inhuman little box into a home. The Morlocks had kept back my poker – as I might have anticipated – but much of the other equipment had been left for me. Even my clasp-knife was there. With this, and using a Morlock tray as a crude mirror, I hacked off my irritating growth of beard, and shaved as close as I could. I was able to discard my underwear and don fresh – I would never have anticipated that the feeling of truly clean socks would invoke such feelings of sensual pleasure in me! – and I thought fondly of Mrs Watchets, who had packed these invaluable items for me.

Finally – and most pleasurably – I took a pipe from the knapsack, packed it with tobacco, and lit it from the candle flame.

It was in this condition, with my few possessions around me, and the rich scent of my finest tobacco still lingering, that I lay down on the little bed, pulled the blanket over me and slept.

I awoke in the dark.

It was an odd thing to wake without daylight – like being disturbed in the small hours – and I never felt refreshed by a sleep, the whole time I was in the Morlocks' Dark Night; it was as if my body could not calculate what time of day it was.

I had told Nebogipfel that I should like to inspect

146

the Time Machine, and I felt a great nervousness as I went through a brief breakfast and toilet. My plan did not amount to much in the way of strategy: it was merely to take the machine, at the first opportunity! I was gambling that the Morlocks, after millennia of sophisticated machines which could change their very shapes, would not know what to make of a device as crude, in its construction, as my Time Machine. I thought they would not expect that so simple an act as the reattachment of two levers could restore the machine's functionality – or so I prayed!

I emerged from the shelter. After all my adventures, the levers to the Time Machine were safe in my jacket's inside pocket.

Nebogipfel walked towards me, his thin feet leaving their sloth-like footprints in the sand, and his two hands empty. I wondered how long he had been near, waiting for my emergence.

We walked along the flank of the Hill together, heading south in the direction of Richmond Park. We set off without preamble, for the Morlocks were not give to unnecessary conversation.

I have said that my house had stood on the Petersham Road, on the stretch below Hill Rise. As such it had been halfway up the shoulder of Richmond Hill, a few hundred yards from the river, with a good westerly prospect – or it would have had, if not for the intervening trees – and I had been able to see something of the meadows at Petersham beyond the river. Well, in the Year A.D. 657,208, all of the intervening clutter had been swept away; and I was able to see down the flank of a deepened valley to where the Thames lay in its new bed, glittering in the star-light. I could see, here and there, the coal-hot mouths of the Morlocks' heat-wells, puncturing the darkened land. Much of the hill-side was bare sand, or given over to moss; but I could see patches of what looked like the soft glass which had carpeted the Sphere, glittering in the enhanced star-light.

The river itself had carved out a new channel a mile or so from its nineteenth-century position; it appeared to have cut off the bow from Hampton to Kew, so that Twickenham and Teddington were now on its east side, and it seemed to me that the valley was a good bit deeper than in my day – or perhaps Richmond Hill had been lifted up by some other geological process. I remembered a similar migration of the Thames in my first voyage into time. Thus, it seemed to me, the discrepancies of human History are mere froth; under it all, the slow processes of geology and erosion would continue their patient work regardless.

I spared a moment to glance up the Hill towards the Park, for I wondered for how long those ancient woodlands and herds of red and fallow deer had survived the winds of change. Now, the Park could be no more than a darkened desert, populated only by cacti and a few olives. I felt my heart harden. Perhaps these Morlocks were wise and patient – perhaps their industrious pursuit of knowledge on the Sphere was to be applauded – but their neglect of the ancient earth was a shame!

We reached the vicinity of the Park's Richmond Gate, close to the site of the Star and Garter, perhaps half a mile from the site of my house. On a level patch of land, a rectangular platform of soft glass had been laid; this platform shimmered in the patchy star-light. It appeared to be manufactured of that marvellous, glassy material of which the Sphere Floor was composed; and from its surface had been evoked a variety of the podiums and partitions which I had come to recognize as the characteristic tools of the Morlocks. These were abandoned now; there was nobody about but Nebogipfel and I. And there – at the heart of the platform – I saw a squat and ugly tangle of brass and nickel, with ivory like bleached bone shining in the star-light, and a bicycle-saddle in the middle of it all: it was my Time Machine, evidently intact, and ready to take me home!

22

ROTATIONS AND DECEPTIONS

I felt my heart pump; I found it difficult to walk at a steady pace behind Nebogipfel – but walk I did. I dropped my hands into my jacket pockets and I grasped the two control levers there. I was already close enough to the machine to see the studs on which the levers must be fitted for the thing to work – and I meant to launch the machine as soon as I could, and to get away from this place!

'As you can see,' Nebogipfel was saying, 'the machine is undamaged – we have moved it, but not attempted to pry into its workings . . .'

I sought to distract him from his close attention. 'Tell me: now that you've studied my machine, and listened to my theories on the subject, what is your impression?'

'Your machine is an extraordinary achievement – ahead of its age.'

I have never been one with much patience for compliments. 'But it is the Plattnerite which enabled me to construct it,' I said.

'Yes. I would like to study this "Plattnerite" more closely.' He donned his goggles, and studied the machine's shimmering quartz bars. 'We have talked – a little – of multiple Histories: of the possible existence of several editions of the world. You have witnessed two yourself –'

150

'The history of Eloi and Morlock, and the History of the Sphere.'

'You must think of these versions of History as parallel corridors, stretching ahead of you. Your machine allows you to go back and forth along a corridor. The corridors exist independently of each other: looking ahead from any point, a man looking along one corridor will see a complete and self-consistent History – he can have no knowledge of another corridor, and nor can the corridors influence each other.

'But in some corridors conditions may be very different. In some, even the laws of physics may differ . . .'

'Go on.'

'You said the operation of your machine depended on a twisting about of Space and Time,' he said. 'Turning a journey in Time into one through Space. Well, I agree: that is, indeed, how the Plattnerite exerts its effects. But how is this achieved?

'Picture, now,' he said, 'a universe – another History – in which this Space-Time twisting is greatly pronounced.'

He went on to describe a variant of the universe almost beyond my imagining: in which *rotation* was embedded in the very fabric of the universe.

'Rotation suffuses every point of Space and Time. A stone, thrown outward from any point, would be seen to follow a spiral path: its inertia would act like a compass, swinging around the launch point. It is even thought by some that our own universe might undergo such a rotation, but on an immensely slow scale: taking a hundred thousand million years to complete a single turn . . .

'The rotating-universe idea was first described some decades after your time – by Kurt Gōdel, in fact.'

151

'Gödel?' It took me a moment to place the name. 'The man who will demonstrate the imperfectibility of mathematics?'

'The same.'

We walked around the machine, and I kept my stiff fingers wrapped around the levers. I planned to manoeuvre myself into precisely the most propitious spot to reach the machine. 'Tell me how this explains the operation of my machine.'

'It is to do with axis-twisting. In a rotating universe, *a journey through space, but reaching the past or future*, is possible. Our universe rotates, but so slowly that such a path would be a hundred thousand *million* light years long, and would take the best part of a million million years to traverse!'

'Of little practical use, then.'

'But imagine a universe of greater density than ours: a universe as dense, everywhere, as the heart of an atom of matter. There, a rotation would be complete in mere fractions of a second.'

'But we are not in such a universe.' I waved my hand through empty space. 'That is evident.'

'But perhaps you are! – for fractions of a second, and thanks to your machine – or at least to its Plattnerite component.

'My hypothesis is that, because of some property of the Plattnerite, your Time Machine is flickering back and forth to this ultra-dense universe, and on each traverse is exploiting that reality's axis-twisting to travel along a succession of loops into the past or future! So you spiral through time . . .'

I considered these ideas. They were extraordinary – of course! – but, it seemed to me, no more than a somewhat fantastic extension of my preliminary thoughts of the intertwining of Space and Time, and the fluidity of their relevant axes. And besides, my subjective impression of time travel was bound up with feelings of twisting – of rotation.

'These ideas are startling – but I believe they would bear further examination,' I told Nebogipfel.

He looked up at me. 'Your flexibility of mind is impressive, for a man of your evolutionary era.'

I barely heard his dismissive remark. I was close enough now. Nebogipfel touched a rail of the machine, with one cautious finger. The device shimmered, belying its bulk, and a breeze ruffled the fine hairs on Nebogipfel's arm. He snatched his hand back. I stared at the studs, rehearsing in my mind the simple action of lifting the levers out of my pockets and fitting them to the studs. It would take less than a second! Could I complete the action before Nebogipfel could render me unconscious, with his green rays?

The darkness closed in around me, and the stink of Morlock was strong. In a moment, I thought with a surge of irrepressible eagerness, I might be gone from all this.

'Is something wrong?' Nebogipfel was watching my face with those great, dark eyes of his, and his stance was upright and tense. Already he was suspicious! – had I betrayed myself? And already, in the darkness beyond, I knew, the muzzles of countless guns must be raised towards me – I had bare seconds before I was lost!

Blood roared in my ears – I hauled the levers from my pockets – and, with a cry, I fell forward over the machine. I jammed the little bars down on their studs and with a single motion I wrenched the levers back. The machine shuddered – in that last moment there was a flash of green, and I thought it was all up for me! – and then the stars disappeared, and silence fell on me. I felt an extraordinary twisting sensation, and then that dreadful feeling of plummeting – but I welcomed the discomfort, for this was the familiar experience of time travel!

I yelled out loud. I had succeeded – I was journeying back through time – I was free!

. . . And then I became aware of a coolness around my throat – a softness, as if some insect had settled there, a *rustling*.

I lifted my hand to my neck – and touched Morlock hair!

BOOK TWO

Paradox

1

THE CHRONIC ARGO

I wrapped my hand around that thin forearm and prised it from my neck. A hairy body lay sprawled across the nickel and brass beside me – a thin, goggled face was close to mine – the sweet, foetid smell of Morlock was powerful!

'*Nebogipfel.*'

His voice was small and shallow, and his chest seemed to be pumping. Was he afraid? 'So you have escaped. And so easily –'

He looked like a doll of rags and horse-hair, clinging as he was to my machine. He was a reminder of that nightmarish world which I had escaped – I could have thrown him off in a moment, I am sure – and yet, I stayed my hand.

'Perhaps you Morlocks underestimated my capacity for action,' I snapped at him. 'But you – you *suspected*, didn't you?'

'Yes. Just in that last second . . . I have become adept, I think, at interpreting the unconscious language of your body. I realized you were planning to operate the machine – I had just time to reach you, before . . .

'Do you think we could straighten up?' he whispered. 'I am in some discomfort, and I fear falling off the machine.'

He looked at me as I considered this proposition. I felt that there was a decision I had to make, of sorts;

was I to accept him as a fellow passenger on the machine – or not?

But I would scarce throw him off; I knew myself well enough for that!

'Oh, very well.'

And so we two Chronic Argonauts executed an extraordinary ballet, there amid the tangle of my machine. I kept a grip of Nebogipfel's arm – to save him from falling, and to ensure that he did not try to reach the controls of the machine – and twisted my way around until I was sitting upright on the saddle. I was not a nimble man even when young, and by the time I had achieved this goal I was panting and irritable. Nebogipfel, meanwhile, lodged himself in a convenient section of the machine's construction.

'Why did you follow me, Nebogipfel?'

Nebogipfel stared out at the dark, attenuated landscape of time travel, and would not reply.

Still, I thought I understood. I remembered his curiosity and wonder at my account of futurity, while we shared the inter-planetary capsule. It had been an impulse for the Morlock to climb after me – to discover if time travel was a reality – and an impulse driven by a curiosity descended, like mine, from a monkey's! I felt obscurely moved by this, and I warmed to Nebogipfel a little. Humanity had changed much in the years that separated us, but here was evidence that curiosity, that relentless drive to *find out* – and the recklessness that came with it – had not died completely!

And then we erupted into light – above my head I saw the dismantling of the Sphere – bare sunlight flooded the machine, and Nebogipfel howled.

I discarded my goggles. The uncovered sun, at first, hung stationary in the sky, but before long it had begun to drift from its fixed position; it arced across the heavens, more and more rapid, and the flapping of day and night returned to the earth. At last the sun shot across the sky too rapidly to follow, and it became a band of light, and the alternation of day and night was replaced by that uniform, rather cold, pearl-like glow.

So, I saw, the regulation of the earth's axis and rotation was undone.

The Morlock huddled over himself, his face buried against his chest. He had his goggles on his face, but their protection did not seem to be enough; he seemed to be trying to burrow into the machine's innards, and his back glowed white in the diluted sunlight.

I could not help but laugh. I remembered how he had failed to warn me when our earth-bound capsule had dropped out of the Sphere and into space: well, here was retribution! 'Nebogipfel, it is only sunlight.'

Nebogipfel lifted his head. In the increased light, his goggles had blackened to impenetrability; the hair on his face was matted and appeared to be tearstained. The flesh of his body, visible through the hair, glowed a pale white. 'It is not just my eyes,' he said. 'Even in this attenuated state the light is painful for me. When we emerge, into the full glare of the sun . . .'

'Sun-burn!' I exclaimed. After so many generations of darkness, this Morlock would be more vulnerable, even to the feeble sun of England, than would the palest redhead in the Tropics. I pulled off my jacket. 'Here,' I said, 'this should help protect you.'

Nebogipfel pulled the garment around him, huddling under its folds.

'And besides,' I said, 'when I stop the machine, I will ensure we arrive when it is night, so we can find you shelter.' As I thought about this, I realized that to arrive in the hours of darkness would be a good idea in any event: a fine sight I should have made, appearing on Richmond Hill with this monster from the future, in the middle of a crowd of gaping promenaders!

The permanent greenery receded from the hillside and we returned to a cycle of seasons. We began our passage back through the Age of Great Buildings which I have described before. Nebogipfel, with the jacket draped over his head, peered out with obvious fascination as bridges and pylons passed over the flickering landscape like mist. As for me, I felt an intense relief that we were approaching my own century.

Suddenly Nebogipfel hissed – it was a queer, cat-like sound – and pressed himself closer to the fabric of the machine. He stared ahead, his eyes huge and fixed.

I turned from him, and I realized that the extraordinary optical effects which I had observed during my voyage to the year A.D. 657,208 were again becoming apparent. I had the impression of star-fields, gaudy and crowded, trying to break through the diluted surface of things, all about me . . . And here, hovering a few yards before the machine, was the Watcher: my impossible companion. Its eyes were fixed on me, and I grabbed at a rail. I stared at that distorted parody of a human face, and those dangling tentacles – and again I was struck by the similarity with the flopping creature I had seen on that remote beach thirty million years hence.

It is an odd thing, but my goggles – which had been so useful in resolving the Morlock darkness – were of no help to me as I studied this creature; I saw it no more clearly than I could with my naked eyes.

I became aware of a low mumbling, like a whimper. It was Nebogipfel, clinging to his place in the machine with every evidence of distress.

'You've no need to be afraid,' I said, a little clumsily. 'I told you of my encounter with this creature on my way to your century. It is a strange sight, but it seems to be without harm.'

Through his shuddery whimpering, Nebogipfel said, 'You do not understand. What we see is *impossible*. Your Watcher apparently has the ability to *cross* the corridors – to traverse between potential versions of History . . . even to enter the attenuated environs of a travelling Time Machine. It is impossible!'

And then – as easily as it had arisen – the star-glow faded, and my Watcher receded into invisibility, and the machine surged on its way into the past.

At length I said to the Morlock harshly, 'You must understand this, Nebogipfel: I have no intention of returning to the future, after this last trip.'

He wrapped his long fingers around the machine's struts. 'I know I cannot return,' he said. 'I knew that even as I hurled myself onto the machine. Even if your intention was to return to the future –'

'Yes?'

'By its return through time once more, this machine of yours is bound to force another adjustment of History, in an unpredictable way.' He turned to me, his eyes huge behind the goggles. 'Do you understand? My History, my home, is lost – perhaps destroyed. I have already become a refugee in time . . . Just as you are.'

His words chilled me. Could he be right? Could I be inflicting more damage on the carcass of History with this new expedition, even as I sat here?

My resolve to put all of this right – to put a stop to the Time Machine's destructiveness – hardened in me!

'But if you knew all this was so, your recklessness in following me was folly of the first order –'

'Perhaps.' His voice was muffled, for he sheltered

161

his head beneath his arms. 'But to see such sights as I have already witnessed – to travel in time – *to gather such information* . . . none of my species has ever had such an opportunity!'

He fell silent, and my sympathy for him grew. I wondered how *I* might have reacted, had I been presented with a single second of opportunity – as the Morlock had!

The chronometric dials continued to wind back, and I saw that we were approaching my own century. The world assembled itself into a more familiar configuration, with the Thames firmly set in its old bank, and bridges I thought I recognized flickering into existence over it.

I pulled the levers over. The sun became visible as a discrete object, flying over our heads like a glowing bullet; and the passage of night was a perceptible flickering. Two of the chronometric dials were already stationary; only thousands of days – a mere few years – remained to be traversed.

I became aware that Richmond Hill had congealed around me, in more or less the form I recognized from my own day. With the obstructing trees reduced to transient transparency by my travel, I took in a good view of the meadows of Petersham and Twickenham, and all dotted about with stands of ancient trees. It was all reassuring and familiar – despite the fact that my velocity through time was still so high that it was impossible to make out people, or deer, or cows, or other denizens of the Hill, meadows or river; and the flickering of night and day bathed the whole scene in an unnatural glow – despite all this, I was nearly home!

I watched my dials as the thousands hand approached its zero – I was home, and it took all my determination not to halt the machine there and then, for my longing to return to my own Year was strong in the extreme – but I kept the levers pressed over, and watched the dials run on into their negative region.

Around me the Hill flickered through night and day, with here and there a splash of colour as some picnic party stayed on the grass long enough for them to register on my vision. At last, with the dials reading six thousand, five hundred and sixty days *before* my departure, I pressed the levers again.

I brought the Time Machine to rest, in the depths of a cloudy, moonless night. If I had got my calculations right, I had landed in July of 1873. With my Morlock goggles, I saw the slope of the Hill, and the river's flank, and dew glittering on the grass; and I could see that – although the Morlocks had deposited my machine on an open stretch of hill-side, a half-mile from my house – there was nobody about to witness my arrival. The sounds and scents of my century flooded over me: the sharp tang of wood burning in some grate somewhere, the distant murmur of the Thames, the brush of a breeze through the trees, the naphtha flares of hawkers' barrows. It was all delicious, and familiar, and welcome!

Nebogipfel stood up cautiously. He had slipped his arms into my jacket sleeves, and now that heavy garment hung from him as if he were a child. 'Is this 1891?'

'No,' I said.

'What do you mean?'

'I mean that I have brought us back *further* in time.' I glanced along the Hill, in the direction of my house. 'Nebogipfel, in a laboratory up there, a brash young man is embarking on a series of experiments which will lead, ultimately, to the creation of a Time Machine . . .'

'You are saying –'

'That this is the year 1873 – and I anticipate, soon, meeting myself as a young man!'

His goggled, chinless face swivelled towards me in what appeared to be astonishment.

'Now come, Nebogipfel, and assist me in finding a place of concealment for this contraption.'

2

HOME

I cannot describe how odd it seemed to me to walk through the night air along the Petersham Road, coming at last to my own house – with a Morlock at my side!

The house was an end terrace, with big bay windows, rather unambitious carvings about the door frame, and a porch with mock-Grecian pillars. At the front there was an area with steps which went down to the basement, railed off by a bit of delicate, black-painted metal-work. The whole effect was really a sort of imitation of the genuinely grand houses on the Green, or in the Terrace at the top of the Hill; but it was a big, roomy, comfortable place which I had bought as a bargain as a younger man, and from which I had had no thoughts of moving away.

I walked past the front door and around towards the rear of the house. At the rear there were balconies, with delicate iron pilasters painted white, giving a view to the west. I could make out the windows of the smoking-room and dining-room, darkened now (it occurred to me that I was not sure what time of the night it was), but I was aware of an odd absence to the rear of the smoking-room. It took me some moments to remember what this repre-sented – an unexpected *absence* of something is so much harder to identify than an incongruous *presence* – it was, in fact, the site of the bathroom which I

165

would later have built there. Here, in 1873, I was still forced to wash in a hip-bath brought into my bedroom by a servant!

And, in that ill-proportioned conservatory protruding from the rear of the house, there was my laboratory, where – I saw with a thrill of anticipation – a light still burned. Any dinner guests had gone, and the servants had long retired; but still he – *I* – was working on.

I suffered a mixture of emotions I imagine no man has shared before; here was my home, and yet I could lay no claim to it!

I returned to the front door. Nebogipfel was standing a little way into the deserted road; he seemed cautious of approaching the area steps, for the pit into which they descended was quite black, even with the goggles.

'You don't need to be fearful,' I said. 'It's quite common to have kitchens and the like underground in houses like this . . . The steps and railings are sturdy enough.'

Nebogipfel, anonymous behind his goggles, inspected the steps suspiciously. I supposed his caution came from an ignorance of the robustness of nineteenth-century technology – I had forgotten how strange my crude era must seem to him – but, nevertheless, something about his attitude disturbed me.

I was reminded, and it disconcerted me, of an odd fragment of my own childhood. The house where I grew up was large and rambling – impractical, actually – and it had underground passages which ran from the house to the stable block, larder and the like: such passages are a common feature of houses of that age. There were gratings set in the ground at intervals: black-painted, round things, covering shafts which led down to the passages, for ventilation. I recalled, now, my own fear, as a child,

166

of those enclosed pits in the ground. Perhaps they *had* been simple air-shafts; but what, my childish imagination had prompted me, if some bony Hand came squirming through those wide bars and grabbed my ankle?

It occurred to me now – I think something in Nebogipfel's cautious stance was triggering all this – that there was something of a similarity between those shafts in the grounds of my childhood, and the sinister wells of the Morlocks . . . Was *that* why, in the end, I had lashed out so at that Morlock child, in A.D. 657,208?

I am not a man who enjoys such insights into his own character! Quite unfairly, I snapped at Nebogipfel, 'Besides, I thought you Morlocks liked the dark!' And I turned from him and walked up to the front door.

It was all so familiar – and yet disconcertingly *different*. Even at a glance I could see a thousand small changes from my day, eighteen years into the future. There was the sagging lintel I would later have replaced, for instance, and there the vacant site which would hold the arched lamp-holder I would one day install, at the prompting of Mrs Watchets.

I came to realize, anew, what a remarkable business this time travelling was! One might expect the most dramatic changes in a flight across thousands of centuries – and such I had found – but even this little hop, of mere decades, had rendered me an anachronism.

'What shall I do? Should I wait for you?'

I considered Nebogipfel's silent presence beside me. Wearing his goggles and with my jacket still drooped about him, he looked comical and alarming in equal measure! 'I think there is more danger in the situation if you stay outside. What if a policeman were to spot you? – he might think you were some odd burglar. If you were arrested –' I was unsure whether the possibilities of a Morlock in a police station of 1873, were alarming or comic! Without his web of Morlock machinery, Nebogipfel was quite defenceless; he had launched himself into History quite as unprepared as I had been on my first jaunt. 'And what of dogs? Or cats? I wonder what the average Tom of the eighteen-seventies would make of a Morlock. A fine meal, I should think ... No, Nebogipfel. All in all, I think it would be safer if you stayed with me.'

'And the young man you are visiting? What of his reaction?'

I sighed. 'Well, I have always been blessed by an open and flexible mind. Or so I like to think! ... Perhaps I am soon to find out. Besides, your presence might convince me – him – of the veracity of my account.'

And, without allowing myself any further hesitation, I tugged at the bell-pull.

From within the house, I heard doors slamming, an irritable shout: 'It's all right, I'll go!' – and then footsteps which clattered along the short corridor linking the rest of the house to my laboratory.

'It's me,' I hissed at Nebogipfel. '*Him*. It must be late – the servants are abed.'

A key rattled in the lock of the door.

Nebogipfel hissed: 'Your goggles.'

I snatched the offending anachronisms from my face, and jammed them into my trouser pocket – just as the door swung open.

A young man stood there, his face glowing like a moon in the light of the single candle he carried. His glance over me, in my shirt-sleeves, was cursory; and the inspection he gave Nebogipfel was even more superficial. (So much for the powers of observation I prized!) 'What the Devil do you want? It's after one in the morning, you know.'

I opened my mouth to speak – but my little rehearsed preamble disappeared from my mind.

Thus I confronted myself at the age of twenty-six!

3

MOSES

Since this experience I have become convinced that we all, without exception, use the mirror to deceive ourselves. The reflection we see there is so much *under our control*: we favour our best features, if unconsciously, and adjust our mannerisms into a pattern which our closest friend would not recognize. And, of course, we are under no compulsion to consider ourselves from less favourable angles: such as from the back of the head, or with our prominent nose in full, glorious profile.

Well, here was one reflection which was *not* under my control – and a troubling experience it was.

He was my height, of course: if anything, I was startled to find, I had shrunk a little in the intervening eighteen years. His forehead was odd: peculiarly broad, just as many people have pointed out to me, unkindly, through my life, and dusted with thin, mouse-brown hair, yet to recede or show any streaks of grey. The eyes were a clear grey, the nose straight, the jaw firm; but I had hardly been a handsome devil: he was naturally pale, and that pallor was enhanced by the long hours he had spent, since his formative years, in libraries, studies, teaching-rooms and laboratories.

I felt vaguely repulsed; there was indeed a little of the Morlock in me! And had my ears *ever* been so prominent?

But it was the clothes which caught my eye. *The clothes!*

He wore what I remembered as the costume of a *masher*: a short, bright red coat over a yellow and black waistcoat fixed with heavy brass buttons, boots tall and yellow, and a nosegay adorning his lapel.

Had *I* ever worn such garments? I must have done! – but anything further from my own sober style would have been difficult to imagine.

'Confound it,' I couldn't help but say, 'you're dressed like a circus clown!'

He seemed uncertain – he saw something odd about my face, evidently – but he replied briskly enough: 'Perhaps I should close this door in your face, sir. Have you climbed the Hill just to insult my clothing?'

I noticed that his nosegay was rather wilted, and I thought I could smell brandy on his breath. 'Tell me. Is this Thursday?'

'That's a very odd question. I ought to . . .'

'Yes?'

He held up the candle and peered into my face. So fascinated was he by me – by his own, dimly perceived self – that he ignored the Morlock: a man-thing from the distant future, standing not two yards away from him! I wondered if there was some clumsy Metaphor buried in this little scene: had I travelled into time, after all, only to seek out myself?

But I have no time for irony, and I felt rather embarrassed at even having framed such a Literary thought!

'It *is* Thursday, as it happens. Or was – we're in Friday's small hours now. What of it? And why don't you know in the first place? Who *are* you, sir?'

'I'll tell you who I am,' I said. 'And –' I indicated the Morlock, and evoked widened eyes from our reluctant host '– and who *this* is. And why I'm not

171

sure what hour it is, or even what day. But first – may we come inside? For I would relish a little of your brandy.'

He stood there for perhaps half a minute, the candle wick sputtering in its pool of wax; and, in the distance, I heard the sigh of the Thames as it made its languid way through the bridges of Richmond. Then, at length, he said: 'I should throw you into the street! – but . . .'

'I know,' I said gently. I regarded my younger self with indulgence; I have never been shy of feverish speculation, and I could imagine what wild hypotheses were already fomenting in that fecund, undisciplined mind!

He came to his decision. He stepped back from the door.

I gestured Nebogipfel forward. The Morlock's feet, bare save for a coat of hair, padded on the hall's parquetry floor. My younger self stared anew – Nebogipfel returned his gaze with interest – and he said: 'It's – ah – it's late. I don't want to get the servants up. Come on through to the dining-room; it's probably the warmest place.'

The hall was dark, with a painted dado and a row of hat-pegs; our reluctant host's broad skull was silhouetted by his single candle as he led the way past the door to the smoking-room. In the dining-room, there was still a glow of coals in the fireplace. Our host lit candles from the one he carried, and the room emerged into brightness, for there were a dozen or so candles in there: two in brass sticks on the mantel, with a tobacco jar plump and complacent between, and the rest in sconces.

I gazed around at this warm and comfortable room – so familiar, and yet made so different by the most subtle of rearrangements and redecoration! There was the little table at the door, with its pile of newspapers – replete, no doubt, with gloomy analyses of Mr Disraeli's latest pronouncements, or perhaps some dreadfully dreary stuff about the Eastern Question – and there was my armchair close to the fire, low and comfortable. But of my set of small octagonal tables, and of my incandescent lamps with their lilies of silver, there was no sign.

Our host came up to the Morlock. He leaned forward, resting his hands on his knees. 'What is this? It looks like some form of ape – or a deformed child. Is this your jacket it's wearing?'

I bridled at this tone – and surprised myself for doing so. '"It",' I said, 'is actually a "he". And he can speak for himself.'

'Can it?' He swivelled his face back to Nebogipfel. 'I mean, can you? Great Scott.'

He kept on staring into poor Nebogipfel's hairy face, and I stood there on the carpet of the dining-room, trying not to betray my impatience – not to say embarrassment – at this ill-courtesy.

He remembered his hospitable duties. 'Oh,' he said, 'I'm sorry. Please – here. Sit down.'

Nebogipfel, swamped by my jacket, stood in the middle of the hearth-rug. He glanced down at the floor, and then around the room. He seemed to be waiting for something – and in a moment, I understood. So used was the Morlock to the technology of his time, he was waiting for furniture to be extruded from the carpet! Although, later in our acquaintance, the Morlock was to show himself rather knowledgeable about things and flexible of mind, just then he was as baffled as I might have been had I searched for a gas mantle on the wall of some Stone Age cave.

'Nebogipfel,' I said, 'these are simpler times. The forms are *fixed*.' I pointed to the dining-table and chairs. 'You must select one of these.'

My younger self listened to this exchange with evident curiosity.

The Morlock, after a few more seconds' hesitation, made for one of the bulkier chairs.

I got there before him. 'Actually, not this one, Nebogipfel,' I said gently. 'I don't think you'd find it comfortable – it might try to give you a massage, you see, but it's not designed for your weight . . .'

My host looked at me, startled.

Nebogipfel, under my guidance – I felt like a clumsy parent as I fussed about him – pulled out a simple upright and climbed up into it; he sat there with his legs dangling like some hairy child.

'How did you know about my Active Chairs?' my host demanded. 'I've only demonstrated them to a few friends – the design isn't even patented yet –'

I did not answer: I simply held his gaze, for long seconds. I could see that the extraordinary answer to his question was already forming in his mind.

He broke the gaze. 'Sit down,' he said to me. 'Please. I'll fetch the brandy.'

I sat with Nebogipfel – at my own transmuted dining-table, with a Morlock for company! – and I glanced around. In one corner of the dining-room, on its tripod, sat the old Gregorian telescope which I had brought from my parents' home – a simple thing capable of delivering only cloudy images, and yet a window for me as a child into worlds of wonder in the sky, and into the intriguing marvels of physical optics. And, beyond this room, there was the dark passage to the laboratory, with the doors left care-lessly open; through the passage I caught tantalizing glimpses of my workshop itself: the clutter of appara-tuses on the benches, sheets of drawings laid across the floor, and various tools and appliances.

Our host rejoined us; he carried, clumsily, three glasses for brandy, and a carafe. He poured out three

174

generous measures, and the liquor sparkled in the light of the candles. 'Here,' he said. 'Are you cold? Would you like the fire?'

'No,' I said, 'thank you.' I raised the brandy, sniffed at it, then let it roll over my tongue.

Nebogipfel did not pick up his glass. He dipped a pallid finger into the stuff, withdrew it, and licked a drop from his fingertip. He seemed to shudder. Then, delicately, he pushed the glass away from him, as if it were full to the brim with the most noxious ale imaginable!

My host watched this curiously. Then, with an evident effort, he turned to me. 'You have me at a disadvantage. I don't know you. But you know me, it appears.'

'Yes.' I smiled. 'But I'm at something of a quandary as to what to call you.'

He frowned, looking uneasy. 'I don't see why that's any sort of a problem. My name is –'

I held up my hand; I had an inspiration. 'No. I will use – if you will permit – *Moses.*'

He took a deep pull on his brandy, and gazed at me with genuine anger in his grey eyes. 'How do you know about that?'

Moses – my hated first name, for which I had been endlessly tormented at school – and which I had kept a secret since leaving home!

'Never mind,' I said. 'Your secret is safe with me.'

'Look here, I'm growing tired of these games. You turn up here with your – companion – and make all sorts of disparagements about my clothes. And I still don't even know your name!'

'But,' I said, 'perhaps you do.'

His long fingers closed around his glass. He knew something strange, and wonderful, was going on – but what? I could see in his face, as clear as day, that mixture of excitement, impatience and a little fear which I had felt so often when confronting the Unknown.

'Look,' I said, 'I'm prepared to tell you everything you want to know, just as I promised. But first –'

'Yes?'

'I would be honoured to view your laboratory. And I'm sure Nebogipfel would be curious. Tell us something of *you*,' I said. 'And in the course of that, you will learn about *me*.'

He sat for a while, clutching his drink. Then, with a brisk motion, he recharged our glasses, stood up, and took his candle from the mantel.

'Come with me.'

THE EXPERIMENT

Bearing his candle aloft, he led us down the cold passage-way to the laboratory. Those few seconds are vivid in my memory: the light of the candle casting huge shadows from Moses's wide skull, and his jacket and boots glimmering in the uncertain light; behind me the Morlock's feet padded softly, and in the enclosed space his rotten-sweet stench was strong.

At the laboratory Moses made his way around the walls and benches, lighting candles and incandescent lamps. Soon the place was brilliantly lit. The walls were whitewashed and free of ornamentation – save for some of Moses's notes, crudely pinned there – and the single book-case was crammed with journals, standard texts and volumes of mathematical tables and physical measurements. The place was cold; in my shirtsleeves, I found myself shivering, and wrapped my arms about my body.

Nebogipfel padded across the workshop floor towards the book-case. He crouched down and studied the battered spines of the volumes there. I wondered if he could read English; for I had seen no evidence of books or papers in the Sphere, and the lettering on those ubiquitous panels of blue glass had been unfamiliar.

'I'm not very interested in giving you a biographical summary,' Moses said. 'And nor –' more sharply '– do I understand yet why you are so interested in me.

But I'm willing to play your game. Look here: suppose I run you through my most recent experimental findings. How does that sound?'

I smiled. How in keeping with my – his – character, with little to the surface of the mind but the current puzzle!

He went to a bench, on which stood a haphazard arrangement of retort stands, lamps, gratings and lenses. 'I'd be grateful if you wouldn't touch anything here. It may look a little random, but I assure you there's a system! I have the devil of a time keeping Mrs Penforth and her dusters and brooms out of here, I can tell you.'

Mrs Penforth? I had an impulse to ask after Mrs Watchets – but then I remembered that Mrs Penforth had been Mrs Watchets's predecessor. I had released her some fifteen years before my departure into time, after I had caught her pilfering from my small stock of industrial diamonds. I thought of warning Moses of this little occurrence, but no real harm had been done; and – I thought with an oddly paternal mood towards my younger self – it would probably do Moses good to take a closer interest in the affairs of his household for once in a while, and not leave it all to chance!

Moses went on, 'My general field is physical optics – that is to say, the physical properties of light, which –'

'We know,' I said gently.

He frowned. 'All right. Well, recently, I've been somewhat diverted by an odd conundrum – it's the study of a new mineral, a sample of which I came upon by chance two years ago.' He showed me a common eight-ounce graduated medicine bottle, plugged with rubber; the bottle was half-full of a fine, greenish powder, oddly shining. 'Look here: can you see how there is a faint translucence about it, as if it were glowing from within?' And indeed the material

178

shone as if it were composed of fine glass beads. 'But where,' Moses went on, 'is the energy source for such illumination?

'So I began my researches – at first in odd moments, for I have my work to do! – I depend on grants and commissions, which depend in turn on my building up a respectable flow of research results. I have no time for chasing wild geese ... But later,' he admitted, 'this Plattnerite came to absorb a great deal of my time – for such I had decided to call the stuff, after the rather mysterious chap – Gottfried Plattner, he called himself – who donated it to me.

'I'm no chemist – even within the limits of the Three Gases my practical chemistry has always been a little tentative – but still, I set to with a will. I bought test tubes, a gas supply and burners, litmus paper, and all the rest of that smelly paraphernalia. I poured my green dust into test tubes and tried it with water, and with acids – sulphuric, nitric and hydrochloric – learning nothing. Then I emptied out a heap onto a slate and held it over my gas burner.' He rubbed his nose. 'The resulting bang blew out a skylight and made a fearful mess of one wall,' he said.

It had been the south-western wall which had sustained damage, and now – I could not help myself – I glanced that way, but there was nothing to distinguish it, for the repair work had been thorough. Moses noted my glance, curiously, for he had not indicated which wall it had been.

'After this failure,' he went on, 'I was still no closer to unravelling the mysteries of Plattnerite. Then, however –' his tone grew more animated '– I began to apply a little more reason to the case. The translucence is an optical phenomenon, after all. So – I reasoned – perhaps the key to the secrets of Plattnerite lay not in its chemistry, but in its optical properties.'

I felt a peculiar satisfaction – a kind of remote self-regard – at hearing this summary of my own clear thinking processes! And I could tell that Moses was enjoying the momentum of his own narrative: I have always enjoyed recounting a good tale, to whatever audience – I think there is something of the showman in me.

'So I swept aside my clutter of Schoolboy Chemistry,' Moses went on, 'and began a new series of tests. And very quickly I came upon striking anomalies: bizarre results concerning Plattnerite's refractive index – which, you may know, depends on the velocity of light within the substance. And it turned out that the behaviour of light rays passing through Plattnerite is highly peculiar.' He turned to the experiment on the bench-top. 'Now, look here; this is the clearest demonstration of Plattnerite's optical oddities which I have been able to devise.'

Moses had set up his test in three parts, in a line. There was a small electric lamp with a curved mirror behind it, and, perhaps a yard away, a white screen, held upright by a retort stand; between these two, clamped in the claws of another retort, was a cardboard panel which bore the evidence of fine scoring. Beside the lamp, wires trailed to an electromotive cell beneath the bench.

The set-up was lucidly simple: I have always sought as straightforward as possible a demonstration of any new phenomenon, the better to focus the mind on the phenomenon itself, and not on deficiencies in the experimental arrangement, or – it is always possible – some trickery on behalf of the experimenter.

Now Moses closed a switch, and the lamp lit; it was a small yellow star in the candle-lit room. The cardboard panel shielded the screen from the light, save for a dim central glow, cast by rays admitted by the scoring in the panel. 'Sodium light,' Moses said. 'It is nearly a pure colour – as opposed, say, to white sunlight, which is a mixture of all the colours. This mirror behind the lamp is parabolic, so it casts all the lamp's light towards the interposed card.'

He traced the paths of the light rays towards the card. 'On the card I have scored two slits. The slits are a mere fraction of an inch apart – but the structure of light is so fine that the slits are, nevertheless, some three hundred wavelengths apart. Rays emerge from the two slits –' his finger continued on '– and travel onwards to the screen, here. Now, the rays from the two slits *interfere* – their crests and troughs reinforce and cancel each other out, at successive places.' He looked at me uncertainly. 'Are you familiar with the idea? You would get much the same effect if you were to drop two stones into a still pond, and watch how the spreading ripples coalesced . . .'

'I understand.'

'Well, in just the same way, these waves of light – ripples in the ether – interfere with each other, and set up a pattern which one may observe, here on this screen beyond.' He pointed to the patch of yellow illumination which had reached the screen beyond the slits. 'Can you see? – one really needs a glass – right at the heart of it, there, you'll see bands of illumination and darkness, alternating, a few tenths of an inch apart. Well, those are the spots where the rays from the two slits are combining.'

Moses straightened up. 'This interference is a well-known effect. Such an experiment is commonly used to determine the wavelength of the sodium light – it works out at a fifty-thousandth part of an inch, if you're interested.'

'And the Plattnerite?' Nebogipfel asked.

Moses started at hearing the Morlock's liquid tones, but he carried on gamely. From another part of the bench he produced a glass slide, perhaps six

181

inches square, held upright in a stand. The glass appeared to be stained green. 'Here I have some Plattnerite – actually, this slide is a sandwich of two glass sheets, with the Plattnerite sprinkled and scattered between – do you see? Now, watch what happens when I interpose the Plattnerite between card and screen . . .'

It took him some adjusting, but he arranged affairs so that one of the slits in the cards remained clear, and the other was covered by the Plattnerite slide. Thus, one of the two interfering sets of rays would have to pass through Plattnerite before reaching the screen.

The image of interference bands on the screen was made fainter – it was tinged with green – and the pattern was shifted and distorted.

Moses said, 'The rays are rendered less pure, of course – some of the sodium light is scattered from the Plattnerite itself, and so emerges with wavelengths appropriate to the greener part of the spectrum – but still, enough of the original sodium light passes through the Plattnerite without scattering to allow the interference phenomenon to persist. But – can you see the changes this has made?'

Nebogipfel bent closer; the sodium light shone from his goggles.

'The shifting of a few smears of light on a card may not seem so important to the layman,' Moses went on, 'but the effect is of great significance, if analysed closely. For – and I can show you the mathematics to prove it,' he said, waving unconvincingly at a heap of notes on the floor, 'the light rays, passing through the Plattnerite, undergo a *temporal distortion*. It is a tiny effect, but measurable – it shows up in a distortion of the interference pattern, you see.'

'A "temporal distortion"?' Nebogipfel said, looking up. 'You mean . . .'

'Yes.' Moses's skin was coldly illuminated in the sodium light. 'I believe that the light rays – in passing through the Plattnerite – *are transferred through time.*'

I gazed with a sort of rapture at this crude demonstration, of bulb and cards and clamps. For this was the start – it was from this naïve beginning that the long, difficult experimental and theoretical trail would lead, at last, to the construction of the Time Machine itself!

5

HONESTY AND DOUBT

I could not betray how much I knew, of course, and
I did my best to simulate surprise and shock at his
pronouncement. 'Well,' I said vaguely,'well – Great
Scott . . .'

He looked at me, dissatisfied. He was evidently
forming the opinion that I was something of an
unimaginative fool. He turned away and began to
tinker with his apparatus.

I took the opportunity to draw the Morlock to one
side. 'What did you make of that? An ingenious
demonstration.'

'Yes,' he said, 'but I am surprised he has not
noticed the radio-activity of your mysterious
substance, Plattnerite. The goggles show clearly –'

'*Radio-activity?*'

He looked at me. 'The term is unfamiliar?' He
gave me a quick survey of this phenomenon, which
involves, it seems, elements which break up and fly
into pieces. All elements do this – according to
Nebogipfel – at more or less perceptible rates; some,
like radium, do it in a manner spectacular enough to
be measurable – if one knows what to look for!

All this stirred up some memories. 'I remember a
toy called a spinthariscope,' I told Nebogipfel.
'Where radium is held in close proximity to a screen,
coated with sulphide of zinc –'

'And the screen fluoresces. Yes. It is the disintegration of the cores of radium atoms which causes this,' he said.

'But the atom is indivisible – or so it is thought –'

'The phenomenon of subatomic structure will be demonstrated by Thomson at Cambridge, no more than a few years – if I recall my studies – after your departure into time.'

'Subatomic structure – by Thomson! Why, I've met Joseph Thomson myself, several times – a rather pompous buffer, I always thought – and only a handful of years younger than me . . .'

Not for the first time I felt a deep regret at my precipitate plummeting into time! If only I had stayed to take part in such intellectual excitement – I could have been at the thick of it, even without my experiments in time travel – surely that would have been adventure enough, for any one lifetime.

Now Moses seemed to be done, and he reached out to turn off the sodium lamp – but he snatched his hand back with a cry.

Nebogipfel had touched Moses's fingers with his own, hairless palm. 'I am sorry.'

Moses rubbed his hand, as if trying to wipe it clean. 'Your touch,' he said. 'It's so – *cold*.' He stared at Nebogipfel as if seeing him, in all his strangeness, for the first time.

Nebogipfel apologized again. 'I did not mean to startle you. But –'

'Yes?' I said.

The Morlock reached out with one worm-like finger, and pointed at the slab of Plattnerite. '*Look*.'

With Moses, I bent down and squinted into the illuminated slab.

At first I could make out nothing but the speckled reflection of the sodium bulb, a sheen of fine dust on the surface of the glass slides . . . and then I became aware of a growing light, a glow from deep within the substance of the Plattnerite itself: a green illumination that shone as if the slide was a tiny window into another world.

The glow intensified further, and evoked glittering reflections from the test tubes and slides and other paraphernalia of the laboratory.

We retired to the dining-room. It was now long hours since the fire had died, and the room was growing chilly, but Moses did not show any awareness of my discomfort. He supplied me with another brandy, and I accepted an offer of a cigar; Nebogipfel asked for some clear water. I lit up my cigar with a sigh, while Nebogipfel watched me with what I took to be blank astonishment, all his acquired human mannerisms forgotten!

'Well, sir,' I said, 'when do you intend to publish these remarkable findings?'

Moses scratched his scalp and loosened his gaudy tie. 'I'm not certain,' he said frankly. 'What I have amounts to little more than a catalogue of observations of anomalies, you know, of a substance whose provenance is uncertain. Still, perhaps there are brighter fellows than me out there who might make something out of it – learn how to manufacture more Plattnerite, perhaps . . .'

'No,' Nebogipfel said obscurely. 'The means to manufacture radio-active material will not exist for another several decades.'

Moses looked at the Morlock curiously, but did not take up the point.

I said bluntly, 'But you've no intention of publishing.'

He gave me a conspiratorial wink – another grating mannerism! – and said, 'All in good time. You know, in some ways I'm not quite like a True Scientist – you know what I mean, the careful,

186

miniature sort of chap who ends up known in the Press known as a "distinguished scientist". You see such a chap giving his little talk, on some obscure aspect of toxic alkaloids, perhaps, and floating out of the magic-lantern darkness you might hear the odd fragment the chap imagines himself to be reading audibly; and you might catch a glimpse of gold-rimmed spectacles and cloth boots cut open for corns . . .'

I prompted, 'But you –'

'Oh, I'm not meaning to decry the patient plodders of the world! – I daresay I have my share of plodding to do in the years to come – but I also have a certain impatience. I always want to know how things turn out, you see.' He sipped his drink. 'I do have some publications behind me – including one in the *Philosophical Transactions* – and a number of other studies which should yield papers. But the Plattnerite work . . .'

'Yes?'

'I have an odd notion about that. I want to see how far I can take it myself . . .'

I leaned forward. I saw how the bubbles in his glass caught the candlelight, and his face was animated, alive. It was the quietest part of the night, and I seemed to see every detail, hear the tick of every clock in the house, with preternatural clarity. 'Tell me what you mean.'

He straightened his ridiculous masher's jacket. 'I've told you of my speculation that a ray of light, passing through Plattnerite, is temporally transferred. By that I mean that the ray moves between two points in space without any intervening interval in time. But it seems to me,' he said slowly, 'that if *light* can move through these time intervals in such a fashion – then so, perhaps, can *material objects*. I have this notion that if one were to mix up the Plattnerite with some appropriate crystalline substance – quartz, perhaps, or some rock crystal – then . . .'

'Yes?'

He seemed to recover himself. He put his brandy-glass down on a table close to his chair, and leaned forward; his grey eyes seemed to shine in the candle-light, pale and earnest. 'I'm not sure I want to say any more! Look here: I've been very open with you. And now, it's time for you to be just as open with me. Will you do that?'

For answer, I looked into his face – into eyes which, though surrounded by smoother skin, were undeniably my own, the eyes which stared out from my shaving-mirror every day!

Evidently unable to look away, he hissed: '*Who are you?*'

'You *know* who I am. Don't you?'

The moment stretched on, still and silent. The Morlock was a wraith-like presence, hardly noticed by either of us.

At length, Moses said: 'Yes. Yes, I think I do.'

I wanted to give him room to take in all of this. The reality of time travel – for any object more substantial than a light ray – was still in the realms of half-fantasy for Moses! To be confronted, so abruptly, with its physical proof – and worse, to be faced by one's own self from the future – must be an immense shock.

'Perhaps you should regard my presence here as an inevitable consequence of your own researches,' I suggested. 'Is not a meeting like this *bound* to happen, if you carry on down the experimental path you've set yourself?'

'Perhaps . . .'

But now I became aware that his reaction – far from remaining awe-struck, as I might have expected – seemed rather less respectful. He seemed to be inspecting me anew; his gaze travelled, appraising, over my face, my hair, my clothes.

I tried to see myself through the eyes of this brash twenty-six-year-old. Absurdly, I felt self-conscious; I brushed back my hair – which had not been combed since the Year A.D. 657,208 – and sucked in my stomach, which was rather less well-defined than once it had been. But that disapproval lingered in his face.

'Have a good look,' I said with feeling. 'This is how it turns out for you!'

He stroked his chin. 'Don't take a lot of exercise, do you?' He jerked his thumb. 'And him – Nebogipfel. Is he –'

'Yes,' I said. 'He is a Man from the Future – from the Year A.D. 657,208, and much evolved from our present state – *who I have brought back on my Time Machine*: on the machine whose first, dim blueprint you are already conceiving.'

'I am tempted to ask you how it all turns out for me – am I a success? will I marry? – and so forth. But I suspect I'm better off without such knowledge.' He eyed Nebogipfel. 'The future of the species, though, is another matter.'

'You do believe me – don't you?'

He picked up his brandy-glass, found it empty, and set it down again. 'I don't know. I mean, it is all very easy for a fellow to walk into a house and say that he is one's Future Self –'

'But you have already conceived of the possibility of time travel yourself. And – look at my face!'

'I admit there's a certain superficial resemblance; but it's also quite possible that this is all some sort of a prank, set up – maybe with malicious intent – to expose me as a quack.' He looked at me sternly. 'If you are who you say you are – if you are *me* – then you have surely travelled here with a purpose.'

'Yes.' I tried to put aside my anger; I tried to

189

remember that my communication with this difficult and rather arrogant young man was of vital importance. 'Yes. I have a mission.'

He pulled at his chin. 'Dramatic words. But how can I be so vital? I am a scientist – not even that, probably; I am a tinkerer, a dilettante. I am not a politician or a prophet.'

'No. But you are – or will be – the inventor of the most potent weapon that could be devised: I mean the Time Machine.'

'What is it you've come to tell me?'

'That you must destroy the Plattnerite; find some other line of research. You must *not* develop the Time Machine – that is essential!'

He steepled his fingers and regarded me. 'Well. Evidently you have a story to tell. Is it to be a long narrative? Do you want some more brandy – or some tea, perhaps?'

'No. No, thank you. I will be as brief as I can manage.'

And so I began my account, with a short summary of the discoveries that had led me to the final construction of the machine – and how I had boarded it for the first time, and launched myself into the History of Eloi and Morlock – and what I discovered when I returned, and tried to go forward in time once more.

I suppose I spoke wearily – I could not remember how many hours had elapsed since I had last slept – but as my account developed I grew more animated, and I fixed on Moses's sincere, round face in the bright circle of the candlelight. At first I was aware of Nebogipfel's presence, for he sat silently by throughout my account, and at times – during my first description of the Morlocks, for example – Moses turned to Nebogipfel as if for confirmation of some detail.

But after a while he ceased to do even that; and he looked only at my face.

6

PERSUASION AND SCEPTICISM

The early dawn of summer was well advanced by the time I was done.

Moses sat in his chair, his eyes still set on me, his chin cupped in his hand. Then, at length: 'Well,' he said, as if to break a spell – 'Well.' He stood up, stretched his back, and crossed the room to the windows; he pulled them back to reveal a cloudy but lightening sky.

'It's a remarkable account.'

'It's more than that,' I said, my voice hoarse. 'Don't you see? On my second journey into the future, I travelled into a *different History*. The Time Machine is a Wrecker of History – a Destroyer of Worlds and Species. Don't you see why it must *not* be built?'

Moses turned to Nebogipfel. 'If you are a Man from the Future – what do you have to say to all this?'

Nebogipfel's chair was still in shadow, but he cowered from the encroaching daylight. 'I am not a Man,' he said in his cold, quiet voice. 'But I am from *a* Future – one of an infinite number, perhaps, of possible variants. And it seems true – it is certainly logically possible – that a Time Machine can change History's course, thus generating new variants of events. In fact the very principle of the Machine's operation appears to rely on its extension, through the properties of Plattnerite, into another, parallel History.'

Moses went to the window, and the rising sun caught his profile. 'But to abandon my research, just on your uncorroborated say-so –'

'*Say-so*? I think I deserve a little more respect than that,' I said, in rising anger. 'After all, I am you! Oh, you are so stubborn. I've brought a Man from the Future – what more persuasion do you want?'

He shook his head. 'Look,' he said, 'I'm tired – I've been up all night, and all that brandy hasn't helped much. And you two look as if you could do with some rest as well. I have spare rooms; I'll escort you –'

'I know the way,' I said with some frost.

He conceded the point with some humour. 'I'll have Mrs Penforth bring you breakfast . . . or,' he went on, looking at Nebogipfel again, 'perhaps I'll have it served in here.'

'Come,' he said. 'The Destiny of the Race can wait for a few hours.'

I slept deeply – remarkably so. I was wakened by Moses, who brought me a pitcher of hot water.

I'd folded up my clothes on a chair; after my adventures in time, they were rather the worse for wear. 'I don't suppose you could lend me a suit of clothes, could you?'

'You can have a house-coat, if you like. I'm sorry, old man – I hardly think anything of mine would fit you!'

I was angered by this casual arrogance. 'One day, you too will grow a little older. And then I hope you remember – Oh – never mind!' I said.

'Look – I'll have my man brush out these clothes for you, and patch the worst damage. Come down when you're ready.'

In the dining-room, breakfast had been set out as a

sort of buffet. Moses and Nebogipfel were already there. Moses wore the same costume as yesterday – or at least, an identical copy of it. The bright morning sun turned the parakeet colours of his coat into a clamour even more ghastly than before. And as for Nebogipfel, the Morlock was now dressed – ludicrously! – in short trousers and battered blazer. He had a cap tucked over his goggled, hairy face, and he stood patiently by the buffet.

'I told Mrs Penforth to keep out of here,' Moses said. 'As for Nebogipfel, that battered jacket of yours – it's over the back of that chair, by the way – seemed hardly sufficient for him. So I dug out an old school uniform – the only thing I could find that might fit him: he reeks of moth-balls, but he seems a little happier.'

'Now then.' He walked up to Nebogipfel. 'Let me help you, sir. What would you like? You can see we have bacon, eggs, toast, sausages –'

In his quiet, fluid tones, Nebogipfel asked Moses to explain the provenance of these various items. Moses did so, in graphic terms: he picked up a slice of bacon on his fork, for example, and described the Nature of the Pig.

When Moses was done, Nebogipfel picked up a single piece of fruit – an apple – and walked with that, and a glass of water, to the room's darkest corner.

As for me, after subsisting for so long on a diet of the Morlocks' bland stuff, I could not have relished my breakfast more if I had known – which I did not – that it was the last nineteenth-century meal I should ever enjoy!

With breakfast done, Moses escorted us to his smoking-room. Nebogipfel installed himself in the darkest corner, while Moses and I sat on opposed armchairs.

Moses dug out his pipe, filled it from a small pouch in his pocket, and lit it.

I watched him, seething. He was so maddeningly calm! 'Do you have nothing to say? I have brought you a dire warning from the future – from several futures – which –'

'Yes,' he said, 'it is dramatic stuff. But,' he went on, tamping down his pipe, 'I'm still not sure if –'

'Not sure?' I cried, jumping to my feet. 'What more proof – what persuasion – do you want?'

'It seems to me that your logic has a few holes. Oh, do sit down.'

I sat, feeling weak. 'Holes?'

'Look at it this way. You claim that I'm you – and you're me. Yes?'

'Exactly. We are two slices of a single Four-Dimensioned entity, taken at different points, and juxtaposed by the Time Machine.'

'Very well. But let us consider this: if you were once me, *then you should share my memories.*'

'I –' I fell silent.

'Then,' Moses said with a note of triumph, 'what memories do you have of a rather burly stranger, and an odd companion of this sort, turning up on the door-step one night? Eh?'

The answer, of course – horrifying! impossible! – was that I had *no* such memories. I turned to Nebogipfel, stricken. 'How can this not have occurred to me? Of *course*, my mission is impossible. It always was. I could never persuade young Moses, because I have no memories of how I, when I was Moses, was persuaded in my turn!'

The Morlock retorted, 'Cause and Effect, when Time Machines are about, are rather awkward concepts.'

Moses said, with more of that insufferable cockiness, 'Here's another puzzle for you. Suppose I agree

194

with you. Suppose I accept your story about your trips into time and your visions of Histories and so forth. Suppose I agree to destroy the Time Machine.'

I could anticipate his argument. 'Then, if the Time Machine were never built –'

'You would not be able to return through time, to put a stop to its building –'

'– and so the machine would be built after all . . .'

'– and you would return through time to stop the building once more – and on it would go, like an endless merry-go-round!' he cried with a flourish.

'Yes. It is a pathological causal loop,' Nebogipfel said. 'The Time Machine must be built, in order to put a stop to its own building . . .'

I buried my face in my hands. Apart from my despair at the destruction of my case, I had the uncomfortable feeling that young Moses was more *intelligent* than I. I should have spotted these logical difficulties! – perhaps it was true, horribly, that intelligence, like more gross physical faculties, declines as age comes on.

'But – despite all this logic-chopping – *it is nevertheless the truth*,' I whispered. 'And the machine must never be built.'

'Then you explain it,' Moses said with less sympathy. '"To Be, or Not To Be" – that, it seems, is *not* the question,' Moses said. 'If you are me, you will remember being forced to play the part of Hamlet's Father in that dire production at school.'

'I remember it well.'

'The question is more, it seems to me: How can things *Be* and – simultaneously – *Not Be*?'

'But it is true,' Nebogipfel said. The Morlock stepped forward a little way, into the light, and looked from one to the other of us. 'But we must construct, it seems to me, a *higher* logic – a logic which can take account of the interaction of a Time

195

Machine with History – a logic capable of dealing with a *Multiplicity* of Histories . . .'

And then – just at that moment, when my own uncertainty was greatest – I heard a roar, as of some immense motor, which echoed up the Hill, outside the house. The ground seemed to shudder – it was as if some monster were walking there – and I heard shouting, and – though it was quite impossible that such a thing should happen here, in sleepy, early-morning Richmond! – *the rattle of a gun.*

Moses and I looked wildly at each other. 'Great Scott,' Moses said. 'What is that?'

I thought I heard the gun clatter again, and now a shout turned to a scream, suddenly cut off.

Together, we ran out of the smoking-room and into the hall. Moses pulled open the door – it was already unlatched – and we spilled into the street. There was Mrs Penforth, thin and severe, and Poole, Moses's manservant of the time. Mrs Penforth carried a duster, bright yellow, and she clutched at Poole's arm. They glanced perfunctorily at us, but then looked away – ignoring a Morlock as if he were no more odd than a Frenchman, or Scotsman!

There were a number of people in the Petersham Road, standing there staring. Moses touched my sleeve, and he pointed down the road in the direction of the town. '*There,*' he said. 'There's your anomaly.'

It was as if an ironclad had been lifted out of the sea and deposited by some great wave, high on Richmond Hill. It was perhaps two hundred yards from the house: it was a great box of metal which lay along the length of the Petersham Road like some immense, iron insect, at least eighty feet long.

But this was no stranded monster: it was, I saw now, crawling towards us, slow but quite deliberate, and where it passed I saw that it had scored the road surface with a series of linked indentations, like the trail of a bird. The ironclad's upper surface was a complex speckle of ports – I took them to be gun ports, or telescope holes.

The morning traffic had been forced to make way for the thing; two dog-carts lay overturned in the road ahead of it, as did a brewer's dray, with a distressed horse still caught between the shafts, and beer spilling from broken barrels.

One youth in a cap, foolhardy, hurled a lump of churned-up cobble at the thing's metal hide. The stone bounced off the hull without leaving so much as a scratch, but there was a response: I saw a rifle poke its snout out of one of those upper ports, and fire off with a crack at the youth.

He fell where he had stood, and lay still.

At that, the crowd dispersed quickly, and there were more screams. Mrs Penforth seemed to be weeping into her duster; Poole escorted her into the house.

A hatch in the front of the land ironclad opened with a clang – I caught a brief impression of a dim interior – and I saw a face (I thought masked) peer out towards us.

'It is Out of Time,' Nebogipfel said. 'And it has come for us.'

'Indeed.' I turned to Moses. 'Well,' I said to him. '*Now* do you believe me?'

THE JUGGERNAUT
LORD RAGLAN

Moses's grin was tight and nervous, his face paler than usual and his broad brow slick with sweat. 'Evidently you are not the only Time Traveller!'

The mobile fort – if that was what it was – toiled its way up the road towards my house. It was a long, flat box, with something of the aspect of a dish-cover. It was painted in patches of green and mud-brown, as if its natural habitat were some broken-up field. There was a skirt of metal around its base, perhaps to shield its more vulnerable parts from the rifle-shots and shrapnel of opponents. I should say the fort was moving at around six miles per hour, and – thanks to some novel method of locomotion whose details I could not make out, because of that skirt – it managed to keep itself pretty level, in spite of the Hill's incline.

Save for the three of us – and that wretched brewer's horse – there was not a living soul left in the road now, and there was a silence broken only by the deep grumbling of the fort's engines, and the distressed whinnying of the trapped horse.

'I don't remember this,' I told Nebogipfel. 'Any of it – this didn't happen, in *my* 1873.'

The Morlock studied the approaching fort through his goggles. 'Once again,' he said evenly, 'we have to consider the possibility of a Multiplicity of Histories. You have seen more than one version of

A.D. 657,208: now, it seems, you must endure new variants on your *own* century.'

The fort came to a halt, its engine growling like some immense stomach; I could see masked faces peering out from the various ports at us, and a pennant fluttered languid above its hull.

'Do you think we can run for it?' Moses hissed.

'I doubt it. See the rifle-barrels protruding from those port-holes? I don't know what the game is here – but these people clearly have the means, and the will, to detain us.

'Let's show a little dignity. We will go forward,' I said. 'Let us demonstrate we are not afraid.'

And so we stepped out, across the mundane cobbles of the Petersham Road, towards the fort.

The various rifles and heavier guns tracked us as we walked, and masked faces – some using field-glasses – marked our progress.

As we neared the fort, I got a better view of its general layout. As I have said it was more than eighty feet long, and perhaps ten feet tall; the flanks looked like sheets of thick gun-metal, although the arrangement of ports and scopes at the fort's upper rim gave it a mottled impression there. Jets of steam squirted into the air from the rear of the machine. I have mentioned the foot-tall skirt which surrounded the base; now I was able to see that the skirt was lifted away from the ground, and that the machine stood – not on wheels, as I had assumed – but on feet! These were flat, broad things, about the shape of elephant's feet, but much larger; from the indentations they left in the road behind, I could infer that the lower surfaces of these feet must be grooved for traction. This arrangement of feet was, I realized now, how the fort was keeping itself more-or-less level on the slope of the road.

There was a device like a flail fixed to the front of the fort: it consisted of lengths of heavy chain attached to a drum, which was held out on two metal frames before the fort's prow. The drum was held up, so that the chains dangled in the air, like carters' whips, and they made an odd clanking noise as the fort travelled along; but the drum was clearly capable of being lowered, to allow the chains to beat against the ground as the fort advanced. I could not fathom the purpose of this arrangement.

We stopped perhaps ten yards from the blunt prow of the machine. Those rifle-men kept their muzzles trained on us. Steam wafted towards us, on a stray breeze.

I was suffering a deep horror at this latest unre-membered turn of events. Now, it seemed, *even my past* was no longer a place of reliability and stability: even that was subject to change, at the whims of Time Travellers! I had no escape from the influence of the Time Machine: it was as if, once invented, its ramifications were spreading into past and future, like ripples from a stone thrown into the placid River of Time.

'I think it's British,' Moses said, breaking into my introspection.

'What? Why do you say that?'

'Do you think that's a regimental badge, there above the skirt?'

I peered more closely; evidently Moses's eyes were sharper than mine. I've never been much interested in military paraphernalia, but it looked as if Moses might be right.

Now he was reading off other bits of text, sten-cilled in black on that formidable hull. '"Live Muni-tions",' he read. '"Fuel Access". It's either British colonial or American – and from a future close enough that the language hasn't changed much.'

There was a scrape of metal on metal. I saw that a wheel, set in one flank of the fort, was turning. When the wheel was fully turned, a hatch-door was pushed open – its polished metal rim gleamed against the dun hull – and I caught a glimpse of a dark interior, like a cave of steel.

A rope-ladder was dropped down from the frame. A trooper clambered out and came walking up the road towards us. He wore a heavy canvas suit, sewn up into one piece; it was open at the neck, and I could see a lining of khaki cloth. There were spectacularly huge metal epaulettes across his shoulders. He wore a black beret, with a regimental badge affixed to the front. He carried a pistol in a web holster which dangled before him; there was a small pouch above this, evidently for ammunition. I saw how the holster flap was open, and his gloved hands never strayed far from his weapon.

And – most striking of all – the trooper's face was hidden by the most extraordinary mask: with wide, blackened goggles and a muzzle like the proboscis of a fly over the mouth, the mask enclosed the head beneath the beret.

'Great Scott,' Moses whispered to me. 'What a vision!'

'Indeed,' I said grimly, for I had seen the significance of this apparition immediately. 'He has protection against gas – see that? There is not a square inch of the fellow's bare flesh showing. And those epaulettes must be to protect him against darts, perhaps also bearing poison – I wonder what other layers of protection he is wearing under that bulky canvas.

'What kind of Age believes it necessary to send such a brute as this, back through time to the innocence of 1873? Moses, this fort comes to us from a very dark future – a Future of War!'

The trooper stepped a little closer to us. In clipped tones – which were muffled by the mask, but were otherwise absolutely characteristic of the Officers' class – he called out a challenge to us, in a language which, at first, I failed to recognize.

Moses leaned towards me. 'That was German! And a damn poor accent too. What on earth is this all about – eh?'

I stepped forward, my hands raised in the air. 'We are English. Do you understand?'

I could not see this trooper's face, but I thought I saw, in the set of his shoulders, evidence of some relief. His voice sounded youthful. This was but a young man, I realized, trapped in a warlike carapace. He said briskly: 'Very well. Please come with me.'

We had little choice, it seemed.

The young trooper stood by his fort, his hands resting on the hilt of his pistol, as we climbed the few steps into the interior.

'Tell me one thing,' Moses demanded of the trooper. 'What is the purpose of that contraption of chains and drum at the front of the vehicle?'

'That's the anti-mine flail,' the masked fellow said.

'*Anti-mine?*'

'The chains whip at the ground, as the *Raglan* advances.' He mimed with his gloved hands, although he kept a careful eye on Moses. He was quite evidently British; he had thought *we* might be Germans! 'See? It's all about blowing up the mines buried there before we get to them.'

Moses thought it over, then climbed after me into the fort. 'A charming use of British ingenuity,' he said to me. 'And – look at the thickness of this hull! Bullets would splash off this hide like rain-drops – surely only a field-gun could slow such a creature.'

The heavy hatch door was swung to behind us; it

202

'He called out a challenge to us in a language which,
at first, I failed to recognize.'

settled into its socket with a heavy thud, and rubber seals settled against the hull.

Thus, the daylight was excluded.

We were escorted to the centre of a narrow gallery which ran the length of the fort. In that enclosed space the noise of engines was loud and resonant. There was a smell of engine-oil and petrol, and the thin stink of cordite; it was exceeding hot, and I felt the perspiration start about my collar immediately. The only illumination came from two electric lamps – quite inadequate to illuminate that long, compact space.

The fort's interior sketched itself into my mind, in fleeting impressions of half-light and shadows. I could see the outlines of eight great wheels – each ten feet in diameter – lining the fort's flanks, and shielded within the hull. At the front of the fort, within the prow, was a single trooper in a high canvas chair; he was surrounded by levers, dials and what looked like the lenses of periscopes; I took this to be the driver. The fort's rear compartment was an engine and transmission centre. There I could see the hulking forms of machinery; in that darkness, the engines were more like the brooding forms of great beasts than anything contrived by the hand of man. Troopers moved around the machines, masked and heavy-gloved, for all the world like attendants serving some idols of metal.

Little cabins, cramped and uncomfortable-looking, were slung from the long ceiling; and in each of these I could see the shadowy profile of a single trooper. Each soldier had a variety of guns and optical instruments, most of them of unfamiliar design to me, which protruded through the hull of the ship. There must have been two dozen of these rifle-men and engineers – they were all masked, and wore the characteristic canvas suits and berets – and, to a man, they stared openly down at us. You may imagine how the Morlock attracted their gaze!

This was a bleak, intimidating place: a mobile temple, dedicated to Brute Force. I could not help but contrast this with the subtle engineering of Nebogipfel's Morlocks.

Our young trooper came up to us; now that the fort was sealed up again, he had discarded his mask – it dangled at his neck, like a flayed face – and I saw that indeed he was quite young, his cheeks rimmed by sweat. 'Please come forward,' he said. 'The Captain would like to welcome you aboard.'

At his guidance, we formed into a line, and began to make our cautious way – under the unrelenting and silent gaze of the troopers – towards the prow of the fort. The floor was open, and we were forced to clamber along narrow metal cat-walks; Nebogipfel's bare feet pattered over the ribbed metal, almost noiseless.

Near the prow of this land boat, and a little behind the driver, there was a cupola of brass and iron which extended up through the roof. Below the cupola stood an individual – masked, hands clasped to rear – with the demeanour of the controller of this fort. The Captain wore a beret and coverall of much the same type as the trooper who had greeted us, with those metal epaulettes and a hand-weapon at the waist; but this superior officer also wore a criss-cross of leather belt, cross strap and sword frog, and also other rank insignia, including cloth formation signs and shoulder flashes. Campaign-ribbons, thick inches of them, decorated the uniform's chest.

Moses was staring around with avid curiosity. He pointed to a ladder-arrangement set above the Captain. 'Look there,' he said. 'I'll wager that he can summon down that ladder, by means of those levers in the rail beside him – see? – and then ascend up to that cupola above. Thus he would be able to see all around this fortress, the better to guide the engineers and gunners.' He sounded impressed by the ingenuity that had gone into this monster of War.

The Captain stepped forward, but with a noticeable limp. Now the mask was pulled back and the Captain's face was revealed. I could see that this person was still quite young, evidently healthy enough – although extraordinarily pallid – and of a type that one associates with the Navy: alert, calm, intelligent – profoundly competent. A glove was pulled off and a hand extended to me. I took the proffered hand – it was small, and my own palm enveloped it like a child's – and I stared, with an astonishment I could not disguise, into that clear face.

The Captain said: 'I wasn't expecting quite such a crowd of passengers – I don't suppose we knew *what* we were expecting – but you're all welcome here, and I'll ensure you're treated well.' The voice was light, but raised to a bray above the rumble of the engines. Pale blue eyes swept over Moses and Nebogipfel, with a hint of humour. 'Welcome to the *Lord Raglan*. My name is Hilary Bond; I'm a Captain in the Ninth Battalion of the Royal Juggernaut Regiment.'

It was true! This Captain – experienced and wounded soldier, and commander of a deadlier fighting machine than I could ever have envisaged – was a *woman*.

8

OLD ACQUAINTANCE RENEWED

She smiled, revealing a scar about her chin, and I saw that she could be no more than twenty-five years of age.

'Look here, Captain,' I said, 'I demand to know by what right you're holding us.'

She was unruffled. 'My mission is a priority for the National Defence. I'm sorry if –'

But now Moses stepped forward; in his gaudy masher's outfit he looked strikingly out of place in that drab, military interior. 'Madam Captain, there is no *need* for National Defence in the Year 1873!'

'But there is in the Year 1938.' This Captain was quite immovable, I saw; she radiated an air of unshakeable command. 'My mission has been to safeguard the scientific research which is proceeding in that house on Petersham Road – in particular, to discourage anachronistic interference with its due process.'

Moses grimaced. '"Anachronistic interference" – I take it you are talking of Time Travellers.'

I smiled. 'A lovely word, that *discourage*! Have you brought back enough guns, do you think, effectively to *discourage*?'

Now Nebogipfel stepped forward. 'Captain Bond,' the Morlock said slowly, 'surely you can see that your mission is a logical absurdity. Do you know who these men are? How can you safeguard the research when

207

its prime progenitor –' he pointed to Moses with one hairy hand '– is being abducted from his rightful time?'

At that Bond stared at the Morlock for long seconds; and then she turned her attention to Moses – and to me – and I thought she saw, as if for the first time, our resemblance! She snapped out questions to us all, aimed at confirming the truth of the Morlock's remark, and Moses's identity. I did not deny it – I could see little advantage to us either way – perhaps, I calculated, we should be treated with more consideration if we were thought to be historically significant; but I made as little as I could of my shared identity with Moses.

At last, Hilary Bond whispered brief instructions to the trooper, and he went off to another part of the craft.

'I'll inform the Air Ministry of this when we get back. I'm sure they will be more than interested in you – and you'll have plenty of opportunity to debate the issue with the authorities on our return.'

'*Return?*' I snapped. '*Return* – do you mean, to your 1938?'

She looked strained. 'The paradoxes of time travel are a bit beyond me, I'm afraid; no doubt the clever chaps at the Ministry will untangle it all.'

I was aware of Moses laughing beside me – loudly, and with a touch of hysteria. 'Oh, this is rich!' he said. 'Oh, it's rich – now I needn't bother building the wretched Time Machine at all!'

Nebogipfel regarded me sombrely. 'I'm afraid these multiple blows to causality are moving us further and further from the primal version of History – that which existed before the first operation of the Time Machine . . .'

Now Captain Bond cut us short. 'I can understand your consternation. But I can assure you you'll not be harmed in any way – on the contrary, my mission is to protect you. Also,' she said with an easy grace, 'I've gone to the trouble of bringing along someone to help you settle in with us. A native of the period, you might say.'

Another figure made its slow way towards us from the darkened rear of the passage. It came to us wearing the ubiquitous epaulettes, hand-weapon and mask dangling at the waist; but the uniform – a drab, black affair – bore no military insignia. This new person moved slowly, quite painfully, along the awkward cat-walks, with every sign of age; I saw how uniform fabric was stretched over a sagging belly.

His voice was feeble – barely audible above the din of the engines. 'Good God, it's you,' he called to me. 'I'm armed to the teeth for Germans – but do you know, I scarcely expected you to turn up again, after that last Thursday dinner-party – and not in circumstances like these!'

As he came into the light, it was my turn for another shock. For, though the eyes were dulled, the demeanour stooped, and barely a trace of red left in that shock of grey hair – and though the man's forehead was disfigured by an ugly scar, as if he had been burned – this was, unmistakably, *Filby*.

I told him I was damned.

Filby snickered as he came up to me. I grasped his hand – it was fragile and liver-spotted – and I judged him to be aged no less than seventy-five. 'Damned you may be. Damned we all are, perhaps! – but it's good to see you, nevertheless.' He gave Moses some odd looks: not surprising, I thought!

'Filby – Great Scott, man – I'm teeming with questions.'

'I'll bet you are. That's why they dug me out of my old people's shelter in the Bournemouth Dome. I'm

209

in charge of Acclimatization, they call it – to help you natives of the period adjust – do you see?'

'But Filby – it seems only yesterday – how did you come to –'

'*This*?' He indicated his withered frame with a dismissive, cynical gesture. 'How did I come to this? *Time*, my friend. That wonderful River on whose breast, you would have us believe, you could skate around like a water-boatman. Well, time is no friend of the common man; *I've* been travelling through time the hard way, and here is what the journey has done to me. For me, it's been forty-seven years since that last session in Richmond, and your bits of magic quackery with the model Time Machine – do you remember? – and your subsequent disappearance into the Day After Tomorrow.'

'Still the same old Filby,' I said with affection, and I grasped his arm. 'Even you have to admit – at last – that I was right about time travel!'

'Much good it's done any of us,' he growled.

'And now,' the Captain said, 'if you'll excuse me, gentlemen, I've a 'Naut to command. We'll be ready to depart in a few minutes.' And, with a nod to Filby, she turned to her crew.

Filby sighed. 'Come on,' he said. 'There's a place at the back where we can sit; it's a little less noisy, and dirty, than this.'

We made our way towards the rear of the fort.

As we walked through the central passage I was able to get a closer look at the fort's means of loco-motion. Below the central cat-walks I could see an arrangement of long axles, each free to swivel about a common axis, with a metal floor beneath; and the axles were hitched up to those immense wheels. Those elephantine feet we had spotted earlier dangled from the wheels on stumps of legs. The wheels dripped mud and bits of churned-up road surface into the engineered interior. By means of the axles, I saw, the wheels could be raised or lowered relative to the main body of the fort, and it seemed that the feet and legs could also be raised, on pneumatic pistons. It was through this arrangement that the fort's variable pitch was achieved, enabling it to travel across the most uneven ground, or hold itself level on steep hills.

Moses pointed out the sturdy, box-shaped steel framework which underpinned the construction of the fort. 'And look,' he said quietly to me, 'can you see something odd about that section? – and that, over there? – the rods which look rather like quartz. It's hard to see what structural purpose they serve.'

I looked more closely; it was difficult to be certain in the light of the remote electric lamps, but I thought I could see an odd green translucence about the sections of quartz and nickel – a translucence which looked more than familiar!

'It is *Plattnerite*,' I hissed at Moses. 'The rods have been doped . . . Moses, I am convinced – I cannot be mistaken, despite the uncertain light – those are components taken from my own laboratory: spares, prototypes and discards I produced during the construction of my Time Machine.'

Moses nodded. 'So at least we know these people haven't learned the technique of manufacturing Plattnerite for themselves, yet.'

The Morlock came up to me and pointed at something stored in a darkened recess in the engine compartment. It took some squinting, but I could make out that that bulky shape was my own Time Machine! – whole and unbroken, evidently extracted from Richmond Hill and brought into this fort, its rails still stained by grass. The machine was wrapped about by ropes as if confined in a spider-web.

I felt a powerful urge, at the sight of that potent symbol of safety, to break free of these soldiers – if I could – and make for my machine. Perhaps I could reach my home, even now . . .

But I knew it would be a futile attempt, and I stilled myself. Even if I could reach the machine – and I could not, for these troopers would gun me down in a moment – I could not find my home again. After this latest incident, no version of 1891 which I could reach could bear any resemblance to the safe and prosperous Year I had abandoned so foolishly. I was stranded in time!

Filby joined me. 'What do you think of the machinery – eh?' He punched me in the shoulder, and his touch had the withered feebleness of an old man. He said, 'The whole thing was designed by Sir Albert Stern, who has been prominent in these things since the early days of the War. I've taken quite an interest in these beasts, as they've evolved over the years . . . You know I've always had a fascination for things mechanical.

'Look at that.' He pointed into the recesses of the engine compartment. 'Rolls Royce "Meteor" engines – a whole row of 'em! And a Merrit-Brown gear-box – see it, over there? We've got Horstmann suspension, with those three bogeys to either side . . .'

'Yes,' I cut in, 'but – dear old Filby – what is it all *for*?'

'*For*? It's *for* the prosecution of the War, of course.' Filby waved his hand about. 'This is a Juggernaut: Kitchener-class; one of the latest models. The main purpose of the 'Nauts is to break up the Siege of Europe, you see; they can negotiate all but the widest trench-works with alacrity – although they are expensive, prone to malfunction, and vulnerable to shelling. *Raglan* is rather an appropriate name, don't you think? – For Lord Fitzroy Raglan was the old

212

devil who made such a hash of the siege of
Sebastopol, in the Crimea. Perhaps poor old Raglan
would have –'

'*The Siege of Europe?*'

He looked at me sadly. 'I'm sorry,' he said. 'Perhaps
they shouldn't have sent me after all – I keep forget-
ting how little you must know! I've turned into the
most awful old buffer, I'm afraid. Look here – I've got
to tell you that we've been at War, since 1914.'

'*War?* With whom?'

'Well, with the Germans, of course. Who else? And
it really is a terrible mess . . .'

These words, this casual glimpse of a future Europe
darkened by twenty-four years of War, chilled me to
the core!

9

INTO TIME

We came to a chamber perhaps ten feet square; it was little more than a box of metal bolted to the inner hull of the 'Naut. A single electric bulb glowed in the ceiling, and padded leather coated the walls, alleviating the metal bleakness of the fort and suppressing the noise of the engines – although a deeper throb could be felt through the fabric of the vessel. There were six chairs here: simple upright affairs that were bolted to the floor, facing each other, and fitted with leather harnesses. There was also a low cabinet.

Filby waved us to the chairs and started fussing around the cabinet. 'I should strap yourselves in,' he said. 'This time-hurdling nonsense is quite vertiginous.'

Moses and I sat down to face each other. I fastened the restraints loosely around me; Nebogipfel had some trouble with his buckles, and the straps dangled about him until Moses helped him adjust their tightness.

Now Filby came pottering up to me with something in his hand; it was a cup of tea in a cracked china saucer, with a small biscuit to one side of the cup. I could not help but laugh. 'Filby, the turns of fate never cease to amaze me. Here we are, about to journey through time in this menacing mobile fort – and you serve us with tea and biscuits!'

'Well, this business is quite difficult enough without life's comforts. *You* must know that!'

I sipped the tea; it was lukewarm and rather stewed. Thus fortified, I became, incongruously, rather mischievous – I think on reflection my mental state was a little fragile, and I was unwilling to face my own future, or the dire prospect of this 1938 War. 'Filby,' I teased him, 'do you not observe anything – ah – *odd* about my companions?'

'Odd?'

I introduced him to Moses – and poor Filby began a staring session which resulted in him dribbling tea down his chin.

'And *there* is the true shock of time travel,' I said to Filby with feeling. 'Forget all this stuff about the Origin of the Species, or the Destiny of Humanity – it's only when you come face to face with yourself as a young man that you realize what *shock* is all about!'

Filby questioned us on this issue of our identity for a little longer – good old Filby, sceptical to the last! 'I thought I'd seen enough changes and wonders in my life, even without this time business. But now – well!' He sighed, and I suspected that he had actually seen a little *too much* in his long lifetime, poor fellow; he always had been prone to a certain brain-weariness, even as a young man.

I leaned forward, as far as my restraints allowed. 'Filby, I can scarce believe that men have fallen so far – become so blind. Why, from my perspective, this damnable Future War of yours sounds pretty much like the end of civilization.'

'For men of our day,' he said solemnly, 'perhaps it is. But this younger generation, who've grown up to know nothing but War, who have never felt the sun on their faces without fear of the air-torpedoes – well! I think they're inured to it; it's as if we're turning into a subterranean species.'

I could not resist a glance at the Morlock.

'Filby, why this mission through time?'

'It isn't so much *you*, as the *Machine*. They had to *ensure* the construction of the Time Machine, you see,' Filby began. 'Time technology is so vital to the War Effort. Or so some of them feel.

'They knew pretty much how you went about your research, from the bits of notes you left behind – although you never published anything on the subject; there was only that odd account you left with us of your first trip into the remote future, on your brief return. And so the *Raglan* has been sent to guard your house against any intrusion by a Time Traveller – like you . . .'

Nebogipfel lifted his head. 'More confusion about causality,' he said. 'Evidently the scientists of 1938 have still not begun to grasp the concept of Multiplicity – that one cannot *ensure* anything about the past: one cannot change History; one can only generate new versions of –'

Filby stared at him – this chattering vision in a school uniform, with hair sprouting from every limb!

'Not now,' I said to Nebogipfel. 'Filby, you keep saying *they*. Who are *they*?'

He seemed surprised by the question. 'The Government, of course.'

'Which party?' snapped Moses.

'Party? Oh, all of *that* is pretty much a thing of the past.'

He gave us that chilling news – of the death of Democracy in Britain – with just those casual words!

He went on, 'I think we have all been expecting to find *die Zeitmaschine* here, rolling around Richmond Park and hoping for a bit of assassination . . .' He looked mournful. 'It's the Germans, you know. The blessed Germans! They're making the most frightful mess of everything . . . Just as they've always done!'

And with that, the single electric bulb dimmed, and I heard the engines roar; I felt the familiar, helpless plummeting which told me that this *Raglan* had launched me into time once more.

BOOK THREE

The War with the Germans

1

A NEW VISION OF RICHMOND

My latest trip through time was bumpy and even more disorienting than usual, I judged because of the uneven distribution of those scraps of Plattnerite about the 'Naut. But the journey was brief, and at length the sense of plummeting faded.

Filby had been sitting there with arms folded and jowls tucked against his chest, the perfect picture of misery. Now he glanced up at what I had taken to be a clock on the wall, and he slapped his hand against his bony knee. 'Ha! – here we are; once more, it is the Sixteenth of June, A.D. 1938.' He began to unravel his constraints.

I got out of my chair and took a closer look at that 'clock'. I found that – although the hands made up a conventional clock face – the device also featured several little chronometric dials. I snorted and tapped the glass face of the thing with my finger. I said to Moses, 'Look at this! It is a chronometric clock, but it shows *years and months* – over-engineering, Moses; a characteristic of Government projects. I'm surprised it doesn't feature little dolls with rain-coats and sun-hats, to show the passing of the seasons!'

After a few minutes we were joined by Captain Hilary Bond, and the young trooper who had collected us from Richmond Hill (whose name, Bond told us, was Harry Oldfield). The little cabin became rather crowded. Captain Bond said, 'I've received

221

instructions about you. My mission is to escort you to Imperial College, where research into Chronic Displacement Warfare is being conducted.'

I had not heard of this college, but I did not inquire further.

Oldfield was carrying a box of gas-masks and metallic epaulettes. 'Here,' he said to us, 'you'd better put these on.'

Moses held up a gas-mask with distaste. 'You cannot expect me to insert my head into such a contraption.'

'Oh, you must,' Filby said anxiously, and I saw he was already buttoning his own mask about his jowly face. 'We've a little way to go in the open out there, you know. And it's not safe. Not safe!'

'Come on,' I said to Moses, as I grimly took a set of mask and epaulettes for myself. 'We're not at home any more, I'm afraid, old man.'

The epaulettes were heavy, but clipped easily to my jacket; but the mask Oldfield gave me, though roomy and well-fitting, was most uncomfortable. I found the twin eye-goggles fogging up almost immediately, the rubber and leather ridges of its construction soon pooling with sweat. 'I shall never get used to this.'

'I hope we're not here long enough to have to,' Moses hissed with feeling, his voice muffled by his own mask.

I turned to Nebogipfel. The poor Morlock – already trussed up in his schoolboy's uniform – was now topped by a ridiculous mask several sizes too big for him: when he moved his head, the insectile filter on the front of the thing actually wobbled.

I patted his head. 'At least you'll blend with the crowds now, Nebogipfel!'

He forbore to reply.

We emerged from the metallic womb of the *Raglan*

222

into a bright summer's day. It was around two in the afternoon, and the sunlight splashed from the drab colours of the 'Naut. My mask immediately filled with perspiration and fog, and I longed to take the heavy, tight thing off my head.

The sky overhead was immense, a deep blue and free of cloud – although here and there I could see thin white lines and swirls, tracings of vapour or ice crystals etched across the sky. I saw a glint at one end of such a trail – perhaps it was sunlight shimmering from some metal Flying Machine.

The Juggernaut was perched on a version of the Petersham Road which was much changed from 1873, or even 1891. I recognised most of the houses from my day: even my own still stood behind an area-rail that was corroded and covered in verdigris. But the gardens and verges seemed uniformly to have been dug over, and given up to a crop of a vegetable I did not know. And I saw that many of the houses had suffered great damage. Some had been reduced to little more than facia, with their roofs and interior partitioning blasted in: here and there, buildings had been blackened and hollowed out by fire; and others were reduced quite to rubble. Even my own house was broken up, and the laboratory was quite demolished. And the damage was not recent: resurgent life, green and vital, had reclaimed the interior of many of the houses; moss and young plants carpeted the remnants of living-rooms and hall-ways, and ivy hung like bizarre curtains over the gaping windows.

I was able to see that the trees still fell away down the same sylvan slope to the Thames, but even the trees showed signs of damage: I saw the stumps of snapped-off branches, scorched boles, and the like. It was as if a great wind, or fire, had passed by here. The Pier was undamaged, but of Richmond Bridge only the haunches remained now, blackened and trun-

223

cated, with the span quite demolished. Much of the river-side meadows towards Petersham had been given over to the same peculiar crop which had inhabited the gardens, I saw, and there was a brown scum floating down the river itself.

There was nobody about. No traffic moved; the weeds pushed through the broken-up road surfaces. I heard no people – no laughing or shouting, no children playing – no animals, no horses, no birds singing.

Of the gaiety which had once characterized a June afternoon from this prospect – the flashing of oars, the laughter of pleasure-seekers floating up off the river – none of that remained.

All of that was gone now, in this grim Year; and perhaps forever. This was a deserted Richmond, a dead place. I was reminded of the splendid ruins in the garden-like world of A.D. 802,701. I had thought all of that remote from me; I had never imagined to see my own familiar England in such a state!

'Great God,' Moses said. 'What a catastrophe – what destruction! Is England abandoned?'

'Oh, no,' Trooper Oldfield put in brightly. 'But places like this just aren't safe any more. There's the gas, and the aerial torpedoes – most people have gone in, to the Domes, do you see?'

'But it's all so broken-down, Filby,' I protested. 'What's become of the spirit of our people? Where's the will to set to and repair all this? It could be done, you know –'

Filby rested a gloved hand on my arm. 'One day – when this wretched business is done – then we'll revive it all. Eh? And it shall be just as it was. But for now . . .' His voice broke off, and I wished I could see his expression. 'Come on,' he said. 'We'd better get out of the open.'

*

We left the *Raglan* behind and hurried along the road towards the town centre: Moses, Nebogipfel and I, with Filby and the two soldiers. Our companions from 1938 walked in a kind of crouch, with endless, nervous glances at the sky. I noted again how Bond walked with a pronounced limp favouring her left leg.

I glanced back with longing at the Juggernaut, for within, I knew, was my Time Machine – my only possible way home, out of this unfolding nightmare of Multiple Historics – but I knew there was no prospect of reaching the machine now; all I could do was to wait on events.

We walked along Hill Street, and then turned into George Street. There was none of the bustle and elegance which had characterized this shopping street in my Year. The department stores, like Gosling's and Wright's, were boarded up, and even the planks which sealed up their windows had faded with years of sunlight. I saw how one corner of Gosling's window had been prised open, evidently by looters; the hole that had been made looked as if it had been gnawed by a rat the size of a human. We passed a squat shelter with a beetling cover, and a pillar beside it with chequered markings and a glass face, now cracked. This too looked abandoned, and the bright yellow-and-black paintwork of the pillar was chipped and peeling.

'It is a shelter against air-raids,' Filby told me in answer to my query. 'One of the early designs. Quite inadequate – if ever a direct impact had come . . . Well! And the pillar marks a first-aid point, equipped with respirators and masks. Hardly used, before the great retreat into the Domes began.'

'*Air-raids* . . . This is not a happy world, Filby, to have coined such terms.'

He sighed. 'They have aerial torpedoes, you see.

The Germans, I mean. Flying machines, which can go to a spot two hundred miles away, drop a Bomb and return! – all mechanical, without the intervention of a man. It's a world of marvels, for War is a terrific motivation for the inventive mind, you know. You'll love it here!'

'The Germans . . .' Moses said. 'We've had nothing but trouble with the Germans since the emergence of Bismarck. Is that old scoundrel still alive?'

'No, but he has able successors,' Filby said grimly.

I had no comment to make. From my perspective, so detached now from Moses's, even such a brute as Bismarck scarcely seemed to warrant the loss of a single human life.

Filby was telling me, in breathless fragments, of more of the marvellous War-faring gargantua of this benighted age: of raider submarines, designed to prosecute the gas battles, with practically unlimited cruising range, and containing half a dozen air missiles each, all packed with a formidable supply of gas bombs; of a torrent of ironmongery which I imagined tearing its way across the battered plains of Europe; of more 'Juggernauts' which could go underwater, or float, or burrow; and all of it was opposed by an equally formidable array of mines and guns of all sorts.

I avoided Nebogipfel's eyes; I could not face his judgement! For this was no patch on a Sphere in the sky, populated by ab-human descendants remote from me: this was *my* world, *my* race, gone mad with War! For my part, I retained something of that greater perspective I had acquired in the Interior of that great construct. I could scarcely bear to see my own nation given over to such folly, and it pained me to hear Moses's contributions, bound up as they were by the petty preconceptions of his day. I could hardly

226

blame *him*! – but it distressed me to think that my own imagination had ever been so limited, so *malleable*.

2

A TRAIN JOURNEY

We reached a crude rail station. But this was not the station I had used in 1891 to ride from Richmond into Waterloo, through Barnes; this new construction was away from the centre of the town, being located just off the Kew Road. And it was an odd sort of station: there was nothing in the way of ticket collection points or destination boards, and the platform was a bare strip of concrete. A new line was crudely laid out. A train waited for us: the locomotive was a drab, dark affair which puffed steam mournfully about its soot-smeared boiler, and there was a single carriage. There were no lights on the locomotive, nor any insignia of the governing Railway Company.

Trooper Oldfield pulled open the carriage door; it was heavy, with a rubber seal around the edge. Oldfield's eyes, visible behind their goggles, flicked about. Richmond, on a sunny afternoon in 1938, was not a safe place to be!

The carriage was plain: there were rows of hard wooden benches – that was all – nothing in the way of padding, or any decoration. The paint-work was a uniform dull brown, without character. The windows were sealed shut, and there were blinds which could be pulled down over them.

We settled into our places, facing each other

rather stiffly. The heat inside the carriage on that sunny day was stifling.

Once Oldfield had closed the door, the train started into motion immediately, with something of a lurch.

'Evidently we're the only passengers,' Moses murmured.

'Well, it's a rum sort of train,' I said. 'Rather bare amenities, Filby – eh?'

'It isn't much of an age for comforts, old man.'

We passed through some miles of the desolate sort of countryside we had seen around Richmond. The land had been given over almost entirely to agriculture, it seemed to me, and was mostly deserted of people, although here and there I saw a figure or two scraping at some field. It might have been a scene from the fifteenth century, not the twentieth – save for the ruined and bombed-out houses which littered the countryside, with, here and there, the imposing brow of bomb shelters: these were great carapaces of concrete, half-submerged in the ground. Soldiers with guns patrolled the perimeters of these shelters, glaring at the world through their bug-faced gas-masks, as if daring any refugee to approach.

Near Mortlake I saw four men hanging from telegraph poles by a road-side. Their bodies were limp and blackened, and evidently the birds had been at them. I remarked on this horrifying sight to Filby – he and the soldiers had not even noticed the presence of the corpses – and he turned his watery gaze in that direction, and muttered something about how 'no doubt they were caught stealing swedes, or some such'.

I was given to understand such sights were common, in this England of 1938.

Just then – quite without warning – the train plunged down a slope and into a tunnel. Two weak electric bulbs set in the ceiling cut into operation, and we sat there in their yellow glow, lowering at each other.

I asked Filby, 'Is this an Underground train? We are on some extension of the Metropolitan Line, I imagine.'

Filby seemed confused. 'Oh, I imagine the line has some Number or other . . .'

Moses began to fumble with his mask. 'At least we can be shut of these terrible things.'

Bond laid a hand on his arm. 'No,' she said. 'It isn't safe.'

Filby nodded his agreement. 'The gas gets everywhere.' I thought he shuddered, but in that drab, loose outfit of his it was difficult to be sure. 'Until you've been through it –'

Then, in brief, vivid words, he painted a picture of a gas raid he had witnessed in the early stages of the War, in Knightsbridge, when bombs had still been tipped by hand from floating balloons, and the population was not yet accustomed to it all.

And such ghastly scenes had become commonplace, Filby implied, in this world of endless War!

'It's a wonder to me that morale hasn't cracked altogether, Filby.'

'People aren't like that, it seems. People endure. Of course there have been low moments,' he went on. 'I remember August of 1918, for instance . . . It was a moment when it seemed the Western Allies might get on top of the damn Germans, after so long, and get the War completed. But then came the Kaiser's Battle: the *Kaiserschlacht*, Ludendorff's great victory, in which he smashed his way between the British and French lines . . . After four years of Trench War, it was a great breakthrough for them. Of course the bombing in Paris, which killed so many of the French general staff, didn't help us . . .'

230

Captain Bond nodded. 'The rapid victory in the West enabled the Germans to turn their attentions to the Russians in the East. Then, by 1925 –'

'By 1925,' said Filby, 'the blessed Germans had established their dreamed-of *Mitteleuropa*.'

He and Bond sketched the situation for me. *Mitteleuropa*: Axis Europe, a single market stretching from the Atlantic coast to beyond the Urals. By 1925 the Kaiser's control extended from the Atlantic to the Baltic, through Russian Poland as far as the Crimea. France had become a weakened rump, shorn of much of its resources. Luxembourg was turned, by force, into a German federal state. Belgium and Holland were compelled to put their ports at German disposal. The mines of France, Belgium and Rumania were exploited to fuel further expansion of the Reich, to the East, and the Slavs were pushed back, and millions of non-Russians were 'freed' from Moscow's dominance . . .

And so on, in all its meaningless detail.

'Then, in 1926,' said Bond, 'the Allies – Britain with her Empire, and America – opened up the Front in the West again. It has been the Invasion of Europe: the greatest transportation of troops and materiel across water, and through the air, ever seen.

'At first it went well. The populations of France and Belgium rose up, and the Germans were thrown back –'

'But not far,' Filby said. 'Soon it was 1915 all over again, with two immense armies bogged down in the mud of France and Belgium.'

So the Siege had begun. But now, the resources available to make War were so much greater: the life-blood of the British Empire and the American continent on the one hand, and of *Mitteleuropa* on the other, was all poured into that awful sink of War.

And then came the War on Civilians, waged in earnest: the aerial torpedoes, the gassing . . .

'"*The wars of peoples will be more terrible than those of kings*",' Moses quoted grimly.

'But the people, Filby – what of the people!'

His voice, obscured by the mask, was at once familiar, yet removed from me. 'There have been popular protests – especially in the late Twenties, I remember. But then they passed Order 1305, which made strikes and lockouts and the rest of it illegal. And that was the end of that! Since then – well, we've all simply got on with things, I suppose.'

I became aware that the walls of the tunnel had receded from the window, as if the tunnel were opening out. We seemed to be entering a large, underground chamber.

Bond and Oldfield unbuttoned their masks, with every expression of relief; Filby, too, released his straps, and when his poor old head came free of its moist prison, I could see white marks in his chin where the seal of the mask had dug into him. '*That's* better,' he said.

'We're safe now?'

'Should be,' he said. 'Safe as anywhere!'

I unbuttoned my mask and pulled it free; Moses shed his quickly, then helped the Morlock. When Nebogipfel's little face was exposed, Oldfield, Bond and Filby all stared quite openly – I could not blame them! – until Moses helped him restore his cap and goggles to their appointed sites.

'Where are we?' I asked Filby.

'Don't you recognize it?' Filby waved his hand at the darkness beyond the window.

'I –'

'It's Hammersmith, old man. We've just crossed the river.'

Hilary Bond explained to me, 'It is the Hammersmith Gate. We have reached the Dome of London.'

3

LONDON AT WAR

The London Dome!
  Nothing in my own time had prepared me for this stupendous feat of construction. *Picture it*: a great pie-dish of concrete and steel almost two miles across, stretching across the city from Hammersmith to Stepney, and from Islington to Clapham. . . The streets were broken everywhere by pillars, struts and buttresses which thrust down into the London clay, dominating and confining the populace like the legs of a crowd of giants.

The train moved on, beyond Hammersmith and Fulham, and deeper into the Dome. As my eyes adjusted to the gloom, I began to see how the street-lights traced out an image of a London I could still recognize: 'Here is Kensington High Street, beyond this fence! And is that Holland Park?' – and so forth. But for all the familiar landmarks and street names, this was a new London: a London of permanent night, a city which could never enjoy the glow of the June sky outside – but a London which had accepted all this as the price for survival, Filby told me; for bombs and torpedoes would roll off that massive Roof, or burst in the air harmlessly, leaving Cobbett's 'Great Wen' unmarked beneath.

Everywhere, Filby said, the cities of men – which had once blazed with light, turning the night-side of our turning world into a glowing jewel – had been covered by such brooding, obscuring Shells; now, men hardly moved between the great Dome-cities, preferring to cower in their man-made Darkness.

Our new train line appeared to have been slashed through the old pattern of streets. The roads we passed over were quite crowded, but with people on foot or on bicycles; I saw no carriages, drawn either by horse or by motor, as I had expected. There were even rickshaws! – light carriages, pulled by sweating, scrawny Cockneys, squirming around the obstacles posed by the Dome's pillars.

Watching the crowds from the window of my slowing train, I caught a sense, despite the general bustle and busy-ness, of despondency, down-heartedness, disillusion . . . I saw down-turned heads, slumped shoulders, lined, weary faces; there was a certain doggedness, it seemed to me, as people went about their lives; but there seemed to me – and it was not surprising – little *joy*.

It was striking that there were no children, anywhere to be seen. Bond told me that the schools were mostly underground now, for greater protection against the possibility of bombs, while the parents worked in the munitions factories, or in the huge aerodromes which had sprung up around London, at Balham, Hackney and Wembley. Well, perhaps that was a safer arrangement – but what a bleak place the city was without the laughter of running children! – as even I, a contented bachelor, was prepared to concede. And what kind of preparation for life were those poor subterranean mites receiving?

Again, I thought, my travels had landed me in a world of rayless obscurity – a world a Morlock would have enjoyed. But the people who had built this great edifice were no Morlocks: they were my own species, cowed by War into relinquishing the Light which was their birthright! A deep and abiding depression settled over me, a mood which was to linger for much of my stay in 1938.

Here and there, I saw rather more direct evidence of the horror of War. In Kensington High Street I saw one chap making his way along the road – he had to be helped, by a thin young woman at his side – his lips were thin and stretched, and his eyes were like beads in shrunken sockets. The skin of his face was a pattern of marks in purple and white on the underlying grey.

Filby sniffed when I pointed this out. '*War Burns*,' he said. 'They always look the same . . . An aerial fighter, probably – a young gladiator, whose exploits we all adore when the Babble Machines shout about them! – and yet where is there for them to go afterwards?' He glanced at me, and laid a withered hand on my arm. 'I don't mean to sound unfeeling, my dear chap. I'm still the Filby you used to know. It's just – God! – it's just that one has to steel oneself.'

Most of the old buildings of London seemed to have survived, although, I saw, some of the taller constructions had been torn down to allow the concrete carapace to grow over – I wondered if Nelson's Column still stood! – and the new buildings were small, beetling and drab. But there were some scars left by the early days of the War, before the Dome's completion: great bomb-sites, like vacant eye-sockets, and mounds of rubble which no-one had yet had the wit or energy to fill.

The Dome reached its greatest height of two hundred feet or so directly above Westminster at the heart of London; as we neared the centre of town, I saw beams of brilliant lights flickering up from the central streets and splashing that universal Roof with illumination. And everywhere, protruding from the streets of London and from immense foundation-

235

rafts on the river, there were those pillars: rough-hewn, crowding, with splayed and buttressed bases – ten thousand concrete Atlases to support that roof, pillars which had turned London into an immense Moorish temple.

I wondered if the basin of chalk and soft clay in which London rested could support this colossal weight! What if the whole arrangement were to sink into the mud, dragging its precious cargo of millions of lives with it? I thought with some wistfulness of that Age of Building which was to come, when the glimpses I had seen of the mastery of gravity would render a construction like this Dome into a trivial affair . . .

Yet, despite the crudity and evident haste of its construction, and the bleakness of its purpose, I found myself impressed by the Dome. Because it was all hewn out of simple stone and fixed to the London clay with little more than the expertise of my own century, that brooding edifice was more remarkable to me than all the wonders I had seen in the Year A.D. 657,208!

We travelled on, but we were evidently close to journey's end, for the train moved at little more than walking pace. I saw there were shops open, but their windows were scarcely a blaze of light; I saw dummies wearing more of the drab clothes of the day, and shoppers peering through patched-up glass panes. There was little left of luxury, it seemed, in this long and bitter War.

The train drew to a halt. 'Here we are,' said Bond. 'This is Canning Gate: just a few minutes' walk to Imperial College.' Trooper Oldfield pushed at the carriage door – it opened with a distinct pop, as if the pressure in this Dome were high – and a flood of noise burst in over us. I saw more soldiers, these dressed in the drab olive battle-dress of infantrymen, waiting for us on the platform.

So, grasping my borrowed gas-mask, I stepped out into the London Dome.

The noise was astonishing! – that was my first impression. It was like being in some immense crypt, shared with millions of others. A hubbub of voices, the squealing of train wheels and the hum of trams: all of it seemed to rattle around that vast, darkened Roof and shower down over me. It was immensely hot – hotter than the *Raglan* had been. There was a warm array of scents, not all of them pleasant: of cooking food, of ozone from some machinery, of steam and oil from the train – and, above all, of *people*, millions of them breathing and perspiring their way through that great, enclosed blanket of air.

There were lights placed here and there in the architecture of the Dome itself: not enough to illuminate the streets below, but enough that one could make out its shape. I saw little forms up there, fluttering between the lights: they were the pigeons of London, Filby told me – still surviving, though now etiolated by their years of darkness – and the pigeons were interspersed with a few colonies of bats, who had made themselves unpopular in some districts.

In one corner of the Roof, to the north, a projected light-show was playing. I heard the echoing of some amplified voice from that direction, too. Filby called this the 'Babble Machine' – it was a sort of public kinematograph, I gathered – but it was too remote to make out any details.

I saw that our new light rail track had been gouged, quite crudely, through the old road surface; and that this 'station' was little more than a splash of concrete in the middle of Canning Place. Everything about the changes which had wrought this new world spoke of haste and panic.

The soldiers formed up into a little diamond around us, and we walked away from the station and along Canning Place towards Gloucester Road. Moses had his fists clenched. In his bright-coloured masher's costume he looked scared and vulnerable, and I felt a pang of guilt that I had brought him to this harsh world of metal epaulettes and gas-masks.

I glanced along De Vere Gardens to the Kensington Park Hotel, where I had been accustomed to dine in happier times; the pillared porticoes of that place still stood, but the front of the building had become shabby, and many of the windows were boarded up, and the Hotel appeared to have become part of the new railway terminus.

We turned into Gloucester Road. There were many people passing here, on the pavement and in the road, and the tinkling of bicycle bells was a cheerful counterpoint to the general sense of despondency. Our tight little party – and Moses in his gaudy costume in particular – were treated to many extended stares, but nobody came too close, or spoke to us. There were plenty of soldiers hereabouts, in drab uniforms similar to those of the 'Naut crew, but most of the men wore suits which – if rather plain and ill-cut – would not have looked out of place in 1891. The women wore delicate skirts and blouses, quite plain and functional, and the only source of shock in this was that most of the skirts were cut quite high, to within three or four inches of the knee, so that there were more feminine calves and ankles on display in a few yards than, I think, I had ever seen in my life! (This latter was not of much interest to me, against the background of so much Change; but it was, apparently, of rather more fascination to Moses, and I found the way he stared rather ungentlemanly.)

238

But, uniformly, all the pedestrians wore those odd metal epaulettes, and all lugged about, even in this summer heat, heavy webbing cases bearing their gas-masks.

I became aware that our soldiers had their holsters open, to a man; I realized that the weapons were not intended for us, for I could see the thin eyes of the soldiers as they surveyed the crush of people close to us.

We turned east along Queen's Gate Terrace. This was a part of London I had been familiar with. It was a wide, elegant street lined by tall terraces; and I saw that the houses here were pretty much untouched by the intervening time. The fronts of the houses still sported the mock Greco-Roman ornamentation I remembered – pillars carved with floral designs, and the like – and the pavement was lined by the same black-painted area rails.

Bond stopped us at one of these houses, half-way along the street. She climbed the step to the front door and rapped on it with a gloved hand; a soldier – another private, in battle-dress – opened it from within. Bond said to us, 'All the houses here were requisitioned by the Air Ministry, a while ago. You'll have everything you need – just ask the privates – and Filby will stay with you.'

Moses and I exchanged glances. 'But what are we to *do* now?' I asked.

'Just wait,' she said. 'Freshen up – get some sleep. Heaven knows what hour your bodies think it is! . . . I've had instructions from the Air Ministry; they are very interested in meeting you,' she told me. 'A scientist from the Ministry is taking charge of your case. He will be here to see you in the morning.

'Well. Good luck – perhaps we'll meet again.' And with that, she shook my hand, and Moses's, in a manly fashion, and she called Trooper Oldfield to her; and they set off down the Mews once more, two young warriors erect and brave – and every bit as fragile as that War-Burned wretch I had seen earlier in Kensington High Street.

4

THE HOUSE IN QUEEN'S GATE TERRACE

Filby showed us around the house. The rooms were large, clean and bright, though the curtains were drawn. The house was furnished comfortably but plainly, in a style that would not have seemed out of place in 1891; the chief difference was a proliferation of new electrical gadgets, especially a variety of lights and other appliances, such as a large cooker, refrigerating boxes, fans and heaters.

I went to the window of the dining-room and pulled back its heavy curtain. The window was a double layer of glass, sealed around its rim with rubber and leather – there were seals around the door-frames too – and beyond, on this English June evening, there was only the darkness of the Dome, broken by the distant flickering of light beams on the roof. And under the window I found a box, disguised by an inlaid pattern, which contained a rack of gas-masks.

Still, with the curtains drawn and the lights bright, it was possible to forget, for a while, the bleakness of the world beyond these walls!

There was a smoking-room which was well stocked with books and newspapers; Nebogipfel studied these, evidently uncertain as to their function. There was also a large cabinet faced with multiple grilles: Moses opened this up, to find a bewildering land-scape of valves, coils and cones of blackened paper.

This device turned out to be called a phonograph. It was the size and shape of a Dutch clock, and down the front of it were electric barometric indicators, an electric clock and calendar, and various engagement reminders; and it was capable of receiving speech, and even music, broadcast by a sophisticated extension of the wireless-telegraphy of my day, with high faithfulness. Moses and I spent some time with this device, experimenting with its controls. It could be tuned to receive radio-waves of different frequencies by means of an adjustable capacitor – this ingenious device enabled the resonant frequency of the tuned circuits to be chosen by the listener – and there turned out to be a remarkable number of broadcasting stations: three or four at least!

Filby had fixed himself a whisky-and-water, and he watched us experiment, indulgent. 'The phonograph is a marvellous thing,' he said. 'Turns us all into one people – don't you think? – although all the stations are MoI, of course.'

'MoI?'

'Ministry of Information.' Filby then tried to engage our interest by telling us of the development of a new type of phonograph which could carry pictures. 'It was a fad before the War, but it never caught on because of the distortion of the Domes. And if you want pictures, there's always the Babble Machine – eh? All MoI stuff again, of course – but if you like stirring speeches by politicians and soldiers, and encouraging homilies from the Great and Good, then it's your thing!' He swigged his whisky and grimaced. 'But what can you expect? – it's a War, after all.'

Moses and I soon tired of the phonograph's stream of bland news, and of the sounds of rather feeble orchestras drifting in the air, and we turned the device off.

We were given a bedroom each. There were changes of underclothes for us all – even the Morlock – though the garments were clearly hastily assembled and ill-fitting. One private, a narrow-faced boy called Puttick, was to stay with us in the house; although he wore his battle-dress whenever I saw him, this Puttick served pretty well as a manservant and cook. There were always other soldiers outside the house, though, and in the Terrace beyond. It was pretty clear we were under guard – or prisoners!

Puttick called us into the dining room for dinner at around seven. Nebogipfel did not join us. He asked only for water and a plate of uncooked vegetables; and he stayed in the smoking-room, his goggles still clamped to his hairy face, and he listened to the phonograph and studied magazines.

Our meal proved to be plain though palatable, with as centrepiece a plate of what looked like roast beef, with potatoes, cabbage and carrots. I picked at the meat-stuff; it fell apart rather easily, and its fibres were short and soft. 'What's this?' I asked Filby.

'Soya.'

'What?'

'*Soya-beans.* They are grown all over the country, out of the Domes – even the Oval cricket ground has been given over to their production! – for meat isn't so easy to come by, these days. It's hard to persuade the sheep and cattle to keep their gas-masks on, you know!' He cut off a slice of this processed vegetable and popped it into his mouth. 'Try it! – it's palatable enough; these modern food mechanics are quite ingenious.'

The stuff had a dry, crumbling texture on my tongue, and its flavour made me think of damp cardboard.

'It's not so bad,' Filby said bravely. 'You'll get used to it.'

I could not find a reply. I washed the stuff down with the wine – it tasted like a decent Bordeaux, though I forbore to ask its provenance – and the rest of the meal passed in silence.

I took a brief bath – there was hot water from the taps, a liberal supply of it – and then, after a quick round of brandy and cigars, we retired. Only Nebogipfel stayed up, for Morlocks do not sleep as we do, and he asked for a pad of paper and some pencils (he had to be shown how to use the sharpener and eraser).

I lay there, hot in that narrow bed, with the windows of my room sealed shut, and the air becoming steadily more stuffy. Beyond the walls the noise of this War-spoiled London rattled around the confines of its Dome, and through gaps in my curtains I saw the flickering of the Ministry news lamps, deep into the night.

I heard Nebogipfel moving about the smoking-room; strange as it may seem, I found something comforting in the sounds of narrow Morlock feet as they padded about, and the clumsy scratching of his pencils across paper.

At last I slept.

There was a small clock on a table beside my bed, which told me that I woke at seven in the morning; though, of course, it was still as black as the deepest night outside.

I hauled myself out of bed. I put on that battered light suit which had already seen so many adventures, and I dug out a fresh set of underclothes, shirt and tie. The air was clammy, despite the earliness of the hour; I felt cotton-headed and heavy of limb.

I opened the curtain. I saw Filby's Babble Machine still flickering against the roof; I thought I heard snatches of some stirring music, like a march, no

244

doubt intended to hasten reluctant workers to another day's toil on behalf of the War Effort.

I made my way downstairs to the dining room. I found myself alone save for Puttick, the soldier-manservant, who served me with a breakfast of toast, sausages (stuffed with some unidentifiable substitute for meat) and – this was a rare treat, Puttick gave me to believe – an egg, softly fried.

When I was done, I set off, clutching a last piece of toast, for the smoking room. There I found Moses and Nebogipfel, hunched over books and piles of paper on the big desk; cold cups of tea littered the desk's surface.

'No sign of Filby?' I asked.

'Not yet,' Moses told me. My younger self wore a dressing gown; he was unshaven, and his hair was mussed.

I sat down at the desk. 'Confound it, Moses, you look as if you haven't slept.'

He grinned and drew a hand through the peak of hair over his broad forehead. 'Well, so I haven't. I just couldn't settle – I think I've been through rather too much, you know, and my head's been in something of a spin . . . I knew Nebogipfel was still up, so I came down here.' He looked at me out of eyes that were red and black-lined. 'We've had a fascinating night – fascinating! Nebogipfel's been introducing me to the mysteries of *Quantum Mechanics.*'

'Of *what?*'

'Indeed,' Nebogipfel said. 'And Moses, in his turn, has been teaching me to read English.'

'He's a damned fast learner, too,' said Moses. 'He needed little more than the alphabet and a quick tour of the principles of phonetics, and he was off.'

I leafed through the detritus on the desk. There were several sheets of note-paper covered in odd, cryptic symbols: Nebogipfel's writing, I surmised.

When I held up a sheet I saw how clumsily he had used the pencils; in several places the paper was torn clean through. Well, the poor chap had never before had to make do with any implement so crude as a *pen* or *pencil*; I wondered how *I* should have got on with wielding the flint tools of my own ancestors, who were less remote in time from me than was Nebogipfel from 1938!

'I'm surprised you've not been listening to the phonograph,' I said to Moses. 'Are you not interested in the details of this world we find ourselves in?'

Moses replied, 'But much of its output is either music or fiction – and *that* of the Moralizing, Uplifting sort which I have never found palatable – as *you* know! – and I have become quite overwhelmed with the stream of trivia which masquerades as news. One wants to deal with the great Issues of the Day – *Where are we? How did we get here? Where are we headed?* – and instead one is inundated with a lot of nonsense about train delays and rationing shortfalls and the obscure details of remote military campaigns, whose general background one is expected to know already.'

I patted his arm. 'What do you expect? Look here: we're dipping into History, like temporal tourists. People *are* generally obsessed by the surface of things – and rightly so! How often in your own Year do you find the daily newspapers filled with deep analyses of the Causes of History? How much of your own conversation is occupied with explanations as to the general pattern of life in 1873? . . .'

'Your point is taken,' he said. He showed little interest in the conversation; he seemed unwilling to engage much concentration in the world around him. Instead: 'Look,' he said, 'I must tell you something of what your Morlock friend has related of this

246

new theory.' His eyes were brighter, his voice clear, and I saw that this was an altogether more palatable subject for him – it was an escape, I supposed, from the complexities of our predicament into the clean mysteries of science.

I resolved to humour him; there would be time enough for him to confront his situation in the days to come. 'I take it this has some bearing on our current plight –'

'Indeed it does,' said Nebogipfel. He ran his stubby fingers over his temples, in a gesture of evident, and very human, weariness. 'Quantum Mechanics is the framework within which I must construct my understanding of the Multiplicity of Histories which we are experiencing.'

'It's a remarkable theoretical development,' Moses enthused. 'Quite unforeseen in my day – even unimaginable! – it's astonishing that the order of things can be overturned with such speed.'

I put down Nebogipfel's bit of paper. 'Tell me,' I said.

5

THE MANY WORLDS INTERPRETATION

Nebogipfel made to speak, but Moses held up his hand. 'No – let me; I want to see if I've got it straightened out. Look here: You imagine the world is made up, pretty much, of *atoms*, don't you? You don't know the composition of these things, for they are far too fine to see, but that's pretty much all there is to it: a lot of little hard Particles bouncing around like billiard balls.'

I frowned at this over-simplification. 'I think you should remember who you're talking to.'

'Oh – let me do this my own way, man! Follow me closely, now: for I have to tell you that this view of things is *wrong*, in every particular.'

I frowned. 'How so?'

'To begin with, you can put aside your Particle – *for there is no such animal*. It turns out that – despite the confidence of Newton – one can never tell, *precisely*, where a Particle is, or where it is heading.'

'But if one had microscopes fine enough, surely, to inspect a Particle, any degree of accuracy one desired –'

'Put it aside!' he commanded. 'There is a fundamental limitation on measurement – called the Uncertainty Principle, I gather – which places a sort of bottom level to such exercises.

'We have to forget about any definiteness about the world, you see. We must think in terms of

Probability – the chance of finding a physical object at such-and-such a place, with a speed of so-and-so – et cetera. There's a sort of fuzziness about things, which –'

I said bluntly, 'But look here – let's suppose I perform some simple experiment. I will measure, at some instant, the position of a Particle – with a microscope, of an accuracy I can name. You'll not deny the plausibility of such an experiment, I hope. Well, then: I have my measurement! Where's the uncertainty in that?'

'But the point is,' Nebogipfel put in, 'there is a finite chance that if you were able to go back and repeat the experiment, you would find the Particle in some other place – perhaps far removed from the first location . . .'

The two of them kept up the argument in this vein for some time.

'Enough,' I said. 'I concede the point, for the sake of the discussion. But what is the relevance for us?'

'There is – will be – a new philosophy called the *Many Worlds Interpretation of Quantum Mechanics*,' Nebogipfel said, and the sound of his queer, liquid voice, delivering such a striking phrase, sent shivers along my spine. 'There is another ten or twenty years to elapse before the crucial papers are published – I remember the name of Everett . . .'

'It's like this,' Moses said. 'Suppose you have a Particle which can be in just two places – *here* or *there*, we will say – with some chance associated with each place. All right? Now you take a look with your microscope, and find it *here* . . .'

'According to the Many Worlds idea,' Nebogipfel said, '*History splits into two* when you perform such an experiment. In the other History, there is *another you* – who has just found the object *there*, rather than *here*.'

'Another History?'

Moses said, 'With all the reality and consistency of

this one.' He grinned. 'There is another you – there is an *infinite* number of "you's" – propagating like rabbits at every moment!'

'What an appalling thought,' I said. 'I thought two were more than enough. But look, Nebogipfel, couldn't we *tell* if we were being split up in this way?'

'No,' he said, 'because any such measurement, in either History, would have to come *after* the split. It would be impossible to measure the consequences of the split itself.'

'Would it be possible to detect if these other Histories were there? – or for me to travel there, to meet another of this sheaf of twin selves you say I have?'

'No,' Nebogipfel said. 'Quite impossible. Unless –'

'Yes?'

'Unless some of the tenets of Quantum Mechanics prove to be false.'

Moses said, 'You can see why these ideas could help us make sense of the paradoxes we have uncovered. If more than one History can indeed exist –'

'Then causality violations are easily dealt with,' Nebogipfel said. 'Look: suppose you had returned through time with a gun, and shot Moses summarily.' Moses paled a little at this. Nebogipfel went on: 'So there we have a classic Causality Paradox in its simplest terms. If Moses is *dead*, he will *not* go on to build the Time Machine, and become you – and so he cannot travel back in time to do the murder. But if the murder *does not* take place, Moses lives on to build the machine, travels back – and kills his younger self. And *then* he cannot build the machine, and the murder cannot be committed, and –'

'Enough,' I said. 'I think we understand.'

'It is a pathological failure of causality,' Nebogipfel said, 'a loop without termination.

'But if the Many Worlds idea is right, *there is no*

paradox. History splits in two: in one edition, Moses lives; in the second, he dies. You, as a Time Traveller, have simply crossed from one History into the other.'

'I see it,' I said in wonder. 'And surely this Many Worlds phenomenon is precisely what we have witnessed, Nebogipfel and I – we have already watched the unfolding of more than one edition of History . . .' I felt enormously reassured by all this – for the first time, I saw that there might be a glimmer of logic about the blizzard of conflicting Histories which had hailed about my head since my second launch into time! Finding some sort of theoretical structure to explain things was as important to me as finding solid ground beneath his feet might be to a drowning man; though what practical application we might make of all this I could not yet imagine.

And – it occurred to me – if Nebogipfel was right, perhaps I was *not* responsible for the wholesale destruction of Weena's history after all. Perhaps, in some sense, that History still existed! I felt a little of my guilt and grief lift at the thought.

Now the smoking-room door clattered open, and in bustled Filby. It was not yet nine in the morning; Filby was unwashed and unshaven, and a battered dressing gown clung to his frame. He said to me: 'There's a visitor for you. That scientist chap from the Air Ministry Bond mentioned . . .'

I pushed back my chair and stood. Nebogipfel returned to his studies, and Moses looked up at me, his hair still tousled. I regarded him with some concern; I was beginning to realize that he was taking all this dislocation in time quite hard. 'Look,' I said to him, 'it seems I have to go to work. Why don't you come with me? I'd appreciate your insights.'

He smiled without humour. '*My* insights are *your* insights,' he said. 'You don't need me.'

'But I'd like your company . . . After all, this may be your future. Don't you think you'll be better off if you stir yourself a bit?'

His eyes were deep, and I thought I recognized that longing for home which was so strong in me. 'Not today. There will be time . . . perhaps tomorrow.' He nodded to me. 'Be careful.'

I could think of no more to say – not then.

I let Filby lead me to the hall. The man waiting for me at the open front door was tall and ungainly, with a shock of rough, greying hair. A trooper stood in the street behind him.

When the tall chap saw me, he stepped forward with a boyish clumsiness incongruous in such a big man. He addressed me by name, and pumped my hand; he had strong, rather battered hands, and I realised that this was a practical experimenter – perhaps a man after my own heart! 'I'm glad to meet you – so glad,' he said. 'I work on assignment to the DChronW – that's the Directorate of Chronic-Displacement Warfare, of the Air Ministry.' His nose was straight, his features thin, and his gaze, behind wire-rimmed spectacles, was frank. He was clearly a civilian, for, beneath the universal epaulettes and gas-mask cache, he wore a plain, rather dowdy suit, with a striped tie and yellowing shirt beneath. He had a numbered badge on his lapel. He was perhaps fifty years old.

'I'm pleased,' I said. 'Although I fear your face isn't familiar . . .'

'Why on earth should it be? I was just eight years old when your prototype CDV departed for the future . . . I apologize! – that's "Chronic Displacement Vehicle". You may get the hang of all these acronyms of ours – or perhaps not! I never have; and they say Lord Beaverbrook himself struggles to remember all the Directorates under his Ministry.

'I'm not well-known – not nearly so famous as you! Until a while ago, I worked as nothing more grand than Assistant Chief Designer for the Vickers-Armstrong Company, in the Weybridge Bunker. When my proposals on Time Warfare began to get some notice, I was seconded to the headquarters of the DChronW, here at Imperial. Look,' he said seriously, 'I really am so glad you're here – it's a remarkable chance that brought you. I believe that *we* – you and I – could forge a partnership that might change History – that might resolve this damned War forever!'

I couldn't help but shudder, for I had had my fill of changing History already. And this talk of Time Warfare – the thought of my machine, which had already done so much damage, deployed deliberately for destruction! The idea filled me with a deep dread, and I was unsure how to proceed.

'Now – where shall we talk?' he asked. 'Would you like to retire to my room at Imperial? I have some papers which –'

'Later,' I said. 'Look – this may seem odd to you – but I'm still newly arrived here, and I'd appreciate seeing a little more of your world. Is that possible?'

He brightened. 'Of course! We can have our talk on the way.' He glanced over his shoulder at the soldier, who nodded his permission.

'Thank you,' I said, 'Mr –'

'Actually, it's *Dr* Wallis,' he said. 'Barnes Wallis.'

6

HYDE PARK

Imperial College, it turned out, was situated in South Kensington – it was a few minutes' walk from Queen's Gate Terrace. The College had been founded a little after my time, in 1907, from three principal constituent colleges, with which I was familiar: they were the Royal College of Chemistry, the Royal School of Mines and the City and Guilds College. As it happened, in my younger days I had done a little teaching at the Normal School of Science, which had also been absorbed into Imperial; and, emerging now into South Kensington, I was reminded of how I had made the most of my time in London, with many visits to the delights of such establishments as the Empire, Leicester Square. At any rate, I had got to know the area well – but what a transformation I found now!

We walked out through Queen's Gate Terrace towards the College, and then turned up Queen's Gate to Kensington Gore, at the southern edge of Hyde Park. We were escorted by a half-dozen soldiers – quite discreet, for they moved about us in a rough circle – but I wondered at the size of the force that might be brought down on us if anything went awry. It did not take long before the sticky heat started to sap my strength – it was like being in a large, hot building – and I took off my jacket and loosened my tie. On Wallis's advice, I clipped my heavy epaulettes to my shirt, and reattached my gas-mask bag to my trouser-belt.

The streets were much transformed, and it struck me that not all the changes between my day and this had been for ill. The banishment of the insanitary horse, the smoke of domestic fires and the fumes of the motor-car – all for reasons of the quality of the air under the Dome – had resulted in a certain freshness about the place. In the major avenues, the roadway was surfaced over by a new, more resilient, glassy material, kept clean by a chain of workmen who pushed about trolley-carts fixed with brushes and sprinklers. The roads were crowded with bicycles, rickshaws and electrical trams, guided by wires which hissed and sparked blue flashes in the gloom; but there were new ways for pedestrians, called the Rows, which ran along the front of the houses at the height of the first storey – and on the second or even third storeys in some places. Bridges, light and airy, ran across the roads to join up these Rows at frequent intervals, giving London – even in this Stygian darkness – something of an Italian look.

Moses later saw a little more of the life of the city than I did, and he reported bustling shops in the West End – despite the privations of the War – and new theatres around Leicester Square, with frontages of reinforced porcelain, and the whole glowing with reflections and illuminated advertisements. But the plays performed were of a dull, educational or improving variety, Moses complained, with two theatres given over to nothing but a perpetual cycle of Shakespeare's plays.

Wallis and I came past the Royal Albert Hall, which I have always regarded as a monstrosity – a pink hatbox! In the obscurity of the Dome, this pile was picked out by a row of brilliant light beams (projected by *Aldis lamps*, Wallis said), which made that memorable heap seem still more grotesque, as it sat and shone complacently. Then we cut into the Park at the Alexandra Gate, walked back to the Albert Memorial, and set off along the Lancaster Walk to the north. Ahead of us I could see the flickering of the Babble Machine beams against the Roof, and hear the distant boom of amplified voices.

Wallis kept up a descriptive chatter as we walked. He was good enough company, and I began to realize that he was indeed the sort of man who – in a different History – I might have called a friend.

I remembered Hyde Park as a civilized place: attractive and calm, with its wide walkways and its scattering of trees. Some of the features I had known were still there – I recognized the copper-green cupola of the Bandstand, where I could hear a choir of Welsh miners singing hymns in gusty unison – but this version of the Park was a place of shadows, broken by islands of illumination around lamp-standards. The grass was gone – dead, no doubt as soon as the sun was occluded – and much of the bare earth had been covered with sheets of timber. I asked Wallis why the Park had not simply been given over to concrete; he gave me to understand that Londoners liked to believe that one day the ugly Dome over their city could safely be demolished, and their home restored to the beauty it had once known – Parks and all.

One part of the Park, near the Bandstand, had been given over to a sort of shanty-town. There were tents, hundreds of them, clustered around crude concrete buildings which turned out to be communal kitchens and bath-houses. Adults, children and dogs picked across the dry, hard-trodden ground between the tents, making their way through the endless, dull processes of living.

'Poor old London has soaked up a lot of refugees

256

in recent years,' Wallis explained. 'The population density is so much higher than it was. . . and yet there's useful work for them all. They do suffer in those tents, though – and yet there's nowhere else to keep them.'

Now we cut off Lancaster Walk and approached the Round Pond at the heart of the Park. This had once been an attractive, uncluttered feature, offering a fine view of Kensington Palace. The Pond was still there, but fenced off; Wallis told me it served as a reservoir to serve the needs of the increased populace. And of the Palace there was only a shell, evidently bombed-out and abandoned.

We stopped at a stand, and were served rather warm lemonade. The crowds milled about, some on bicycles. There was a game of football going on in one corner, with gas-masks piled up to serve as posts; I even heard speckles of laughter. Wallis told me that people would still turn out to the Speakers' Corner, to hear the Salvation Army, the National Secular Society, the Catholic Evidence Guild, the Anti-Fifth Column League (who waged a campaign against spies, traitors and anyone who might give comfort to the enemy), and so forth.

This was the happiest I had seen people in this benighted time; save for the universal epaulettes and masks – and the deadness of the ground beneath, and that awful, looming Roof over all our heads – this might have been a Bank Holiday crowd from any age, and I was struck again by the resilience of the human spirit.

7

THE BABBLE MACHINE

To the north of the Round Pond rows of dingy canvas deck-chairs had been set out, for the use of those wishing to view the news projected on the roof above us. The chairs were mostly occupied; Wallis paid an attendant – the coins were metal tokens, much smaller than the currency of my day – and we settled in two seats with our heads tipped back.

Our silent soldier-attendants moved into place around us, watching us and the crowd.

Dusty fingers of light reached up from Aldis lamps situated (Wallis said) in Portland Place, and splashed grey and white tones across the Roof. Amplified voices and music washed down over the passive crowd. The Roof had been white-washed hereabouts and so the kinematographic images were quite sharp. The first sequence showed a thin, rather wild-looking man shaking hands with another, and then posing beside what looked like a pile of bricks; the voices were not quite lined up with the movements of the mouths, but the music was stirring, and the general effect was easy to follow.

Wallis leaned over to me. 'We're in luck! – it is a feature on Imperial College. That's Kurt Gödel – a young scientist from Austria. You may meet him. We managed to retrieve Gödel recently from the Reich; apparently he wished to defect because he has some crazy notion that the Kaiser is dead, and has been replaced by an impostor . . . Rather an odd chap, between you and me, but a great mind.'

'*Gödel?*' I felt a flicker of interest. 'The chap behind the Incompleteness of Mathematics, and all of that?'

'Why, yes.' He looked at me curiously. 'How do you know about that? – It's after your time. Well,' he said, 'it's not his achievements in mathematical philosophy we want him for. We've put him in touch with Einstein in Princeton –' I forbore to ask who this *Einstein* was '– and he's going to start up on a line of research he was pursuing in the Reich. It'll be another way into time travel for us, we hope. It was quite a coup – I imagine the Kaiser's boys are furious with each other . . .'

'And the brick construction beside him? What's that?'

'Oh, an experiment.' He glanced around with caution. 'I shouldn't say too much – it's only on the Babble for a bit of show. It's all to do with *atomic fission* . . . I can explain later, if you're interested. Gödel is particularly keen, apparently, to run experiments with it; in fact I believe we've started some tests for him already.'

We were presented, now, with a picture of a troop of rather elderly-looking men in ill-fitting battle-dress, grinning towards the camera. One of them was picked out, a thin, intense-looking chap. Wallis said, 'The Home Guard . . . men and women out of serviceable age, who nevertheless do a bit of soldiering, in case the Invasion of England ever comes. That's Orwell – George Orwell. A bit of a writer – don't suppose you know him.'

The news seemed to be finished for now, and a new entertainment blossomed over our heads. This turned out to be a *cartoon* – a kind of animated drawing, with a lively musical backing. It featured a character called Desperate Dan, I gathered, who lived in a crudely-drawn cartoon Texas. After eating a huge cow pie, this Dan tried to knit himself a jumper of wires, using telegraph poles as needles. Inadvertently he created a chain; and when he threw it away in the sea, it sank. Dan fished the chain out – and found that he had snagged no less than three German undersea Juggernauts. A naval gentleman, observing this, gave Dan a reward of fifty pounds . . . and so forth.

I had supposed this entertainment to be fit only for children, but I saw that adults laughed at it readily enough. I found it all rather crude and coarsely imagined propaganda, and I decided that the common slang epithet of 'Babble Machine' suited this kinematographic show rather well.

After this entertainment we were treated to some more snippets of news. I saw a burning city – it might have been Glasgow, or Liverpool – where a glow filled the night sky, and the flames were gigantic. Then there were pictures of children being evacuated from a collapsed Dome in the Midlands. They looked like typical town children to me, grinning into the camera, with their outsize boots and dirty skin – waifs, quite helpless in the tide of this War.

Now we entered a section of the show entitled, according to a caption, 'Postscript'. First there was a portrait of the King; he was, disconcertingly for me, a skinny chap called Egbert, who turned out to be a remote relation of the old Queen I remembered. This Egbert was one of the few members of the family to have survived audacious German raids in the early days of the War. Meanwhile a plum-voiced actor read us a poem:

'. . . *All shall be well and/ All manner of thing shall be well/ When the tongues of flame are in-folded/ Into the crowned knot of fire/ And the fire and the rose are one* . . .'

And so on! As far as I could make out the piece

was representing the effects of this War as a kind of Purgatory, which in the end would cleanse the souls of Humanity. Once I might have agreed with this argument, I reflected; but after my time in the Sphere's Interior, I think I had come to regard War as no more or less than a dark excrescence, a flaw of the human soul; and any justification for it was just that – justification, after the fact of it.

I gathered Wallis didn't make much of this sort of stuff. He shrugged his shoulders. 'Eliot,' he said, as if that explained it all.

Now there came an image of a man: a rather care-worn, jowly old fellow with an unruly moustache, tired eyes, ugly ears and a fierce, frustrated sort of manner. He sat with his pipe in his hand, by a fire-place – the pipe was rather obviously unlit – and he began to proclaim in a frail voice a kind of commentary on the day's events. I thought the chap looked familiar, but at first I couldn't place him. He wasn't much impressed by the efforts of the Reich, it seemed – 'That vast machine of theirs can't create a glimmer of that poetry of action which distinguishes War from Mass Murder. It's a machine – and therefore has no soul.'

He evoked us all to still sterner efforts. He worked the myths of the English countryside – 'the round green hills dissolving into the hazy blue of the sky' – and asked us to imagine that English scene torn apart 'to reveal the old Flanders Front, trenches and bomb craters, ruined towns, a scarred countryside, a sky belching death, and the faces of murdered children' – all this last pronounced with something of an apoc-alyptic glee, I thought.

In a burst of realization, I remembered him. It was my old friend the Writer, withered into an old man! 'Why, isn't that Mr –?' I said, naming him.

'Yes,' he said. 'Did you know him? I suppose you could have . . . Of course you did! For he wrote up

261

that popular account of your travels in time. It was serialized in *The New Review*, as I recall; and then put out as a book. That was quite a turning point for me, you know, to come across that . . . Poor chap's getting on now, of course – I don't think he was ever all that healthy – and his fiction isn't what it was, in my view.'

'No?'

'Too much lecturing and not enough action – you know the type! Still, his works of popular science and history have been well received. He's a good friend of Churchill – I mean the First Lord of the Admiralty – and I suspect your pal has had a great deal of influence on official thinking on the shape of things to come, after the War is done. You know – when we reach the "Uplands of the Future",' Wallis said, quoting some other speech of my former friend's. 'He's working on a Declaration of Human Rights, or some such, to which we all must adhere after the War – you know the sort of dreamy affair. But he's not so effective a speaker. Priestley's my favourite of that type.'

We listened to the Writer's perorations for several minutes. For my part, I was gladdened that my old friend had survived the vicissitudes of this grisly history, and had even found a meaningful role for himself – but I was helplessly saddened to see what time had done to the eager young man I had known! As when I had met Filby, I felt a stab of pity for the anonymous multitudes around me, embedded in slow-oozing time and doomed to inexorable decay. And it was a ghastly irony, I thought, that a man with such strong faith in the perfectibility of man should find the greater part of his lifetime dominated by the greatest War in history.

'Come on,' Wallis said briskly. 'Let's walk some more. The shows here repeat themselves pretty quickly anyway . . .'

*

Wallis told me more of his background. In the Weybridge Bunker, working for the Vickers-Armstrong Company, he had become a designer of aeronautical devices of some reputation – he was known as a 'wizard boffin', in his words.

As the War had dragged on, Wallis's evidently fertile brain had turned to schemes of how its end might be accelerated. He had considered, for instance, how one might go about destroying the enemy's sources of energy – reservoirs, dams, mines and such-like – by means of massive explosives to be dropped from the stratosphere by 'Monster Bomber' flying machines. To this end he had gone into studies of the Variation of Wind Speed with Height, the Visibility of Objects from Great Heights, and the Effect of Earth Waves on Coal-mine Shafts, and so forth. '*You* can see the possibilities of such things, can't you? One just needs the right sort of imagination. With ten tons of explosives one could divert the course of the Rhine!'

'And what was the reaction to these proposals?'

He sighed. 'Resources are always scarce during wars – even for priority schemes – and for unproven ventures like this . . . "Moonshine", they called it. "Tripe of the wildest description . . ." and there was a lot of talk from the military types about "inventors" like me "throwing away" the lives of "their boys".' I could see he was hurt by this memory. '*You* know that men such as you and I must expect scepticism . . . but still!'

But Wallis had persevered with his studies, and at last he had been given the go-ahead to build his 'Monster Bomber'. 'It is called the *Victory*,' he said. 'With a bomb-load of twenty thousand pounds, and operating at forty thousand feet, it can travel at over three hundred miles per hour and has a range of four thousand miles. It is a magnificent sight at take-

263

off – with its six Hercules engines blazing away, it takes no less than two-thirds of a mile to lumber into the air . . . and the Earthquake Bombs it can deliver have already begun to wreak havoc, deep in the heart of the Reich!' His deep, handsome eyes gleamed behind his dusty glasses.

Wallis had thrown himself into the development of the *Victory* air machine for some years. But then his track had turned, for he came across that popular account of my time travels, and he had immediately seen the possibilities of adapting my machine for War.

This time his ideas had received a decent hearing – his stock was high, and it didn't take much imagination to see the limitless military potential of a Time Machine – and the Directorate of Chronic-Displacement Warfare was set up with Wallis as the civilian head of research. The first action of the DChronW was to sequestrate my old house, which had stood abandoned in Richmond since my departure into time, and the relics of my research were dug out.

'But what do you want of me? You have a Time Machine already – the Juggernaut that brought me here.'

He clasped his hands behind his back, his face long and serious. 'The *Raglan*. Of course – but you've seen that beast for yourself. As far as its time-travelling abilities go, it was constructed solely with the scrap that was found in the ruins of your laboratory. Bits of quartz and brass, doped with Plattnerite – impossible to balance or calibrate – the *Raglan* is a lumbering beast which can reach barely a half-century away from the present. We dared risk the 'Naut for no more than to try to ensure that there was no anachronistic interference by our enemies with the development of your original machine. But now – by chance! – it has brought us you.

'Already we can do more, of course: we have stripped the Plattnerite from your old machine, and have lodged the hull in the Imperial War Museum. Would you like to see it? It will be an honoured exhibit.'

I was pained at the thought of such an end for my faithful chariot – and disturbed at the destruction of my only route away from 1938! I shook my head stiffly.

Wallis went on, 'We need you to generate more of the substance you called Plattnerite – tons of it – show us how!' So Wallis thought *I* had manufactured the Plattnerite? . . . I kept the thought to myself. He went on, 'We want to take your Time Machine technology, and extend it – put it to uses beyond, perhaps, your most extraordinary dreams . . .

'With a CDV one might bomb History and change its course – it is just like my scheme to divert the Rhine! Why not? – if it can be conceived, it should be done. It's the most exciting technical challenge you can imagine – *and* it's all for the benefit of the War Effort.'

'*Bomb* History?'

'Think of it – one might go back and intervene in the early stages of the War. Or assassinate Bismarck – why not? what a prank that would be – and put a stop to the formation of Germany in the first place.

'Can you see it, sir? *A Time Machine is a weapon against which there can be no defence.* Whoever first develops a reliable Chronic-Displacement technology will be the Master of the World – and that Master must be Britain!'

His eyes shone, and I began to find his high-altitude enthusiasm for all of this destruction and power rather disturbing.

8

THE UPLANDS OF
THE FUTURE

We reached the Lancaster Walk and began our
stroll back to the southern boundary of the
Park. We were still flanked by our discreet soldiers.

I said, 'Tell me more of what will be done when
Britain and her Allies win this Time War – tell me
about your "Uplands of the Future".'

He rubbed his nose and looked uncertain. 'I'm no
politician, sir. I can't –'

'No, no. Give me your own words.'

'Very well.' He looked up at the Dome. 'To begin
with – this War has stripped away a lot of our fond
illusions, you know.'

'It has?' I thought that an ominous preamble – and
my fears were soon justified!

'The Fallacy of Democracy, for one thing. You see,
it is now clear that is no good *asking* people what they
want. You have first to think out what they *ought* to
want if society is to be saved. Then you have to *tell*
them what they want and see that they get it.

'I know this may seem odd for a man of your
century,' he said, 'but it's the modern thinking – and
I've heard your famous friend espouse much the
same views on the phonograph before! – and he's of
your time, isn't he?

'I know little of History, but it seems to me that the
Modern State which we're developing in Britain and
America – the form of things we intend to share with

266

the rest of the world – is more like the Republics of antiquity – Carthage, Athens, Rome – which were essentially aristocratic, you see. We have Members of Parliament still, but they are no longer nominated by anything so crude as popular suffrage.

'And all that old business of Opposition – well! We've given all of that up. Look, men like you and me know that about most affairs there can be no two respectable and opposed opinions. There is one sole *right* way and endless *wrong* ways of doing things. A government is trying to go the right way, or it is criminal. That is all there is to it. The Opposition of the past was mostly just a spoiling job done for advancement. And the sabotage must cease.

'And some of the younger folk are going much further, in their thinking on the future. The family, for instance, is dissolving – so they say. It was the common social cell, if you like, through all our agricultural past. But now, in our modern world, the family is losing its distinctness, and has been dissolving into larger systems of relationships. The domestication of all our young people, including the women, is diminishing greatly.'

I thought, at that, of Captain Hilary Bond. 'But what's to *replace* the family?'

'Well, the outlines aren't clear, but the youngsters are talking of a *re-nucleation* of society around different seeds: teachers, writers, talkers, who will lead us into a new way of thinking – and get us away from this old tribalism and into a better way.'

'"Uplands", indeed.' I doubted that much – or any! – of this philosophizing originated with Wallis himself; he was acting simply as a mirror of his times, as moulded by the chattering opinion-makers in Government and beyond. 'And how do *you* feel about all this?'

'Me?' He laughed, self-deprecating. 'Oh, I'm too

267

old to change – and,' his voice was uneven, 'I'd hate to lose my daughters . . . But, likewise, I don't want to see them growing up in a world like –' he waved a hand at the Dome, the dead Park, the soldiers '– like this! And if that means changing the heart of man, then so be it.

'Now,' he said, 'can you see why we need your co-operation? With such a weapon as a CDV – a Time Machine – the establishment of this Modern State becomes, not trivial, but more achievable. And if we fail –'

'Yes?'

He stopped; we were approaching the south wall of the Park now, and there were few people around. He said in a low voice, 'We have rumours that the Germans are building a Time Machine of their own. And if they succeed *first* – if the Reich gets function-ing Chronic-Displacement Warfare capabilities . . .'

'Yes?'

And he painted, for my benefit, a brief but chilling portrait, evidently informed by years of propaganda, of the Time War to come. The old Kaiser's cold-eyed staff officers would be planning how to project into our noble History their half-doped, crazy lads – their *Time Warriors*. Wallis portrayed these soldiers as if they were bombs with legs; they would swarm forward into a hundred of our ancient battles as if they were death-dealing dolls . . .

'They would destroy England – strangle it in its cot. And that's what we have to stop,' he said to me. 'You see that, don't you? You see it?'

I gazed into his deep, earnest face, quite unable to respond.

Wallis returned me to the house in Queen's Gate Terrace. 'I don't want to press you for a decision on working with me, old man – I know how difficult all this must be for you; after all, it isn't your War – but time is short. And yet, what does "time" mean, in such a circumstance? Eh?'

I rejoined my companions in the smoking room. I accepted a whisky-and-water from Filby and threw myself into a chair. 'It's so close out there,' I said. 'More like Burma! – that damned Dome. And doesn't it feel odd? Pitch dark outside, and yet it's only lunch-time.'

Moses glanced up from the volume he was reading. '"Experience is as to intensity and not as to duration",' he quoted. He grinned at me. 'Wouldn't that be a perfect epitaph for a Time Traveller? *Intensity* – that's what counts.'

'Who's the author?'

'Thomas Hardy. Close to a contemporary of yours, wasn't he?'

'I've not read him.'

Moses checked the preface. 'Well, he's gone now. . . 1928.' He closed the book. 'What did you learn from Wallis?'

I summarized my conversations for them. I concluded, 'I was glad to get away from him. What a farrago of propaganda and half-baked politics . . . not to mention the most perfect muddle about causality, and so forth.'

Wallis's words had deepened the sense of depression I had endured since my arrival here in 1938. It seems to me that there is a fundamental conflict in the heart of man. He is swept along by the forces of his own nature – more than anyone, I have witnessed the remorseless action of the evolutionary currents which pulse through Humanity, deriving even from the primal seas – and yet here were these bright young Britons and Americans, hardened by War, determined to Plan, to Control, to fight against Nature and set themselves and their fellows in a sort of stasis, a frozen Utopia!

269

If I were a citizen of this new Modern State they intended, I knew, I should soon have become one of the protesting spirits who squirmed in its pitilessly benevolent grip.

But, even as I reflected thus, I wondered, deep in my heart, to what extent I would have fallen into Wallis's way of thinking – of this Modern State, with its Controls and Plans – before my time-travelling had opened up my eyes to the limitations of Humanity.

'By the way, Nebogipfel,' I said, 'I came across an old friend of ours – Kurt Gödel –'

And the Morlock uttered a queer, gurgling word in his own language; he spun in his chair and stood up in a rapid, liquid movement that made him seem more animal than human. Filby blanched, and I saw Moses's fingers tighten around the book he held.

'*Gödel* – is he here?'

'He's in the Dome, yes. In fact, he's not a quarter-mile from this spot – in Imperial College.' I described the Babble Machine show I had seen.

'*A fission pile*. That is it,' hissed Nebogipfel. 'I understand now. He is the key – Gödel is the key to everything. It must have been him, with his insights into rotating universes –'

'I don't see what you're talking about.'

'Look: do you want to escape from this dreadful History?'

I did – of course I did! – for a thousand reasons: to escape this dreadful conflict, to try to get home, to put a stop to time travelling before the inception of the insanity of Time War . . . 'But for that we must find a Time Machine.'

'Yes. Therefore you must get us to Gödel. You *must*. Now I see the truth.'

'What truth?'

'Barnes Wallis was wrong about the Germans.

270

Their Time Machine is more than a threat. *It has already been built!*

Now we were all on our feet, and talking at once. 'What?' 'What are you saying?' 'How –'

'Already,' the Morlock said, 'we are in a strand of History which has been engineered by the Germans.'

'How do you know?' I demanded.

'Remember that I studied your era in my history,' he said. 'And – in *my* history – there was no such European War as this, which has already spanned decades. In my History, there *was* a War in 1914 – but it finished in 1918, with a victory for the Allies over the Germans. A new War started up in 1939, but under a new form of government in Germany. And –'

I felt odd – dizzy – and I felt behind me for a chair and sat down.

Filby looked terrified. 'Those confounded Germans – I told you! I told you they'd cause trouble!'

Moses said, 'I wonder if that final battle which Filby described – the *Kaiserschlacht* – was somehow modified in the Germans' favour. Perhaps the assassination of an Allied commander might have done it . . .'

'The bombing in Paris,' Filby said, confused and wondering. 'Could that have been it?'

I remembered Wallis's horrid descriptions, of robotic German soldiers dropping into British History. 'What are we to do? We must stop this dreadful Time War!'

'*Get us to Gödel*,' the Morlock said.

'But why?'

'Because it can only be Gödel who has manufactured the Germans' Plattnerite!'

9

IMPERIAL COLLEGE

Wallis called for me again after lunch. Immediately he started pressing me for a decision as to whether I would throw in my lot with his Time War project.

I requested that I be taken into Imperial College, to visit this Kurt Gödel. At first Wallis demurred: 'Gödel is a difficult man – I'm not sure what you'd gain out of the meeting – and the security arrangements are pretty elaborate . . .' But I set my jaw, and Wallis soon caved in. 'Give me thirty minutes,' he said, 'and I'll make the arrangements.'

The fabric of Imperial College seemed largely untouched by the intervening years, or by its reestablishment from the constituent colleges I remembered. Here was Queen's Tower, the central monument of white cut stone flanked by lions, and surrounded by the rather dowdy red brick buildings that comprised this functional place of learning. But I saw that some neighbouring buildings had been appropriated for the College's expanded War-time purposes: in particular the Science Museum had been given over to Wallis's Directorate of Chronic-Displacement Warfare, and there were several newer structures on the campus – mostly squat, plain and evidently thrown up in haste and without much regard for the architectural niceties – and all of these buildings were joined together by a new warren of closed-over corridors, which ran across the campus like huge worm-casts.

Wallis glanced at his watch. 'We've a short while yet before Gödel will be ready for us,' he said. 'Come this way – I've got clearance to show you something else.' He grinned, looking boyish and enthusiastic. 'Our pride and joy!'

So he led me into the warren of worm-cast corridors. Inside, these proved to be walled with untreated concrete and illuminated at sparse intervals by isolated light bulbs. I remember how the uneven light caught the lie of Wallis's clumsy shoulders and his awkward gait as he preceded me deeper into that maze. We passed through several gates, at each of which Wallis had his lapel-badge checked, was required to produce various papers, provide thumb- and finger-prints, have his face compared to photographs, and so forth; I, too, had to be validated against pictures; and we were both searched, bodily, twice.

We took several twists and turns on the way; but I took careful note of my bearings, and built up a map of the College's various annexes in my head.

'The College has been expanded quite a bit,' Wallis said. 'I'm afraid we've lost the Royal College of Music, the College of Art, and even the Natural History Museum – this damned War, eh? And you can see they've had to clear a lot of ground for this new stuff.

'There are still a good few scientific facilities scattered around the country, including the Royal Ordnance factories at Chorley and Woolwich, the Vickers-Armstrong facilities at Newcastle, Barrow, Weybridge, Burhill and Crawford, the Royal Aircraft Establishment at Farnborough, the Armament and Aeronautical Experimental Establishment at Boscombe Down. . . and so forth. Most of these have been relocated into Bunkers and Domes. Nevertheless, Imperial – enhanced as it has been – has become Britain's primary centre for scientific research into Military Technology.'

After more security checks, we entered a kind of hanger, brightly lit, about which there was a healthy smell of engine grease, rubber and scorched metal. Motor vehicles sat about on the stained concrete floor in various states of disassembly; overall-clad men moved amongst them, some of them whistling. I felt my spirits lift a little from my habitual Dome-induced oppression. I have often observed that nothing much perturbs a man who has the opportunity to work with his hands.

'This,' Wallis announced, 'is our CDV Development Division.'

'CDV? Ah! – I remember. *Chronic Displacement Vehicle.*'

In this hangar, these cheerful workmen were labouring to construct Time Machines – and on an industrial scale, it seemed!

Wallis led me to one of the vehicles, which looked pretty much complete. This Time-Car, as I thought of it, stood about five feet tall, and was an angular box shape; the cabin looked big enough to carry four or five people, and it sat on three pairs of wheels, about which tracks looped. There were lamps, brackets and other pieces of equipment dotted about. In each corner of the hull was bolted a flask a couple of inches wide; these flasks were evidently hollow, for they had screw caps. The whole was unpainted, and its gun-metal finish reflected the light.

'It looks a little different from your prototype design, doesn't it?' Wallis said. 'It's actually based on a standard military vehicle – the Carrier, Universal – and it functions as a motor-car as well, of course. Look here: there's a Ford V8 engine driving the

274

tracks by these sprockets – see? And you can steer by displacement of this front bogie unit –' he mimed it '– like this; or, if you must make a more savage turn, you can try track braking. The whole thing's pretty much armoured.. . .'

I pulled at my chin. I wondered how much I would have seen of the worlds I had visited if I had peered at them anxiously from within such an armoured Time-Car as this!

'Plattnerite is essential, of course,' Wallis went on, 'but we don't think there's any need to go doping components of the machine with the stuff, as you did. Instead, it should be sufficient to fill up these flasks with the raw stuff.' He unscrewed a cap from one of the corner units to show me. 'See? And then the thing can be steered through time, if *steer* is the right verb, from within the cabin.'

'And have you tried it out?'

He ran his fingers through his hair, making a lot of it stand on end. 'Of course not! – for we have no Plattnerite.' He clapped me on the shoulder. 'Which is where you come in.'

Wallis took me to another part of the complex. After more security checks we entered a long, narrow chamber, like a corridor. This chamber had one wall made entirely of glass, and beyond the glass I could see into a larger room, about the size of a tennis court. That larger room was empty. In our narrower companion chamber there were six or seven researchers sitting at desks; each wore the characteristic dirty white coat into which every experimentalist seems born, and they hunched over dials and switches. The researchers looked around at me as we entered – three of them were women – and I was struck by their drawn faces; there was a sort of nervous fatigue about them, despite their apparent youth. One class of instrument kept up a soft click-ing, the whole time we were there; this was the sound of 'radiation counters', Wallis told me.

The larger chamber beyond the glass was a simple box of concrete, with unpainted walls. It was quite empty, save for a monolith of bricks perhaps ten feet tall and six wide, which stood, square and silent, at the chamber's centre. The bricks were of two sorts, light and dark grey, alternating in a neat pattern. This monolith was held up from the floor on a layer of thicker slabs, and wires trailed from it to sealed orifices in the walls of the room.

Wallis stared through the glass. 'Remarkable – isn't it? – that something so ugly, so *simple*, should have such profound implications. We should be safe here – the glass is leaded – and besides, the reaction is subdued at present.'

I recognized the heap from the Babble Machine show. 'This is your fission machine?'

'It is the world's *second* Graphite Reactor,' Wallis said. 'It's pretty much a copy of the first, which Fermi built at the University of Chicago.' He smiled. 'He put it up in a squash court, I understand. It's a remarkable story.'

'Yes,' I said, becoming irritated, 'but *what* is Reacting with *what*?'

'Ah,' he said, and he took off his spectacles and polished the lenses on the end of his tie. 'I'll try to explain. . .'

Needless to say, he took some time about this, but I managed to distil the essence of it for my under-standing.

I had already learned from Nebogipfel that there is a sub-structure within the atom – and that Thomson would take one of the first steps to this understanding. Now I learned that this sub-structure can be *changed*. This may happen through a coalesc-

276

ing of one atomic core with another, or perhaps spontaneously, through the breaking-up of a massive atom; and this disintegration is called atomic fission.

And, since the sub-structure determines the identity of the atom, the result of such changes is nothing less, of course, than the transmutation of one element into another – the ancient dream of the Alchemists!

'Now,' said Wallis, 'you won't be surprised to learn that on each atomic disintegration, some energy is released – for the atoms are always seeking a more stable, lower energy state. Do you follow?'

'Of course.'

'So, in this pile, we have six tons of Carolinum, fifty tons of uranium oxide, and four hundred tons of graphite blocks . . . and it is producing a flood of invisible energy, even as we look at it.'

'*Carolinum?* I have not heard of that.'

'It is a new, artificial element, produced by bombardment. Its half period is seventeen days – that is, it loses half its store of energy in that period.'

I looked again at that nondescript heap of bricks: it looked so plain, so unprepossessing! – and yet, I thought, if what Wallis said about the energy of the atomic core was true . . .

'What are the applications of this energy?'

He popped his glasses back onto his nose. 'We see three broad areas. First, the provision of energy from a compact source: with such a pile aboard, we can envisage submarine Juggernauts which could spend months below the ocean, without the need to refuel; or we could build high-altitude Bombers which could circle the earth dozens of times before having to land – and so forth.

'Second, we're using the pile to *irradiate* materials. We can use the by-products of uranium fission to transmute other materials – in fact, a number of samples are being run in there for Professor Gödel just now, to support some obscure experiment of his. You can't see them, of course – the sample bottles are within the pile itself . . .'

'And the third application?'

'Ah,' he said, and once more his eyes took on that remote, calculating look.

'I see it already,' I said grimly. 'This atomic energy would make a fine *Bomb*.'

'Of course there are severe practical problems to solve,' he said. 'The production of the right isotopes in sufficient quantities . . . the timing of preliminary explosions. . . but, yes; it looks as if one could make a Bomb powerful enough to flatten a city – Dome and all – *a Bomb small enough to fit into a suitcase.*'

10

PROFESSOR GÖDEL

We set off through more of the narrow concrete corridors, emerging at last in the College's main office block. We came to a corridor carpeted in plush pile, with portraits of eminent men of the past on the walls – you know the sort of place: a Mausoleum for Dead Scientists! There were soldiers about, but they were discreet in their presence.

It was here that Kurt Gödel had been awarded an office.

With quick, efficient strokes, Wallis sketched out Gödel's life for me. He was born in Austria, and took his degree, in mathematics, in Vienna. Influenced by the gaggle of Logical Positivist Thinkers he found there (I have never had much time for Philosophizing myself), Gödel's interests drifted towards logic and the foundations of mathematics.

By 1931 – he was just twenty-five – Gödel had published his startling thesis on the eternal Incompleteness of Mathematics.

Later, he showed interest in the physicists' newly emerging studies of Space and Time, and he produced speculative papers on the possibility of time travel. (These must have been the published studies to which Nebogipfel had referred, I thought.) Soon, under pressure from the Reich, he was moved to

Berlin, where he began work on the military applications of time travelling.

We reached a door on which a brass plate bearing Gödel's name had been fixed – so recently, in fact, that I spotted spindles of wood from the drilling on the carpet below.

Wallis warned me that I could have only a few minutes on this visit. He knocked on the door.

A thin, high, voice within called: 'Come!'

We entered a roomy office with a high ceiling, fine carpet and rich wall-paper, and a desk inlaid with green leather. Once this room must have been sunny, I realized, for the wide windows – now curtained – faced westwards: in fact, in the direction of the Terrace where I was lodged.

The man at the desk continued to write as we entered; he kept his arm tucked around the page, evidently lest we see. He was a short, thin, sickly-looking man, with a high, fragile forehead; his suit was of wool and quite crumpled. He was in his thirties, I judged.

Wallis cocked an eyebrow at me. 'He's a rum cove,' he whispered, 'but a *remarkable* mind.'

There were book-shelves all around the room, though currently bare; the carpet was piled high with crates, and books and journals – mostly in German – had spilled out in uneven piles. In one crate I caught a glimpse of scientific equipment, and various sample bottles – and in one such, I saw something which made my heart pound with excitement!

I turned resolutely from the crate, and tried to conceal my agitation.

At last, with a gasp of exasperation, the man at the desk hurled his pen from him – it clattered against a wall – and he crumpled the written pages within his fists, before discarding the whole lot – everything he had written – in a waste-bin!

Now he glanced up, as if noticing we were there for the first time. 'Ah,' he said. 'Wallis.' He tucked his hands behind his desk and seemed to shrink inside himself.

'Professor Gödel, it's good of you to let us visit you. This is –' He introduced me.

'*Ah*,' Gödel said again, and he grinned, showing uneven teeth. 'Of course.' Now he stood, in angular jerks, and stepped around the desk and proffered his hand. I took it; it was thin, bony and cold. He said, 'The pleasure is mine. I anticipate we will have many engrossing discussions.' His English was good, lightly accented.

Wallis took the initiative and waved us to a set of arm-chairs close to the window.

'I hope you find a place for yourself in this New Age,' Gödel said to me sincerely. 'It may be a little more savage than the world you remember. But perhaps, like me, you will be tolerated as a useful Eccentric. Yes?'

Wallis blustered, 'Oh, come now, Professor –'

'Eccentric,' he snapped. '*Ekkentros* – out of the centre.' His eyes swivelled to me. 'That's what we both are, I suspect – a little out of the centre of things. Come, Wallis, I know you steady British think I'm a little odd.'

'Well –'

'Poor Wallis can't get used to my habit of my drafting and re-drafting my correspondence,' Gödel said to me. 'Sometimes I will go through a dozen drafts or more – and still finish by abandoning the piece altogether – as you saw! Is that strange? Well. So be it!'

I said, 'You must have some regrets at leaving your home, Professor.'

'None. *None*. I had to get away from Europe,' he said to me, and his voice was low, like a conspirator's.

'Why?'

281

'*Because of the Kaiser*, of course.'

Barnes Wallis shot me warning glares.

'I have evidence, you know,' Gödel said intently. 'Take two photographs – one from 1915, say, and one from this year, of the man *purporting* to be Kaiser Wilhelm. If you measure the length of the nose, and take its ratio with the distance from the tip of the nose to the point of the chin – you'll find it different!'

'I – ah – Great Scott!'

'Indeed. And with such a simulacrum at the helm – *who knows* where Germany is heading? Eh?'

'Quite,' said Wallis hastily. 'Anyway, whatever your motives, we're glad you accepted our offer of a Professorship here – that you chose Britain to make your home.'

'Yes,' I said, 'couldn't you have found a place in America? Perhaps at Princeton, or –'

He looked shocked. 'I'm sure I could. But it would be quite impossible. *Quite* impossible.'

'Why?'

'Because of the Constitution, of course!' And now this extraordinary chap went into a long and rambling discourse on how he had discovered a logical loop-hole in the American Constitution, which would allow the legal creation of a dictatorship!

Wallis and I sat and endured this.

'Well,' Gödel said when he had run down, 'what do you think of that?'

I got more stern looks from Wallis, but I decided to be honest. 'I can't fault your logic,' I said, 'but its application strikes me as outlandish in the extreme.'

He snorted. 'Well – perhaps! – but logic is everything. Don't you think? The axiomatic method is very powerful.' He smiled. 'I also have an ontological proof for the existence of God – quite faultless, as far as I can see – and with honourable antecedents, going back eight hundred years to Archbishop Anselm. You see –'

'Perhaps another time, Professor,' Wallis said.

'Ah – yes. Very well.' He looked from one to other of us – his gaze was piercing, quite unnerving. 'So. *Time travel.* I'm really quite envious of you, you know.'

'For my travelling?'

'Yes. But not for all this tedious hopping about through History.' His eyes were watery; they gleamed in the strong electric light.

'What, then?'

'Why, for the glimpses of other Worlds than this – other Possibilities – do you see?'

I felt chilled; his grasp seemed extraordinary – almost telepathic. 'Tell me what you mean.'

'The reality of other Worlds, containing a *meaning* beyond that of our brief existence, seems evident to me. Anyone who has experienced the wonder of mathematical discovery must *know* that mathematical Truths have an independent existence from the minds in which they lodge – that the Truths are splinters of the thoughts of some higher Mind.. . .

'Look: our lives, here on Earth, have but a dubious meaning. And so their true significance *must* lie outside this world. Do you see? So much is mere logic. And the idea that everything in the world has an ultimate Meaning is an exact analogue of the principle that everything has a Cause – a principle on which rests all of science.

'It follows, immediately, that somewhere beyond our History is the Final World – the World where all Meaning is resolved.

'Time travel, by its very nature, results in the perturbation of History, and hence the generation, or discovery, of Worlds other than this. Therefore the task of the Time Traveller is to *search* – to search on, until that Final World is found – or built!'

By the time we left Gödel, my thoughts were racing. I resolved never to mock Mathematical Philosophers again, for this odd little man had journeyed further in Time, Space and Understanding, without leaving his office, than I ever had in my Time Machine! And I knew that I must indeed visit Gödel again soon . . . for I was convinced that I had seen a flask of raw Plattnerite, tucked inside his crate!

11

THE NEW WORLD ORDER

I was returned to our lodging at about six. I came in calling halloos, and found the rest of my party in the smoking-room. The Morlock was still poring over his notes – he seemed to be trying to reconstruct the whole of this future science of Quantum Mechanics from his own imperfect memory – but he jumped up when I came in. 'Did you find him? Gödel?'

'I did.' I smiled at him. 'And – yes! – you were right.' I glanced at Filby, but the poor old chap was dozing over a magazine, and could not hear us. '*I think Gödel has some Plattnerite.*'

'*Ah.*' The Morlock's face was as inexpressive as ever, but he thumped one fist into the other palm in a decidedly human gesture. 'Then there is hope.'

Now Moses walked up to me; he handed me a glass of what proved to be whisky-and-water. I gulped at the drink gratefully, for the day had stayed as hot as in the morning.

Moses moved a little closer to me, and the three of us bent our heads together and spoke quietly. 'I've come to a conclusion as well,' Moses said.

'Which is?'

'That we must indeed get out of here – by any means possible!'

Moses told me the story of his day. Growing bored with his confinement, he had struck up conversations with our young soldier-guards. Some of these were privates, but others were Officer-class; and all of those assigned to guard us and to other duties in this scientific campus area were generally intelligent and well-educated. They seemed to have taken a liking to Moses, and had invited him to a nearby hostelry – the Queen's Arms in Queen's Gate Mews – and later they had taken rickshaws into the West End. Over several drinks, these young people had evidently enjoyed arguing through their ideas – and the concepts of their new Modern State – with this stranger from the past.

For my part I was pleased that Moses seemed to be shaking off his timidity, and was showing interest in the world in which we found ourselves. I listened to what he had to say with fascination.

'These youngsters are all highly likeable,' Moses said. 'Competent – practical – clearly brave. But their views!'

The great concept of the future – Moses had learned – was to be *Planning*. When the Modern State was in place, as directed by a victorious Britain and her Allies, an Air and Sea Control would take effective possession of all the ports, coal mines, oil wells, power stations and mines. Similarly a Transport Control would take over the world's shipyards and turn them away from warships to manufacturing steel cargo ships by the score. The Allied Supply Control would organize the production of iron, steel, rubber, metals, cotton, wool and vegetable substances. And the Food Control . . .

'Well!' Moses said. 'You get the picture. It's an end of Ownership, you see; all these resources will be owned by the new Allied World State. The resources of the world will be made to work together, at last, for the repair of the War-ravaged lands – and later, for the betterment of Humanity. All *Planned*, you see, by an all-wise, all-knowing Fellowship – who, by the by, will elect themselves!'

'Aside from that last, it doesn't sound so bad,' I mused.

'Maybe – but this Planning isn't to stop with the physical resources of the planet. It includes the *human* resources as well.

'And that's where the problems start. First of all there is *behaviour*.' He looked at me. 'These youngsters don't look back with much favour on our times,' he said. 'We suffer from a "profound laxity of private conduct" – so I was informed! These new types have gone back the other way: towards a severe austerity – particularly regarding sexual excitement. Decent busy-ness! – that is the order of the day.'

I felt a twinge of nostalgia. 'I suppose this bodes ill for the future of the Empire, Leicester Square.'

'Closed already! Demolished! – to make way for a *Railway Planning Office.*

'And it goes on. In the *next* phase, things will get a little more active. We will see the painless destruction of the more "pitiful sorts of defectives" – these are not my words! – and also the sterilization of some types who would otherwise have transmitted tendencies that are, I quote, "plainly undesirable".

'In some parts of Britain, it seems, this cleansing process has already begun. They have a type of gas called Pabst's Kinetogens . . .

'Well. You can see that they are making a start here at directing Humanity's racial heredity.'

'Hum,' I said. 'I find myself with a deep distrust of such *normalizing*. Is it really so desirable that the future of the human species should be filtered through the "tolerance" of the Englishman of 1938? Should *his* long shadow stretch down, through all the millions of years to come?'

'It's all *Planning*, you see,' Moses said. 'And, they

say, the only alternative is a relapse through chaotic barbarism – to final extinction.'

'Are men – modern men – capable of such epochal deeds?'

Moses said, 'There will surely be bloodshed and conflict on a scale not yet envisaged – even by the standards of this dull, ghastly War – as the majority of the world resists the imposition of a flawed Plan by these Allied technocrats.'

I met Moses's eyes, and I recognized there a certain righteous anger, an infuriation at the foolishness of mankind, which had informed my own, younger soul. I had always had a distrust of the advancement, willy-nilly, of civilization, for it seemed to me an unstable edifice which must one day collapse about the foolish heads of its makers; and this Modern State business seemed about the most extreme folly, short of actual War, I had heard in a while! It was as if I could see Moses's thoughts in his grey eyes – he had thrown off his funk, and become a younger, more determined version of me – and I had not felt closer to him since we met.

'Well, then,' I said, 'the matter is decided. I don't think any of us can tolerate such a future.' Moses shook his head – Nebogipfel appeared to acquiesce – and, for my part, I renewed my resolve to put an end to this time-travelling business once and for all. 'We must escape. But how –'

And then, even before I could finish framing the question, the house shook.

I was hurled down, nearly catching my head on the desk. There was a rumble – a deep boom, like the slamming of a door, deep inside the earth. The lamps flickered, but did not die. All around me there were cries – poor Filby whimpered – and I heard the tinkle of glass, the clatter of falling furniture.

The building seemed to settle. Coughing, for an

inordinate quantity of dust had been raised, I struggled to my feet. 'Is everyone all right? Moses? Morlock?'

Moses had already turned to help Nebogipfel. The Morlock seemed unhurt, but he'd got himself caught under a fallen bookcase.

I let them be and looked for Filby. The old chap had been lucky; he'd not even been thrown out of his chair. But now he stood up and made his way to the window, which was cracked clean across.

I reached him and put my arms around his bowed shoulders. 'Filby, my dear chap – come away.'

But he ignored me. His rheumy eyes streaming with water, and his face caked with dust, he raised a crooked finger to the window. '*Look.*'

I leaned closer to the glass, cupping my hand against the reflection of the electric lamps. The Babble Machine Aldis lamps had died, as had many of the street-lamps. I saw people running, distraught – an abandoned bicycle – a soldier with his mask over his face, firing shots into the air . . . and there, a little further in the distance, was a shaft of brilliant light, a vertical slice of scudding dust-motes; it picked out a cross-section of streets, houses, a corner of Hyde Park. People stood in its glare, blinking like owls, their hands before their faces.

The shaft of brilliancy was daylight. The Dome was breached.

12

THE GERMAN ASSAULT
ON LONDON

Our street door was hanging from its hinges, evidently shaken open by the concussion. There was no sign of the soldiers who had been guarding us – not even of the faithful Puttick. Outside in the Terrace, we heard the clatter of running footsteps, screams and angry shouts, the shrill of whistles, and we could smell dust, smoke and cordite. That fragment of June daylight, bright and sharp, hung over everything; the people of cara-paced London blinked like disturbed owls, baffled and terrified.

Moses clapped me on the shoulder. 'This chaos won't last long; now's our chance.'

'Very well. I'll fetch Nebogipfel and Filby; you collect some supplies from the house –'

'Supplies? What supplies?'

I felt impatient and irritated: what fool would proceed into time equipped with nothing more than a house-coat and slippers? 'Oh – candles. And matches! As many as you can find. Any fashion of a weapon – a kitchen knife will do if there's nothing better.' *What else – what else?* 'Camphor, if we have it. Underwear! – fill your pockets with the stuff . . .'

He nodded. 'I understand. I'll pack a satchel.' He turned from the door and made for the kitchen.

I hurried back to the smoking room. Nebogipfel had donned his schoolboy's cap; he had gathered up his notes and was slipping them into a cardboard file. Filby – poor old devil! – was down on his knees beneath the window-frame; he had his bony knees tucked up against his concave chest, and his hands were up before his face, like a boxer's guard.

I knelt before him. 'Filby. Filby, old chap –' I reached out to him but he flinched from me. 'You must come with us. It's not safe here.'

'Safe? And will it be safer with you? Eh? You . . . *conjurer*. You *quack*.' His eyes, flooded with tears from the dust, were bright, like windows, and he hurled those words at me as if they were the vilest insults imaginable. 'I remember you – when you scared the life out of all of us with that damned ghost trick of yours, that Christmas-time. Well, I'll not be fooled again!'

I restrained myself from shaking him. 'Oh, have some sense, man! Time travel is no trick – and certainly this desperate War of yours isn't!'

There was a touch on my shoulder. It was Nebogipfel; his pale fingers seemed to glow in the fragments of daylight from the window. 'We cannot help him,' he said gently.

Filby had dropped his head into his trembling, liver-spotted hands now, and I was convinced he could no longer hear me.

'But we can't leave him like this!'

'What will you do – restore him to 1891? The 1891 you remember doesn't even exist any more – except across some unreachable Dimension.'

Now Moses burst into the smoking room, a small, crammed knapsack in his hand; he had donned his epaulettes and his gas mask was at his waist. 'I'm ready,' he gasped. Nebogipfel and I did not respond immediately, and Moses glanced from one to the other of us. 'What is it? What are you waiting for?'

I reached out and squeezed Filby's shoulder. At

least he did not resist, and I took this as a last shred of friendly contact between us.

That was the last I saw of him.

We looked out into the street. This had been a comparatively quiet part of London, to my memory; but today people poured through the Queen's Gate Terrace, running, stumbling, bumping up against each other. Men and women had simply decanted from their homes and work-places. Most of them had their heads hidden by gas masks, but where I could see faces, I read pain, misery and fear.

There seemed to be children everywhere, mostly in drab school uniforms, with their small, shaped gas masks; for the schools had evidently been closed up. The children wandered about the street, crying for their parents; I considered the agony of a mother searching for a child in the huge, teeming ant-hill which London had become, and my imagination recoiled.

Some people carried the paraphernalia of the working day – briefcases and handbags, familiar and useless – and others had already gathered up bundles of household belongings, and bore them in bulging suitcases or wrapped up in curtains and sheets. We saw one thin, intense man stumbling along with an immense dresser, packed no doubt with valuables, balanced on the handlebars and saddle of a bicycle. The wheel of his cycle bumped against backs and legs. 'Go on! Go on!' he cried, to those ahead of him.

There was no evidence of authority or control. If there were policemen, or soldiers, they must have been overwhelmed – or had torn off their insignia and joined the rush. I saw a man in the uniform of the Salvation Army; he stood on a step and bawled: 'Eternity! Eternity!'

Moses pointed. 'Look – the Dome is breached to the east, towards Stepney. So much for the impregnability of this marvellous Roof!'

I saw that he was right. It looked as if a great Bomb had punched an immense hole in the concrete shell, close to the eastern horizon. Above that main wound, the Dome had cracked like an eggshell, and a great irregular ribbon of blue sky was visible, almost all the way up to the Dome's zenith above me. I could see that the damage hadn't settled yet, for bits of masonry – some the size of houses – were raining down, all over that part of the city, and I knew that the damage and loss of life on the ground must be vast.

In the distance – to the north, I thought – I heard a sequence of dull booms, like the footsteps of a giant. All around us the air was rent by the wail of sirens – 'ulla, ulla, ulla' – and by the immense groans of the broken Dome above us.

I imagined looking down from the Dome, on a London transformed in moments from a fearful but functioning city to a bowl of chaos and terror. Every road leading west, south or north, away from the Dome breach, would be stippled black with streaming refugees, with each dot in that stippling representing a human being, a mote of physical suffering and misery: each one a lost child, a bereft spouse or parent.

Moses had to shout over the cacophony of the street. 'That confounded Dome is going to come down on us all, any minute!'

'I know. We must get to Imperial College. Come on – use your shoulders! Nebogipfel, help us if you can.'

We stepped to the middle of the crowded street. We had to go eastwards, against the flow of the crowd. Nebogipfel, evidently dazzled by the daylight, was almost knocked down by a running, moon-faced man in a business suit and epaulettes who shook his fist at the Morlock. After that, Moses and I kept the Morlock between us, each with a skinny arm clamped in one fist. I collided with a cyclist, almost knocking him off his vehicle; he screamed at me, incoherent, and swung a bony punch, which I ducked; then he wobbled on into the press of people behind me, his tie draped over his shoulder. Now there came a fat woman who stumbled backwards up the street, lugging a rolled-up carpet behind her; her skirt had ridden up over her knees, and her calves were streaked with dust. Every few feet, some other refugee would stand on her carpet, or a cyclist's wheel would run over it, and the woman would stumble; she wore her mask, and I could see tears pooling behind those goggles as she struggled with the unreasonable, unmanageable mass that was so important to her.

Where I could see a human face it didn't seem so bad, for I could feel a shard of fellow feeling for this red-eyed clerk, or that tired shopgirl; but, with the gas masks, and in that patchy, shadowed illumination, the crowd was rendered anonymous and insectile; it was as if I had once more been transported away from the earth to some remote planet of nightmares.

Now there came a new sound – a thin, shrill monotone, which pierced the air. It seemed to me it came from that breach to the east. The crowds around us seemed to pause in their scrambling past each other, as if listening. Moses and I looked at each other, baffled as to the meaning of this new, menacing development.

Then the whistling stopped.

In the silence that followed, a single voice set up a call: 'Shell! That's a bloomin' shell –'

Now I knew what those distant giant's footsteps to

294

the north had signified: it was the landing of an artillery barrage.

The pause broke. The panic erupted around us, more frantic than ever. I reached over Nebogipfel and grabbed at Moses's shoulders; without ceremony I wrestled him, and the Morlock, to the ground, and a layer of people stumbled around us, covering us with warm, squirming flesh. In that last moment, as limbs battered against my face, I could hear the thin voice of that Salvation Army man, still shrieking out his call: 'E-ternity! E-ternity!'

And then there was a flash, bright even under that heap of flesh, and a surge of motion through the earth. I was lifted up – my head cracked against another man's – and then I was cast to the ground, for the moment insensible.

THE SHELLING

I awoke to find Moses with his hands under my arm-pits, dragging me from beneath fallen bodies. My foot caught on something – I think it was a bicycle-frame – and I cried out; Moses gave me a moment to twist my foot free of the obstruction, and then he hauled me free.

'Are you all right?' He touched my forehead with his finger-tips, and they came away bloody. He had lost his knapsack, I saw.

I felt dizzy, and a huge pain seemed to be hovering around my head, waiting to descend; I knew that when I lost this momentary numbness, I should suffer indeed. But there was no time. 'Where's Nebogipfel?'

'Here.'

The Morlock stood in the street, unharmed; he had lost his cap, though, and his goggles were starred by some flying fragment. His notes were scattered about, their file having burst, and Nebogipfel watched the pages blow away.

People had been scattered like skittles by the blast and concussion. All round us, they lay in awkward positions, with body on top of body, flung arm, twisted feet, open mouth, staring eyes, old men on top of young women, a child lying on a soldier's back. There was much stirring and groaning, as people struggled to rise – I was reminded of nothing so much as a heap of insects, squirming over each other – and here and there I saw splashes of blood, dark against flesh and clothing.

'My God,' Moses said with feeling. 'We have to help these people. Can you see –?'

'No,' I snapped at him. 'We *can't* – there are too many; there's nothing we can do. We're lucky to be alive – don't you see that? And now that the guns have got their range – Come! We have to stick to our intention; we have to escape from here, and into time.'

'I can't bear it,' Moses said. 'I've never seen such sights.'

The Morlock came up to us now. 'I fear there's worse to see before we're done with this century of yours,' he said grimly.

So we went on. We stumbled over a road surface become slippery with blood and excrement. We passed a boy, moaning and helpless, evidently with a shattered leg; despite my earlier admonitions, Moses and I were quite unable to resist his plaintive weeping and cries for help, and we bent to lift him from where he lay, close to the body of a milkman, and we sat him up against a wall. A woman emerged from the crowd, saw the child's plight and came to him; she began to wipe his face with a handkerchief.

'Is she his mother?' Moses asked me.

'I don't know. I –'

That odd, liquid voice sounded behind us, like a call from another world. '*Come.*'

We went on, and at length we reached the corner of Queen's Gate with the Terrace; and we saw how this had been the epicentre of the blast.

'No gas, at least,' I said.

'No,' Moses said, his voice tight. 'But – oh, God! – this is enough!'

There was a crater, torn into the road surface, a few

297

feet across. Doors were beaten in, and there was not a window left intact as far as I could see; curtains dangled, useless. There were subsidiary craters in the pavements and walls, left by bits of shrapnel from the exploded shell.

And the people . . .

Sometimes language is incapable of portraying the full horror of a scene; sometimes the communication of remembered events between humans, which is the basis of our shared society, breaks down. This was one such time. I could not communicate the horror of that London street to anyone who did not witness it.

Heads were blown off. One lay on the pavement, quite neatly, beside a small suitcase. Arms and legs littered the scene, most still clothed; here I saw one outstretched limb with a watch at the wrist – I wondered if it was still working! – and here, on a small, detached hand which lay close to the crater, I saw fingers curled upwards like a flower's petals. To describe it so sounds absurd – comical! Even at the time I had to force myself to understand that these detached *components* had comprised, a few minutes ago, conscious human beings, each with a life and hope of his own. But these bits of cooling flesh seemed no more human to me than the pieces of a smashed-up bicycle, which I saw scattered across the road.

I had never seen such sights before; I felt detached from it all, as if I were moving through the landscape of a dream – but I knew that I should forever revisit this carnage in my soul. I thought of the Interior of the Morlocks' Sphere, and imagined it as a bowl filled with a million points of horror and suffering, each as ghastly as this. And the thought that such madness could descend on London – *my* London –

298

filled me with an anguish that caused a sensation of actual physical pain in my throat.

Moses was pallid, and his skin was covered by a sheen of fine sweat and dust; his eyes were huge and flickered about, staring. I glanced at Nebogipfel. Behind his goggles, his large eyes were unblinking as he surveyed that awful carnage; and I wondered if he had begun to believe that I had transported him – not into the past – but to some lower Circle of Hell.

14

THE ROTA-MINE

We struggled through the last few dozen yards to the walls of Imperial College; and there we found, to my dismay, our way blocked by a soldier, masked and with a rifle. This fellow – stout-hearted, but evidently quite without imagination – had stayed at his post, while the gutters of the street before him had turned red with blood. His eyes became huge, behind their protective discs of glass, at the sight of Nebogipfel.

He did not recognize me, and he adamantly would not let us pass without the proper authority.

There was another whistle in the air; we all cringed – even the soldier clutched his weapon to his chest like a totemic shield – but, this time, the shell fell some distance from us; there was a flash, a smash of glass, a shudder of the ground.

Moses stepped up to the soldier with his fists clenched. His distress at the bombing seemed to have metamorphosed into anger. 'Did you hear that, you confounded uniformed flunky?' he bellowed. 'It's all chaos anyway! What are you guarding? What's the point any more? Can't you *see* what's happening?'

The guard pointed his rifle at Moses's chest. 'I'm warning you, chappy –'

'No, he *doesn't* see.' I interposed myself between Moses and the soldier; I was dismayed by Moses's evident lack of control, regardless of his distress.

Nebogipfel said, 'We may find another way. If the College walls are breached –'

'No,' I said with determination. 'This is the route I know.' I stepped up to the soldier. 'Look, Private, I don't have authority to pass you – but I have to assure you I'm important for the War Effort.'

Behind the soldier's mask, his eyes narrowed.

'Make a call,' I insisted. 'Send for Dr Wallis. Or Professor Gödel. They'll vouch for me – I'm sure of it! Please check, at least.'

At length – and with his gun pointed at us – the trooper backed into his doorway, and lifted a light telephone receiver from the wall.

It took him several minutes to complete the call. I waited with mounting anguish; I could not have borne to be kept away from an escape into time by such a pettifogging obstacle – not after having made it through so much! At last, grudgingly, he said: 'You're to go to Dr Wallis's office.' And with that our simple, brave soldier stood aside, and we stepped out of the chaos of that street and into the comparative calm of Imperial College.

'We'll report to Wallis,' I told him. 'Don't worry. Thank you . . .!'

We entered that maze of enclosed corridors I have described earlier.

Moses let out a grunt of relief. 'Just our luck,' he said, 'to come up against the only soldier still at his post in all of confounded London! The hopeless little fool –'

'How can you be so contemptuous?' I snapped. 'He is a common man, doing the job he's been given as best he can, in the middle of all this – a madness not of his making! What more do you want from a man? Eh?'

'Huh! How about imagination? Flair, intelligence, initiative –'

We had come to a halt and stood nose to nose.

'*Gentlemen,*' Nebogipfel said. 'Is this the time for such navel-gazing?'

Moses and I stared at the Morlock, and at each other. In Moses's face, I saw a sort of vulnerable fear which he masked with this anger – looking into his eyes was like peering into a cage at a terrified animal – and I nodded at him, trying to transmit reassurance.

The moment passed, and we moved apart.

'Of course,' I said in an attempt to break the tension, 'you never do any navel-gazing, do you, Nebogipfel?'

'No,' the Morlock said easily. 'For one thing I do not have a navel.'

We hurried on. We reached the central office block and set off in search of Wallis's room. We moved through carpeted corridors, past rows of brass-plated doors. The lights were still burning – I imagined the College had its own, secured supply of electricity – and the carpet deadened our footsteps. We saw no one about. Some of the office doors were open, and there were signs of hasty departure: a spilled cup of tea, a cigarette burning down in an ash tray, papers scattered across floors.

It was hard to believe that carnage reigned only a few dozen yards away!

We came to an opened door; a bluish flicker emanated from it. When we reached the doorway, the single occupant – it was Wallis – was perched on the corner of the desk. 'Oh! – it's you. I'm not sure I expected to see you again.' He wore his wire spectacles, and a tweed jacket over a woollen tie; he had one epaulette attached and his gas mask on the desk beside him; he was evidently in the midst of preparations to evacuate the building with the rest, but he had let himself be distracted. 'This is a desperate business,' he said. 'Desperate!' Then he looked at us more closely – it was as if he was seeing us for the first time. 'Good God, you're in a state!'

We moved into the room, and I could see that the blue flickering came from the screen of a small, glass-fronted box. The screen showed a view down a stretch of river, presumably the Thames, in rather grainy detail.

Moses leaned forward, with his hands on his knees, the better to see the little set. 'The focus is pretty poor,' he said, 'but it's quite a novelty.'

Despite the urgency of the moment, I too was intrigued by the device. This was evidently the picture-carrying development of the phonograph which Filby had mentioned.

Wallis snapped a switch on his desk, and the picture changed; it was the same in its broad details – the river, winding through built-over landscape – but the lighting was a little brighter. 'Look here,' he said, 'I've been watching this film over and over since it happened. I really can't quite believe my eyes . . . Well,' he said, 'if we can dream up such things, I suppose *they* can too!'

'Who?' Moses asked.

'The Germans, of course. The blessed Germans! Look: this view is from a camera fixed up at the top of the Dome. We're looking east, beyond Stepney – you can see the curve of the river. Now: look here – in she comes –'

We saw a flying machine, a black, cross-shaped craft, sweeping low over the shining river. It came in from the east.

'You see, it's not easy to Bomb a Dome,' Wallis said. 'Well, that's the point, of course. The whole thing's pretty much solid masonry, and it's all held together by gravity as much as by steel; any small breaches tend to heal themselves . . .'

Now the flying machine dropped a small package

towards the water. The image was grainy, but the package looked cylindrical, and it was glinting in the sunlight, as if spinning as it fell.

Wallis went on, 'The fragments from an air-burst will simply hail off the concrete, by and large. Even a Bomb placed, somehow, directly against the face of the Dome won't harm it, in ordinary instances, because so much of the blast goes off into the air – do you see?

'But there is a way. I knew it! *The Rota-Mine* – or Surface Torpedo . . . I wrote up a proposal myself, but it never progressed, and I had no energy – not with this DChronW business as well . . . Where the Dome meets the river, you see, the carapace extends *beneath* the surface of the water. The purpose is to keep out attack by submersibles and so forth. Structurally the whole thing is like a dam.

'Now – if you can place your Bomb against the part of the Dome *beneath* the water . . .' Wallis spread his large, cultured hands to mime it. 'Then the water will *help* you, you see; it contains the blast and directs the energy inward, into the structure of the Dome.'

On the screen, the package – the German Bomb – struck the water. And it *bounced*, in a mist of silvery spray, and leapt on, over the surface of the water, towards the Dome. The flying machine tipped to its right and swept away, quite graceful, leaving its Rota-Mine to stride on towards the Dome in successive parabolic arcs.

'But how to deliver a Bomb, accurately, to such an inaccessible place?' Wallis mused. 'You can't simply drop the thing. Sticks end up scattered all over the shop . . . If you drop a mine even from a modest height of, say, fifteen thousand feet, a crosswind of just ten miles an hour will create two hundred yards' inaccuracy.

'But then it came to me,' he said. 'Give it a bit of back-spin, and your Bomb could *bounce* over the water – one can work out the laws of ricochet with a bit of experiment and make it all quite accurate . . . Did I tell you about my experiments at home on this subject, with my daughter's marbles?

'The Mine bounces its way to the foot of the Dome, and then slides down its face, *under* the water, until it reaches the required depth . . . And there it is. A perfect placement!' He beamed, and with his shock of white hair and those uneven glasses, he looked quite avuncular.

Moses squinted at the imprecise images. 'But this Bomb looks to me as if it's going to fail . . . Its bounces will surely leave it short . . . *ah.*'

Now a plume of smoke, brilliant white even in the poor image, had burst from the back of the Rota-Mine. The Bomb leapt across the water, as if invigorated.

Wallis smiled. 'Those Germans – you have to admire them. Even *I* never thought of that little wrinkle . . .'

The Rota-Mine, its rocket-engine still blazing, passed beneath the curve of the Dome and out of sight of the camera. And then the image shuddered, and the screen filled with a formless blue light.

Barnes Wallis sighed. 'They've done for us, it looks like!'

'What about the German shelling?' Moses asked.

'The guns?' Wallis scarcely sounded interested. 'Probably hundred-and-five-mil Light-Gun 42s, dropped in by paratroop units. All in advance of the Invasion by Sea and Air that's to follow, I don't doubt.' He took off his glasses and began to polish them on the end of his tie. 'We're not finished yet. But this is a desperate business. Very bad indeed . . .'

'Dr Wallis,' I said, 'what about Gödel?'

'Hum? Who?' He looked at me from large, fatigue-rimmed eyes. 'Oh, Gödel. What about him?'

'Is he here?'

'Yes, I should think so. In his office.'

Moses and Nebogipfel made for the door; Moses indicated, urgently, that I should follow. I held up my hand.

'Dr Wallis – won't you come with us?'

'Whatever for?'

'We might be stopped before we reach Gödel. We must find him.'

He laughed and thrust his glasses back over his nose. 'Oh, I don't think security and any of *that* matters very much any more. Do you? Anyway – here.' He reached up to his lapel and tugged free the numbered button that was clipped there. 'Take this – tell them I'm authorizing you – if you meet anyone mad enough to be at his post.'

'You might surprised,' I said with feeling.

'Hum?' He turned back to his television set. Now it was showing a random assortment of scenes, evidently taken from a series of cameras about the Dome: I saw flying machines take to the air like black gnats, and lids in the ground which were drawn back to reveal a host of Juggernaut machines which toiled out of the ground, spitting steam, to draw up in a line which stretched, it seemed to me, from Leytonstone to Bromley; and all this great horde pressed forward, breaking up the earth, to meet the invading Germans. But then Wallis pressed a switch, and these fragments of Armageddon were banished, as he made his record of the Rota-Mine run through again.

'A desperate business,' he said. 'We could have had it first! But what a marvellous development . . . even I wasn't sure if it could be *done*.' His gaze was locked on the screen, his eyes hidden by the flickering, meaningless reflection of the images.

And that was how I left him; with an odd impulse towards pity, I closed his office door softly behind me.

15

THE TIME-CAR

Kurt Gödel stood at the uncurtained window of his office, his arms folded. 'At least the gas hasn't come yet,' he said without preamble. 'I once witnessed the result of a gas attack, you know. Delivered by English bombers on Berlin, as it happens. I came down the *Unter den Linden* and along the *Sieges Allee*, and there I came upon it . . . So undignified! The body corrupts so quickly, you know.' He turned and smiled sadly at me. 'Gas is very *democratic*, do you not think?'

I walked up to him. 'Professor Gödel. Please . . . We know you have some Plattnerite. I saw it.'

For answer, he walked briskly to a cupboard. As he passed a mere three feet from Nebogipfel, Gödel did no more than glance at him; of all the men I met in 1938, Gödel showed the coolest reaction to the Morlock. Gödel took a glass jar from the cupboard; it contained a substance that sparkled green, seeming to retain the light.

Moses breathed, '*Plattnerite.*'

'Quite so. Remarkably easy to synthesize from Carolinum – if you know the recipe, and have access to a fission pile for irradiation.' He looked mischievous. 'I wanted you to see it,' he said to me; 'I hoped you would recognize it. I find it delightfully easy to tweak the nose of these pompous Englishmen, with their Directorates of This and That, who could not recognize the treasure under their own noses! And now it will be your passage out of this particular Vale of Tears – yes?'

'I hope so,' I said fervently. 'Oh, I hope so.'

'Then come!' he shouted. 'To the CDV workshop.' And he held the Plattnerite up in the air like a beacon, and led us out of the office.

Once more we entered that labyrinth of concrete corridors. Wallis had been right: the guards had universally left their posts, and, although we came across one or two white-coated scientists or technicians hurrying through the corridors, they made no attempt to impede us, nor even to inquire where we were going.

And then – *whump!* – a fresh shell hit.

The electric lights died, and the corridor rocked, throwing me to the ground. My face collided with the dusty floor, and I felt warm blood start from my nose – my face must have presented a fine sight by now – and I felt a light body, I think Nebogipfel's, tumble against my leg.

The shuddering of the foundations ceased within a few seconds. The lights did not return.

I was taken by a fit of coughing, for concrete dust was thick on the air, and I suffered a remnant of my old terror of darkness. Then I heard the fizz of a match – I caught a brief glimpse of Moses's broad face – and I saw him apply the flame to a candle wick. He held up the candle, cupping the flame in his hands, and its yellow light spread in a pool through the corridor. He smiled at me. 'I lost the knapsack, but I took the precaution of loading some of those supplies you recommended in my pockets,' he said.

Gödel got to his feet, a little stiffly; he was (I saw with gratitude) cradling the Plattnerite against his chest, and the jar was unbroken. 'I think that one must have been in the grounds of the College. We must be grateful to be alive; for these walls could easily have collapsed in on us.'

So we progressed through those gloomy corridors. We were impeded twice by fallen masonry, but with a little effort we were able to clamber through. By now I was disoriented and quite lost; but Gödel – I could see him ahead of me, with the Plattnerite jar glowing under one arm – made his way quite confidently.

Within a few more minutes we reached the annexe Wallis had called the CDV Development Division. Moses lifted his candle up, and the light glimmered about the big workshop. Save for the lack of lights, and one long, elaborate crack which ran diagonally across the ceiling, the workshop remained much as I remembered it. Engine parts, spare wheels and tracks, cans of oil and fuel, rags and overalls – all the paraphernalia of a workshop – lay about the floor; chains dangled from pulleys fixed to brackets on the ceiling, casting long, complex shadows. In the centre of the floor I saw a half-drunk mug of tea, apparently set down with some care, with a thin layer of concrete dust scumming the liquid's surface.

The one almost-complete Time-Car sat in the centre of the floor, its bare gun-metal finish shining in the light of Moses's candle. Moses stepped up to the vehicle and ran a hand along the rim of its boxy passenger compartment. 'And this is it?'

I grinned. 'The pinnacle of 1930s technology. A "Universal Carrier," I think Wallis called it.'

'Well,' Moses said, 'it's scarcely an elegant design.'

'I don't think elegance is the point,' I said. 'This is a weapon of war: not of leisure, exploration or science.'

Gödel moved to the Time-Car, set the Plattnerite jar on the floor, and made to open one of the steel flasks welded to the hull of the vehicle. He wrapped his hands around the screw-cap lid and grunted with exertion, but could not budge it. He stepped back, panting. 'We must prime the frame with Plattnerite,' he said. 'Or –'

Moses set his candle on a shelf and cast about in the piles of tools, and emerged with a large adjustable wrench. 'Here,' he said. 'Let me try with this.' He closed the clamps about the cap's rim and, with a little effort, got the cap unstuck.

Gödel took the Plattnerite jar and tipped the stuff into the flask. Moses moved around the Time-Car, unfixing the caps of the remaining flasks.

I made my way to the rear of the vehicle, where I found a door, held in place by a metal pin. I removed the pin, folded the door downwards, and clambered into the cabin. There were two wooden benches, each wide enough to take two or three people, and a single bucket seat at the front, facing a slit window. I sat in the driver's bucket seat.

Before me was a simple steering wheel – I rested my hands on it – and a small control panel, fitted with dials, switches, levers and knobs; there were more levers close to the floor, evidently to be operated by the feet. The controls had a raw, unfinished look; the dials and switches were not labelled, and wires and mechanical transmission levers protruded from the rear of the panel.

Nebogipfel joined me in the cabin, and he stood at my shoulder; the strong, sweet smell of Morlock was almost overpowering in that enclosed space. Through the slit window I could see Gödel and Moses, filling up the flasks.

Gödel called, 'You understand the principle of the CDV? This is all Wallis's design, of course – I've had nothing much to do with the construction of it –'

I brought my face up against the slit window. 'I am at the controls,' I said. 'But they're not labelled. And

I can see nothing resembling a chronometric gauge.'

Gödel did not look up from his careful pouring. 'I've a suspicion such niceties as chronometric dials aren't yet fitted. This is an incomplete test vehicle, after all. Does that trouble you?'

'I have to admit the prospect of losing my bearings in time does not appeal to me very much,' I said, 'but – no – it is scarcely important . . . One can always ask the natives!'

'The principle of the CDV is simple enough,' Gödel said. 'The Plattnerite suffuses the sub-frames of the vehicle through a network of capillaries. It forms a kind of circuit . . . When you close the circuit, you will travel in time. Do you see? Most of the controls you have are to do with the petrol engine, transmission, and so forth; for the vehicle is also a functioning motor-car. But to close the time-circuit there is a blue toggle, on your dashboard. Can you recognize it?'

'I have it.'

Now Moses had fixed the last of the flask caps back into place, and he walked around the car to the door at its rear. He clambered in and placed his wrench on the floor, and he pounded his fists against the cabin's inner walls. 'A good, sturdy construction,' he said.

I said, 'I think we are ready to depart.'

'But where – *when* – are we going *to*?'

'Does it matter? *Away from here* – that's the only significant thing. Into the past – to try to rectify things . . .

'Moses, we are done with the Twentieth Century. Now we must take another leap into the dark. Our adventure is not over yet!'

His look of confusion dissolved, and I saw a reck-less determination take its place; the muscles of his jaw set. 'Then let's do it, or be damned!'

Nebogipfel said: 'I think we quite possibly will be.'

I called: 'Professor Gödel – come aboard the car.'

'Oh, no,' he said, and he held his hands up before him. 'My place is here.'

Moses pushed into the cabin behind me. 'But London's walls are collapsing around us – the German guns are only a few miles away – it's hardly a safe place to be, Professor!'

'I do envy you, of course,' Gödel said. 'To leave this wretched world with its *wretched* War . . .'

'Then come with us,' I said. 'Seek that Final World of which you spoke –'

'I have a wife,' he said. His face was a pale streak in the candle-light.

'Where is she?'

'I lost her. We did not succeed in getting out together. I suppose she is in Vienna . . . I cannot imagine they would harm her, as punishment for my defection.'

There was a question in his voice, and I realized that this supremely logical man was looking to me, in that extreme moment, for the most illogical reassurance! 'No,' I said, 'I am sure she –'

But I never completed my sentence, for – without even the warning of a whistle in the air – a new shell fell, and this was the closest of all!

The last flicker of our candle showed me, in a flash-bulb slice of frozen time, how the westerly wall of the workshop burst inwards – simply that; it turned from a smooth, steady panel into a billowing cloud of fragments and dust, in less than a heartbeat.

Then we were plunged into darkness.

The car rocked, and – '*Down!*' Moses called – I ducked – and a hail of masonry shards, quite lethal, rattled against the shell of the Time-Car.

Nebogipfel climbed forward; I could smell his

313

sweet stink. His soft hand grasped my shoulder. 'Close the switch,' he said.

I peered through the slit-window – and into utter darkness, of course. 'What of Gödel?' I cried. 'Professor!'

There was no reply. I heard a creak, quite ominous and heavy, from above the car, and there was a further clatter of falling masonry fragments.

'*Close the switch,*' Nebogipfel said urgently. 'Can you not hear? The roof is collapsing – we will be crushed!'

'I'll get him,' Moses said. In pitch darkness, I heard his boots clump over the car's panels as he made his way to the rear of the cabin. 'It will be fine – I've more candles . . .' His voice faded as he reached the rear of the cabin, and I heard his feet crunch on the rubble strewn floor –

– and then there was an immense groan, like a grotesque gasp, and a rushing from above. I heard Moses cry out.

I twisted, intending to dive out of the cabin after Moses – and I felt a nip of small teeth in the soft part of my hand – Morlock teeth!

At that instant, with Death closing in around me, and plunged into primal darkness once more, the presence of the Morlock, his teeth in my flesh, the brush of his hair against my skin: it was all unbearable! I roared and drove my fist into the soft flesh of the Morlock's face.

. . . But he did not cry out; even as I struck him, I felt him reach past me to the dash-board.

The darkness fell from my eyes – the roar of collapsing concrete diminished into silence – and I found myself falling once more into the grey light of time travel.

16

FALLING INTO TIME

The Time-Car rocked. I grasped for the bucket seat, but I was thrown to the floor, clattering my head and shoulders against a wooden bench. My hand ached, irrelevantly, from the Morlock's nip.

White light flooded the cabin, bursting upon us with a soundless explosion. I heard the Morlock cry out. My vision was blurred, impeded by the mats of blood which clung to my cheeks and eyebrows. Through the rear door and the various slit-windows, a uniform, pale glow seeped into the shuddering cabin; at first it flickered, but it soon settled to a washed-out grey glow. I wondered if there had been some fresh catastrophe: perhaps this workshop was being consumed by flames . . .

But then I recognized that the quality of light was too steady, too neutral for that. I understood that we had already gone far beyond that War-time laboratory.

The glow was, of course, daylight, rendered featureless and bland by the overlaying of day and night, too fast for the eye to follow. We had indeed fallen into time; this car – though crude and ill-balanced – was functioning correctly. I could not tell if we were falling into future or past, but the car had already taken us to a period beyond the existence of the London Dome.

I got my hands under me and tried to rise, but

there was blood – mine or the Morlock's – on my palms, and they slid out from under me. I tumbled back to the hard floor, thumping my head on the bench once more.

I fell into a huge, bone-numbing fatigue. The pain of my rattling about during the shellings, deferred by the scramble I had been through, now fell on me with a vengeance. I let my head rest against the floor's metal ribs and closed my eyes. 'What's it all for, anyhow?' I asked, of no-one in particular. *Moses was dead* . . . lost, with Professor Gödel, under tons of masonry in that destroyed lab. I had no idea whether the Morlock was alive or dead; nor did I care. Let the Time-Car carry me to future or past as it would; let it go on forever, until it smashed itself to pieces against the walls of Infinity and Eternity! Let there be an end to it – I could do no more. 'It's not worth the candle,' I muttered. 'Not worth the candle . . .'

I thought I felt soft hands on mine, the brush of hair against my face; but I protested, and – with the last of my strength – pushed the hands away.

I fell into a deep, dreamless, comfortless darkness.

I was woken by a severe buffeting.

I was rattled against the floor of the cabin. Something soft lay under my head, but that slipped away, and my skull banged against the hard corner of a bench. This renewed hail of pain brought me to my senses, and, with some reluctance, I sat up.

My head ached pretty comprehensively and my body felt as if it had been through a gruelling boxing-bout. But, paradoxically, my mood seemed a little improved. The death of Moses was still there in my mind – a huge event, which I knew I must confront, in time – but after those moments of blessed unconsciousness I was able to look away from

316

it, as one might turn away from the blinding light of the sun, and consider other things.

That dim, pearly mixture of day and night still suffused the interior of the car. It was quite remarkably cold; I felt myself shiver, and my breath fogged before my face. Nebogipfel sat in the pilot's bucket seat, his back turned to me. His white fingers probed at the instruments in the rudimentary dash-board, and he traced the wires which dangled from the steering column.

I got to my feet. The car's swaying, together with the battering I had endured in 1938, left me uncertain on my feet; to steady myself I had to cling to the cabin's ribbed framework, and found the metal ice-cold under my bare hands. The soft item which had been cushioning my head, I found, was the Morlock's blazer. I folded it up and placed it on a bench. I also saw, dropped on the floor, the heavy wrench which Moses had used to open the Plattnerite flasks. I picked it up with my fingertips; it was splashed with blood.

I still wore my heavy epaulettes; disgusted by these bits of armour, I ripped them from my clothes and dropped them with a clatter.

At the noise, Nebogipfel glanced towards me, and I saw that his blue goggles were cracked in two, and that one huge eye was a mess of blood and broken flesh. 'Prepare yourself,' he said thickly.

'What for? I –'

And the cabin was plunged into darkness.

I stumbled backwards, almost falling again. An intense cold sucked the remaining warmth out of the cabin air, and from my blood; and my head pounded anew. I wrapped my arms around my torso. 'What has happened to the daylight?'

The voice of the Morlock seemed almost harsh in that swaying blackness. 'It will last only a few seconds. We must endure . . .'

And, as quickly as it had come, the blackness receded, and the grey light seeped into the cabin once more. Some of the edge of that immense cold was blunted, but still I shivered violently. I knelt on the floor beside Nebogipfel's seat. 'What is happening? What was that?'

'*Ice*,' he said. 'We are travelling through an Age of Periodic Glaciation; ice-sheets and glaciers are sweeping down from the north and covering the land – overwhelming us in the process – and then melting away. At times, I would hazard, there is as much as a hundred feet of ice above us.'

I peered through the slit-windows in the car's front panel. I saw a Thames valley made over into a bleak tundra inhabited only by tough grass, defiant blazes of purple heather, and sparse trees; these latter shivered through their annual cycles too fast for me to follow, but they looked to me like the hardier varieties: oak, willow, poplar, elm, hawthorn. There was no sign of London: I could make out not even the ghosts of evanescent buildings, and there was no evidence of man in all that grey landscape, nor indeed of any animal life. Even the shape of the landscape, the hills and valleys, seemed unfamiliar to me, as it was remade over and again by the glaciers.

And now – I saw it approach in a brief flood of white brilliance, before it overwhelmed us – the great Ice came again. In darkness, I cursed, and dug my hands into my arm-pits; my fingers and toes were numb, and I began to fear frostbite. When the glaciers receded once more, they left a landscape inhabited by much the same variety of hardy plants, as far as I could see, but with its contours adjusted: evidently the intervals of Ice were remaking the landscape, though I could not tell if we were proceeding into future or past. As I watched, boulders taller than men seemed to migrate across the landscape, taking slow slithers or rolls; this was clearly some odd effect of the erosion of the land.

'For how long was I unconscious?'

'Not long. Perhaps thirty minutes.'

'And is the Time-Car taking us into the future?'

'We are penetrating the past,' the Morlock said. He turned to face me, and I saw how his graceful movements had been reduced to stiff jerks by the fresh pummelling I had inflicted on him. 'I am confident of it. I caught a few glimpses of the recession of London – its withering, back to its historical origins . . . From the intervals between Glaciations, I should say we are travelling at some tens of thousands of years every minute.'

'Perhaps we should work out how we might stop this car's headlong drive into time. If we find an equable age –'

'I do not think we have any way *of* terminating the flight of the car.'

'*What?*'

The Morlock spread his hands – I saw how the hair on the back of them was sprinkled with a light frost – and then we were plunged once more into a darkened sepulchre of Ice, and his voice floated out of the obscurity. 'This is a crude, unfinished test vehicle, remember. Many of the controls and indicators are disconnected; those that *do* have connections largely appear non-functional. Even if we knew how to modify the workings without wrecking the vehicle, I can see no way for us to get out of the cabin and to reach the inner mechanism.'

We emerged from the Ice into that reshaped tundra once more. Nebogipfel watched the landscape with some fascination. 'Think of it: the fjords of Scandinavia are not yet cut, and the lakes of Europe and North America – deposited by melting ice – are phantasms of the future.

'Already, we have passed beyond the dawn of human history. In Africa we might find races of Australopithecines – some of them clumsy, some gracile, some carnivorous, but all with a bipedal gait and ape-like features: a small brain-case and large jaws and teeth . . .'

A great, cold loneliness descended on me. I had been lost in time before, but never, I thought, had I suffered quite this intensity of isolation! Was it true – *could* it be true – that Nebogipfel and I, in our damaged Time-Car, represented the only candle-flames of intelligence on the whole of the planet?

'So we are out of control,' I said. 'We may not stop until we reach the beginning of time . . .'

'I doubt it will come to that,' Nebogipfel said. 'The Plattnerite must have some finite capacity. It cannot propel us deeper into time, *forever*; it must exhaust itself. We must pray that it does so before we pass through the Ordovician and Cambrian time-layers – before we reach an Age in which there is no oxygen to sustain us.'

'That's a cheerful prospect,' I said. 'And things may become worse still, I suppose.'

'How?'

I got my stiff legs out from under me and sat on the cold, ribbed metal floor. 'We have no provisions, of any kind. No water, no food. And we're both injured. We don't even have warm clothing! How long can we survive, in this freezing time-barque? A few days? Less?'

Nebogipfel did not reply.

I am not a man to submit easily to Fate, and I invested some energy in studying Nebogipfel's controls and wires. I soon learned he was right – there was no way I could find to build this tangle of components into a dirigible vehicle – and my energy,

320

sapped as it was, was soon spent: I reverted to a sort of dull apathy.

We passed through one more brief, brutal Glaciation; and then we entered a long, bleak winter. The seasons still brought snow and ice flickering across the land, but the Age of Permanent Ice lay in the future now. I saw little change in the nature of the landscape, millennium on millennium: perhaps there was a slow enrichment of the texture of the blur of greenery that coated the hills. An immense skull – it reminded me of an elephant's – appeared on the ground not far from the Time-Car, bleached, bare and crumbled. It persisted long enough for me to make out its contours, a second or so, before it vanished as fast as it had appeared.

'Nebogipfel – about your face. I – you have to understand . . .'

He regarded me from his one good eye. I saw he had reverted to his Morlock mannerisms, losing the human coloration he had adopted. '*What?* What must I understand?'

'I didn't mean to injure you.'

'You do not *now*,' he said with a surgeon's precision. 'But you did *then.* Apology is futile – absurd. You are what you are . . . we are different species, as divergent from each other as from the Australopithecines.'

I felt like a clumsy animal, my huge fists stained once more with the blood of a Morlock. 'You shame me,' I said.

He shook his head, a brief, curt gesture. 'Shame? The concept is without meaning, in this context.'

I should no more feel *shame* – I saw he meant – than should some savage animal of the jungle. If attacked by such a creature, would I argue the morals of the case with it? No – without intelligence, it could not help its behaviour. I should merely deal with its actions.

To Nebogipfel, I had proved myself – again! – to be little better than those clumsy brutes of the African plains, the precursors of men in this desolate period.

I retreated to the wooden benches. I lay there, cradling my aching head with my arm, and watched the flicker of Ages beyond the still-open door of the car.

17

THE WATCHER

The bleak, wintry cold passed, and the sky took on a more complex, mottled texture. Occasionally the rocking sun-band would be blotted out by a shell of dark cloud, for as long as a second. New species of trees flourished in this milder climate: deciduous types, as best I could make out, maple, oak, poplar cedars and others. Sometimes these antique forests lapped over the car, shutting us into a twilight of flickering green-brown, and then receded, as if a curtain had been drawn aside.

We had entered a time of powerful earth movements, Nebogipfel said. The Alps and Himalayas were being forced out of the ground, and immense volcanoes were spewing ash and dust into the air, sometimes obscuring the sky for years on end. In the oceans – the Morlock said – great sharks cruised, with teeth like daggers. And in Africa, the ancestors of Humanity were shrivelling back into primitive mindlessness, with shrinking brains, stooping gait and blunted, clumsy fingers.

We fell through that long, savage Age for perhaps twelve hours.

I tried to ignore the hunger and thirst that clawed at my belly, while centuries and forests flickered past the cabin. This was the longest journey through time I had taken since my first plunge into the remote future beyond Weena's History, and the immense, futile emptiness of it all – for hour after unchanging hour – began to depress my soul. Already the brief flourishing of humanity was a remote sliver of light, far away in time; even the distance between man and Morlock – of whatever variety – was but a fraction of the great distance I had travelled.

The hugeness of time, and the littleness of man and his achievements, quite crushed me; and my own, petty concerns seemed of absurd insignificance. The story of Humanity seemed trivial, a flash-lamp moment lost in the dark, mindless halls of Eternity.

The earth's crust heaved like the chest of a choking man, and the Time-Car was lifted or dropped with the evolving landscape; it felt like the swell of an immense sea. The vegetation grew more lush and green, and new forests pressed up against the Time-Car – I thought they were deciduous trees by now, though flowers and leaves were reduced to a uniform green blur by our velocity – and the air grew warmer.

The ache of those aeons of cold left my fingers at last, and I discarded my jacket and loosened the buttons of my shirt; I abandoned my boots and flexed the circulation back into my toes. Barnes Wallis's numbered security badge fell out of my jacket pocket. I picked it up, this little symbol of man's suspicious fencing-off of his fellow man, and I do not think I could have found, in that primeval greenness, a more perfect symbol of the narrowness and absurdity on which so much human energy is wasted! I threw the badge into a dark corner of the car.

The long hours, suspended in that cloaking greenery, passed more slowly than ever, and I slept for a while. When I woke, the quality of the greenness around me seemed to have changed – it was more translucent, with something of the shade of Plattnerite, and I thought I saw a hint of star-fields –

it was like being immersed in emeralds, rather than leaves.

Then I saw it: it hovered in the moist, gloomy air of the cabin, immune to the rocking of the car, with its huge eyes, fleshy 'V' of a mouth, and those articulated tentacles which trailed towards, but did not touch, the floor. This was no phantasm – I could not see *through* it, to details of the forest beyond – and it was as real as me, Nebogipfel, or the boots I had set on the bench.

The Watcher regarded me with a cool analysis.

I felt no fear. I reached out towards it, but it bobbled away through the air. I had no doubt that its grey eyes were fixed on my face. 'Who are you?' I asked. 'Can you help us?'

If it could hear, it did not respond. But the illumination was already changing; that light-suffused quality of the air was fading back to a vegetable greenness. I caught a sensation, then, of *spinning* – that great skull was like some improbable toy, turning on its axis – and then it was gone.

Nebogipfel walked up to me, his long feet picking over the floor's ribs. He had discarded his nineteenth-century clothes, and he went naked, save for his battered goggles and the coat of white hair on his back, now tangled and grown out. 'What is it? Are you ill?'

I told him of the Watcher, but he had seen nothing of it. I returned to my rest on the bench, uncertain if what I had witnessed was real – or a lingering dream.

The heat was oppressive, and the air in the cabin grew stifling.

I thought of Gödel, and of Moses.

That unprepossessing man, Gödel, had *deduced* the existence of Multiple Histories, purely from ontological principles – while I, poor fool that I am, had

'The Watcher regarded me with a cool analysis.'

needed several trips through time before the possibility had even occurred to me! But now, that man who had dreamed his magnificent dreams of the Final World, a world in which all Meaning is resolved, lay crushed and broken under a heap of masonry – killed by the narrowness and stupidity of his fellow men.

And as for Moses: for him, I simply grieved. It was something of the desolation one might feel if a child is killed, I think, or a younger brother. Moses was dead at twenty-six; and yet I – *the same person* – breathed on at four-and-forty! My past had been cut out from under me; it was as if the ground had evaporated, leaving me stranded in the air. But beyond this I had come to know Moses, if briefly, as a person in his own regard. He had been cheerful, erratic, impulsive, a little absurd – just like me! – and immensely likeable.

It was another death on my hands!

All Nebogipfel's double-talk of a Multiplicity of Worlds – all the possible arguments that the Moses I had known was never, in the end, destined to be *me*, but some other *variant* of me – none of that made any difference to the way it felt to have lost *him*.

My thoughts dissolved into half-coherent fragments – I struggled to keep my eyes open, fearing I should not wake again – but, once more, consumed by confusion and grief, I slept.

I was woken by my name, pronounced in the Morlock's odd, liquid guttural. The air was as foul as before, and a new throb, caused by the heat and lack of oxygen, was jostling for room in my skull with the residue of my earlier injuries.

Nebogipfel's battered eyes were huge in that arboreal gloom. 'Look around,' he said.

The greenery pressed about us with as much persistence as before – and yet now the texture seemed

different. I found that – with care – I was able to
follow the evolution of single leaves on the crowding
branches. Each leaf sprang from the dust, went
through a sort of reverse withering, and crumpled
into its bud in less than a second, but even so –

'We are slowing,' I breathed.

'Yes. The Plattnerite is losing its potency, I think.'

I uttered a prayer of thanks – for my strength had
recovered sufficiently that I no longer wished to die
on some airless, rocky plain at the dawn of the earth!

'Do you know where we are?'

'Somewhere in the Palaeocene Era. We've been
travelling for twenty hours. We are perhaps fifty
million years before the present . . .'

'Whose present? – mine, of 1891, or yours?'

He touched the blood still matted over his face.
'On such timescales it scarcely matters.'

The blossoming of leaves and flowers was now
quite slow – almost stately. I became aware of a
flickering, of impermanent intrusions of deeper
darkness, superimposed on the general green
gloom. 'I can distinguish night and day,' I said.
'We're slowing.'

'Yes.' The Morlock sat on the bench opposite me
and gripped its edge with his long fingers. I
wondered if he was afraid – he had every right to be!
I thought I saw a motion in the floor of the car, a
gentle, upward bulging below Nebogipfel's bench.

'What should we do?'

He shook his head. 'We can only wait on events.
We are hardly in a controlled situation . . .'

The flapping of night and day slowed further, until
it became a steady pulse around us, like a heartbeat.
The floor creaked, and I saw stress-marks appear in
its steel plates . . .

Suddenly I understood!

I cried, 'Look out!' I stood, reached over and

grabbed Nebogipfel by the shoulders. He did not resist. I lifted him as if he were a skinny, hairy child, and stumbled backwards –

– and a tree accreted out of the air before me, ripping the car's metal like paper. One immense branch probed towards the controls like the arm of some huge, purposeful man of wood, and smashed through the casing's front panel.

We were evidently arriving in the space occupied by this tree, in this remote era!

I fell backwards against a bench, cradling Nebogipfel. The tree shrank a little, as we receded towards the moment of its birth. The flapping of night and day grew slower, still more ponderous. The trunk narrowed further – and then, with an immense crack, the cabin of the car broke in two, snapped open from within like an egg-shell.

I lost hold of Nebogipfel, and the Morlock and I tumbled to the soft, moist earth, amid a hail of metal and wood.

BOOK FOUR

The Palaeocene Sea

1

DIATRYMA GIGANTICA

I found myself on my back, peering up at the tree which had riven through our Time-Car as we fell out of diluted presentation. I heard Nebogipfel's shallow breathing close by, but I could not see him.

Our tree, now frozen in time, soared up to join its fellows in a canopy, thick and uniform, far above me, and shoots and seedlings sprouted from the ground around its base, and through the wrecked components of the car. The heat was intense, the air moist and difficult for my straining lungs, and the world around me was filled with the coughs, trills and sighs of a jungle, all overlaid on a deep, richer rumble which made me suspect the presence of a large body of water nearby: either a river – some primeval version of the Thames – or a sea.

It was more like the Tropics than England!

Now, as I lay there and watched, an animal came clambering down the trunk towards us. It was something like a squirrel, about ten inches long, but its coat was wide and loose, and hung about its body like a cloak. It carried a fruit in its little jaws. Ten feet from the ground this creature spotted us; it cocked its sharp head, opened its mouth – dropping its fruit – and hissed. I saw that its incisor teeth divided at their tips, into five-pronged combs. Then it leapt headlong from its tree trunk. It spread its arms and legs wide and its cloak of skin opened out with a snap, turning the animal into a sort of fur-covered kite. It soared away into the shadows, and was lost to my view.

'Quite a welcome,' I gasped. 'It was like a flying lemur. But did you see its teeth?'

Nebogipfel – still out of my sight – replied, 'It was a *planetatherium*. And the tree is a *dipterocarps* – not much changed from the species which will survive in the forests of your own day.'

I pushed my hands into the mulch under me – it was quite rotten and slippery – and endeavoured to turn so that I could see him. 'Nebogipfel, are you injured?'

The Morlock lay on his side, his head twisted so that he was staring at the sky. 'I am not hurt,' he whispered. 'I suggest we begin a search for –'

But I was not listening; for I had seen – just behind him – a beaked head, the size of a horse's, pushing through the foliage, and dipping down towards the Morlock's frail body!

For an instant I was paralysed by shock. That hooked beak opened with a sort of liquid pop, and disc-shaped eyes fixed on me with every evidence of intelligence.

Then, with a heavy swoop, the great head ducked down and clamped its beak over the Morlock's leg. Nebogipfel screamed, and his small fingers scrabbled at the ground, and bits of leaf clung to his coat of hair.

I scrambled backwards, kicking at the leaves to get away, and finished up against a tree trunk.

Now, with a crackle of smashed branches, the beast's body came lumbering through the greenery and into my view. It was perhaps seven feet tall, and coated with black, scaly feathers; its legs were stout, with strong, clawed feet, and covered with a sagging yellow flesh. Residual wings, disproportionately small on that immense torso, beat at the air. This bird-monster hauled its head back, and the poor Morlock was dragged across the mulchy ground.

'Nebogipfel!'

'It is a *Diatryma*,' he gasped. 'A *Diatryma Gigantica*, I – *oh!*'

'Never mind its phylogeny,' I cried, 'get away from it!'

'I am afraid – I have no way to – *oh!*' Again his speech disintegrated into that wordless yowl of anguish. Now the creature twisted its head from side to side. I realized that it was endeavouring to club the Morlock's skull against a tree trunk – no doubt as a preliminary to making a feast of his pale flesh!

I needed a weapon, and could think only of Moses's wrench. I got to my feet and scrambled into the wreckage of our Time-Car. A profusion of struts, panels and wires lay about, and the steel and polished wood of 1938 looked singularly out of place in this antique forest. I could not see the wrench! I plunged my arms, up to the elbows, into the decaying ground cover. It took long, agonizing seconds of searching; and all the while the *Diatryma* dragged its prize further towards the forest.

And then I had it! – my right arm emerged from the compost clasping the handle of the wrench.

With a roar, I raised the wrench to shoulder height and plunged through the mulch. *Diatryma*'s bead-like eyes watched me approach – it slowed its head-shaking – but it did not loosen its grip on Nebogipfel's leg. It had never seen men before, of course; I doubted that it understood that I could be a threat to it. I kept up my charge, and tried to ignore the awful, scaly skin around the claws of the feet, the immensity of the beak, and the whiff of decaying meat that hung about the thing.

In the manner of a cricket stroke, I swung my

makeshift club – *thump* – into *Diatryma*'s head. The blow was softened by feathers and flesh, but I felt a satisfying collision with bone.

The bird opened its beak, dropping the Morlock, and squawked; it was a noise like sheet-metal tearing. That huge beak was poised above *me* now, and every instinct told me to run – but I knew that if I did we should both be done for. I raised my wrench back over my head, and launched it towards the crown of the *Diatryma*'s skull. This time the creature ducked, and I caught it only a glancing blow; so, after completing my swing, I lifted up my wrench and smote against the underside of the beak.

There was a splintering noise, and *Diatryma's* head snapped back. It reeled, then it gazed at me with eyes alight with calculation. It emitted a squawk so deep-pitched it was more like a growl.

Then – quite suddenly – it shivered up its black feathers, turned, and hobbled away into the forest.

I tucked the wrench into my belt and knelt beside the Morlock. He was unconscious. His leg was a crushed, bloody mess, the hair on his back soaked by the bird-monster's looping spittle.

'Well, my companion in time,' I whispered, 'perhaps there are occasions when it is useful to have an antique savage on hand, after all!'

I found his goggles in the mulch, wiped them clear of leaves on my sleeve, and placed them over his face.

I peered into the forest's gloom, wondering what I should do next. I may have travelled in time, and across space to the Morlocks' great Sphere – but in my own century, I had never journeyed to any of the Tropical countries. I had only dim recollections of travellers' tales and other popular sources to guide me now in my quest for survival.

But at least, I consoled myself, the challenges that

lay ahead would be comparatively *simple!* I would not be forced to face my own younger self – nor, since the Time-Car was wrecked, would I have to deal with the moral and philosophical ambiguities of Multiple Histories. Rather, I must simply seek food, and shelter against the rain, and to protect us against the beasts and birds of this deep time.

I decided that finding fresh water must be my first mission; even leaving aside the needs of the Morlock, my own thirst was raging, for I had had no sustenance since before the shelling of London.

I placed the Morlock in the midst of the Time-Car's wreckage, close to the tree trunk. I thought it as safe a place as anywhere from the predations of the monsters of this Age. I doffed my jacket and placed it under his back, to protect him from the moisture of the mulch – and anything that crawled and chewed that might live therein! Then, after some hesitation, I took the wrench from my belt and laid it over the Morlock, so that his fingers were wrapped around the weapon's heavy shaft.

Reluctant to leave myself weaponless, I cast about in the car's wreckage until I found a short, stout piece of iron ribbing, and I bent this sideways until it broke free from the frame. I hefted this in my hand. It did not have the satisfying solidity of my wrench, but it would be better than nothing.

I decided to make for that sound of water; it seemed to lie in a direction away from the sun. I rested my club on my shoulder and struck out through the forest.

2

THE PALAEOCENE SEA

It was not difficult to make my way, as the trees grew from loose, mixed stands, with plenty of level earth between; the thick, even canopy of leaves and branches excluded the light from the ground, and seemed to be suppressing growth there.

The canopy swarmed with vigorous life. Epiphytes – orchids and creepers – clung to the trees' bark surfaces, and lianas dangled from branches. There were a variety of birds, and colonies of creatures living in the branches: monkeys, or other primates (I thought, at that first glance). There was a creature something like a pine marten, perhaps eight inches long, with flexible shoulders and joints and a rich, bushy tail, which scampered and leapt through the branches, emitting a cough-like cry. Another climbing animal was rather larger – perhaps a yard long – with grasping claws and a prehensile tail. This did not flee at my approach; rather it clasped the underside of a branch and peered down at me with unnerving calculation.

I walked on. The local fauna were ignorant of man, but had evidently developed strong preservation instincts thanks to the presence of Nebogipfel's *Diatryma*, and no doubt other predators, and they would be wary of my attempts to hunt them.

As my eyes became attuned to the general forest background, I saw that camouflage and deception

338

were everywhere. Here was a decaying leaf, for instance, clinging to the trunk of a tree – or so I thought, until, at my approach, the 'leaf' sprouted insectile legs, and a cricket-like creature hopped away. Here, on an outcropping of rock, I saw what looked like a scattering of raindrops, glinting like little jewels in the canopy-filtered light. But when I bent to inspect them, I saw these were a clutch of beetles, with transparent carapaces. And here was a splash of guano on a tree-trunk, a stain of white and black – and I was scarcely surprised to see it uncurl languid spider-legs.

After perhaps half a mile of this, the trees thinned; I walked through a fringe of palm trees and into the glare of sunlight, and rough, young sand scraped against my boots. I found myself at the head of a beach. Beyond a strip of white sand a body of water glittered, so wide I could not see its far side. The sun was low in the sky behind me, but quite intense; I could feel its warmth pressing on the flesh of my neck and scalp.

In the distance – some way from me, along the long, straight beach – I saw a family of *Diatryma* birds. The two adults preened, wrapping their necks around each other, while three fledglings waded about on their ungainly legs, splashing and hooting, or sat in the water and shivered moisture into their oily feathers. The whole ensemble, with their black plumage, clumsy frames and minuscule wings, looked comical, but I kept a careful eye on their movements while I was there, for even the smallest of the youngsters was three or four feet tall, and quite muscular.

I walked to the edge of the water; I moistened my fingers and licked them. The water was salty: *sea water.*

I thought the sun had dipped lower, behind the forest, and it must be descending into the west. Therefore I had walked perhaps half a mile to the *east* of the Time-Car's position, so here I was – I pictured it – somewhere near the intersection of Knightsbridge and Sloane Street. And, in this Palaeocene Age, it was the fringe of a Sea! I was looking across this ocean, which appeared to cover all of London to the east of Hyde Park Corner. Perhaps, I mused, this Sea was some extension of the North Sea or Channel, which had intruded into London. If I was right, we had been quite lucky; if the level of the seas had raised itself just a little further, Nebogipfel and I should have emerged into the depths of the ocean, and not at its shore.

I took off my boots and socks, tied them to my belt by their laces, and waded a short way into the water. The liquid was cool as it worked around my toes; I was tempted to dip my face into it, but I refrained, for fear of the interaction of the salt with my wounds. I found a depression in the sand, which looked as if it would form a pool at low tide. I dug my hands into the sand here, and came up immediately with a collection of creatures: burrowing bivalves, gastropods, and what looked like oysters. There seemed to be a small variety of species, but there was evidently a high abundance of specimens in this fertile Sea.

There at the fringe of that ocean, with the gurgling water lapping about my toes and fingers, and with the sun warm on my neck, a great feeling of peace descended on me. As a child I had been taken for day-trips by my parents to Lympne and Dungeness, and I would walk to the edge of the Sea – just as I had today – and imagine I was alone in the world. But now, it was nearly true! It was remarkable to think that no ships sailed this new ocean, anywhere in the world; that there were no cities of men on the other side of the jungle behind me – indeed, the only flickers of intelligence on the planet were myself, and the poor, wounded Morlock. But it was not a forbidding prospect – not a bit of it – not after the awful darkness and chaos of 1938, which I had so recently escaped.

I straightened up. The Sea was charming, but we could not drink salt water! I took careful note of the point at which I had emerged from the jungle – I had no wish to lose Nebogipfel in that arboreal gloom – and I struck barefoot out along the water's edge, away from the family of *Diatryma*.

After perhaps a mile, I came to a brook which bubbled out of the forest, and came trickling down the beach to the Sea. When I tested this, I found it to be fresh water, and it seemed quite clear. I felt a great access of relief: at least we should not die today! I dropped to my knees and plunged my head and neck in the cool, bubbling stuff. I drank down great gulps, and then took off my jacket and shirt and bathed my head and neck. Crusted blood, stained brown by exposure to the air, swirled away towards the Sea; and when I straightened up I felt much refreshed.

Now I faced the challenge of how to transport this bounty to Nebogipfel. I needed a cup, or some other container.

I spent some minutes sitting by the side of that stream, peering about in a baffled fashion. All my ingenuity seemed to have been exhausted by my latest tumble through time, and this final puzzle was one step too far for my tired brain.

In the end, I took my boots from my belt, rinsed them out as well as I could, and filled them up with stream water; then I transported them back along the beach and through the forest, to the waiting Morlock. As I bathed Nebogipfel's battered face, and tried to rouse him to drink, I promised myself that the next day I should find something rather more suitable than an old boot to use as a dinner service.

Nebogipfel's right leg had been mangled by the assault of the *Diatryma*; the knee seemed crushed, and the foot was resting at an unnatural angle. Using a sharp fragment of Time-Car hull – I had no knife – I made a rudimentary effort to shave his flaxen hair from the damaged areas. I washed off the exposed flesh as best I could: at least the surface wounds seemed to have closed, and there was no sign of infection.

During my clumsy manipulations – I am no medical man – the Morlock, still unconscious, grunted and mewled with pain, like a cat.

Having cleaned the wounds, I ran my hands along the leg, but could detect no obvious break in the shin or calf bones. As I had noted before, the main damage seemed to be in the knee and ankle areas, and I registered this with dismay, for, while I might have been able to set a broken tibia by touch, I could see no way I could treat such damage as Nebogipfel had sustained. Still, I rummaged through the wreckage of our car until I had found two straight sections of framework. I took my improvised knife to my jacket – I did not anticipate the garment being terribly useful in such a climate as this – and produced a set of bandages, which I washed off.

Then, taking my courage in my hands, I straightened out the Morlock's leg and foot. I bound his leg tight to the splints, strapping it for support against the other, uninjured leg.

The Morlock's screams, echoing from the trees, were terrible to hear.

Exhausted, I dined that night on oysters – raw, for I had no strength to construct a fire – and I propped myself up, close to the Morlock, with my back against a tree trunk and Moses's wrench in my hand.

3

HOW WE LIVED

I established a camp on the shore of my Palaeocene Sea, close to that fresh-water brook I had found. I decided we should be healthier, and safer from attack, there rather than in the gloom of the forest. I set up a sunshade for Nebogipfel, using bits of the Time-Car with items of clothing stretched over them.

I carried Nebogipfel to this site in my arms. He was as light as a child, and still only half conscious; he looked up at me, helpless, through the ruins of his goggles, and it was hard for me to remember that he was a representative of a species which had crossed space, and tamed the sun!

My next priority was fire. The available wood – fallen branches and so forth – was moist and mouldy, and I took to carrying it out to the edge of the beach, to allow it to dry. With some fallen leaves to act as kindling, and a spark from a stone beaten against Time-Car metal, I was able to ignite a flame readily enough. At first I went through the ritual of restarting the fire daily, but soon discovered the doubtless ancient trick of keeping coals glowing in the fire's pit during the day, with which it was a simple matter to re-ignite the blaze as required.

Nebogipfel's convalescence progressed slowly. Enforced unconsciousness, to a member of a species who do not know sleep, is a grave and disturbing thing, and on his revival he sat in the shade for some days, passive and unwilling to talk. But he proved able to eat the oysters and bivalves I fetched up from the Sea, albeit with a deep reluctance. In time I was able to vary our diet with the cooked flesh of turtle – for that creature was quite abundant, all along the shore. After some practice, I succeeded in bringing down clusters of the fruits of the shoreline palm trees by hurling lumps of metal and rocks high into the branches. The nuts proved very useful: their milk and flesh varied our diet; their empty shells served as containers for a variety of purposes; and even the brown fibres which clung to the shells were capable of being woven into a crude cloth. However I have no great facility for such fine work, and I never got much further than making myself a cap – a broad-brimmed affair, like a coolie's.

Still, despite the munificence of the Sea and the palms, our diet was monotonous. I looked with envy at the succulent little creatures which clambered, out of my reach, through the branches of the trees above me.

I explored the shore of the Sea. Many types of creature inhabited that oceanic world. I observed wide, diamond-shaped shadows skimming the surface, which I believe were rays; and twice I saw upright fins – beating with purpose through the water, at least a foot high – which could only be the signs of huge sharks.

I spotted an undulating form, cruising through the surface of the water perhaps a half mile from land. I made out a wide, hinged jaw, inset with small, cruel teeth, and white flesh behind. This beast was perhaps five feet long, swimming by means of undulations of its sinuous body. I reported this sighting to Nebogipfel, who – retrieving a little more of that encyclopaedic body of data stored in his little skull – identified it as *Champsosaurus*: an ancient creature, related to the crocodile, and in fact a survivor of the Age of the Dinosaurs – an Age already long vanished by this Palaeocene period.

Nebogipfel told me that in this period, the ocean-going mammals of my century – whales, sea-cows and so forth – were in the midst of their evolutionary adaptation to the Sea, and lived still as large, slow-moving land animals. I kept a wary eye out for a basking land-whale, for surely I should be able to hunt down such a slow-moving animal – but I never saw one.

When I removed Nebogipfel's splints for the first time, the broken flesh showed itself to be healing. Nebogipfel probed at his joints, however, and pronounced that they had been set incorrectly. I was not surprised, but neither of us could think of a way to improve the situation. Still, after some time, Nebogipfel was able to walk, after a fashion, by using a crutch made of a shaped branch, and he took to hobbling about our little encampment like some desiccated wizard.

His eye, however – which I had ruined with my assault in the Time-Car workshop – did not recover, and remained without sight, to my deep regret and shame.

Being a Morlock, poor Nebogipfel was far from comfortable in the intensity of the daytime sun. So he took to sleeping through the day, within the shelter I constructed, and moving about during the hours of darkness. I stuck to the daylight, and so each of us spent most of his waking hours alone. We met and talked at twilight and dawn, although I have to admit that after a few weeks of open air, heat and hard physical labour, I was pretty much spent by the time the sun fell.

The palms had broad fronds, and I determined to

retrieve some of these, intent on using them to construct a better shelter. But all my efforts at hurling artefacts up into the trees were of no avail at fetching down the fronds, and I had no means of cutting down the palms themselves. So I was forced to resort to stripping down to my trousers and shinning up the trees like a monkey. Once at the crown of a tree, it was the work of moments to strip the fronds from the trunk and hurl them to the ground. I found those climbs exhausting. In the fresh sea air and sunshine, I was growing healthier and more robust; but I am not a young man, and I soon found a limit to my athletic ability.

With the retrieved fronds I constructed us a more substantial shelter, of fallen branches roofed over by plaited fronds. I made a wide hat of fronds for Nebogipfel. When he sat in the shade with this affair tied under his chin, and otherwise naked, he looked absurd.

As for me, I have always been pale of complexion, and after the first few days I suffered greatly from my exposure to the sun, and I learned caution. The skin peeled from my back, arms and nose. I grew a thick beard to protect my face, but my lips blistered in a most unsightly fashion – and the worst of it was the intense burning of the bald patch at my crown. I took to bathing my burns, and to wearing my hat and what remained of my shirt at all times.

One day, after perhaps a month of this, while I was shaving (using bits of Time-Car as blade and mirror), I realized, suddenly, how much I had changed. My teeth and eyes shone, brilliant white, from a mahogany-brown face, my stomach was as flat as it had been during my College days, and I walked about in a palm frond hat, cut-off trousers, and barefoot, as naturally as if I had been born to it.

I turned to Nebogipfel. 'Look at me! My friends

346

would barely recognize me – I'm becoming an aboriginal.'

His chinless face showed no expression. 'You *are* an aboriginal. This is England, remember?'

Nebogipfel insisted that we retrieve the components of our smashed Time-Car from the forest. I could see the logic of this, for I knew that in the days to come we should need every scrap of raw materials, particularly metals. So we salvaged the car, and assembled the remnants in a pit in the sand. When the more urgent of our survival needs were satisfied, Nebogipfel took to spending a great deal of time with this wreckage. I did not inquire too closely at first, supposing that he was constructing some addition to our shelter, or perhaps a hunting weapon.

One morning, however, after he had fallen asleep, I studied his project. He had reconstructed the frame of the Time-Car; he had laid out the shattered floor section, and built up a cage of rods around it, tied together with bits of wire salvaged from the steering column. He had even found that blue toggle switch which had closed the Plattnerite circuit.

When he next woke, I confronted him. 'You're trying to build a new Time Machine, aren't you?'

He dug his small teeth into palm-nut flesh. 'No. I am *rebuilding* one.'

'Your intention is obvious. You have remade the frame which bore the essential Plattnerite circuit.'

'As you say, that is obvious.'

'But it's futile, man!' I looked down at my callused and bleeding hands, and found myself resenting this diversion of his effort, while *I* was struggling to keep us alive. 'We don't have any Plattnerite. The stuff we arrived with is exhausted, and scattered about in the jungle anyway; and wc've no possible means of manufacturing any more.'

'If we build a Time Machine,' he said, 'we *may* not be able to escape from this Age. But if we do not build one, we *certainly* will not be able to escape.'

I growled. 'Nebogipfel, I think you should face facts. We are stranded, here in deep time. We will never find Plattnerite here, as it is not a naturally occurring substance. We can't make it, and no one will bring a sample to us, for no one has the faintest inkling that we are within ten million years of this era!'

For reply, he licked at the succulent meat of his palm-nut.

'*Pah!*' Frustrated and angry, I stalked about the shelter. 'You'd be better advised to spend your ingenuity and effort in making me a gun, so I can bag some of those monkeys.'

'They are not monkeys,' he said. 'The most common species are *miacis* and *chriacus* –'

'Well – whatever they are – *oh!*'

Infuriated, I stalked away.

My arguments made no difference, of course, and Nebogipfel continued with his patient rebuilding. But he did assist me in many ways in my quest to keep us alive, and after a time I grew to accept the presence of the rudimentary machine, glittering and complicated and exquisitely useless, there on that Palaeocene beach.

We all need hope, to give purpose and structure to our lives, I decided – and that machine, as flightless as great *Diatryma*, represented Nebogipfel's last hope.

4

ILLNESS AND RECUPERATION

I fell ill.

I was unable to rise from the crude pallet of fronds and dried leaves I had made for myself. Nebogipfel was forced to nurse me, which duty he performed without much in the way of bedside manner, but with patience and persistence.

Once, in the dark pit of night, I came to a state of half-consciousness with the Morlock's soft fingers probing at my face and neck. I imagined I was once more entrapped in the pedestal of that White Sphinx, with the Morlocks crowding around to destroy me. I cried out, and Nebogipfel scurried backwards; but not before I was able to lift my fist and strike him a blow in the chest. Enfeebled as I was, I retained sufficient strength to knock the Morlock off his feet.

That done, my energy was spent, and I lapsed into unconsciousness.

When I next came to wakefulness, there was Nebogipfel at my side again, patiently trying to induce me to take a mouthful of shellfish chowder.

At length my senses returned, and I found myself propped up on my pallet. I was alone in our little hut. The sun was low, but the heat of the day still lay on me. Nebogipfel had left a nutshell of water close to my pallet; I drank this.

The sunlight seeped away, and the warm, Tropical

darkness of evening settled over our lean-to. The sunset was tall and magnificent: this was because of a surplus of ash in the atmosphere, Nebogipfel had told me, deposited by volcanoes to the west of Scotland. This vulcanism would one day lead to the formation of the Atlantic Ocean; lava was flowing as far as the Arctic, Scotland and Ireland, and the warm climatic zone in which we found ourselves stretched as far north as Greenland.

Britain was already an island, in this Palaeocene, but compared to its configuration in the nineteenth century, its north-west corner was tipped up to a greater altitude. The Irish Sea had yet to form, so that Britain and Ireland formed a single landmass; but the south-east of England was immersed beneath the Sea whose margins we inhabited. My Palaeocene Sea was an extension of the North Sea; if we could have made a boat, we could have travelled across the English Channel and sailed into the heart of France through the Aquitaine Basin, a tongue of water which connected in turn to the Tethys Sea – a great ocean swamping the Mediterranean countries.

With the coming of night, the Morlock emerged from a deeper shade in the forest. He stretched – working his muscles more as a cat will than a human – and he massaged his injured leg. Then he spent some minutes on finger-combing the hair on his face, chest and back.

At length he came hobbling over to me; the purple light of the sunset glinted from his starred and cracked goggles. He fetched me more water, and with my mouth moistened, I whispered, 'How long?'

'Three days.'

I had to suppress a shudder at the sound of his queer, liquid voice. You might have thought I would be used to Morlocks by now; but after three days spent lying helpless, it came as something of a shock to be reminded that I was isolated in this hostile world, save only for this alien of the far future!

Nebogipfel made me some chowder. By the time I had eaten, the sunset was gone, and the only illumination came from a sliver of young moon which hung low in the sky. Nebogipfel had discarded his goggles, and I could see his huge, grey-red eye, hovering like the moon's translucent shadow in the dark of the hut.

'What I want to know is,' I said, 'what made me ill?'

'I am not certain.'

'Not certain?' I was surprised at this unusual admission of limitation, for Nebogipfel's breadth and depth of knowledge were extraordinary. I pictured the mind of a nineteenth-century man as something analogous to my old workshop: full of information, but stored in a quite haphazard way, with open books and scraps of notes and sketches scattered over every flat surface. By comparison with this jumble, the mind of a Morlock – thanks to the advanced educational techniques of the Year 657,208 – was ordered like the contents of a fine encyclopaedia, with the books of experience and learning indexed and shelved. All this raised the *practical* level of intelligence and knowledge to heights undreamed of by men of my time. 'Still,' he said, 'we should not be surprised at the *fact* of illness. I am, in fact, surprised you have not succumbed earlier.'

'What do you mean?'

He turned to me. '*That you are a man out of your time.*'

In a flash, I understood what he meant.

The germs of disease have taken toll of Humanity since the beginning – indeed, were cutting down the prehuman ancestors of man even in this ancient Age. But because of this grim winnowing of our kind we have developed resisting power. Our bodies struggle against all germs, and are altogether immune to some.

I pictured all those human generations which still lay ahead of this deep Age, those firefly human souls which would flicker in the darkness like sparks, before being extinguished forever! But those tiny struggles would not be in vain, for – by this toll of a billion deaths – man would buy his birthright of the earth.

It was different for the Morlock. By Nebogipfel's century, there was little left of the archetypal human form. Everything in the Morlock's body – bones, flesh, lungs, liver – had been adjusted by machinery to permit, Nebogipfel said, an ideal balance between longevity and richness of life. Nebogipfel could be wounded, as I had seen, but – according to him – his body was no more likely to catch a germ infection than was a suit of armour. And indeed, I had detected no signs of infection about his injured leg, or his eye. The original world of Eloi and Morlock had devised a different solution, I remembered, for I had seen no disease or infection there either, and little decay, and I had surmised that that was a world cleansed of harmful bacteria.

I, however, had no such protection.

After my first brush with illness, Nebogipfel turned his attention to more subtle aspects of our survival needs. He sent me foraging for supplements for our diet, including nuts, tubers, fruit, and edible fungi, all of which were added to our staples of sea food and the flesh of those animals and birds stupid enough to allow themselves to be entrapped by my clumsy hunting with slings and stones. Nebogipfel also attempted to derive simple medicines: poultices, herbal teas, and the like.

My illness filled me with a deep and abiding gloom, for this was a danger of time travel which had not occurred to me before. I shivered, and wrapped my arms around my still feeble body. My strength and intelligence could beat off *Diatryma*, and other massive natives of the Palaeocene, but they would offer me no defence against the predations of the invisible monsters borne by air, water and flesh.

5

THE STORM

Perhaps if I had had some experience of Tropical conditions before our stranding in the Palaeocene, I might have been prepared for the Storm.

The day had been heavy and more humid than usual, and the air near the Sea had that odd, light-impregnated quality one associates with a forthcoming change of weather. That evening, exhausted by my labours and uncomfortable, I was glad to fall into my pallet; at first, though, the heat was so great that sleep was slow to come.

I was woken by a slow patter of raindrops falling onto our loose roof of palm fronds. I could hear the rain coming down into the forest behind us – bullets of water hammering against the leaves – and pounding into the sand of the beach. I could not hear, or see, Nebogipfel; it was the darkest part of the night.

And then the Storm *fell* on us.

It was as if some lid had been opened up in the sky; gallons of rainwater came hurtling down, pushing in our palm-frond roof in a moment. The wreckage of our flimsy hut clattered down around me, and I was drenched to the skin; I was still on my back, and lay staring up into the rod-like paths of the raindrops, which receded into a cloud-obscured heaven.

I struggled to get up, but soaked roof-fronds impeded me, and my pallet turned into a muddy swamp. Soon I was coated in mud and filth, and with the water hammering at my scalp and trickling into my eyes, I was all but blind.

By the time I reached my feet, I was dismayed at the alacrity with which our shelter was collapsing; all its struts had fallen, or were leaning crazily. I could make out the boxy structure of Nebogipfel's recon-structed time-device, but it was already all but buried by bits of the hut.

I cast about in that sodden, slippery wreckage, dragging away fronds and bits of cloth. I found Nebogipfel: he looked like an oversize rat, with his hair plastered against his body and his knees tucked up against his chest. He had lost his goggles and was quivering, quite helpless. I was relieved to find him so easily; for the night was his normal time of operation, and he might have been anywhere within a mile or so of the hut.

I bent to scoop him up, but he turned to face me, his ruined eye a pit of darkness. 'The Time-Car! We must save the Time-Car!' His liquid voice was almost inaudible against the Storm. I reached for him again, but, feebly, he struggled away from me.

With the raindrops hammering against my scalp, I growled in protest; but, gamely, I waded through the litter of our home to Nebogipfel's device. I hauled great handfuls of fronds from it, but found the frame-work embedded in a deepening mud, all tangled up with clothes and cups and the remnants of our attempts at furniture. I took hold of the frame's uprights and tried to haul the whole thing free of the mud by main force, but succeeded only in bending the shape of the frame, and then in snapping open its corners.

I straightened up and looked about. The hut was quite demolished now. I saw how the water was begin-ning to run out of the forest, over the sand and down to the ocean. Even our friendly fresh-water stream was becoming broader and more angry, and itself threatened to burst its shallow banks and overrun us.

I abandoned the Time-Car and stalked over to Nebogipfel. 'It's all up,' I shouted to him. 'We have to get away from here.'

'But the time-device –'

'We have to chuck it! Can't you see? We're going to get washed into the Sea, at this rate!'

He strove to rise to his feet, with lanks of his hair dangling like bits of sodden cloth. I made to grab him, and he tried to wriggle out of my grasp; if he had been healthy, perhaps, he could have evaded me, but his damaged leg impeded him, and I caught him.

'I can't save it!' I shouted into his face. 'We'll be lucky to get out of this lot with our blessed lives!'

And with that I threw him over my shoulder, and stalked out of our hut and towards the forest. Instantly I found myself wading through inches of cold, muddy water. I slipped more than once on the squirming sand, but I kept one arm wrapped around the wriggling body of the Morlock.

I reached the fringe of the forest. Under the shelter of the canopy, the pressure of the rain was lessened. It was still pitch black, and I was forced to stumble forward into darkness, tripping on roots and colliding with boles, and the ground under me was sodden and treacherous. Nebogipfel gave up his struggling and lay passive over my shoulder.

At last I reached a tree I thought I remembered: thick and old, and with low side-branches that spread out from the trunk at a little above head-height. I hooked the Morlock over a branch, where he hung like a soaked-through coat. Then – with some effort, for I am long past my climbing days – I hauled myself off the ground and got myself sat on a branch with my back against the trunk.

And there we stayed as the Storm played itself out. I kept one hand resting on the Morlock's back, to ensure he did not fall or strive to return to the hut; and I was forced to endure a sheet of water which ran down the trunk of the tree and over my back and shoulders.

As the dawn approached, it picked out an eerie beauty in that forest. Peering up into the canopy I could make out how the rain trickled across the engineered forms of the leaves, and was channelled down the trunks to the ground; I am not much of a botanist but now I saw that the forest was like a great machine designed to survive the predations of such a Storm as this, far better than man's crude constructions.

As the light increased I tore a strip from the remains of my trousers – I was without a shirt – and tied it over Nebogipfel's face, to protect his naked eye. He did not stir.

The rains died at midday, and I judged it safe to descend. I lifted Nebogipfel to the ground, and he could walk, but I was forced to lead him by the hand, for he was blind without his goggles.

The day beyond the jungle was bright and fresh; there was a pleasant breeze off the Sea, and light clouds scudded across an almost English sky. It was as if the world was remade, and there was nothing left of yesterday's oppressiveness.

I approached the remains of the hut with some reluctance. I saw scraps – bits of smashed-up structure, the odd nut-shell cup, and so forth – all half-buried in the damp sand. In the midst of it all was a baby *Diatryma*, pecking with its great clumsy beak at the rubble. I shouted, 'Hoi!' – and ran forward, clapping my hands over my head. The bird-beast ran off, the loose yellow flesh of its legs wobbling.

I poked through the debris. Most of our possessions were lost – washed away. The shelter had been a mean thing, and our few belongings mere shards of improvisation and repair; but it had been our home – and I felt a shocking sense of violation.

'What of the device?' Nebogipfel asked me, turning his blinded face this way and that. 'The Time-Car – what of it?'

After some digging about, I found a few struts and tubes and plates, bits of battered gun-metal now even more twisted and damaged than before; but the bulk of the car had been swept into the sea. Nebogipfel fingered the fragments, his eyes closed. 'Well,' he said, 'well, this will have to do.'

And he sat down on the sand and cast about blindly for bits of cloth and vine, and he began the patient construction of his time-device once more.

6

HEART AND BODY

We never managed to retrieve Nebogipfel's goggles after the Storm, and this proved to be a great handicap to him. But he did not complain. As before, he restricted himself to the shade during the hours of daylight, and if he was forced to emerge into the light of twilight or dawn he would wear his wide-brimmed hat and, over his eye, a slitted mask of animal skin which I made for him, to afford him some sight.

The Storm was a mental as well as a physical shock to me, for I had begun to feel as if I had protected myself against such calamities as this world might throw at me. I decided that our lives must be put on a more secure footing. After some thought I decided that a hut of some form, solidly founded, and placed on stilts – that is, above the run-off from future monsoons – was the thing to aim for. But I could not rely on fallen branches for my construction material, for these, by their nature, were often irregular of form and sometimes rotten. I needed tree-trunks – and for *that* I would need an axe.

So I spent some time as an amateur geologist, hunting about the countryside for suitable rock formations. At last I found, in a layer of gravelly debris in the area of Hampstead Heath, some dark, rounded flints, together with cherts. I thought this debris must have been washed here by some vanished river.

I carried these treasures back to our encampment with as much care as if they were made of gold – or more; for that weight of gold would not have been of any value to me.

I took to bashing up the flint on open spaces on the beach. It took a good deal of experimentation, and a considerable wasting of flint, before I found ways to crack open the nodules in sympathy with the planes of the stone, to form extensive and sharp edges. My hands felt clumsy and inexpert. I had marvelled before at the fine arrow-heads and axe blades which are displayed in glass cases in our museums, but it was only when I tried to construct such devices for myself that I understood what a deep level of skill and engineering intuition our fore-fathers had possessed in the Age of Polished Stone.

At last I constructed a blade with which I was satis-fied. I fixed it to a short length of split wood, binding it in with strips of animal-skin, and I set off with a high mood for the forest.

I returned not fifteen minutes later with the frag-ments of my axe-head in my hand; for it had shat-tered on the second blow, with barely a cut made in the tree's bark!

However, with a little more experimentation I got it correct, and soon I was chopping my way through a forest of young, straight trees.

For our permanent encampment, we would stay on our beach, but I ensured we were well above the tidal line, and away from the possibilities of flood from our stream. It took me some time to dig pits for the founds, deep enough to satisfy me; but at last I had erected a square framework of upright posts, securely fixed, and with a platform of thin logs attached at perhaps a yard above the ground. This floor was far from even, and I planned to acquire the skills of better plank-making one day; but when I laid

360

down on it at night the floor felt secure and solid, and I had a measure of security that we were raised above the various perils of the ground. I almost wished another Storm down on our heads, so that I could test out my new design!

Nebogipfel hauled his fragments of Time-Car up onto the floor by a little ladder I made for him, and continued his dogged reconstruction there.

One day, as I made my way through the forest, I became aware of a pair of bright eyes studying me from a low branch.

I slowed, taking care not to make any jerky movements, and slipped my bow from my back.

The little creature was perhaps four inches long, and rather like a miniature Lemur. Its tail and face were rodent-like, with gnawing incisors quite clear at the front; it had clawed feet and suspicious eyes. It was either so intelligent that it thought it should fool me into ignoring it by its immobility – or else so stupid that it did not recognize any danger from me.

It was the work of a moment to fit the string of the bow into the notch of an arrow, and fire it off.

Now my hunting and trapping skills had improved with practice, and my slings and traps had become moderately successful; but my bows and arrows much less so. The construction of my arrows was sound enough, but I could never find wood of the right flexibility for the bows. And generally, by the time my clumsy fingers had loaded up the bow, most of my targets, bemused by my antics, were well able to scamper for cover.

Not so this little fellow! He watched with no more than dim curiosity as my skewed arrow limped through the air towards him. For once my aim was true, and the flint head pinned his little body to the tree-trunk.

I returned to Nebogipfel, proud of my prize, for mammals were useful to us: not just as sources of meat, but for their fur, teeth, fat and bones. Nebogipfel studied the little rodent-like corpse through his slit-mask.

'Perhaps I shall hunt down more of these,' I said. 'The little creature really didn't seem to understand what danger he was in, right until the end. Poor beast!'

'Do you know what this is?'

'Tell me.'

'I believe it is *Purgatorius*.'

'And the significance –?'

'It is a primate: the earliest known.' He let himself sound amused.

I swore. 'I thought I was done with all this. But even in the Palaeocene, one cannot avoid meeting one's relatives!' I studied the tiny corpse. 'So here is the ancestor of monkey, and man, and Morlock! The insignificant little acorn from which will grow an oak which will smother more worlds than this earth . . . I wonder how many men, and nations, and *species*, would have sprung from the loins of this modest little fellow, had I not killed him. Once again, perhaps I have destroyed my own past!'

Nebogipfel said, 'We cannot help but interact with History, you and I. With every breath we take, every tree you cut down, every animal we kill, we create a new world in the Multiplicity of Worlds. That is all. It is unavoidable.'

After that, I could not bring myself to touch the flesh of the poor little creature. I took it into the forest and buried it.

One day I set myself to follow our little fresh-water stream westwards towards its source, in the interior of the country.

I set off at dawn. Away from the coast, the tang of salt and ozone faded, to be replaced by the hot, moist scents of the *dipterocarps* forest, and the over-powering perfume of the crowding flowers. The going was difficult, with heavy growth underfoot. It became much more humid, and my cap of nut-fibre was soon soaked through; the sounds around me, the rustling of vegetation and the endless trills and coughs of the forest, took on a heavier tone in the thickening air.

By mid-morning I had travelled two or three miles, arriving somewhere in Brentford. Here I found a wide, shallow lake, from which flowed our stream and a number of others, and the lake was fed in turn by a series of minor brooks and rivers. The trees grew close around this secluded body of water, and climbing plants clung to their trunks and lower branches, including some I recognized as bottle gourds and loofahs. The water was warm and brackish, and I was wary of drinking it, but the lagoon teemed with life. Its surface was covered by groupings of giant lilies, shaped like upturned bottle-tops and perhaps six feet wide, which reminded me of plants I had once seen in Turner's Waterlily House in the Royal Botanic Gardens at Kew. (It was ironic, I thought, that the eventual site of Kew itself was less than a mile from where I stood!) The lilies' saucers looked strong and buoyant enough for me to stand on, but I did not put this hypothesis to the test.

It was the work of a few minutes to improvise a fishing rod, made from the long, straight trunk of a sapling. I fixed a line to this, and I baited a hook of Time-Car metal with grubs.

I was rewarded within a few minutes by brisk tugs of the line. I grinned to imagine the envy of some of my angling friends – dear old Filby, for instance – at my discovery of this un-fished oasis.

I built a fire and ate well that night of broiled fish and tubers.

A little before dawn I was woken by a strange hooting. I sat up and looked about me. My fire had more or less died. The sun was not yet up; the sky had that unearthly tinge of steel blue which prefigures a new day. There was no wind, and not a leaf stirred; a heavy mist lay immobile on the surface of the water.

Then I made out a group of birds, a hundred yards from me around the rim of the lake. Their feathers were dun brown and each had legs as long as a flamingo's. They stepped about the waters of the lake's margin, or stood poised on one leg like exquisite sculptures. They had heads shaped like those of modern ducks, and they would dip those familiar-looking beaks through the shimmering surface and sweep through the water, evidently filtering for food.

The mist lifted a little, and more of the lake was revealed; I saw now that there was a great flock of these creatures (which Nebogipfel later identified as *Presbyornis*) – thousands of them, in a great, open colony. They moved like ghosts through that vaporous haze.

I told myself that this location was nowhere more exotic than the junction of Gunnersbury Avenue with the Chiswick High Road – but a vision more unlike England it is hard to conjure!

As the days wore on in that sultry, vital landscape, my memories of the England of 1891 seemed more and more remote and irrelevant. I found the greatest of satisfactions in my building, hunting and gathering; and the bathing warmth of the sun and the Sea's freshness were combining to give me a sense of health, strength and immediacy of sensory experience lost since childhood. I had done with *Thinking*, I decided; there were but two conscious Minds in all this elaborate panoply of Palaeocene life, and I could not see that mine would do me much good from now on, save for keeping me alive a little longer.

It was time for the Heart, and the Body, to have their say. And the more the days wore away, the more I gathered a sense of the greatness of the world, the immensity of time – and the littleness of myself and my concerns in the face of that great Multiple panorama of History. I was no longer important, even to myself; and that realization was like a liberation of the soul.

After a time, even the death of Moses ceased to clamour at my thoughts.

7

PRISTICHAMPUS

Nebogipfel's screaming woke me with a start. A Morlock's voice, raised, is a kind of gurgle: queer, but quite chilling to hear.

I sat up in the cool darkness; and for an instant I imagined I was back in my bed in my house on the Petersham Road, but the scents and textures of the Palaeocene night came crowding in on me.

I scrambled out of my pallet and jumped down, off the floor of the shelter, and to the sand. It had been a moonless night; and the last stars were fading from the sky as the sun approached. The sea rolled, placid, and the wall of forest was black and still.

In the midst of this cool, blue-soaked tranquillity, the Morlock came limping towards me along the beach. He had lost his crutch, and, it seemed to me, he could barely stay upright, let alone run. His hair was ragged and flying, and he had lost his face-mask; even as he ran I could see how he was forced to raise his hands to cover his huge, sensitive eye.

And behind him, chasing –

It was perhaps ten feet in length, in general layout something like a crocodile; but its legs were long and supple, giving it a raised, horse-like gait, quite unlike the squat motion of the crocodiles of my time – this beast was evidently adapted to running and chasing. Its slit eyes were fixed on the Morlock, and when it opened its mouth I saw rows of saw-edge teeth.

This apparition was bare yards from Nebogipfel!

I screamed and ran at the little tableau, waving my arms, but even as I did so I knew it was all up for Nebogipfel. I grieved for the lost Morlock, but – I am ashamed to record it – my first thought was for myself, for with his death I should be left alone, here in the mindless Palaeocene . . .

And it was at that moment, with a startling clarity, that a rifle-shot rang out from the margin of the forest.

The first bullet missed the beast, I think; but it was enough to make that great head turn, and to slow the pumping of those mighty thighs.

The Morlock fell, now, and went sprawling in the sand; but he pushed himself up on his elbows and squirmed onwards, on his belly.

There was a second shot, and a third. The crocodile flinched as the bullets pounded into its body. It faced the forest with defiance, opened his saw-toothed mouth and emitted a roar which echoed like thunder from the trees. Then it set off on its long, determined legs towards the source of these unexpected stings.

A man – short, compact, wearing a drab uniform – emerged from the forest's margin. He raised the rifle again, sighted along it at the crocodile, and held his nerve as the beast approached.

I reached Nebogipfel now and hauled him to his feet; he was shivering. We stood on the sand together, and waited for the drama to play itself out.

The crocodile could have been no more than ten yards away from the man when the rifle spoke again. The crocodile stumbled – I could see blood streaming from its mouth – but it raised itself up with barely a sliver of its momentum lost. The rifle shouted, and bullet after bullet plunged into that immense carcase.

At last, less than ten feet from the man, the thing tumbled, its great jaws snapping at the air; and the man – as cool as you like! – stepped neatly aside to let it fall.

I found Nebogipfel's mask for him, and the Morlock and I followed the trail of the crocodile up the slope of the beach. Its claws had scuffed up the sand, and the last few pace-marks were strewn with saliva, mucus and steaming blood. Close to, the crocodile-thing was even more intimidating than from a distance; the eyes and jaw were open and staring, and as the last echoes of life seeped from the monster the huge muscles of its rear legs twitched, and hoofed feet scuffed at the sand.

The Morlock studied the hot carcass. '*Pristichampus*,' he said in his low gurgle.

Our saviour stood with his foot on the twitching corpse of the beast. He was aged perhaps twenty-five: he was clean-jawed and with a straightforward gaze. Despite his brush with death, he looked quite relaxed; he favoured us with an engaging, gap-toothed grin. His uniform consisted of brown trousers, heavy boots, and a brown khaki jacket; a blue beret perched jauntily on his head. This visitor could have come from any Age, or any variant of History, I supposed; but it did not surprise me at all when this young man said, in straightforward, neutrally-accented English, 'Damn ugly thing, isn't it? Tough fellow, though – did you see I had to plug him in the mouth before he fell? And even then he kept on coming. Got to give him credit – he was game enough!'

Before his relaxed, Officer-class manners, I felt clumsy, rather oafish in my skins and beard. I extended my hand. 'Sir, I think I owe you the life of my companion.'

He took the hand and shook it. 'Think nothing of

it.' His grin widened. 'Mr —, I presume,' he said, naming me. 'Do you know, I've always wanted to say that!'

'And you are?'

'Oh, I'm sorry. The name's Gibson. Wing Commander Guy Gibson. And I'm delighted to have found you.'

8

THE ENCAMPMENT

It transpired that Gibson was not alone. He shouldered his rifle, turned and made a beckoning
gesture towards the shadows of the jungle.

Two soldiers emerged from that gloom. Sweat had
soaked through the shirts of these laden fellows, and,
as they stepped into the growing light of the day, they
seemed altogether more suspicious of us, and generally uncomfortable, than had the Wing Commander.
These two were Indians, I thought – sepoys, soldiers
of the Empire – their eyes glittered black and fierce,
and each had a turban and clipped beard. They wore
khaki drill shirts and shorts; one of them carried a
heavy mechanical gun at his back, and bore two
heavy leather pouches, evidently holding ammunition for this weapon. Their heavy, silvery epaulettes
glittered in the Palaeocene sunlight; they scowled at
the corpse of *Pristichampus* with undisguised ferocity.

Gibson told us that he and these two fellows had
been involved on a scouting expedition; they had
travelled perhaps a mile from a main base camp,
which was situated inland from the Sea. (It struck me
as odd that Gibson did not introduce the two soldiers
by name. This little incivility – brought on by an
unspoken recognition, by Gibson, of differences of
rank – seemed to me altogether absurd, there on
that isolated beach in the Palaeocene, with only a
handful of humans anywhere in the world!)

I thanked Gibson again for rescuing the Morlock, and invited him to join us for some breakfast at our shelter. 'It's just along the beach,' I said, pointing; and Gibson peaked his hand over his eyes to see.

'Well, that looks – ah – as if it's going to be a jolly *solid* construction.'

'Solid? I should say so,' I replied, and began a long and rather rambling discourse on the details of our incomplete shelter, of which I felt inordinately proud, and of how we had survived in the Palaeocene.

Guy Gibson folded his hands behind his back and listened, with a set, polite expression on his face. The sepoys watched me, puzzled and suspicious, their hands never far from their weapons.

After some minutes of this, I became aware, rather belatedly, of Gibson's detachment. I let my prattle slow to a halt.

Gibson glanced around brightly at the beach. 'I think you've done remarkably well here. Remarkably. I should have thought that a few weeks of this Robinson Crusoe stuff would pretty much have driven me batty with loneliness. I mean, opening time at the pub won't be for another fifty million years!'

I smiled at this joke – which I failed to follow – and I felt rather embarrassed at my exaggerated pride at such mean achievements, before this vision of dapper competence.

'But look here,' Gibson went on gently, 'don't you think you'd be better off coming back with us to the Expeditionary Force? We have travelled here to find you, after all. And we've some decent provisions there – and modern tools, and so forth.' He glanced at Nebogipfel, and added, a little more dubiously, 'And the doc might be able to do something for this poor chap as well. Is there anything you need here? We can always come back later.'

Of course there was not – I had no need to return

through those few hundred yards along the beach ever again! – but I knew that, with the arrival of Gibson and his people, my brief idyll was done. I looked into Gibson's frank, practical face, and knew that I could never find the words to express such a sense of loss to him.

With the sepoys leading the way, and with the Morlock supporting himself against my arm, we set off into the interior of the jungle.

Away from the coast, the air was hot and clammy. We moved in single file, with the sepoys at front and back, and Gibson, the Morlock, and myself sandwiched between; I carried the frail Morlock in my arms for much of the journey. The two sepoys kept up their suspicious, hooded glares at us, although after a time they allowed their hands to stray from their webbing holsters. They said not a single word to Nebogipfel or me, in the whole time we travelled together.

Gibson's expedition had come from 1944 – six years after our own departure, during the German assault on the London Dome.

'And the War is still continuing?'

'I'm afraid so,' he said, sounding grim. 'Of course we responded for that brutal attack on London. Paid them back in spades.'

'You were involved in such actions yourself?'

As he walked, he glanced down – apparently involuntarily – at the service ribbons sewn to the chest of his tunic. I did not recognize these at the time – I am no military buff, and in any case some of these awards hadn't even been devised in my day – but I learned later that they constituted the Distinguished Service Order, and the Distinguished Flying Cross and Bar: high awards indeed, especially for one so young. Gibson said without drama, 'I saw a bit of action, yes. A good few sorties. Pretty lucky to be here to talk about it – plenty of good chaps who aren't.'

'And these sorties were effective?'

'I'll say. We broke open their Domes for them, without much of a delay after they did us the same favour!'

'And the cities underneath?'

He eyed me. 'What do you think? Without its Dome, a city is pretty much defenceless against attack from the air. Oh, you can throw up a barrage from your eighty-eights –'

'"Eighty-eights"?'

'The Germans have an eight-point-eight centimetre Flat 36 anti-aircraft gun – pretty useful as a field gun and anti-'Naut, as well as its main purpose: good bit of design . . . Anyway, if your bomber pilot can get in under such flak he can pretty much dump what he likes into the guts of an unDomed city.'

'And the results – after six more years of all this?'

He shrugged. 'There's not much in the way of cities left, I suppose. Not in Europe, anyway.'

We reached the vicinity of South Hampstead, I estimated. Here, we broke through a line of trees into a clearing. This was a circular space perhaps a quarter-mile across, but it was not natural: the tree-stumps at its edge showed how the forest had been blasted back, or cut away. Even as we approached, I could see squads of bare-chested infantrymen hacking their way further into the undergrowth with saws and machetes, extending the space. The earth in the clearing was stripped of undergrowth and hardened by several layers of palm fronds, all stamped down into the mud.

At the heart of this clearing sat four of the great Juggernaut machines which I had encountered before, in 1873 and 1938. These beasts sat at four sides of a square a hundred feet across, immobile, their ports gaping like the mouths of thirsty animals; their anti-mine flails hung limp and useless from the drums held out before them, and the mottled green and black coloration of their metal hides was encrusted with guano and fallen leaves.There were a series of other vehicles and items of materiel scattered around the encampment, including light armoured cars, and small artillery pieces mounted on thick-wheeled trolleys.

This, Gibson gave me to understand, would be the site of a sort of graving-yard for time-travelling Juggernauts, in 1944.

Soldiers worked everywhere, and when I walked into the clearing beside Gibson, and with the limping Nebogipfel leaning against me, to a man the troopers ceased their labouring and stared at us with undiluted curiosity.

We reached the courtyard enclosed by the four 'Nauts. At the centre of this square there was a white-painted flag-pole; and from this a Union Flag dangled, gaudy, limp and incongruous. A series of tents had been set up in this yard; Gibson invited us to sit on canvas stools beside the grandest of these. A soldier – thin, pale and evidently uncomfortable in the heat – emerged from one of the 'Nauts. I took this fellow to be Gibson's batman, for the Wing Commander ordered him to bring us some refreshment.

The work of the camp proceeded all around us as we sat there; it was a hive of activity, as military sites always seem endlessly to be. Most of the soldiers wore a full kit of a jungle-green twill shirt and trousers with anklets; on their heads they had soft felt hats with puggrees of light khaki, or else bush hats of (Gibson said) an Australian design. They wore their divisional insignia sewn into their shirts or hats, and most of them carried weaponry: leather bandoliers for small-arms ammunition, web pouches, and the like. They all bore the heavy epaulettes I remembered from 1938. In the heat and moisture, most of these troopers were fairly dishevelled.

I saw one chap in a suit of pure white which enclosed him head to foot; he wore thick gloves, and a soft helmet which enclosed his head, with an inset visor through which he peered. He worked at the opened side-panels of one of the Juggernauts. The poor fellow must have been melting of the heat in such an enclosure, I surmised; Gibson explained that the suit was of asbestos, to protect him from engine fires.

Not all the soldiers were men – I should think two-fifths of the hundred or so personnel were female – and many of the soldiers bore wounds of one sort or another: burn scars and the like, and even, here and there, prosthetic sections of limb. I realized that the dreadful attrition of the youth of Europe had continued since 1938, necessitating the call-up of those wounded already, and more of the young women.

Gibson took off his heavy boots and massaged his cramped feet with a rueful grin at me. Nebogipfel sipped from a glass of water, while the batman provided Gibson and me with a cup of traditional English breakfast tea – *tea*, there in the Palaeocene!

'You have made quite a little colony,' I said to Gibson.

'I suppose so. It's just the drill, you know.' He put down his boots and sipped his tea. 'Of course we're a jumble of Services here – I expect you noticed.'

'No,' I said frankly.

'Well, most of the chaps are Army, of course.' He pointed to a slim young trooper who wore a khaki tag at the shoulders of his Tropical shirt. 'But a few of us, like *him* and myself, are RAF.'

'RAF?'

'Royal Air Force. The men in grey suits have finally worked out that we're the best chaps to drive these great iron brutes, you see.' A trooper of the Army passed by, goggling at Nebogipfel, and Gibson favoured him with an easy grin. 'Of course we don't mind giving these foot-sloggers a lift. Better than leaving you to do it yourselves, eh, Stubbins?'

The man Stubbins – slim, red-haired, with an open, friendly face – grinned back, almost shyly, but evidently pleased at Gibson's attention: all this despite the fact that he must have been a good foot taller than the diminutive Gibson, and some years older. I recognized in Gibson's relaxed manner something of the poise of the natural leader.

'We've been here a week already,' Gibson said to me. 'Surprising we didn't stumble on you earlier, I suppose.'

'We weren't expecting visitors,' I said drily. 'If we had been, I suppose I would have lit fires, or found some other way of signalling our presence.'

He favoured me with a wink. 'We have been occupied ourselves. We had the devil's own work to do in the first day or two here. We have good kit, of course – the boffins made it pretty clear to us before we left that the climate of dear old England is pretty variable, if you take a long enough view of it – and so we've come prepared with an issue of everything from greatcoats to Bombay bloomers. But we weren't expecting quite these Tropical conditions: not here, in the middle of London! Our clothes seem to be falling apart – literally rotting off our backs – and the metal fittings are rusting, and our boots won't grip in this slime: even my bally socks have shrunk! And the whole lot is being gnawed away by rats.' He frowned. 'At least I think they are rats.'

'Probably not, in fact,' I remarked. 'And the Juggernauts? Kitchener class, are they?'

Gibson cocked an eyebrow at me, evidently surprised at my display of this fragment of knowledge. 'Actually we can barely move the 'Nauts: those wretched elephants' feet sink into this endless mud . . .'

And now a clear, familiar voice called out from behind me: 'I'm afraid you're a little out of date, sir. The Kitchener class – including the dear old *Raglan* – has been discarded for a number of years now . . .'

I turned in my chair. Approaching me was a figure dressed in a crisp Juggernaut crew beret and coverall; this soldier walked with a pronounced limp, and a hand was proffered for shaking. I took the hand; it was small but strong.

'Captain Hilary Bond,' I said, and smiled.

She looked me up and down, taking in my beard and animal-skin clothes. 'You're a little more ragged, sir, but quite unmistakeable. Surprised to see me?'

'After a few doses of this time travelling, nothing much surprises me any more, Hilary!'

9

THE CHRONIC
EXPEDITIONARY FORCE

Gibson and Bond explained the purpose of the Chronic Expeditionary Force to me.

Thanks to the development of Carolinum fission piles, Britain and America had managed to achieve the production of Plattnerite in reasonable quantities soon after my escape into time. No longer did the engineers of the day have to rely on the scraps and leavings of my old workshop!

There was still a great fear that German chronic warriors were planning some sneak offensive against Britain's past – and besides, it was known from the wreckage we had left behind in Imperial College, and other clues, that Nebogipfel and I must have travelled some tens of millions of years into the past. So a fleet of time-travelling Juggernauts was rapidly assembled, and equipped with subtle instruments which could detect the presence of Plattnerite traces (based on the radio-active origins of that substance, I was given to understand). And now this Expeditionary Force was proceeding into the past, in great leaps of five million years or more.

Its mission was nothing less than to secure the History of Britain from enemy anachronistic attack!

When stops were made, a valiant effort was made to study the period; and to this end a number of the soldiers had been trained, albeit hastily, to act as amateur scientists: climatologists, ornithologists and the like. These fellows made rapid but effective surveys of the flora, fauna, climate and geology of the Age, and a good deal of Gibson's daily log was given over to summarizing such observations. I saw that the soldiers, common men and women all, accepted this task with good humour and joking, as such people will, and – it seemed to me – they showed a healthy interest in the nature of the strange, Palaeocene Thames valley around them.

But at night sentries patrolled the perimeter of the encampment, and troopers with field-glasses spent a great deal of their time peering at the air, or the Sea. When engaged in these duties, the soldiers showed none of the gentle humour and curiosity which characterized their scientific or other endeavours; rather, their fear and intent was apparent in the set of their faces, and the thinness of their eyes.

This Force was here, after all, not to study flowers, but to seek *Germans*: time-travelling human enemies, here amid the wonders of the past.

Proud as I was of my achievements in surviving in this alien Age, it was with considerable relief that I abandoned my suit of rags and animal pelts and donned the light, comfortable Tropical kit of these time-traversing troopers. I shaved off my beard, washed – in warm, clean water, with soap! – and tucked with relish into meals of tinned soya-meat. And at night, it was with a feeling of peace and security that I lay down under a covering of canvas and mosquito netting, and with the powerful shoulders of the 'Nauts all about me.

Nebogipfel did not settle in the camp. Although our discovery by Gibson was the cause of some celebration and marvelling – for our retrieval had been the primary objective of the Expedition – the Morlock soon became the object of blatant fascination among the troopers, and, I suspected, a little sly goading. So the Morlock returned to our original encampment, by the edge of the Palaeocene Sea. I did not oppose this, for I knew how eager he was to continue the construction of his time-frame – he even borrowed tools from the Expeditionary Force to facilitate this. Recalling his close shave with the *Pristichampus*, however, I insisted that he not stay there alone, but be accompanied either by me or an armed soldier.

As for me, after a day or two I tired of being at leisure in this busy encampment – I am not by nature an idle man – and I asked to participate in the soldiers' chores. I soon proved my worth in sharing my painfully acquired knowledge of the local flora, fauna and surrounding geography. There was a good deal of sickness in the camp – for the soldiers had been no more prepared than I had been for the various infections of the Age – and I lent a hand assisting the camp's solitary doctor, a rather young and perpetually exhausted *naik* attached to the 9th Gurkha Rifles.

After the first day I saw little of Gibson, who was consumed by the minutiae of the daily operation of his Expeditionary Force, and – to his own irritation – by a hefty load of bureaucracy, forms and reports and logs, which he was required to maintain daily: and all for the benefit of a Whitehall which would not exist for another fifty million years! I formed the impression that Gibson was restless and impatient with this time-travelling; he would, I think, have been more content if he could have resumed the bombing raids over Germany which he had led, and which he described to me with startling clarity. Hilary Bond had a deal of free time – her duties were most demanding during those periods when the great time-travelling ironclads pushed through the centuries – and she served as my, and Nebogipfel's, host.

One day the two of us walked along the rim of the forest, close to the shore. Bond pushed her way through the thick patches of undergrowth. She limped, but her gait was blunt and forceful. She described to me the progress of the War since 1938.

'I would have thought the smashing-up of the Domes would have made an end of it,' I said. 'Can't people see – I mean, what is there to fight for after that?'

'It should have been an end of the War, you mean? Oh, no. It's been an end to city life for a time, I imagine. Our populations have taken a fair old battering. But there are the Bunkers, of course – that's where the War is being run from now, and where the munitions factories and so forth are mostly located. It isn't much of a century for cities, I don't think.'

I thought back to what I had seen of the barbarism of the countryside beyond the London Dome, and I tried to imagine permanent life in an underground Bomb Shelter: I conjured up images of hollow-eyed children scurrying through darkened tunnels, and a population reduced by fear to servility and near-savagery.

'And what of the War itself?' I asked. 'The fronts – your great Siege of Europe –'

Bond shrugged. 'Well, you hear a lot on the Babbles about great advances here and there: *One Last Push* – that sort of thing.' She lowered her voice. 'But – and I don't suppose it matters much if we discuss this here – the flyers see a bit of Europe, you know, even if it is by night and lit up by shell-fire, and word gets around. And *I* don't think those trench lines have moved across an inch of mud since 1935. We're stuck, is what we are.'

'I can no longer imagine what you're all fighting

381

for. The countries are all pretty much bashed up, industrially and economically. None of them can pose much of a threat to the rest, surely; and none of them can have assets left that are worth acquiring.'

'Perhaps that's true,' she said. 'I don't think Britain has strength left to do much but rebuild her own smashed-up countryside, once the War is done. We'll not be going conquering for a long time! And, the situation being as even as it is, the view of things from Berlin must be pretty similar.'

'Then why go on?'

'*Because we can't afford to stop.*' Beneath the tan she had acquired in this deep Palaeocene, I could see traces of Bond's former weary pallor. 'There are all sorts of reports – some rumours, but some better substantiated, from what I hear – of German technical developments . . .'

'Technical developments? You mean *weapons.*'

We walked away from the forest, now, and down to the edge of the Sea. The air burned hot against my face, and we let the water lap around the soles of our boots.

I pictured the Europe of 1944: the smashed cities, and, from Holland to the Alps, millions of men and women trying to inflict irreparable damage on each other . . . In this Tropical peace, it all seemed absurd – a fevered dream!

'But what can you possibly hope to invent,' I protested, 'that can do significantly more damage than has already been achieved?'

'There is talk of Bombs. A new sort – more powerful than anything we've yet seen . . . Bombs containing Carolinum, they say.' I remembered Wallis's speculations on those lines in 1938. 'And, of course,' Bond said, 'there is Chronic-Displacement warfare.

'You see, we can't stop fighting if it means letting the Germans have a monopoly on such weapons.'

Her voice had a sort of quiet desperation. 'You *can* see that, can't you? That's why there's been such a rush to build atomic piles, to acquire Carolinum, to produce more Plattnerite . . . that's why so much expense and resource has been invested in these time-travelling Juggernauts.'

'And all to leap back in time before the Germans? To do unto them *before* they get the chance to do unto you?'

She lifted her chin and looked defiant. 'Or to fix the damage they do. That's another way of looking at it, isn't it?'

I did not debate, as Nebogipfel might have done, the ultimate futility of this quest; for it was clear that the philosophers of 1944 had not yet come to such an understanding of the Multiplicity of Histories as I had, under the Morlock's tuition.

'But,' I protested, 'the past is a pretty huge place. You came looking for us, but how could you know we would end up here – how could you settle near us, even to within a million years or so?'

'We had clues,' she said.

'What sort of clues? You mean the wreckage left behind in Imperial?'

'Partly. But also archaeological.'

'*Archaeological?*'

She looked at me quizzically. 'Look here, I'm not sure you'd want to hear this –'

That, of course, made my curiosity burn! I insisted she told me.

'Very well. They – the boffins – knew the general area where you had left for the past – in the grounds of Imperial College, of course – and so they began an intensive archaeological survey of the area. Pits were dug –'

'Good heavens,' I said. 'You were looking for my fossilized bones!'

'And Nebogipfel's. It was reasoned that if any anomalies were found – bones, or tools – we should be able to place you tolerably well by your position in the strata . . .'

'And were they? Hilary –' She held back again, and I had to insist she answer.

'They found a skull.'

'Human?'

'Sort of.' She hesitated. 'Small, and rather misshapen – placed in a stratum fifty million years older than any human remains had a right to be – *and bitten clean in two.*'

Small and misshapen – it must, I realized, have been Nebogipfel's! Could that have been the relic of his encounter with *Pristichampus* – but in some other History, in which Gibson did not intervene?

And did *my* bones lie, crushed and turned to stone, in some neighbouring, undiscovered pit?

I felt a chill, despite the heat of the sun on my back and head. Suddenly this brilliant Palaeocene world seemed faded – a transparency, through which shone the pitiless light of time.

'So you detected your traces of Plattnerite, and you found us,' I said. 'But I imagine you were disappointed merely to find me – again! – and no horde of warmongering Prussians. But – look here – can't you see there is a certain paradox?

'You develop your time ironclads because you fear the Germans are doing the same. Very well. But the situation is symmetrical: from *their* point of view, the Germans must fear that *you* will exploit such time machinery first. Each side is behaving precisely in such a way as to provoke the worst reaction in its opponents. And so you both slide towards the worst situation for all.'

'That's as may be,' Bond said. 'But the possession

of time technology by the Germans would be cata-
strophic for the Allied Cause. The role of this
Expedition is to hunt down German travellers, and to
avert any damage the Germans inflict on History.'

I threw my hands in the air, and Palaeocene water
rippled about my ankles. 'But – confound it, Captain
Bond – it is fifty million years until the birth of Christ!
What meaning can that firefly struggle between
England and Germany – in such a remote future –
have *here*?'

'We cannot relax,' she said with a grim weariness.
'Can't you see that? We must hunt the Germans, right
back to the dawn of Creation – if necessary.'

'And where will this War stop? Will you consume all
of Eternity before you are done? Don't you see that
that –' I waved a hand, meaning to summarize all of
that awful future of shattered cities and populations
huddling in subterranean caves. '– all that – is impossible? Or will you go on until there are two men left –
just two – and the last turns to his neighbour and
bashes out his brain with a lump of shattered
masonry? Eh?'

Bond turned away – the light of the Sea picked out
the lines in her face – and she would not reply.

This period of calm, after our first encounter with
Gibson, lasted five days.

10

THE APPARITION

It was noon of a cloudless, brilliant day, and I had spent the morning putting my clumsy nursing skills at the service of the gurkha doctor. It was with a sense of relief that I accepted Hilary Bond's invitation to join her for another of our walks to the beach.

We cut through the forest easily enough – by now, the troopers had cleared respectable paths radiating from the central encampment – and, when we reached the beach, I hauled off my boots and socks and dumped them at the fringe of the forest, and I scampered down to the water's edge. Hilary Bond discarded her own footwear, a little more decorously, and she piled it on the sand with the hand-weapon she carried. She rolled up the legs of her trousers – I was able to see how her left leg was misshapen, the skin shrunken by an ancient burn – and she waded into the foamy surf after me.

I stripped off my shirt (we were pretty much informal in that camp in the ancient forest, men and women all) and I dunked my head and upper body in the transparent water, disregarding the soaking my trouser legs were receiving. I breathed deep, relishing it all: the heat of the sun prickling on my face, the sparkle of the water, the softness of the sand between my toes, the sharp scents of salt and ozone.

'You're glad to get here, I see,' Hilary said with a tolerant smile.

'Indeed I am.' I told her how I had been assisting the doctor. 'You know I'm willing enough – more than willing – to help. But by about ten o'clock today my head had got so full of the stench of chloroform, of ether, of various antiseptic fluids – as well as more earthy smells! – that –'

She held her hands up. 'I understand.'

We emerged from the Sea, and I towelled myself dry with my shirt. Hilary picked up her gun, but we left our boots piled on the beach, and we strolled by the water's edge. After a few dozen yards I spotted the shallow indentations which betrayed the presence of *corbicula* – those burrowing bivalves which inhabited that beach in such numbers. We squatted on the sand; and I showed her how to dig out the compact little creatures. Within a few minutes we had built up a respectable haul; and a heap of bivalves sat drying in the sun beside us.

As she picked over the bivalves with the fascination of a child, Hilary's face, with her cropped hair plastered flat by the water, shone with pleasure at her simple achievement. We were quite alone on that beach – we might have been the only two humans in all that Palaeocene world – and I could feel the sparkle of every bead of perspiration on my scalp, the rasp of every grain of sand against my shins. And it was all suffused by the animal warmth of the woman beside me; it was as if the Multiple Worlds through which I had travelled had collapsed down to this single moment of vividness – to Here and Now.

I wanted to communicate something of this to Hilary. 'You know –'

But she had straightened up, and turned her face to the Sea. 'Listen.'

I gazed about, baffled, at the forest's edge, the lapping Sea, the lofty emptiness of the sky. The only sounds were the rustle of a soft breeze in the forest canopy, and the gentle gurgle of the lapping wavelets. 'Listen to what?'

Her expression had become hard and suspicious – the face of the soldier, intelligent and fearful. '*Single-engined*,' she said, her concentration apparent. 'That's a Daimler-Benz DB – a twelve-cylinder, I think . . .' She jumped to her feet and pressed her hands to her brow, shielding her eyes.

And then I heard it too, my older ears following hers. It was a distant *thrum* – like some immense, remote insect – which came drifting to us off the Sea.

'Look,' Hilary said, pointing. 'Out there. Can you see it?'

I sighted along Hilary's arm, and was rewarded with a glimpse of something: a distortion, hanging over the Sea, far to the east. It was a patch of *otherness* – a whorl no bigger than the full moon, a kind of sparkling refraction tinged with green.

Then I had an impression of something *solid* in the middle of it all, congealing and spinning – and then there was a hard, dark shape, like a cross, which came hurtling low out of the sky – from the east, from the direction of a Germany yet to be born. That thrumming noise grew much louder.

'My God,' Hilary Bond said. 'It is a Messerschmitt – an Eagle; it looks like a Bf 109F . . .'

'*Messerschmitt* . . . That's a German name,' I said, rather stupidly.

She glanced at me. 'Of *course* it's a German name. Don't you understand?'

'What?'

'That's a German plane. It is *die Zeitmaschine*, come to hunt us down!'

*

388

As it approached the coast, the craft tipped in the air, like a seagull in flight, and began to run parallel to the Sea's edge. With a noisy whoosh, and so fast that Hilary and I were forced to swivel on the sand to follow its progress, it passed over our heads, not a hundred feet from the ground.

The machine was some thirty feet long, and perhaps a little more from wing-tip to wing-tip. A propeller whirled at its nose, blurred by speed. The craft's underside was painted blue-grey, and its upper sections were done out in mottled brown and green. Strident black crosses on the fuselages and wings marked the craft's country of origin, and there were more gaudy militaristic designs on the painted skin, of an eagle's head, an upraised sword, and so on. The underside was quite smooth, save for the craft's single load: a tear-drop mass of metal perhaps six feet long, painted in the ubiquitous blue.

For some moments Bond and I stood there, as stunned by this sudden apparition as if by some religious visitation.

The excitable young man buried inside me – the shade of poor, lost Moses – thrilled at the sight of that elegant machine. What an adventure for that pilot! What a glorious view! And what extraordinary courage it must have taken to haul that machine into the smoke-blackened air of 1944 Germany – to take that plane so high that the landscape of the heart of Europe would be reduced to a kind of map, a textured table-top coated with sand and sea and forest, and tiny, doll-like people – and *then* to close the switch which launched the craft into time. I imagined how the sun would arc over the ship like a meteorite, while beneath the prow, the landscape, made plastic by time, would flow and deform . . .

Then the gleaming wings tipped again, and the propeller's noise came crashing down over us. The craft swooped upwards and away, over the forest and in the direction of the Expeditionary Force.

Hilary ran up the beach, and her uneven limping left asymmetric craters in the sand.

'Where are you going?'

She reached her boots, and began to haul them on roughly, ignoring her socks. 'To the camp, of course.'

'But . . .' I stared at our small, pathetic pile of bivalves. 'But you can't outrun that Messerschmitt. What will you do?'

She picked up her hand-gun and stood up straight. For answer, she looked at me, her expression blank. And then she turned and shoved her way through the fringe of palm trees which lined the edge of the forest, and disappeared into the shadows of the *dipterocarps*.

The noise of the Messerschmitt aircraft was fading, absorbed by the forest canopy. I was alone on the beach, with the bivalves and the lapping of the surf.

It all seemed quite unreal: *War*, imported to this Palaeocene idyll? I felt no fear – nothing but a sense of bizarre dislocation.

I shook off my immobility, and prepared to follow Bond into the forest.

I had not even reached my boots when a small, liquid voice came floating across the sand to me: '. . . No! . . . go to the water . . . no! . . .'

It was Nebogipfel: the Morlock came stumbling across the sand towards me, his improvised crutch digging a series of deep, narrow pits. I saw how a loose edge of his face-mask flapped as he staggered along.

'What is it? Can't you see what's happening? *Die Zeitmaschine –*'

'The water.' He leaned on his crutch, as limp as a rag doll, and his panting tore at his frame. His wheezing had grown so pronounced that his syllables were barely distinguishable. 'The water . . . we must get in the . . .'

'This is no time for a swim, man!' I bellowed, indignant. 'Can't you see –'

'Do not understand,' he gasped. 'You. You do not . . . Come . . .'

I turned, abstracted, and looked over the forest. Now I could see the elusive form of *die Zeitmaschine* as it skimmed over the tree-tops, its green and blue paint making vivid splashes against the foliage. Its speed was extraordinary, and its distant noise was like an insect's angry buzz.

Then I heard the staccato cough of artillery pieces, and the whistle of shells.

'They're fighting back,' I said to Nebogipfel, caught up by this spark of War. 'Can you see? The flying machine has evidently spotted the Expeditionary Force, but they are firing off their guns at it . . .'

'*The Sea*,' Nebogipfel said. He plucked at my arm with fingers as feeble as a baby's, and it was a gesture of such immediacy, such pleading, that I had to tear my eyes from the aerial battle. The grubby slit-mask exposed mere slivers of his eyes, and his mouth was a down-turned, quivering gash. 'It is the only shelter close enough. It might be sufficient . . .'

'Shelter? The battle is two miles away. How can we be hurt, standing here on this empty beach?'

'But the Bomb . . . the Bomb carried by the German; did you not see it? . . .' His hair was lank against his small skull. 'The Bombs of this History are not sophisticated – little more than lumps of pure Carolinum . . . But they are effective enough, for all that.

'There is nothing you can do for the Expedition! – not now . . . we must wait until the battle is done.' He stared up at me. 'Can you see that? Come,' he said, and he tugged, again, at my arm. He had dropped his crutch, now, so that my arm was supporting him.

Like a child, I allowed myself to be led into the water.

Soon we had reached a depth of four feet or more. The Morlock was covered up to his shoulders; he bade me crouch down, so that I, too, was more or less immersed in salt water.

Over the forest, the Messerschmitt banked and came back for another pass, swooping like some predatory bird of metal and oil; the artillery pieces shouted up at *die Zeitmaschine*, and shells burst into clouds of smoke, which drifted off through the Palaeocene air.

I admit that I thrilled to this aerial contest – the first I had witnessed. My mind raced with visions of the extended conflicts in the air which must have filled the skies over Europe in 1944: I saw men who rode upon the wind, and slew and fell like Milton's angels. This was the Apotheosis of War, I thought: what was the brutish squalor of the trenches beside this lofty triumph, this headlong swoop to glory or death?

Now the Messerschmitt spiralled away from the bursting shells, almost lazily, and began to climb higher. At the top of this manoeuvre, it seemed to hover – just for a moment, hundreds of feet above the earth.

Then I saw the Bomb – that deadly blue-painted metal pod – detach from its parent, quite delicately, and it began its fall to earth.

A single shell arced up, out of the forest, and it punched a hole in the wing of the flying machine. There was an eruption of flame, and *die Zeitmaschine* looped crazily away, enveloped by smoke.

I emitted a whoop. 'Good shooting! Nebogipfel – did you see that?'

But the Morlock had reached up out of the Sea, and hauled with his soft hands at my head. 'Down,' he said. 'Get down into the water . . .'

My last glimpse of the battle was of the trail of smoke which marked the path of the tumbling Messerschmitt – and, before it, a glowing star, already almost too bright to look at, which was the falling Bomb.

I ducked my head into the Sea.

11

THE BOMB

In an instant, the gentle light of the Palaeocene sun was banished.

A crimson-purple glare flooded the air above the water's surface. An immense, complex sound crashed over me: it was founded on the crack of a great explosion, but all overlaid by a roaring, and by a noise of smashing and tearing. All of this was diluted by the few inches of water above me, but still it was so loud that I was forced to press my hands to my ears; I called out, and bubbles escaped from my mouth and brushed against my face.

That initial crack subsided, but the roaring went on and on. My air was soon done, and I was forced to push my head above the water. I gasped, and shook water from my eyes.

The noise was extraordinarily loud. The light from the forest was too bright to look into, but my dazzled eyes had an impression of a great ball of crimson fire that seemed to be whirling about, in the middle of the forest, almost like a living thing. Trees had been smashed down like skittles, all around that pirouetting fire, and huge shards of the broken-up *diptero-carps* were picked up and thrown around in the air as easily as match-stalks. I saw animals tumbling from the forest, fleeing in terror from the Storm: a family of *Diatryma*, their feathers ruffled and scorched, stumbled towards the water; and there came a

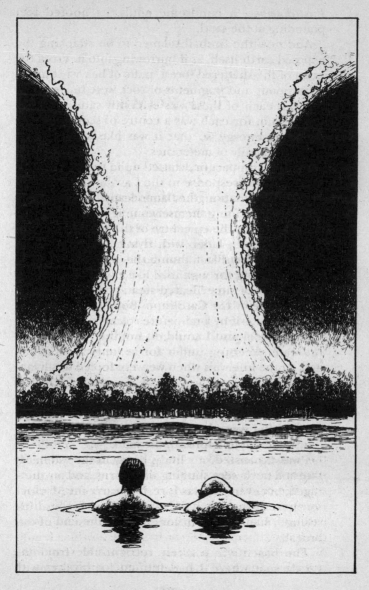

'Nebogipfel and I could do nothing but cower in the water.'

Pristichampus, a handsome adult, its hoofed feet pounding at the sand.

And now the fireball seemed to be attacking the exposed earth itself, as if burrowing into it. From the heart of the shattered forest, puffs of heavy incandescent vapour and fragments of rock were hurled high and far; each of these was evidently saturated with Carolinum, for each was a centre of scorching and blistering energy, so that it was like watching the birth of a family of meteorites.

A huge, compact fire started up in the heart of the forest now, in response to the Carolinum's god-like touch of destruction; the flames leaped up, hundreds of feet tall, forming themselves into a cone of billowing light about the epicentre of the blast. A cloud of smoke and ash, laden with flying lumps of debris, began to collect like a thunderhead above the blaze. And, punching through it all like a fist of light, there was a pillar of superheated steam, rising out of the crater made by the Carolinum Bomb, a pillar red-lit from below as if by a miniature volcano.

Nebogipfel and I could do nothing but cower in the water, keeping under for as long as we could, and, in the intervals when we were forced to surface for air, holding our arms above our heads for fear of the shower of scorched, falling debris.

At last, after some hours of this, Nebogipfel decreed it safe enough to approach the land.

I was exhausted, my limbs heavy in the water. My face and neck were stinging with burns, and my thirst raged; but even so I was forced to carry the Morlock for most of the way back to the shore, for his little strength had given out long before the end of our ordeal.

The beach was scarcely recognizable from the gentle spot where I had hunted for bivalves with

Hilary Bond, mere hours before. The sand was strewn with debris from the forest – much of it smashed-up branches and bits of tree-trunk, some of it still smouldering – and muddy rivulets worked their way across the pocked surface. The heat emanating from the forest was still all but unbearable – fires burned on in many sections of it – and the tall, purple-red glow of the Carolinum column shone out over the agitated waters. I stumbled past a scorched corpse, I think it was a *Diatryma* chick, and I found a reasonably clear patch of sand. I brushed away a coating of ash which had settled there, and dumped the Morlock on the ground.

I found a little rill and cupped my hand to catch the water. The liquid was muddy and flecked with black soot – the stream was polluted by the burnt flesh of trees and animals, I surmised – but my thirst was so great that I had no choice but to drink it down, in great, dirty handfuls.

'Well,' I said, and my voice was reduced to a croak by the smoke and my exertions, '*this* is a damned fine fist of things. Man has been present in the Palaeocene for less than a year . . . and, already – this!'

Nebogipfel was stirring. He tried to get his arms under him; but he could barely lift his face from the sand. He had lost his face-mask, and the huge, soft lids of his delicate eyes were encrusted with sand. I felt touched by an odd tenderness. Once again, this wretched Morlock had been forced to endure the devastation of War among humans – among members of my own, shoddy race – and had suffered as a consequence.

As gently as if I were lifting a child, I lifted him from the sand, turned him over, and sat him up; his legs dangled like lengths of string. 'Take it easy, old man,' I said. 'You're safe now.'

His blind head swivelled towards me, his functioning eye leaking immense tears. He murmured liquid syllables.

'What?' I bent to hear. 'What are you saying?'

He broke into English. '. . . not safe . . .'

'What?'

'We are not safe here – not at all . . .'

'But why? The fire can't reach us now.'

'Not the fire . . . *the radiations* . . . Even when the glow is finished . . . in weeks, or months, still the radiative particles will linger . . . the radiations will eat into the skin . . . It is not a safe place.'

I cupped his thin, papery cheek in my hand; and at that moment – burned, thirsty beyond belief – I felt as if I wanted to chuck it all in, to *sit* on that ruined beach, regardless of fires, Bombs and radiative particles: to sit and wait for the final Darkness to close about me. But some lingering bits of strength coalesced around my concern at the Morlock's feeble agitation.

'Then,' I said, 'we will walk away from here, and see if we can find somewhere we can rest.'

Ignoring the pain of the cracked skin of my own shoulders and face, I slipped my arms under his limp body and picked him up.

It was late afternoon by now, and the light was fading from the sky. After perhaps a mile, we were far enough from the central blaze that the sky was clear of smoke, but the crimson pillar above the Carolinum crater illuminated the darkling sky, almost as steadily as the Aldis lamps which had lit up the London Dome.

I was startled by a young *Pristichampus* who came bursting from the forest's rim. The yellow-white mouth of the beast was gaping wide as it tried to cool itself, and I saw that it dragged one hind leg quite badly; it looked as if it was almost blind, and quite terrified.

Pristichampus stumbled past us and fled, screeching in an unearthly fashion.

I could feel clean sand under my bare feet once more, and I could smell the rich brine of the Sea, a vapour which began the job of washing the stink of smoke and ash out of my head. The ocean remained placid and immovable, its surface oily in the Carolinum light, despite all the foolishness of Humanity; and I pledged my gratitude to that patient body – for now the Sea had cradled me, saving my life even as my fellow humans had blown each other to bits.

This reverie of walking was broken by a distant call. '*Ha-llooo . . .*'

It came drifting along the beach, and, perhaps a quarter-mile away ahead of me, I made out a waving figure, walking towards me.

For a moment I stood there, quite unable to move; for I suspect that I had assumed, in some morbid recess of my soul, that all the members of the Chronic Expeditionary Force must have been consumed by the atomic explosion, and that Nebogipfel and I had been once more left alone in time.

The other chap was a soldier who had evidently been far enough away from the action to remain unscathed, for he was dressed in the trooper's standard jungle-green twill shirt, rifle-green felt hat and trousers with anklets. He carried a light machine-gun, with leather ammunition pouches. He was tall, wire-thin, and red-haired; and he seemed familiar. I had no idea how *I* looked: a frightful mess, I imagine, with scorched and blackened face and hair, white-staring eyes, naked save for my trousers, and with the inhuman bundle of the Morlock in my arms.

The trooper pushed back his hat. 'This is all a fine pickle, isn't it, sir?' He had the clipped, Teutonic accent of the North-East of England.

I remembered him. 'Stubbins, isn't it?'

'That's me, sir.' He turned and waved up the beach. 'I've been map-making up that way. Was six or seven miles away when I saw Jerry coming over the water. As soon as I saw that big column of flame go up – well, I knew what was what.' He looked towards the encampment site uncertainly.

I shifted my weight, trying to hide my fatigue. 'But I shouldn't go back to the encampment yet. The fire's still burning – and Nebogipfel warns of radiative emissions.'

'Who?'

For answer, I lifted the Morlock a little.

'Oh, *him.*' Stubbins scratched the back of his head; the short hairs there rasped.

'There'll be nothing you can do to help, Stubbins – not yet.'

He sighed. 'Well then, sir, what are we to do?'

'I think we should carry on up the beach a little way, and find somewhere to shelter for the night. I expect we'll be safe – I doubt that any Palaeocene animal will be unwise enough to interfere with men tonight, after all *that* – but we perhaps should build a fire. Do you have matches, Stubbins?'

'Oh, yes, sir.' He tapped his breast pocket, and a box rattled. 'Don't you worry about that.'

'I won't.'

I resumed my steady walking along the beach, but my arms were aching uncommonly, and my legs seemed to be trembling. Stubbins noted my distress, and with silent kindness, he hung his machine-gun from his broad back, and lifted the unconscious Morlock from my arms. He had a wiry strength, and did not find, it seemed, Nebogipfel a burden.

We walked until we found a suitable hollow in the forest's fringe, and there we made our camp for the night.

12

THE AFTERMATH OF
THE BOMBING

The morning dawned fresh and clear.

I woke before Stubbins. Nebogipfel remained unconscious. I walked down to the beach and to the fringe of the Sea. The sun was rising over the ocean before me, its warmth already strong. I heard the clicks and trills of the forest fauna, busy already with their little concerns; and a smooth black shape – I thought it was a ray – glided through the water a few hundred yards from land.

In those first moments of the new day, it was as if my Palaeocene world was as vigorous and unscarred as it had been before the arrival of Gibson and his expedition. But that pillar of purple fire still guttered from the central wound in the forest, reaching up through a thousand feet or more. Clots of flame – bits of melted rock and soil – hurled themselves along the flanks of that pillar, following glowing parabolic paths. And over it all there lingered still an umbrella-shaped cloud of dust and steam, its edges frayed by the action of the breeze.

We breakfasted on water and the flesh of nuts from the palms. Nebogipfel was subdued, weakened, and his voice was a scratch; but he counselled Stubbins and me against returning to the devastated camp-site. For all we knew, he said, the three of us might have been left alone, there in the Palaeocene, and we must think of our survival into the future. Nebogipfel argued that we should migrate further away – several miles, he said – and set up camp in some more equable spot, safe from the radiative emissions of the Carolinum.

But I saw in Stubbins's eyes, and in the depths of my own soul, that this course of action was impossible for both of us.

'I'm going back,' Stubbins said at last, with a blunt directness that overcame his natural deference. 'I hear what you're telling me, sir, but the fact is there might be people lying sick and dying back there. I couldn't just leave them to it.' He turned to me, and his open, honest face was crumpled with concern. 'It wouldn't be right, would it, sir?'

'No, Stubbins,' I said. 'Not right at all.'

And so it was, with the day still young, that Stubbins and I set off back along the beach, in the direction of the devastated camp site. Stubbins still wore his jungle-green kit, which had survived the previous day pretty much unscathed; I, of course, was dressed only in the remains of the khaki trousers I had been wearing at the moment of the Bombing. Even my boots were lost, and I felt singularly ill-equipped as we set out. We had no medical supplies whatever, save for the small kit of bandages and ointments Stubbins had been carrying for his own use. But we had gathered some fruit from the palm-trees, emptied out their milk, and filled the shells with fresh water; Stubbins and I each wore five or six such shells around our necks on bits of liana, and we thought with this we might bring some succour to such victims of the Bombing as we found.

There was a steady noise from the Bomb's slow, continuing detonation: a featureless sound, with the ground-shaking quality of a waterfall's roar. Nebogipfel had made us promise that we should approach the central Bomb-site no closer than a

402

mile; and by the time we reached that part of the beach which was, as best as we could judge it, a mile from the epicentre of the blast, the sun was climbing high in the sky. We were already in the shadow of that lingering, poisonous umbrella-cloud; and the crimson-purple glow of the continuing central explosion was so violent that it cast a shadow before me on the beach.

We bathed our feet in the Sea. I rested my aching knees and calves, and relished the warmth of the sunlight on my face. Ironically it remained a beautiful day, with the sky clear and the Sea bathed in light. I observed how the action of the tide had already repaired much of the damage to the beach wrought by the best efforts of we humans the day before: bivalves burrowed again in the sooty sand, and I saw a turtle scampering through the shallows, almost close enough for us to touch.

I felt very old, and immeasurably tired: quite out of place, here at the dawn of the world.

We struck away from the beach and into the forest. I entered the gloom of that battered wood with dread. Our plan was to work through the forest around the camp site, following a circle a safe mile in radius. School-boy geometry was sufficient to provide an estimate of the six-mile hike we would have to complete around the circumference of that circle before we reached the sanctuary of the beach again; but I knew that we would find it difficult, or impossible, to stick to a precise arc, and I expected our full traverse to be considerably longer, and to take some hours.

We were already close enough to the epicentre of the blast that many of the trees had been toppled and smashed up – trees destroyed in a moment, which might otherwise have stood for a century – and we were forced to clamber over the charred, battered remnants of trunks, and through the forest canopy's scorched remains. And, even where the effects of the first blast were less marked, we saw the scars of the storm of fire, which had turned whole stands of *dipterocarps* into clusters of charred, denuded trunks, like immense match-stalks. The canopy was quite disrupted; and the daylight piercing through to the forest floor was much more powerful than I had become accustomed to. But still the forest was a place of shadows and gloom; and the purple glow of that deadly, continuing explosion cast a sickly glow over the scorched remains of trees and fauna.

Not surprisingly, the surviving animals and birds – even the insects – had fled the wounded forest, and we proceeded in an eerie stillness broken only by the rustle of our own footsteps, and by the steady, hot breath of the Bomb's fire-pit.

In some places the fallen wood was still hot enough to steam, or even to glow dull red, and my bare feet were soon blistered and burned. I tied grass around my soles to protect them, and I was reminded of how I had done the same as I made my way out of the forest I had burned in the Year 802,701. Several times we came across the corpse of some poor animal, caught in a disaster beyond its comprehension; despite the blaze, the putrefactive processes of the forest worked vigorously, and we were forced to endure a stink of decay and death as we walked. Once I stepped on the liquefying remains of some little creature – it had been a *planetetherium*, I think – and poor Stubbins was forced to wait for me as, with noises of disgust, I scraped the remains of the little animal from the sole of my foot.

After perhaps an hour, we came across a still, hunched form on the floor of the forest. The stench was so bad that I was forced to hold the remains of my handkerchief over my face. The body was so badly burned and misshapen that at first I thought it might be the corpse of some beast – a young *diatryma* perhaps – but then I heard Stubbins exclaim. I stepped to his side; and there I saw, at the end of a blackened limb stretched out along the ground, the hand of a woman. The hand, by some bizarre accident, was quite undamaged by the fire; the fingers were curled, as if in sleep, and a small gold ring sparkled on the fourth finger.

Poor Stubbins stumbled away into the trees, and I heard him retching. I felt foolish, helpless and desolate, standing there in the ruined forest with those shells of water dangling useless from my neck.

'What if it's all like this, sir?' Stubbins asked. 'You know – *this*.' He could not bear to look at the corpse, or in any way point to it. 'What if we find no-one alive – what if they're all gone, all burnt to a crisp like *this*?'

I laid a hand on his shoulder, and sought a strength I did not feel. 'If that's so, then we'll go back to the beach, and find a way to live,' I said. 'We'll make the best of it; that's what we'll do, Stubbins. But you mustn't give up, man – we've barely started our searching.'

His eyes were white, in a face as soot-dark as a chimney-sweep's. 'No,' he said. 'You're right. We mustn't give up. We'll make the best of it; what else can we do? But –'

'Yes?'

'Oh – *nothing*,' he said; and he began to straighten his kit, in readiness to go on.

He did not have to finish his sentiment for me to understand what he meant! If all the Expedition were finished save the two of us and the Morlock, then, Stubbins knew, the three of us would sit in our huts on the beach, until we died. And then the tide would cover our bones, and that would be that; we should be lucky to leave behind a fossil, to be found by some curious householder digging a garden in Hampstead or Kew, fifty million years from now.

It was a grim, futile prospect; and what – Stubbins would want to know – what was the *best* that could be made out of all that?

In grim silence, we left the girl's charred corpse, and pressed on.

We had no way of judging time in the forest, and the day was long in that grisly wreckage; for even the sun seemed to have suspended his daily traverse around the sky, and the shadows of the broken stumps of trees seemed neither to shorten nor to track across the ground. But in reality it was perhaps only an hour later that we heard a crackling, crashing noise, approaching us from the interior of the wood.

At first we could not see the source of the noise – Stubbins's eyes, wide with fear, were white as ivory in the gloom – and we waited, holding our breath.

A form approached us, coalescing from the charred shadows, stumbling and colliding with the tree stumps; it was a slight figure, clearly in distress but, nonetheless, undoubtedly human.

With my heart in my mouth, I rushed forward, careless now of the crusty, blackened undergrowth under my feet. Stubbins was at my side.

It was a woman, but with her face and upper body burned and so blackened I could not recognize her. She fell into our arms with a gurgled sigh, as if with relief.

Stubbins sat the woman on the ground with her back to a snapped-off tree stump. He muttered clumsy endearments as he worked: 'Don't you worry – you'll be fine, I'll look after you –' and so forth, in a voice that was choked. She still wore the charred remnants of a twill shirt and khaki trousers, but the whole was blackened and torn; and her arms were

406

badly scorched, particularly on the underside of the forearms. Her face was burned – she must have been facing the blast – but there were, I saw now, strips of healthy flesh across her mouth and eyes, which remained comparatively unharmed. I surmised that she had thrown her arms across her face when the blast had come, damaging her forearms, but protecting at least some of her face.

She opened her eyes now: they were a piercing blue. Her mouth opened, and an insect-whisper emerged; I bent close to hear, suppressing my revulsion and horror at the blackened ruin of her nose and ears.

'Water. In the name of God – *water* . . .'

It was Hilary Bond.

13

BOND'S ACCOUNT

Stubbins and I stayed with Hilary for some hours, feeding her sips of water from our shells. Periodically Stubbins set off on little circular tours of the forest, calling boldly to attract the attention of more survivors. We tried to ease Hilary's wounds with Stubbins's medical kit; but the contents of the kit – intended to treat bruises and cuts and the like – were quite inadequate to cope with burns of the extent and severity of Hilary's.

Hilary was weakened, but she was quite coherent, and she was able to give me a sensible account of what she had seen of the Bombing.

After she had left me on the beach, she had plunged through the forest as fast as she could. Even so, she was no closer than a mile to the camp when the Messerschmitt came.

'I saw the Bomb falling through the air,' she whispered. 'I knew it was Carolinum from the way it burned – I've not seen it before, but I've heard accounts – and I thought I was done for. I froze like a rabbit – or like a fool – and by the time I'd got my wits back, I knew I didn't have time to get to the ground, or duck behind the trees. I threw my arms before my face ...'

The flash had been inhumanly bright. 'The light burned at my flesh ... it was like the doors of Hell

opening . . . I could feel my cheeks *melting*; and when
I looked I could see the tip of my nose burning – like
a little candle . . .it was the most extraordinary . . .'
She collapsed into coughing.

Then the concussion came – 'like a great wind' –
and she was knocked backwards. She had tumbled
across the forest floor, until she had collided with a
hard surface – presumably a tree trunk – and, for a
spell, knew no more.

When she came to, that pillar of crimson and
purple flame was rising like a daemon out of the
forest, with its attendant familiars of melted earth and
steam. Around her the trees were smashed and
scorched, although – by chance – she was far enough
from the epicentre to have avoided the worst of the
damage, and she hadn't been further injured by
falling branches or the like.

She had reached up to touch her nose; and she
remembered only a dull curiosity as a great piece of it
came away in her hand. 'But I felt no pain – it is very
odd . . . although,' she added grimly, 'I was compen-
sated for that soon enough . . .'

I listened to this in a morbid silence, and vivid in
my mind's eye was the slim, rather awkward girl with
whom I had hunted bivalves, mere hours before this
terrible experience.

Hilary thought she slept. When she came to her
senses, the forest was a good deal darker – the first
flames had subsided – and, for some reason, her pain
was reduced. She wondered if her very nerves had
been destroyed.

With a huge effort, for she was by now greatly
weakened by thirst, she pulled herself to her feet
and approached the epicentre of the blast.

'I remember the glow of the continuing Carolinum
explosion, that unearthly purple, brightening as I
moved through the trees . . . The heat increased, and

I wondered how close I would be able to come, before I would be forced back.'

She had reached the fringe of the open space around the parked Juggernauts.

'I could barely see, so bright was the glare of the Carolinum fire-pit, and there was a roar, like rushing water,' she said. 'The Bomb had landed slap in the centre of our camp – that German was a good marksman – it was like a toy volcano, with smoke and flame pouring up out of it.

'Our camp is flattened and burned, most of our belongings destroyed. Even the 'Nauts are smashed to bits: of the four, only one has retained its shape, and that is gutted; the others are burst open, toppled like toys, burned and exploded. I saw no people,' she said. 'I think I had expected . . .' She hesitated. 'Horrors: I expected horrors. But there was nothing – nothing left of them. Oh – save for one thing – the strangest thing.' She laid a hand on my arm; it was reduced by flame to a claw. 'On the skin of that 'Naut, most of the paint was blistered away – except in one place, where there was a shaped patch . . . It was like a shadow, of a crouching man.' She looked up at me, her eyes gleaming from her ruined face. 'Do you understand? It *was* a shadow – of a soldier, I don't know who – caught in that moment of a blast so intense that his flesh was evaporated, his bones scattered. *And yet the shadow in the paint remained.*' Her voice remained level, dispassionate, but her eyes were full of tears. 'Isn't that strange?'

Hilary had stumbled about the rim of the encampment for a while. Convinced by now she would not find people alive there, she had a vague idea of seeking out supplies. But, she said, her thoughts were scattered and confused, and her residual pain so intense it threatened to overwhelm her; and, with her damaged hands, she found it impossible to grub

410

through the charred remnants of the camp with any semblance of system.

So she had come away, with the intention of trying to reach the Sea.

After that, she could barely remember anything of her stumble through the forest; it had lasted all night, and yet she had come such a short distance from the explosion site that I surmised she must have been blundering in circles, until Stubbins and I found her.

411

14

SURVIVORS

Stubbins and I resolved that our best course would be to take Hilary out of the forest, away from the damaging Carolinum emissions, and bring her to our encampment along the beach, where Nebogipfel's advanced ingenuity might be able to concoct some way to make her more comfortable. But it was clear enough that Hilary did not have the strength to walk further. So we improvised a stretcher of two long, straight fallen branches, with my trousers and Stubbins's shirt tied between them. Wary of her blistered flesh, we lifted Hilary onto this makeshift construction. She cried out when we moved her, but once we had her settled on the stretcher her discomfort eased.

So we set off back through the forest, towards the beach. Stubbins preceded me, and soon I could see how his bare, bony back prickled with sweat and dirt. He stumbled in the forest's scorched gloom, and lianas and low branches rattled against his unprotected face; but he did not complain, and kept his hands wrapped around the poles of our stretcher. As for me, staggering along in my under-shorts, my strength was soon exhausted, and my emptied-out muscles set up a great trembling. At times, it seemed impossible that I could lift my feet for another step, or keep my stiffening hands wrapped around those rough poles. But, watching the stolid determination of Stubbins ahead of me, I strove to mask my fatigue and to follow his pace.

Hilary lay in a shallow unconsciousness, with her limbs convulsing and mumbled cries escaping her lips, as echoes of pain worked their way through her nervous system.

When we reached the shore we set Hilary down in the shade of the forest's rim, and Stubbins lifted her head, cupping her skull in one hand, as he fed her sips of water. Stubbins was a clumsy man, but he worked with an unconscious delicacy and sensitivity that overcame the natural limitations of his frame; it seemed to me that he was pouring his whole being into those simple acts of kindness for Hilary. Stubbins struck me as fundamentally a good, kind man; and I accepted that his detailed care of Hilary was motivated largely by nothing more nor less than simple compassion. But I saw, too, that it would have been unbearable for poor Stubbins to have survived – thanks only to the lucky chance of following an assignment away from the camp during the disaster – when all of his fellows had perished; and I foresaw that he would spend a good deal of his remaining days on such acts of contrition as this.

When we had done our best we picked up the stretcher and progressed along the beach. Stubbins and I, all but naked, our bodies coated with the soot and ash of the burned forest, and with the broken body of Hilary Bond suspended between us, walked along the firmer, damp sand at the Sea's fringe, with cool, wet sand between our toes and brine wavelets lapping against our shins.

When we reached our small encampment, Nebogipfel took command. Stubbins fussed about, but he impeded Nebogipfel's movements, and the Morlock served me with a series of hostile glares until I took Stubbins's arm and pulled him away.

'Look here, old chap,' I said, 'the Morlock might look a little strange, but he knows a sight more medicine that I do – or you, I should hazard. I think it's best if we keep out of his way for a bit, and let him treat the Captain.'

Stubbins's great hands flexed.

At length I had an idea. 'We still need to seek out any others,' I said. 'Why not build a fire? If you use green wood, and produce enough smoke, you should raise a signal which will be visible for miles.'

Stubbins fell in with this suggestion with alacrity, and he plunged without delay into the forest. He was like some clumsy animal as he hauled out branches from the wood, but I felt relief that I had found a useful purpose for the helpless energy surging within him.

Nebogipfel had prepared a series of opened palm-nut shells, set in little cups in the sand, each filled with a milky lotion he had devised. He asked for Stubbins's clasp-knife; with this, he began to cut away Hilary's clothing. Nebogipfel scooped up handfuls of his lotion and, with his soft Morlock fingers, he began to work it into her worst-damaged flesh.

At first Hilary, still all but unconscious, cried out at these ministrations; but before long her discomfort passed, and she appeared to be passing into a deeper, more peaceful sleep.

'What is the lotion?'

'A salve,' he said as he worked, 'based on palm-nut milk, bivalve oil and plants from the forest.' He pushed his slit-mask more comfortably over his face, and left on it streaks of the sticky lotion. 'It will ease the pain of the burns.'

'I'm impressed by your foresight in preparing the salve,' I said.

'It did not take much *foresight*,' he said coolly, 'to

anticipate such victims, after your self-inflicted catastrophe of yesterday.'

I felt a stab of irritation at this. *Self-inflicted?* None
of us had *asked* the confounded German to come
through time with his Carolinum Bomb. 'Blast you, I
was trying to congratulate you on your efforts for this
girl!'

'But I would much rather not have you bring me
such sad victims of folly, as exercises for my compassion and ingenuity.'

'Oh – confound it!' The Morlock really was impossible at times, I thought – quite un-human!

Stubbins and I maintained our bonfire, feeding it
with wood so green it spat and fractured and sent up
billows of cloudy-white smoke. Stubbins set off for
brief, ineffectual searches of the forest; I was forced
to promise him that if the fire met with no success in
a few days, we should resume our expedition around
the explosion epicentre.

It was on the fourth day after the Bombing that
more survivors began to arrive at our beacon. They
came alone, or in pairs, and they were burned and
beaten up, clothed in the ragged remnants of jungle
kit. Soon Nebogipfel was running a respectable field
hospital – a row of palm-frond pallets, there in the
shade of the *dipterocarps* – while the able-bodied
among us were set to work with rudimentary nursing
duties and the collection of more supplies.

For a while we hoped that there might be, elsewhere, some other encampment better equipped
than ours. Perhaps Guy Gibson had survived, I speculated, and had taken things in hand, in his practical,
level-headed way.

We had a brief burst of optimism along these lines
when a light motor vehicle came bounding along the
beach. The car bore two soldiers, both young women.

But we were to be disappointed. These two girls were merely the furthest-flung of the exploratory expeditions the Force had sent out from its base: they had been following the shore to the west, looking for a way to strike inland.

For some weeks after the attack we maintained patrols along the beach and into the forest. These occasionally turned up the remains of some poor victim of the Bombing. Some of these appeared to have survived for a time after the first blast, but, enfeebled by injuries, had proved unable to save themselves or call for help. Sometimes a bit of kit would be brought back. (Nebogipfel was keen that any scraps of metal should be retrieved, for he argued that it would be some considerable time before our little residual colony would be able to smelt ore.) But of further survivors, we found none; the two women in their car were the last to join us.

We kept the signal fire burning, though, day and night, long after any reasonable hope of more survivors had vanished.

All told, of the hundred or more Expedition members, twenty-one individuals – eleven women, nine men, and Nebogipfel – survived the Bombing and fire-storm. No trace of Guy Gibson was found; and the Gurkha doctor was lost.

So we busied ourselves with caring for injured, with collecting the supplies necessary to keep us alive from day to day, and with assembling our thoughts for how we should build a colony for the future . . . for, with the destruction of the Juggernauts, it was soon evident to us all that we should not be returning to our home centuries: that this Palaeocene earth would, after all, receive our bones.

416

15

A NEW SETTLEMENT

Four of our number died, of burns and other injuries, soon after being brought to the camp. At least their suffering appeared to be slight, and I wondered if Nebogipfel had tempered his improvised drugs in such a way as to shorten the distress of these afflicted.

I kept such speculations to myself, however.

Each loss cast a deep pall over our little colony. For myself I felt numb, as if my soul was replete with horror, and beyond further reaction. I watched the battered young soldiers, in their ragged, bloodied remnants of military kit, go about their dismal chores; and I knew that these new deaths, in the midst of the brutal, primitive squalor within which we now strove to survive, forced each one of them to confront his or her own mortality anew.

To make things worse, after a few weeks a new sickness began to haunt our thinned ranks. It afflicted some of those already wounded, and, disturbingly, others who had seemed, on the surface, to have been left healthy after the Bombing. The symptoms were gross: vomiting, bleeding from the body's orifices, and a loosening of the hair, fingernails and even the teeth.

Nebogipfel took me aside. 'It is as I feared,' he whispered. 'It is a sickness brought on by exposure to Carolinum radiation.'

417

'Are any of us safe – or will we all succumb?'

'We have no way to treat it, save for the alleviation of some of the worst symptoms. And as for safety –'

'Yes?'

He pushed his hands under his slit-mask to rub his eyes. 'There is no such thing as a *safe* level of radio-activity,' he said. 'There are only degrees of risk – of chance. We may all survive – or we may all succumb.'

I found all this most distressing. To see those young bodies, already scarred by years of War, now lying broken on the sand, left this way at the hands of a fellow human, and with only the inexpert ministra-tions of a Morlock – a stranded alien – to treat their wounds . . . It made me ashamed of my race, and of myself.

'Once, you know,' I told Nebogipfel, 'I think a part of me might have argued that War could ultimately be a force for good – because it might break open the ossified ways of the Old Order of things, and open up the world for *Change*. And once I believed in an innate wisdom in Humanity: that, after witnessing so much destruction in a War like this, a certain bluff common sense would prevail, to put a stop to it all.'

Nebogipfel rubbed his hairy face. '"Bluff common sense"?' he repeated.

'Well, so I imagined,' I said. 'But I had had no experience of War – not of the real thing. Once humans start bashing each other up, precious little will stop them until exhaustion and attrition over-came them! Now I can see there's *no* sense in War – not even in the outcome of it . . .'

But on the other hand, I told Nebogipfel, I was struck by the selfless devotion of this handful of survivors to the care and tending of each other. Now that our situation had been reduced to its essentials – to simple human suffering – the tensions of class, race, creed and rank, all of which I had observed in this Expeditionary Force before the Bombing, had dissolved away.

Thus I observed, if I adopted the dispassionate viewpoint of a Morlock, that contradictory complex of strengths and weaknesses that lay at the soul of my species! Humans are at once more brutal, and yet, in some ways, more *angelic*, than the shallow experience of my first four decades of life had led me to believe.

'It's a little late,' I conceded, 'to be learning such deep lessons about the species with whom I have shared the planet for forty-odd years. But nevertheless, there it is. It seems to me now that if man is ever to achieve peace and stability – at least before he evolves into something new, like a Morlock – then the unity of the species will have to start at the bottom: by building on the firmest foundation – the only foundation – the instinctive support of a man for his fellows.' I peered at Nebogipfel. 'Do you see what I'm getting at? Do you think there's any sense in what I say?'

But the Morlock would neither support nor dismiss this latest rationalization. He simply returned my gaze: calm, observant, analytical.

We lost three more souls to the radiative sickness.

Others showed some symptoms – Hilary Bond, for instance, suffered extensive hair loss – but survived; and some, even one man who had been closer to the original blast than most, showed no ill-effects at all. But, Nebogipfel warned me further, we were not done with the Carolinum yet; for other illnesses – cancers and other disorders of the body – might develop in any of us in later life.

Hilary Bond was the senior officer surviving; and, as soon as she was able to raise herself on her pallet, she began to take a calm and authoritative command. A natural military discipline began to assert itself over our group – though much simplified, given that only thirteen had survived of the Expeditionary Force – and I think the soldiers, particularly the younger ones, found much comfort in the restoration of this familiar framework to their world. This military order could not last, of course. If our colony flourished, grew, and survived beyond this generation, then a chain of command along the lines of an Army unit would be neither desirable nor practicable. But for now, I reflected, needs must.

Most of these troopers had spouses, parents, friends – even children – 'back home', in the twentieth century. Now they must come to terms with the fact that none of us were going home – and, as their remaining equipment slowly fell apart in the humidity of the jungle, the troopers came to realize that all that would sustain them in the future was the fruit of their own labour and ingenuity, and their support for each other.

Nebogipfel, still mindful of the dangers of radiative emissions, insisted that we should make a more permanent encampment further along the coast. We sent out scouting parties, making the best use of our motor-car while its fuel lasted. At length, we decided on the delta of the mouth of a broad river, some five miles south-west of the Expedition's original encampment – it was in the vicinity of Surbiton, I suppose. The land bordering our river's plain would be fertile and irrigated, if we chose to develop agriculture in the future.

We made the migration in several stages, for many of the wounded required carrying for much of the journey. At first we used the car, but its supply of petrol soon expired. Nebogipfel insisted we bring the vehicle with us, though, to serve as a mine of rubber, glass, metal and other materials; and so for its final journey we shoved our car like a wheel-barrow along the sand, laden with wounded and with our supplies and equipment.

Thus we limped along the beach, the fourteen of us who had survived, with our ragged clothes and crudely-treated wounds. It struck me that if a dispassionate observer had watched this little trek, he should scarcely have been able to deduce that this ragged band of survivors were the sole representatives, in this Age, of a species which could one day shatter worlds!

Our new colony site was distant enough from the Expedition's first encampment that the forest here showed no significant damage. We could not yet forget the Bombing, though; for at night, that bruised-purple glow to the east still lingered – Nebogipfel said it would remain visible for many years to come – and, exhausted by the work of the day, I often took to sitting at the edge of the camp, away from the lights and talk of the others, and I would watch the stars rise over that man-made volcano.

At first our new encampment was crude: little more than a row of lean-tos lashed up out of windfall branches and palm fronds. But as we settled in, and as our supply of food and water became assured, a more vigorous programme of construction was put underway. The first priority, it was agreed, was a communal Hall, large enough to house us all in the event of a storm or other disaster. The new colonists set to constructing this with a will. They followed the rough outlines I had intended for my own shelter: a wooden platform, set on stilt-like foundations; but its scale was rather more ambitious.

A field beside our river was cleared, so that Nebogipfel could direct the patient cultivation of what might one day become useful crops, bred out of the aboriginal flora. A first boat – a crude dug-out canoe – was constructed, so that the Sea could be fished.

We captured, after much effort, a small family of *Diatryma*, and contained them within a stockade. Although these bird-beasts broke out several times, causing a havoc about the colony, we stuck at containing and taming the birds, for the meat and eggs available from a domesticated flock of *Diatryma* was a pleasant prospect, and there were even experiments in having the *Diatryma* draw ploughs.

From day to day, the colonists treated me with a certain polite deference, as befitted my age – I conceded! – and my greater experience of the Palaeocene. For my part, I found myself in the position of leader of some of our projects in their early days, thanks to my greater experience. But the inventiveness of the younger people, coupled with the jungle survival training they had received, allowed them quickly to surpass my limited understanding; and soon I detected a certain tolerant amusement in their dealings with me. I remained an enthusiastic participant in the colony's burgeoning activities, however.

As for Nebogipfel, he remained, naturally enough, something of a recluse in that society of young humans.

Once the immediate medical problems were resolved, and the demands on his time grew less, Nebogipfel took to spending time away from the colony. He visited our old hut, which still stood some miles to the north-east along the beach; and he went for great explorations into the forest. He did not take me into his confidence as to the purpose of these trips. I remembered the Time-Car he had tried to construct, before the arrival of the Expeditionary Force, and I suspected he was returning to some such project; but I knew that the Plattnerite of the

Force's land-cruisers had been destroyed in the Bombing, so I could see no purpose in his continuing with that scheme. Still, I did not press Nebogipfel on his activities, reasoning that, of all of us, he was the most isolated – the most removed from the company of his fellows – and so, perhaps, the most in need of tolerance.

16

THE ESTABLISHMENT OF FIRST LONDON

Despite the grisly battering they had endured, the colonists were resilient young people, and they were capable of high spirits. Gradually – once we were finished with the Bombing radiation deaths, and once it was clear that we should not immediately starve or get washed into the Sea – a certain good humour became more evident.

One evening, with the shadows of the *dipterocarps* stretching towards the ocean, Stubbins found me sitting, as usual, at the verge of the camp, looking back towards the glow of the Bomb pit. With a painful shyness he – to my astonishment – asked me if I would care to join in a game of football! My protests that I had never played a game in my life counted for nothing, and so I found myself walking back along the beach with him, to where a rough pitch had been marked out in the sand, and posts – scrap timber from the construction of the Hall – had been set up to serve as goals. The 'ball' was a palm-nut shell, emptied of its milk, and eight of us prepared to play out the game, a mixture of men and women.

I scarcely expect that dour battle to go down in the annals of sporting history. My own contribution was negligible, save only to expose that utter lack of physical coordination which had made my days at school such a trial. Stubbins was by far the most skilled of us.

Only three of the players, including Stubbins, were fully fit – and one of those was me, and I was completely done in within ten minutes of the start. The rest were a collection of strapped-up wounds and – comic, pathetic – missing or artificial limbs! But still, as the game wore on, and laughter and shouts of encouragement started to flourish, it seemed to me that my fellow players were really little more than *children*: battered and bewildered, and now stranded in this ancient Age – but children nevertheless.

What kind of species is it, I wondered, that inflicts such damage on its own offspring?

When the game was done, we retired from our pitch, laughing and exhausted. Stubbins thanked me for joining in.

'Not at all,' I said. 'You're a fair old player, Stubbins. Maybe you should have taken it up as a professional.'

'Aye, well, I did, as a matter of fact,' he said wistfully. 'I signed on as an apprentice with Newcastle United . . . but that was in the early days of the War. Pretty soon *that* put a stop to the football. Oh, there's been some competition since – regional leagues, and the League War Cups – but in the last five or six years, even that has been closed down.'

'Well, I think it's a shame,' I said. 'You've a talent there, Stubbins.'

He shrugged, his evident disappointment mingling with his natural modesty. 'It wasn't to be.'

'But now you've done something much more important,' I consoled him. 'You've played in the first football match on the earth – *and* got a hat-trick of goals.' I slapped him on the back. 'Now, *that's* a feather fit for any cap, Albert!'

As time wore on, it became increasingly apparent – I mean, at that level of the spirit below the intellectual where true knowledge resides – that we should, truly, *never* return home. Slowly – inevitably, I suppose – partnerships and ties in the twentieth century became remote, and the colonists formed themselves into couples. This pairing off showed no respect for rank, class or race: sepoy, gurkha and English alike joined in new liaisons. Only Hilary Bond, with her residual air of command, remained aloof from it all.

I remarked to Hilary that she might use her rank as a vehicle for performing marriage ceremonies – much as a sea-captain will join passengers in wedlock. She greeted this suggestion with polite thanks, but I caught scepticism in her voice, and we did not pursue the matter.

A little pattern of dwellings spread along the coast and up the river valley from our Sea-shore node. Hilary viewed all this with a liberal eye; her only rule was that – for now – no dwelling should be out of sight of at least one other, and none should be more than a mile's distance from the site of the Hall. The colonists accepted these strictures with good grace.

Hilary's wisdom regarding the business of marriage – and my converse folly – soon became obvious, for one day I saw Stubbins strolling along the beach with his arms around two young women. I greeted them all cheerfully – but it was not until they had passed that I realized that I did not know which of the women was Stubbins's 'wife'!

I challenged Hilary, and I could tell she was suppressing amusement.

'But,' I protested, 'I've seen Stubbins with Sarah at the barn dance – but then, when I called at his hut that morning last week, there was the *other* girl –'

Now she laughed, and laid her scarred hands on my arms. 'My dear friend,' she said, 'you have sailed the seas of Space and Time – you have changed

426

History many times; you are a genius beyond doubt – and yet, how little you know of people!'

I was embarrassed. 'What do you mean?'

'Think about it.' She ran her hand over her ravaged scalp, where tufts of greyed hair clung. 'We are thirteen – not counting your friend Nebogipfel. And that thirteen is eight women and five men.' She eyed me. 'And that's what we're stuck with. There's no island over the horizon, from whence might come more young men to marry off our girls . . .

'If we all made stable marriages – if we settled into monogamy, as *you* suggest – then our little society would soon tear itself apart. For, you see, eight and five don't match. And so I think a certain *looseness* of our arrangements is appropriate. For the good of all. Don't you think? And besides, it's good for this "genetic diversity" that Nebogipfel lectures us about.'

I was shocked; not (I fondly believed) by any moral difficulties, but by the *calculation* behind all this!

Troubled, I made to leave her – and then a thought struck me. I turned back. 'But – Hilary – *I* am one of the five men you speak of.'

'Of course.' I could see she was making fun of me.

'But I don't – I mean, I haven't –'

She grinned. 'Then perhaps it's time you *did*. You're only making things worse, you know!'

I left in confusion. Evidently, between 1891 and 1944, society had evolved in ways of which I had never dreamed!

Work on the great Hall proceeded quickly, and within no more than a few months of the Bombing, the bulk of the construction was done. Hilary Bond announced that a service of dedication would be held to commemorate the completion. At first Nebogipfel demurred – with characteristic Morlock over-analysis, he could see no purpose to such an

427

exercise – but I persuaded him that it would be politic, as regards future relations with the colonists, to attend.

I washed and shaved, and got myself as smart as it is possible to be when dressed only in a ragged pair of trousers. Nebogipfel combed and trimmed his mane of flaxen hair. Given the practicalities of our situation, many of the colonists went around pretty much nude by now, with little more than strips of cloth or animal skin to cover their modesty. Today, however, they donned the remnants of their uniforms, cleaned up and repaired as far as possible, and, while it was a parade which would have scarce passed muster at Aldershot, we were able to present ourselves with a display of smartness and discipline which I, for one, found touching.

We walked up a shallow, uneven flight of steps and into the new Hall's dark interior. The floor – though uneven – was laid and swept, and the morning sunlight slanted through the glassless windows. I felt rather awed: despite the crudeness of its architecture and construction, the place had a feeling of solidity, of *intent to stay*.

Hilary Bond stood on a podium improvised from the car's petrol tank, and rested her hand for support on Stubbins's broad shoulder. Her ruined face, topped by those bizarre tufts of hair, held a simple dignity.

Our new colony, she announced, was now founded, and ready to be named: she proposed to call it *First London*. Then she asked us all to join her in a prayer. I dropped my head with the rest and clasped my hands before me. I was brought up in a strict High Church household, and Hilary's words now worked nostalgically on me, transporting me back to a simpler part of my life, a time of certainty and surety.

And at length, as Hilary spoke on, simply and effectively, I gave up my attempts at analysis and allowed myself to join in this simple, communal celebration.

17

CHILDREN AND DESCENDANTS

The first fruits of the new unions arrived within the year, under Nebogipfel's supervision.

Nebogipfel inspected our first new colonist carefully – I heard that the mother was most uncertain about allowing a Morlock to handle her baby, and protested; but Hilary Bond was there to calm her fears – and at last Nebogipfel announced that the baby was a perfect girl, and returned her to her parents.

Quite quickly – or so it seemed to me – there were several of the children about the place. It was a common sight to see Stubbins bouncing his baby boy on his shoulders to the little chap's evident delight; and I knew it should not be long before Stubbins would have the little chap kicking bivalve shells for footballs about the beach.

The children were a source of immense joy to the colonists. Before the first births, several of the colonists had been prone to severe bouts of depression, brought on by homesickness and loneliness. Now, though, there were the children to think about: children who would only know First London as their home, and whose future prosperity provided a goal – the greatest goal of all – for their parents.

As for me, as I watched the soft, unmarked limbs of the children, cradled in the scarred flesh of parents who were still young themselves, it was as if I saw the shadow of that dreadful War lifting from these people at last – a shadow banished by the abundant light of the Palaeocene.

Still, though, Nebogipfel inspected each new-born arrival.

The day came, at last, when he would not return a child to its new mother. That birth turned into an occasion of private grief, into which the rest of us did not intrude; and afterwards Nebogipfel disappeared into the forest, following his secret pursuits, for long days.

Nebogipfel spent a good deal of his time running what he called 'study groups'. These were open to any and all of the colonists, though in practice three or four at a time would turn up, depending on interest and other commitments. Nebogipfel held forth on practicalities of life in the conditions of the Palaeocene, such as the manufacture of candles and cloth from the local ingredients; he even devised a sort of soap, a coarse, gritty paste concocted of soda and animal fat. But he also expounded on subjects of broader significance: medicine, physics, mathematics, chemistry, biology, the principles of time travel . . .

I sat in on a number of these sessions. Despite the unearthly nature of his voice and manner the Morlock's exposition was always admirably clear, and he had a knack of asking questions to test the understanding of his audience. Listening to him, I realized that he could have taught the lecturers of the average British university a thing or two!

As for the content, he was careful to restrict himself to the language of his audience – to the vocabulary, if not the jargon, of 1944 – but he summarized for them the main developments in each field in the decades which followed that date. He worked demonstrations where he could, with bits of metal and wood, or produced diagrams sketched in the sand with sticks; he had his 'students' cover every scrap of paper we had been able to retrieve with a codification of his knowledge.

I discussed all this with him around midnight, one dark and moonless night. He had discarded his latest slit-mask, and his grey-red eyes seemed luminescent; he was working with a crude mortar and pestle, in which he was mashing up palm fronds in some liquid. 'Paper,' he said. 'Or at least, an experiment in that direction . . . We must have more paper! Your human verbal memory is not of sufficient fidelity – they will lose everything when I am gone, within a few years . . .'

I took it – wrongly, as it turned out – that he was referring to a fear, or expectation at any rate, of death. I sat down beside him and took the mortar and pestle. 'But is there a point to all this? Nebogipfel, we're still barely subsisting. And you talk to them of Quantum Mechanics, and the Unified Theory of Physics! What need have they of this material?'

'None,' he said. 'But their children will – *if they are to survive*. Look: by accepted theory, one needs a population of several hundred, of any of the large mammalian species, for sufficient genetic diversity to ensure long-term survival.'

'*Genetic diversity* – Hilary mentioned that.'

'Clearly, the available stock of humankind here is far too small for the viability of the colony – even if all the potential genetic material is placed in the pool.'

'And so?' I prompted.

'And so, the only prospect for survival beyond two or three generations is for these people rapidly to attain an advanced grasp of technology. That way, they can become the masters of their own genetic

432

destiny: they need not tolerate the consequences of inbreeding, or the lingering genetic damage inflicted by the Carolinum's radio-activity. So you see, they *do* need Quantum Mechanics and the rest.'

I pushed at the pestle. 'Yes. But there's an implied question here – *should* the human race survive, here in the Palaeocene? I mean, we're not *meant* to be here – not for another fifty million years.'

He studied me. 'But what is the alternative? Do you want these people to die out?'

I remembered my determination to eradicate the existence of the Time Machine before it was ever launched – to put a stop to this endless splintering of Histories. Now, thanks to my blundering about, I had indirectly induced the establishment of this human colony deep in the past, an establishment which would surely cause the most significant Historical fracturing yet! I had a sudden feeling of falling – it was a little like the vertiginous plummeting one feels when Travelling into time – and I felt that this diverging of History must already be far beyond my control.

And then, I thought of the expression on Stubbins's face as he gazed at his first child.

I am man, not a god! I must let myself be influenced by my human instincts, for I was surely incapable of managing the evolution of Histories with any conscious direction. Each of us, I thought, could do little to change the course of things – indeed, anything we tried was likely to be so uncontrolled as to inflict more damage than benefit – and yet, conversely, we should not allow the huge panorama about us, the immensity of the Multiplicity of Histories, to overwhelm us. The perspective of the Multiplicity rendered each of us, and our actions, tiny – *but not without meaning*; and each of us must proceed with our lives with stoicism and fortitude, as if the rest of it – the final Doom of mankind, the endless Multiplicity – were not so.

Whatever the impact on the future of fifty million years hence, there was a sense of health and rightness about this Palaeocene colony, I thought. So my reply to Nebogipfel's question was inevitable.

'No. No, of course we must do all we can to help the colonists, and their descendants, survive.'

'Therefore –'

'Yes?'

'Therefore I must find a way to make paper.'

I ground on with the pestle and mortar.

18

THE FEAST, AND LATER

One day, Hilary Bond announced that the first anniversary of the Bombing was one week away, and that a celebratory Feast would be held to commemorate the founding of our little village.

The colonists fell on this scheme with a will, and preparations were soon well advanced. The Hall was decorated with lianas and immense garlands of flowers, gathered from the forest, and preparations were made to kill and cook one of the colony's precious flock of *Diatryma*.

As for me, I scavenged funnels and lengths of tubing and, in the privacy of an old lean-to, began conducting intense private experiments. The colonists were curious about this, and I was forced to resort to sleeping in the lean-to to keep the secret of my improvised apparatus. It was time, I had decided, to put my scientific understanding to good use – for once!

The day of the Feast dawned. We gathered before the Hall in the bright morning light, and there was an air of great excitement and occasion. Once more the remains of uniforms had been cleaned and donned, and the infants-in-arms were decorated in the new fabrics Nebogipfel had devised of a type of local cotton, coloured bright red and purple by vegetable dyes. I passed through the little knot of people, seeking out my closer friends –

– when there was a crash of twigs, and a deep, creaking bellow.

The cry went up. '*Pristichampus* – it is *Pristichampus*! Look out . . .'

And indeed, the bellow had been characteristic of that great land-running crocodile. People ran around, and I cast about for a weapon, cursing myself for being so unprepared.

Then another voice, gentler and more familiar, came floating to us. 'Hi! Don't be afraid – look!'

The panic subsided, and a sprinkle of laughter broke out.

Pristichampus – a proud male – stalked into the clear space in front of the Hall. We moved back to make room for it, and its hoofed feet left great pockmarks in the sand . . . and there on its back, grinning widely, his red hair flaming in the sunlight, sat Stubbins!

I approached the crocodile. Its scaly hide stank of decaying meat, and one cold eye was fixed on me, swivelling as I walked. Stubbins, bare-backed, grinned down at me; in his wiry hands he held a rein made of plaited lianas, wrapped about *Pristichampus*'s head.

'Stubbins,' I said, 'this is quite an achievement.'

'Aye, well, I know we've set the *Diatryma* to dragging a plough, but this creature is far more agile. Why, we'll be able to travel miles – it's better than a horse . . .'

'Just be careful, even so,' I admonished him. 'And, Stubbins, if you join me later –'

'Yes?'

'I might have a surprise for *you*.'

Stubbins dragged at *Pristichampus*'s head. It took considerable effort, but he managed to get the beast to turn. The great creature stepped its way out of the clearing and back towards the forest, the muscles of its huge legs working like pistons.

Nebogipfel joined me, his head almost lost beneath a huge, broad-brimmed hat.

'That's a fine achievement,' I remarked. 'But – can you see? – he barely had control of the brute . . .'

'He will win,' Nebogipfel said. 'Humans always do.' He stepped closer to me, his white pelt shining in the morning sunlight. 'Listen to me.'

I was startled by this sudden, incongruous whisper. 'What? What is it?'

'I have finished my construction.'

'*What* construction?'

'I leave tomorrow. If you wish to join me, you are welcome.'

And he turned and, noiselessly, walked away towards the forest; in a moment the white of his back was lost in the darkness of the trees. I stood there with the sun at my neck, gazing after the enigmatic Morlock – and it was as if the day had been transformed, for my mind was in a perfect turmoil, for his meaning was utterly clear.

A heavy hand clapped me on the back. 'So,' said Stubbins, 'what's this great secret you have for me?'

I turned to him, but I found it difficult, for some seconds, to focus on his face. 'Come with me,' I said at last, with as much vigour and good humour as I could muster.

A few minutes later, Stubbins – and the rest of the colonists – were raising shells full to the brim with my home-made nut-milk liqueur.

The rest of the day passed in a joyous blur. My liqueur proved more than popular – although for my part I should have much preferred to have been able to improvise a pipe-ful of tobacco! There was much dancing to the sound of inexpert singing and hand-clapping, which impersonated a jolly sort of 1944 music Stubbins called 'swing', that I would like, I think, to have heard more of. I had them sing 'The Land of the Leal' for me, and I performed, with my usual solemnity, one of my patent improvised dances; it evoked great admiration and mirth. The *Diatryma* was roasted on a spit – the cooking of it took most of the day – and the evening saw us sprawled on the scuffed sand, with plates laden with succulent meat.

Once the sun slipped below the tree-line, the party thinned rapidly; for most of us had become accustomed to a dawn-to-dusk existence. I hailed goodnight one final time, and retired to the ruins of my improvised still. I sat in the entrance to the lean-to, sipping at the last of my liqueur, and I watched the shadow of the forest sweep across the Palaeocene Sea. Dark shapes slid through the water: rays, perhaps, or sharks.

I thought over my conversation with Nebogipfel, and tried to come to terms with the decision I must make.

After a time, there was a soft, uneven footstep on the sand.

I turned. It was Hilary Bond – I could barely make out her face in the last of the day-light – and yet, somehow, I was not surprised to see her.

She smiled. 'Can I join you? Do you have any of that moonshine left?'

I waved her to a place in the sand beside me, and I passed her my shell. She drank with some grace. 'It's been a good day,' she said.

'Thanks to you.'

'No. Thanks to all of us.' She reached out and took my hand – quite without warning – the touch of her skin was like an electric jolt. She said, 'I want to thank you for all you've done for us. You and Nebogipfel.'

'We haven't –'

'I doubt if we'd have survived those first few days, without you.' Her voice, soft and level, was nevertheless quite compelling. 'And now, with all *you've* shown us, and all Nebogipfel's taught us – well, I think we've every chance of building a new world here.'

Her fingers were delicate and long against my palm, and yet I could feel the scarring from her burns. 'Thank you for the eulogy. But you speak as if we are going away . . .'

'But you are,' she said. 'Aren't you?'

'You know about Nebogipfel's plans?'

She shrugged. 'In principle.'

'Then you know more than I do. If he has built a Time-Car – where did he get the Plattnerite, for example? The Juggernauts were destroyed.'

'From the wreck of *die Zeitmaschine*, of course.' She sounded amused. 'Didn't you think of that?' She paused. 'And you want to go with Nebogipfel. Don't you?'

I shook my head. 'I don't know. You know, sometimes I feel old – and tired – as if I have seen quite enough already!'

She snorted her contempt for that. 'Baloney. Look: you started it –' She waved a hand. 'All of *this*. Time travelling – and all the changes it's brought about.' She gazed around at the placid Sea. 'And now, this is the biggest *Change* of all. Isn't it?' She shook her head. 'You know, I've had a certain amount of dealing with the strategic planners at the DChronW, and I've come away downcast every time at the smallness of the thinking of such types. To adjust the course of a battle here, to assassinate some tin-pot figure there . . . If you have such a tool as a Chronic-Displacement Vehicle, and if you know that History can be changed, as we do, then would you, *should* you, restrict yourself to such footling goals as that? Why restrict yourself to a few decades, and to fiddling with the boyhood of

439

Bismarck or the Kaiser, when you can go back millions of years – as we have? Now, our children will have *fifty million years* to remake the world . . . We're going to rebuild the human species – aren't we?' She turned to me. 'But *you* haven't reached the end of it yet. What's the Ultimate Change, do you think? Can you go back all the way to the Creation, and start things all over again from there? How far can this – *Changing* – go?'

I remembered Gödel, and his dreams of the Final World. 'I don't know how far it can go,' I said truthfully. 'I can't even imagine it.'

Her face was huge before me, her eyes wells of darkness in the deepening twilight. 'Then,' she said, 'you must travel on and find out. Mustn't you?' She moved closer, and I felt my hand tighten around hers, and her breath was warm against my cheek.

I sensed a stiffness about her – a reticence, which she seemed determined to overcome, if only by force of will. I touched her arm, and I found scarred flesh, and she shuddered, as if my fingers were made of ice. But then she clasped her hand around mine and held it against her arm. 'You must forgive me,' she said. 'It is not easy for me to be close.'

'Why? Because of the responsibilities of your command?'

'No,' she said, and her tone made me feel foolish and clumsy. 'Because of the War. Do you see? Because of all of those who are gone . . . It's hard to sleep, sometimes. You suffer *now*, not *then* – and that's the tragedy of the thing, for those who survive. You feel you can't forget – and that it's wrong of you to go on living, even. *If you break faith with us who died/ We shall not sleep, though poppies grow/ In Flanders field . . .*'

I pulled her closer, and she softened against me, a fragile, wounded creature.

At the last moment, I whispered: 'Why, Hilary? Why now?'

'Genetic diversity,' she said, her breath growing shallow. '*Genetic diversity . . .*'

And soon we travelled on – not to the ends of time – but to the limits of our Humanity, there beside the shore of that primeval Sea.

When I awoke it was still dark, and Hilary had gone.

I came to our old encampment in full daylight. Nebogipfel barely glanced at me through his slit-mask as I entered; evidently he was as unsurprised by my decision as Hilary had been.

His Time-Car was completed. It was a box about five feet square, and around it I saw fragments of an unfamiliar metal: bits, I presumed, of the Messerschmitt, salvaged by the Morlock. There was a bench, lashed up from the wood of the *dipterocarps*, and a small control panel – a crude thing of switches and buttons – that featured the blue toggle switch which Nebogipfel had salvaged from our first Time-Car.

'I have some clothes for you,' Nebogipfel said. He held up boots, a twill shirt, and trousers, all in reasonable order. 'I doubt our colonists will miss them now.'

'Thank you.' I had been wearing shorts made of animal-skin; I dressed rapidly.

'Where do you want to go?'

I shrugged. 'Home. 1891.'

He distorted his face. 'It is lost in the Multiplicity.'

'I know.' I climbed into the frame. 'Let us travel forward anyway, and see what we find.'

I glanced, one last time, at the Palaeocene Sea. I thought of Stubbins, and the tame *Diatryma*, and the light off the Sea in the morning. I knew that I had come close to happiness here – to a contentment that

441

had eluded me all my life. But Hilary was right: it was not enough.

I still felt that great desire for *home*; it was a call in me along the River of Time, as strong, I thought, as the instinct which returns a salmon to its breeding-ground. But I knew, as Nebogipfel had said, that *my* 1891, that cosy world of Richmond Hill, was lost in the fractured Multiplicity.

Well: if I could not go home, I decided, I would go on: I would follow this road of Changing, until it could take me no further!

Nebogipfel looked at me. 'Are you ready?'

I thought of Hilary. But I am not a man to be doing with good-byes.

'I'm ready.'

Nebogipfel climbed stiffly into the frame, favouring his badly-set leg. Without ceremony, he reached for his panel of controls and closed the blue toggle.

19

LIGHTS IN THE SKY

I caught one last glimpse of two people – a man and a woman, both naked – who seemed to hurtle across the beach. A shadow fell briefly over the car, perhaps cast by one of the immense animals of this Age; but soon we were moving too rapidly for such details to be discernible, and we fell into the colourless tumult of time travel.

The heavy Palaeocene sun leapt across the Sea, and I imagined how from the point of view of our transition through time the earth spun like a top on its axis, and rocketed around its star. The moon, too, was visible as a hurtling disc, rendered shadowy by the flickering of its phases. Soon the sun's daily passage merged into the band of silver light which dipped between equinoctial limits, and day and night melted into the uniform blue-grey glow I have described before.

The *dipterocarps* trees of the forest shivered with growth and death, and were shouldered aside by the vigorous growth of younger plants; but the scene around us – the forest, the Sea smoothed by our time-passage to a glassy plain – remained static in its essentials, and I wondered if, despite all my and Nebogipfel's efforts, men had after all failed to survive, here in the Palaeocene.

Then – quite without warning – the forest withered and vanished. It was as if a blanket of greenery had been ripped back from the soil. But the land was scarcely left bare; as soon as the forest was cleared, a melange of blocky brown and grey – the buildings of an expanding First London – swept over the earth. The buildings flowed over the denuded hills and down, past us, to the Sea, there to sprout into docks and harbours. The individual constructions shivered and expired, almost too fast for us to follow, though one or two persisted long enough – I suppose for several centuries – to become almost opaque, like crude sketches. The Sea lost its blue tinge and mutated into a sheet of dirty grey, its waves and tides made into a blur by our passage; the air seemed to take on a brown tinge, like an 1890s London fog, which gave the scene something of a dirty, twilit glow, and the air about us felt warmer.

It was striking that as the centuries fell away, regardless of the fate of individual buildings, the general outlines of the city persisted. I could see how the ribbon of the central river – the proto-Thames – and the scars of major road routes remained, in their essentials, unchanged by time; it was a striking demonstration of how geomorphology, the shape of the landscape, dominates human geography.

'Evidently our colonists have survived,' I said to Nebogipfel. 'They have become a race of New Humans, and they are changing their world.'

'Yes.' He adjusted his skin slit-mask. 'But remember we are travelling at several centuries per second; we are in the midst of a city which has already persisted for some thousands of years. I doubt that little is left of the First London we saw established.'

I peered around, my curiosity strong. Already my little band of exiles must be as remote to these New Humans as had been the Sumerians, say, from 1891. Had any memory persisted, in all this wide and

444

bustling civilization, of the fragile origins of the human species in this antique era?

I became aware of a change in the sky: an odd, green-tinged flickering about the light. I soon realized it was the moon, which still sailed around the earth, waxing and waning through its ancient cycle too fast for me to follow – *but the face of that patient companion was now stained green and blue* – the colours of earth, and life.

An inhabited, earthlike moon! This New Humanity had evidently travelled to the sister world in Space Machines, and transformed it, and colonized it. Perhaps they had developed into a race of moon-men, as tall and spindly as the low-gravity Morlocks I had encountered in the Year 657,208! Of course I could not make out any detail, as the moon's month-long orbit took it spinning across my accelerated sky; and of that I was regretful, for I would have loved to have had a telescope and to make out the waters of new oceans lapping those deep, ancient craters, and the forests spreading across the dust of the great *maria*. How would it be to stand on those rocky plains – to be cut loose of Mother Earth's leading-strings? With every step in that reduced gravity one would fly through the thin, cold air, with the sun fierce and motionless overhead; it would be like the landscape of a dream, I thought, with all that glare, and plants less like earthly flora than the things I imagined among the rocks at the bottom of the sea . . .

Well, it was a sight I should never witness. With an effort, I returned in imagination from the moon, and fixed my attention on our situation.

Now there was some movement in the western sky, low against the horizon: firefly lights flickered into life, jerked across the heavens, and settled into place, there to remain for long millennia, before fading to be replaced by others. There was soon quite a crowd

445

of these sparks, and they coalesced into a sort of bridge, which spanned the sky from horizon to horizon; at its peak, I counted several dozen lights in this city in the sky.

I pointed this out to Nebogipfel. 'Are they stars?'

'No,' he said evenly. 'The earth rotates still, and the true stars must be too obscured to be visible. The lights we see are hanging in a fixed position over the earth . . .'

'Then what are they? Artificial moons?'

'Perhaps. They are certainly placed there by the actions of men. The objects may be artificial – constructed of materials hauled up from the earth, or from the moon, whose gravity well is so much more shallow. Or they may be natural objects towed into place around the earth by rockets: captured asteroids or comets, perhaps.'

I peered at those jostling lights with as much awe as any cave-dweller might stare at the light of a comet beating over his upturned, ignorant head!

'What would be the purpose of such stations in space?'

'Such a satellite is like a tower, fixed over the earth, twenty thousand miles tall . . .'

I grimaced. 'Quite a view! One could sit in it and watch the evolution of weather patterns over a hemisphere.'

'Or the station could serve for the transmission of telegraphic messages from one continent to another. Or, more radically, one could imagine the transfer of great industries – heavy manufacture, or the generation of power, perhaps – to the comparative safety of high earth orbit.'

He opened his hands. 'You can observe for yourself the degradation of the air and water around us. The earth has a limited capacity to absorb the waste products of human industry, and with enough devel-

446

opment, the planet could even be rendered unin-
habitable.

'In orbit, though, the limits to growth are virtually
infinite: witness the Sphere, constructed by my own
species.'

The temperature continued to increase, as the air
grew more foul. Nebogipfel's improvised Time-Car
was functional, but poorly balanced, and it swayed
and rocked; I clung to my bench miserably, for the
combination of the heat, the swaying and the usual
vertigo induced by time travel gave me a most
nauseous feeling.

20

THE ORBITAL CITY

There was a further evolution of our equatorial Orbital City. The chaotic arrangement of those artificial lights had become significantly more regular, I saw. Now there was a band of seven or eight stations, all dazzling bright, positioned at regular intervals around the globe; I imagined that more such stations must be in position below the horizon, continuing their steady march about the waist of the planet.

Now threads of light, fine and delicate, grew steadily down from the gleaming stations, reaching towards the earth like tentative fingers. The motion was even, and slow enough for us to follow, and I realized that I was watching stupendous engineering projects – projects spanning thousands of miles of space, and occupying whole millennia – and I was awed by the dedication and grasp of the New Humans.

After several seconds of this, the leading threads had descended into the obscuring mist of the horizon. Then one such thread disappeared, and the station to which it had been fixed was snuffed out like a candle-flame in a breeze. Evidently the thread had fallen, or broken loose, and its anchoring station was destroyed. I watched the pale, soundless images, wondering what immense disaster – and how many deaths – they represented! Within moments, though, a new station had been fixed into the vacant position in the equator-girdling array, and a fresh thread extended.

'I'm not sure I believe my eyes,' I told the Morlock. 'It looks to me as if they are fixing those cables from space to the earth!'

'So I imagine is happening,' the Morlock said. 'We are witnessing the construction of a Space Elevator – a link, fixed between the surface of the earth and the stations in orbit.'

I grinned at the thought. 'A Space Elevator! I should relish riding such a device: to rise up through the clouds, and into the silent grandeur of space – but, if the Elevator were glass-walled, it would not be a ride for the vertiginous.'

'Indeed not.'

Now I saw that more lines of light were extending *between* the geosynchronous stations. Soon the glowing points were linked, and the traces thickened into a glowing band, as broad and bright as the stations themselves. Again – though I had no real wish to curtail our time-travelling – I wished I could see more of this huge, world-girdling City in the sky.

The development of earth over the same period was scarcely so spectacular, however. Indeed, it seemed to me that First London had become static, perhaps abandoned. Some of the buildings became so long-lived that they seemed almost solid to us, although they were dark, squat and ugly; while others were falling into ruin without replacement. (We saw this process as the appearance, with brutal abruptness, of gaps in the complex sky-line). It seemed to me that the air was becoming still thicker, the patient Sea a drabber grey, and I wondered if the battered earth had been abandoned at last, either for the stars or, perhaps, for more palatable havens beneath the ground.

I raised these possibilities with the Morlock.

'Perhaps,' he said. 'But you must recognize that already more than a million years have passed since the establishment of the original colony, by Hilary Bond and her people. There is more evolutionary distance between you and the New Humans of *this* era, than between you and me. So we can make nothing but educated guesses about the way of living of the races extant here, their motives – even their biological composition.'

'Yes,' I said slowly. 'And yet –'

'Yes?'

'*And yet the sun still shines.* So the tale of these New Humans has diverged from your own. Even though they evidently have Space Machines like yours, *they* have no wish to cloak about the sun, as you Morlocks did.'

'Evidently not.' He raised his pale hand to the heavens. 'In fact, their intent seems altogether more ambitious.'

I turned to see what he was indicating. Once again, I saw, that great Orbital City was showing developments. Now, huge shells – irregular, obviously thousands of miles across – were sprouting around the glowing linear town, like berries on a cane. And as soon as a shell was completed it cast off from earth, blossomed with a fire that illuminated the land, and vanished. From our point of view, the development of such an artefact, from embryonic form to departing fledgling, took a second or less; but each dose of flaring light must, I thought, have bathed the earth for decades.

It was a startling sight, and it continued for some time – for several thousand years, by my estimation.

The shells were, of course, huge ships in space.

'So,' I said to the Morlock, 'men are travelling from the earth, in those great space yachts. But where are they *going*, do you think? The planets? Mars, or Jupiter, or –'

Nebogipfel sat with his masked face tilted up at the sky, and his hands in his lap, and the lights of the ships playing on the hairs of his face. 'One does not need such spectacular energies as we have seen here to travel such petty distances. With an engine like that . . . I think the ambition of these New Humans is wider. I think they are abandoning the solar system, much as they appear to have abandoned the earth.'

I peered after the departing ships in awe. 'What remarkable people these must be, these New Humans! I don't want to be rude about you Morlocks, old chap, but still – what a difference of grasp, of ambition! I mean – a Sphere around the sun is one thing, but to hurl one's children to the stars . . .'

'It is true that *our* ambition was limited to the careful husbandry of a single star – and there was logic to that, for more living space for the species is to be obtained by that means than through a thousand, a *million* interstellar jaunts.'

'Oh, perhaps,' I said, 'but it's scarcely so *spectacular*, is it?'

He adjusted his grubby skin-mask and stared around at the ruined earth. 'Perhaps not. But the husbandry of a finite resource – even this earth – seems to be a competence not shared by your New Humans.'

I saw that he was right. Even as the star-ships' fire splashed across the sea, the remains of First London were decaying further – the crumbling ruins seemed to bubble, as if deliquescing – and the sea became more grey, the air still more foul. The heat was now intense, and I pulled my shirt away from my chest, where it had stuck.

Nebogipfel stirred on his bench, and peered

451

about uneasily. 'I think – if it happens, it will come quickly . . .'

'What will?'

He would not reply. The heat was now more severe than I remembered ever suffering in the jungles of the Palaeocene. The ruins of the city, scattered over the hills of brown dirt, seemed to shimmer, becoming unreal . . .

And then – with a glare so bright it obscured the sun – the city burst into flames!

21

INSTABILITIES

That consuming fire swallowed us, for the merest fraction of a second. A new heat – quite unbearable – pulsed over the Time-Car, and I cried out. But, mercifully, the heat subsided as soon as the city's torching was done.

In that instant of fire, the ancient city had gone. First London was scoured clean of the earth, and left behind were only a few outcroppings of ash and melted brick, and here and there the tracery of a foundation. The bare soil was soon colonized once more by the busy processes of life – a sluggish greenery slid over the hills and about the plain, and dwarfish trees shivered through their cycles at the fringe of the Sea – but the progress of this new wave of life was slow, and seemed doomed to a stunted existence; for a pearl-grey fog lay over everything, obscuring the patient glow of the Orbital City.

'So First London is destroyed,' I said in wonder. 'Do you think there was a war? That fire must have persisted for decades, until there was nothing left to burn.'

'It was not a war,' Nebogipfel said. 'But it *was* a catastrophe wrought by man, I think.'

Now I saw the strangest thing. The new, sparse trees began to die back, but not by withering before my accelerated gaze, like the *dipterocarps* I had watched earlier. Rather, the trees burst into flame –

they burned like huge matches – and then were gone, all in an instant. I saw, too, how a great scorching spread across the grass and shrubs, a blackening which persisted through the seasons, until at last no more grass would grow, and the soil was bare and dark.

Above, those pearl-grey clouds grew thicker still, and the sun- and moon-bands were obscured.

'I think those clouds, above, are ash,' I said to Nebogipfel. 'It is if the earth is burning up ... Nebogipfel – what is happening?'

'It is as I feared,' he said. 'Your profligate friends – these New Humans –'

'Yes?'

'With their meddling and carelessness, *they have destroyed the life-bearing equilibrium of the planet's climate.*'

I shivered, for it had grown colder: it was as if the warmth was leaking out of the world through some intangible drain. At first I welcomed this relief from the scorching heat; but the chill quickly became uncomfortable.

'We are passing through a phase of excess oxygen, of higher sea-level pressure,' Nebogipfel said. 'Buildings, plants and grasses – even damp wood – will combust, spontaneously, in such conditions. But it will not last long. It is a transition to a new equilibrium . . . It is the instability.'

The temperature plummeted now – the area took on an air of chill November – and I pulled my jungle shirt closer around me. I had a brief impression of a white flickering – it was the seasonal blanketing and uncovering of the land by winter's snow and ice – and then the ice and permafrost settled over the ground, unyielding to the seasons, a hard grey-white surface which laid itself down with every impression of permanence.

The earth was transformed. To west, north and south, the contours of the land were masked by that layer of ice and snow. In the east, our old Palaeocene Sea had receded by some several miles; I could see ice on the beach at its fringe, and – far to the north – a glint of steady white that told of bergs. The air was clear, and once more I could see the sun and green moon arcing across heaven, but now the air had about it that pearly-grey light you associate with the depths of winter, just before a snow.

Nebogipfel had huddled over on himself, with his hands tucked into his armpits and his legs folded under him. When I touched his shoulder his flesh was icy to the touch – it was as if his essence had retreated to the warmest core of his body. The hairs over his face and chest had closed over themselves, after the manner of a bird's feathers. I felt a stab of guilt at his distress, for, as I may have indicated, I regarded Nebogipfel's injuries as my responsibility, either directly or indirectly. 'Come now, Nebogipfel. We have been through these Glacial periods before – it was far worse than this – and we survived. We pass through a millennium every couple of seconds. We're sure to move beyond this, and back into the sunshine, soon enough.'

'You do not understand,' he hissed.

'What?'

'This is no mere *Ice Age*. Can't you see that? This is qualitatively different . . . the *instability* . . .' His eyes closed again.

'What do you mean? Is this lot going to last longer than before? A hundred thousand, half a million years? *How long?*'

But he did not answer.

I wrapped my arms around my torso and tried to keep warm. The claws of cold sank deeper into the earth's skin, and the thickness of the ice grew, century on century, like a slowly rising tide. The sky above seemed to be clearing – the light of the sun-band was bright and hard, though apparently without heat – and I guessed that the damage done to that thin layer of life-giving gases was slowly healing, now that man was no longer a force on the earth. That Orbital City still hung, glowing and inaccessible, in the sky over the frozen land, but there were no signs of life on the earth, and still less of humanity.

After a million years of this, I began to suspect the truth!

'Nebogipfel,' I said. 'It is *never* going to end – this Age of Ice. Is it?'

He turned his head and mumbled something.

'What?' I pressed my ear close to his mouth. 'What did you say?'

His eyes had closed over, and he was insensible.

I got hold of Nebogipfel and lifted him from the bench. I laid him out on the Time-Car's wooden floor, and then I lay down beside him and pressed my body against his. It was scarcely comfortable: the Morlock was like a slab of butcher's meat against my chest, making me feel still colder myself; and I had to suppress my residual loathing of the Morlock race. But I bore it all, for I hoped that my body heat would keep him alive a little longer. I spoke to him, and rubbed at his shoulders and upper arms; I kept at it until he was awake, for I believed that – if I let him remain unconscious – he might slip, unknowing, into Death.

'Tell me about this *climatic instability* of yours,' I said.

He twisted his head and mumbled. 'What is the point? Your New Human friends have killed us . . .'

'The point is that I should prefer to know *what* is killing me.'

After rather more of this type of persuasion, Nebogipfel relented.

He told me that the atmosphere of the earth was a dynamic thing. The atmosphere had just two naturally stable states, Nebogipfel said, and neither of these could sustain life; and the air would fall into one of these states, away from the narrow band of conditions tolerable by life, if it were too far disturbed.

'But I don't understand. If the atmosphere is as unstable a mixture as you suggest, how is it that the air has managed to sustain us, as it has, for so many millions of years?'

He told me that the evolution of the atmosphere had been heavily modified *by the action of life itself*. 'There is a balance – of atmospheric gases, temperature and pressure – which is ideal for life. And so life works – in great, unconscious cycles, each involving billions of blindly toiling organisms – to maintain that balance.

'But this balance is inherently *unstable*. Do you see? It is like a pencil, balanced on its point: such a thing is ever likely to fall away, with the slightest disturbance.' He twisted his head. '*We* learned that you meddle with the cycles of life at peril, we Morlocks; *we* learned that if you choose to disrupt the various mechanisms by which atmospheric stability is maintained, then they must be repaired or replaced. What a pity it is,' he said, heavily, 'that these New Humans – these star-faring heroes of yours – had not absorbed similar simple lessons!'

'Tell me about your two stabilities, Morlock; for it seems to me we are going to be visiting one or the other!'

In the first of the lethal stable states, Nebogipfel said, the surface of earth would burn up: the atmosphere could become as opaque as the clouds over

457

Venus, and trap the heat of the sun. Such clouds, miles thick, would obstruct most of the sunlight, leaving only a dull, reddish glow; from the surface the sun could never be seen, nor the planets or stars. Lightning would flash continually in the murky atmosphere, and the ground would be red-hot: scorched bare of life.

'That's as may be,' I said, trying to suppress my shivers, 'but compared to this damned cold, it sounds like a pleasant holiday resort . . . And the second of your stable states?'

'*White Earth.*'

He closed his eyes, and would speak to me no more.

22

ABANDONMENT AND ARRIVAL

I do not know how long we lay there, huddled in the base of that Time-Car, grasping at our remaining flickers of body-warmth. I imagined that we were the only shards of life left on the planet – save, perhaps, for some hardy lichen clinging to an outcropping of frozen rock.

I pushed at Nebogipfel, and kept talking to him.

'Let me sleep,' he mumbled.

'No,' I replied, as briskly as I could. 'Morlocks don't sleep.'

'I do. I have been around humans too long.'

'If you sleep, you'll die . . . Nebogipfel. I think we must stop the car.'

He was silent for a while. 'Why?'

'We must go back to the Palaeocene. The earth is dead – locked into the grip of this wretched winter – so we must return, to a more equable past.'

'That is a fine idea – ' he coughed '– save for the detail that it is impossible. I did not have the means to design complex controls into this machine.'

'What are you saying?'

'That this Time-Car is essentially ballistic. I was able to aim it at future or past, and over a specified duration – we will be delivered to the 1891 of this History, or thereabouts – but then, after the aiming and launch, I have no control over its trajectory.

'Do you understand? The car follows a path

through time, determined by the initial settings, and the strength of the German Plattnerite. We will come to rest in 1891 – a frozen 1891 – and not before . . .'

I could feel my shivering subsiding – but not through any great degree of increasing comfort, but because, I realized, my own strength was at last beginning to be exhausted.

But perhaps we were not finished even so, I speculated wildly: if the planet were not abandoned – if men were to rebuild the earth – perhaps we could yet find a climate we could inhabit.

'And man? What of man?' I pressed Nebogipfel.

He grunted, and his lidded eye rolled. 'How could Humanity survive? Man has surely abandoned the planet – or else become extinct altogether . . .'

'Abandoned the earth?' I protested. 'Why, even you Morlocks, with your Sphere around the sun, didn't go quite so far as that!'

I pushed away from him, and propped myself up on my elbows so I could see out of the Time-Car towards the south. For it was from *there* – I was sure of it now – from the direction of the Orbital City, that any hope for us would come.

But what I saw next filled me with a deep dread.

That girdle around the earth remained in place, the links between the brilliant stations as bright as ever – but I saw now that the downward lines, which had anchored the City to the planet, had *vanished*. While I had been occupied with the Morlock, the orbital dwellers had dismantled their Elevators, thus abandoning their umbilical ties to Mother Earth.

As I watched further, a brilliant light flared from several of the stations. That glow shimmered from the earth's fields of ice, as if from a daisy-chain of miniature suns. The metal ring slid away from its position, over the equator. At first this migration was slow; but then the City appeared to turn on its axis – glowing with fire, like a Catherine Wheel – until it moved so fast that I could not make out the individual stations.

Then it was gone, sliding away from the earth and into invisibility.

The symbolism of this great abandonment was startling, and without the fire from the great engines, the ice fields of the deserted earth seemed more cold, more grey than before.

I settled back into the car. 'It is true,' I said to Nebogipfel.

'What is?'

'That the earth is abandoned – the Orbital City has cut loose and gone. The planet's story is done, Nebogipfel – and so, I fear, is ours!'

Nebogipfel lapsed into unconsciousness, despite all my efforts to rouse him; and after a time, I lacked the strength to continue. I huddled against the Morlock, trying to protect his damp, cold body from the worst of the chill, I feared without much success. I knew that given our rate of passage through time, our journey should last no more than thirty hours in total – but what if the German Plattnerite, or Nebogipfel's improvised design, were faulty? I might be trapped, slowly freezing, in this attenuated Dimension forever – or pitched, at any moment, out onto the eternal Ice.

I think I slept – or fainted.

I thought I saw the Watcher – that great broad head – hovering before my eyes, and beyond his limbless carcase I could see that elusive star-field, tinged with green. I tried to reach out to the stars, for they seemed so bright and warm; but I could not move – perhaps I dreamt it all – and then the Watcher was gone.

*

At last, with a groaning lurch, the power of the Plattnerite expired, and the car fell into History once more.

The pearly glow of the sky was dispersed, and the sun's pale light vanished, as if a switch had been thrown: and I was plunged into darkness.

The last of our Palaeocene warmth fell away into the great sink of the sky. Ice clawed at my flesh – it felt like burning – and I could not breathe, though whether from the cold or from poisons in the air I did not know, and I had a great pressure in my chest, as if I was drowning.

I knew that I should not retain consciousness for many more seconds. I determined that I should at least see this 1891, so wildly changed from my own world, before I died. I got my arms underneath me – already I could not feel my hands – and pushed myself up until I was half-sitting.

The earth lay in a silver light, like moon-light (or so I thought at first). The Time-Car sat, like a crumpled toy, in the centre of a plain of ancient ice. It was night, and *there were no stars* – at first I thought there must be clouds – but then I saw, low in the sky, a sliver of crescent moon, and I could not understand the absence of the stars; I wondered if my eyes were somehow damaged by the cold. That sister world was still green, I saw, and I felt pleased; perhaps people still lived there. How brilliant the frozen earth must be, in the sky of that young world! Close to the moon's limb, a bright light shone: not a star, for it was too close – it was the reflection of the sun from some lunar lake, perhaps.

A corner of my failing brain prompted me to wonder about the source of the silvery 'moonlight', for this now glinted from frost which was gathering already over the frame of the Time-Car. If the moon

462

was verdant still, she could not be the source of this elfish glow. What, then?

With the last of my strength I twisted my head. And there, in the starless sky far above me, was a glowing disc: a shimmering, gossamer thing, as if spun from spider-web, a dozen times the size of the full moon.

And, behind the Time-Car, standing patiently on the plain of ice –

I could not make it out; I wondered if my eyes were indeed failing. It was a pyramidal form, about the height of a man, but its lines were blurred, as if with endless, insectile motion.

'Are you alive?' – I wanted to ask this ugly vision. But my throat was closed up, my voice frozen out of me, and I could ask no more questions.

The blackness closed around me, and the cold receded at last.

BOOK FIVE

White Earth

1

CONFINEMENT

I opened my eyes – or rather, I had the sensation that my eyelids were *lifted* back, or perhaps cut away. My vision was cloudy, my view of the world refracted; I wondered if my eyeballs were iced over – perhaps even frozen through. I stared up into a random point in the dark, starless sky; at the periphery of my vision I saw a trace of green – perhaps the moon? – but I could not turn to see.

I was not breathing. That is easy to record, but it is hard to convey the ferocity of that realization! I felt as if I had been lifted out of my body; there was none of that mechanical business – the clatter of breath and heart, the million tiny aches of muscles and membranes – which makes up, all but unnoticed, the surface of our human lives. It was as if my whole being, all of my identity, had become compressed into that open, staring, fixed gaze.

I should have been frightened, I thought; I should have been struggling for another breath, as if drowning. But no such urgency struck me: I felt sleepy, dream-like, as if I had been etherized.

It was that lack of terror, I think, which convinced me I was dead.

Now a shape moved over me, interposing itself between my line of sight and the empty sky. It was roughly pyramidal, its edges indistinct; it was like a mountain, all in shadow, looming over me.

I recognized this apparition, of course: it was the thing which had stood before me, as we lay exposed on the Ice. Now this machine – for such I thought it must be – swept towards me. It moved with an odd, flowing motion; if you think of how the sand in a glass timer might shift in a composite movement of grains if you tilt the device, you will have something of the effect. I saw, at the corner of my vision, how the blurred edge of the machine's skirt swept over my chest and stomach. Then I felt a series of prickles – tiny jabs – across my chest and belly.

Thus, sensation had returned! – and with the suddenness of a rifle shot. There was a soft scraping against the skin of my chest, as if cloth were being cut away and pulled back. And now the prickles grew deeper; it was as if tiny, insectile palps were reaching below my flesh, infesting me. I felt *pain* – a million tiny needle-jabs, burrowing into my gut.

So much for Death – so much for Discorporeality! And with the realization of my continued existence came the return of Fear – instantly, and in a great flood of spurting chemicals which swilled around inside me with great intensity.

Now the looming shadow of the mountain-creature, blurred and ominous, crept further along my body, in the direction of my head. Soon I should be smothered! I wanted to scream – but I could feel nothing of my mouth and lips and neck.

I had never, in all my travels, felt so helpless as in that moment. I felt splayed out, like a frog on a dissecting table.

In the last moment, I felt something move over my hand. I could feel an etiolated cold there, a brush of hair: it was Nebogipfel's hand, holding mine. I wondered if he were lying beside me, even now, as this ghastly vivisection proceeded. I tried to enclose his fingers, but I could not move a muscle.

And now the pyramidal shadow reached my face, and my friendly patch of sky was obscured. I felt needles burrow into my neck, chin, cheeks and forehead. There was a prickle – an unbearable itch – across the surface of my exposed eyes. I longed to look away, to close my eyes; but I could not: it was the most exquisite torture I can imagine!

Then, with that deep fire penetrating even my eyeballs, my grasp on consciousness slipped mercifully away.

When next I woke, my emergence had none of the nightmarish quality of my first arousal. I surfaced towards the world through a layer of sunlit dreams: I swam through fragmentary visions of sand, forest and ocean; I tasted again tough, salty bivalves; and I lay with Hilary Bond in warmth and darkness.

Then, slowly, full awakening came.

I was lying on some hard surface. My back, which responded with a twinge when I tried to move, was real enough; as were my splayed-out legs, my arms, my tingling fingers, the engine-like whistle of air through my nostrils, and the thrum of blood in my veins. I lay in darkness – utter and complete – but that little fact, which once might have terrified me, now seemed incidental, for I was alive again, surrounded by the familiar mechanical rattle of my own body. I felt an access of relief, pure and intense, and I let out a whoop of joy!

I sat up. When I laid my hands on the floor I found coarse-grained particles there, as if a layer of sand sat over some harder surface. Though I wore only my shirt, trousers and boots, I felt quite warm. I remained in complete darkness; but the echoes of that foolish holler had returned swiftly to my ears, and I had the sensation that I was in some enclosed space.

I turned my head this way and that, seeking a window or door; but this was without avail. However I became aware of a heaviness about my head – something was pinching my nose – and when I lifted my hands to investigate, I found a pair of heavy spectacles sitting on my face, the glass integrated with the frame.

I probed at this clumsy device – and the room was flooded with a brilliant light.

At first I was dazzled, and I squeezed my eyes shut. I snatched off the spectacles – and found that the light disappeared, leaving me sunk in darkness. And when I donned the spectacles, the brightness returned.

It did not tax my ingenuity far to understand that the darkness was the reality; and that the light was being furnished for me by the spectacles themselves, which I had inadvertently activated. The spectacles were some equivalent of Nebogipfel's goggles, which the poor Morlock had lost in the Palaeocene Storm.

My eyes adjusted to the illumination, and I stood up and inspected myself. I was whole, and, it seemed, hale; I could find no trace on my hands or arms of the action of that diffuse pyramid-creature on my skin. I noticed a series of white traces, though, in the fabric of my jungle-twill shirt and trousers; when I ran my finger along these, I found low, ridged seams, as if clumsy repairs had been effected in my clothes.

I was in a chamber perhaps twelve feet across and about as high – and it was the most peculiar room I had visited in all my travels through time so far. To picture it, you must begin with a hotel room of the late nineteenth century. But the room was not constructed on the rectangular pattern common in my day; rather, it was a rounded cone, something like the inside of a tent. There was no door, and no furniture of any sort. The floor was covered by an even layer of sand, in which I could see the indentations where I had slept.

On the walls there was a rather garish paper – a purple, flock concoction – and what looked like window-frames, set about with heavy curtains. But the frames contained not glass, but only panels coated with more of the flock-paper.

There was no light source in the room. Instead, a steady and diffuse glow permeated the air, like the light of a cloudy day. I was by now convinced, however, that the illumination I saw was some artefact of my spectacles rather than anything physical. The ceiling above me was an ornate affair, decorated with the most remarkable paintings. Here and there in that baroque cascade I could make out fragments of the human form, but so jumbled about and distorted that the design was impossible to make out: it was not grotesque, but instead clumsy and confused – as if the artist had the technical ability of a Michelangelo, but the vision of a retarded child. And so you have it: the elements, I suppose, of a cheap hotel room of my day – but transmogrified into this peculiar geometry, like something out of a dream!

I walked about, and my boots crunched on the coarse sand. I found no seam in the walls, no hint of a door. In one part of the room there was a cubicle, about three feet on a side, made of white porcelain. When I stepped off the sand and onto the porcelain platform, steam hissed, quite unexpectedly, from vents in the walls. I stepped back, startled, and the jets desisted; the lingering steam lapped about my face.

I found a series of small bowls set on the sand. They were a hand's-breadth across and had shallow rims, like saucers. Some of the bowls contained water, and others portions of food: simple stuff, fruit and nuts and berries and the like, but nothing I could readily recognize. Finding myself thirsty, I drained a couple of the water-bowls. I found the bowls clumsy to use; their shallow profiles gave them a tendency to dump their contents over my chin, and they were less like cups, I thought, than the dishes one uses to water a dog or cat. I nibbled at a little of the food; the taste of the fruit pieces was bland but acceptable.

After this my hands and lips were left sticky, and I looked about for a sink or toilet facilities. There was none, of course; and I resorted to rinsing myself with the contents of another of the little water-bowls, and drying my face on a corner of my shirt.

I probed at the dummy windows, and leaped up, trying to poke at the clumsy ceiling designs, but to no avail; the surface of the walls and floor was as smooth as an eggshell's but unbreachable. I dug out some of the sand on the floor and found that it penetrated to a depth of nine inches or a foot; under it lay a mosaic of brightly coloured fragments, rather after the Roman style – but, like the ceiling, the mosaic depicted no portrait or scene I could discern, but rather a fragmentary jumble of designs.

I was quite alone, and there was no sound from beyond the walls: no sound in my universe, in fact, save the rustle of my own breathing, the thump of my heart – the very noises which I had welcomed back with such vigour, so recently!

After a time, certain human needs asserted themselves. I resisted these pressures as long as I could, but at last was forced to resort to digging shallow pits in the sand, for the purpose of relieving myself.

As I covered over the first of these pits I felt the most extraordinary shame. I wondered what the Starmen of this remote 1891 were making of this performance!

When I tired, I settled myself in the sand, with my back to the wall of the room. At first I kept the light-spectacles on, but I found the illumination too bright to allow me to rest; so I doffed the spectacles, and kept them wrapped around my hand while I slept.

So began my sojourn in that bizarre cage of a room. As my initial fear subsided, a restless boredom crept over me. It was an imprisonment reminiscent of my time in the Morlocks' Cage of Light, and I had come away from *that* without any wish to repeat the experience. I came to feel that *anything*, even the intrusion of danger, would be preferable to remaining in this dull, seamless prison. My exile in the Palaeocene – fifty million years from the nearest newspaper – had cured me of my old impulse to read, I think; but still, at times I thought I should go mad for lack of someone to talk to.

The bowls of food and water were filled up each time I slept. I never determined the mechanism by which this was done. I saw no evidence of an extruding machinery like the Morlocks'; but neither did I ever witness the refilling of a bowl by any semblance of attendant. Once, as an experiment, I went to sleep with a bowl buried *beneath* my body. I awoke to find a soggy sensation under my ribs. When I lifted myself, I found the bowl had filled with water once more, as if by some miraculous process.

I came to the tentative conclusion that, somehow, a subtle machinery in the bowls themselves was *assembling* the contents – either from the substance of the bowls, or from the material of the air. I thought – though I had no desire to investigate! – that my buried waste was broken down by the same discreet mechanisms. It was a bizarre, and not very appetizing, prospect.

2

EXPERIMENTS AND
REFLECTIONS

After three or four days I felt the need to get myself properly clean. As I have said, there was no semblance of toilet facilities here, and I grew dissatisfied with the cat-licks I was able to perform with my bowls of drinking water. I longed for a bath, or, better still, a swim in my Palaeocene Sea.

It took me some time – you may think me rather dull on this point – before I turned my attention again to that cubicle of porcelain I have described, ignored since my first tentative exploration of the chamber. I approached that cubicle now, and placed one cautious foot onto the porcelain base. Once more, steam spurted from the walls.

Suddenly I understood. With a surge of enthusiasm I stripped off my boots and garments (I retained my spectacles, though) and stepped into the little cubicle. Steam billowed all around me; the perspiration started from my skin, and moisture gathered over my spectacles. I had expected that the steam would blow out around the room, turning it all into something of a sauna. But the steam confined itself to the cubicle area, no doubt thanks to some arrangement involving differences in air pressure.

This was my bath-room, after all: it was not kitted out like the facilities of my own day – but why should it have been? My house in the Petersham Road was lost in a different History, after all. I recalled that the Romans, for example, had known nothing of soap or detergents; they had been forced to resort to this sort of poaching to sweat the dirt out of their pores. And the steam cleansing proved quite effective in my case, although, lacking the scrapers the Romans had used, I was forced to use my finger-nails to drag the accumulated muck off my flesh.

When I stepped away from the sauna, I looked for a way to dry myself off, lacking a towel. I considered, with reluctance, using my clothes; then, with an inspiration, I turned to the sand. I found that the gritty stuff, though coarse against my skin, took away the moisture pretty well.

My experience with the sauna caused me some self-reflection. How could I have been so narrow of mind that it should take me so long to have deduced the function of so obvious a piece of equipment? There had been many parts of the world in my own time, after all, which had not known the pleasures of modern plumbing and china bath-ware – plenty of districts of London, in fact, if one was to believe the more harrowing tales in the *Pall Mall Gazette*.

It was clear that a great deal of effort had been taken, by the unknown Star-men of this Age, to provide me with a room to sustain me. I *was* in a radically different History now, after all; and perhaps the strangeness of this chamber – the lack of recognizable sanitary facilities, the unusual type of food, and so forth – were not so significant or bizarre as they seemed to me.

I had been provided with the elements of a hotel room of my own day, but they were mixed up with what seemed to be sanitary arrangements dating from the birth of Christ; and as for the food, those plates of nuts and fruit which I was expected to nibble seemed more suited to one of my remote, fruit-gathering ancestors – say, from forty thousand years before my birth.

It was a muddle, a melange of fragments from the disparate Ages of man! But I thought I saw a sort of pattern about it.

I considered the separation between myself and the inhabitants of this world. Since the founding of First London there had been fifty million years of development – more than a *hundred times* the evolutionary gap between myself and the Morlock. Over such unimaginable Ages, time is compressed – it is like the squeezing of layers of sedimentary rock by the weight of deposits above – until the interval between myself and Gaius Julius Caesar, or even between myself and the first representatives of genus Homo to walk the earth – which seemed so immense to me, from *my* perspective – dwindles to virtually naught.

Given all *that*, I thought, my unseen hosts had done a pretty good job at guessing at the conditions which might make me comfortable.

In any event it appeared that my expectations, even after all my experiences, were still rooted in my own century, and in one small part of the globe! This was a chastening thought – a recognition of my own smallness of spirit – and I gave up some time, reluctantly, to inward contemplation. But I am not by nature a reflective man, and soon I found myself chafing once more at my conditions of restraint. Ungrateful as it might be, I wanted my liberty back! – though I could see no means of obtaining it.

I think I was in that cage for perhaps a fortnight. When my release came, it was as sudden as it was unexpected.

I awoke in the dark.

I sat up, without my spectacles. At first I could not

476

determine what had disturbed me – and then I heard it: a soft sound, a gentle, remote *breathing*. It was the most subtle of noises – almost inaudible – and I knew that, if it had come floating up from the Richmond streets in the small hours of the morning, I should not have been disturbed by it. But *here* my senses had been heightened in sensitivity by my lengthy isolation: *here* I had heard no sounds for a fortnight – save for the soft hiss of the steam-bath – not generated by myself. I jammed my glasses onto my face. Light flooded my eyes, and I blinked away tears, impatient to see.

The glasses showed me a gentle glow, moonlight-pale, seeping into my room. *A door was open*, in the wall of my cell. It was lozenge-shaped, with a sill perhaps six inches from the floor, and it cut through a fake window-frame.

I got to my feet, pulled on my shirt – for I had become accustomed to sleeping with the shirt as a rough pillow – and stepped towards the door-frame. That soft breathing increased in volume, and – overlaid on it, like the whisper of a brook over a breeze – I heard the liquid gurgle of a voice: an almost-human sound, a voice I recognized instantly!

The door-way led to another chamber, about the size and shape of my own. But here there were no false window-frames, no clumsy attempts at decoration, no sand on the floor; instead the walls were bare, a plain metallic grey, and there were several windows, covered by screens, and a door with a simple handle. There was no furniture here, and the room was dominated by a single, immense artefact: it was the pyramid-machine (or one identical to it) which I had last seen as it began its slow, painful crawl over my body. I have said that it was the height of a man, and was correspondingly broad at the base; its surface was metallic, by and large, but of a complex, shifting texture. If you will picture a great pyramidal frame, six feet tall, and covered with a blur of busy, metallic soldier-ants, then you will have the essence of it.

But this monstrosity barely attracted my attention; for – standing primly before it, and apparently peering into the pyramid's hide with some kind of eye-scope device – there was Nebogipfel.

I stumbled forward, and I held out my arms with pleasure. But the Morlock merely stood, patiently, and did not react to my presence.

'Nebogipfel,' I said, 'I cannot tell you how delighted I am to have found you. I think I was going crazy in there – crazy with isolation!'

I saw now that one of his eyes – the wounded right – was covered by the eye-scope device; this tube extended to the pyramid, merging with the body of that object, and the whole affair crawled with the miniature ant-motion that plastered the pyramid. I looked at this with some revulsion, for I should not have liked to have inserted such a device into *my* eye-socket.

Nebogipfel's other, naked eye swivelled towards me, huge and grey-red. 'Actually it was *I* who found *you*, and asked to see you. And whatever your mental state, I see you are healthy, at least,' he said. 'How is your frost-bite?'

I was confused by this. 'What frost-bite?' I pawed at my skin, but I knew well enough that it was unmarked.

'Then they have done a good job,' Nebogipfel said.

'Who?'

'The Universal Constructors.' By this I took it he meant the pyramid-machine and its cousins.

I noticed how straight was his bearing, how neat

478

and well-groomed his pelt of hair. I realized that in this moonlight glow he needed no goggles here, as *I* did, to aid his vision; evidently these chambers of ours had been designed more with his needs in mind than mine. 'You're looking fine, Morlock,' I said warmly. 'Your leg's been straightened out – and that bad arm too.'

'The Constructors have managed to repair my most ancient of injuries – frankly, I am now as healthy as when I first climbed aboard your Time Machine.'

'All save that eye of yours,' I said with some regret, for I referred to the eye I had all but destroyed in my fear and rage. 'I take it they – these Constructors of yours – were unable to save it.'

'My eye?' He sounded puzzled. He pulled his face from the eye-scope; the tube came away from his face with a soft, pulpy noise, and dangled from the pyramid-thing, retracting into its metallic hide. 'Not at all,' he said. 'I *chose* to have it rebuilt this way. It has certain conveniences, although I admit I had some difficulty explaining my wishes to the Constructors . . .'

He turned to me now. His socket was a bare hole. The ruin of his eye had been scooped out, and it looked as if the bone had been opened up, the hole deepened – and the socket glistened throughout with moist, squirming metal.

3

THE UNIVERSAL
CONSTRUCTOR

In contrast to my sparse cell, Nebogipfel, it turned out, had been provided with a veritable suite. There were four rooms, each as large as mine and roughly conical in form, and fitted with doors and windows, which our hosts had not thought fit to provide for me: it was evident that they had a higher view of his intellect than mine!

There was the same lack of furniture that I had suffered, although Morlocks have simple needs, and it was not such an incongruity for Nebogipfel. In one room, though, I found a bizarre object: a table-like affair perhaps twelve feet long and six wide, topped with a soft orange covering. There were pockets arranged around the rim of this table, all edged with a hard substance that glowed green. The table was an approximate rectangle, although its edges were irregularly shaped; and a single ball – white, of some dense material – sat on the table-top. When I pushed the ball across the table-top it ran well enough, although, without a covering of baize, its speed was a little free, and it caromed off cushions at the rim with a satisfying solidity.

I tried to discern some deeper meaning of this device; but, for all the world – as you will have guessed from my description – it was like nothing so much as a billiards table! I wondered at first if this was some other distorted echo of a nineteenth-century hotel room – but a rather bizarre selection if so, and, lacking anything in the way of cues, and only a single ball, it was not likely to give me much sport.

Baffled, I abandoned the table, and tested the doors and windows. The doors worked by simple handles, to be grasped and turned, but the doors led only to other rooms within the suite, or to my original chamber; there were no ways out to the world beyond. I found, though, that the panels covering the transparent windows could be lifted up, and for the first time I was able to inspect this new 1891, this *White Earth.*

My viewpoint was raised some thousand feet or more from the ground! – we seemed to be at the apex of some immense cylindrical tower, whose flanks I could see sweeping down below me. Everything I saw reinforced the first impression I had gained when I had obtained that last glimpse over the rim of the Time-Car, just before the cold overcame me: that this was a world forever sunk into the Ice. The sky was the colour of gun-metal, and the icebound land a grey-white like exposed bone, with none of that attractive blueness one sees sometimes about prettier snow-fields. Looking out now, I could see quite clearly how dreadfully stable this world-state truly was, just as Nebogipfel had described: the daylight glinted fiercely from the mantle of scarred Ice which sheathed the earth, and the whiteness of that world-wide carapace hurled the warmth of the sun back into the sink of space. The poor earth was dead, caught at the bottom of this pit of icy, climatic stability, for evermore – it was the ultimate Stability of Death.

Here and there I saw a Constructor – in form just like our own, here in Nebogipfel's apartment – standing on the frozen landscape. Each Constructor was always alone, standing there like some ill-wrought monument, a splash of steel grey against the bone white of the ice. I never saw any of them move! It was as if they simply *appeared* in the sites where they stood, reassembling themselves, perhaps, from the air. (Indeed, as I found later, this first assessment of mine was not so far from the truth.)

Dead the land was, but not without the evidence of intelligence. There were more great buildings – like our own – puncturing the landscape. They took simple geometric forms: cylinders, cones and cubes. My vantage point showed me the south and west, and from my eyrie I could see these great buildings scattered as far afield as Battersea, Fulham, Mitcham and beyond. They were spaced perhaps a mile apart on average, as far as I could see; and the whole prospect – the fields of Ice, the mute Constructors, the sparse, anonymous buildings – combined to make up a bleak, inhuman London.

I returned to Nebogipfel, who still stood before his Constructor. The metal pelt of the thing rippled and shone, as if it were the surface of some tilted pond with metal fish moving beneath, and then a protuberance – a tube a few inches wide – thrust out of the surface, glistening with the silvery metal texture of the pyramid, and pressed towards Nebogipfel's waiting face.

I recognized this arrangement, of course; it was the return of the eye-scope device I had seen earlier. In a moment it would be fitted to Nebogipfel's skull.

I prowled around the rim of the Constructor. As I have described, in appearance the Constructor was like a heap of melted slag; it was animate to some degree – and mobile, for I had seen this object, or one similar, crawl over my own body – but I could not begin to guess as to its purpose. Inspecting closely, I saw how the surface was covered by a series of metal hairs: cilia, like iron filings, which waved about in the air, quite active and intelligent. And I had the infuriating, eye-hurting sensation that there were further levels of detail to all this, beyond the grasp of my ageing vision. The texture of this mobile surface was at the same time fascinating and repulsive: mechanical, but with something of the quality of life. I was not tempted to touch it – I could not bear the thought of those squirming cilia latching onto *my* skin – and I had no instruments with which to probe. Without any means of making a closer examination, I was unable to undertake a study of the pyramid's internal structure.

I noticed a certain degree of activity about the lowest rim of the pyramid. Crouching down, I saw how tiny communities of metal cilia – the size of ants, or smaller – were continually breaking away from the Constructor. Generally these fallen pieces seemed to dissolve as they fell against the floor, doubtless breaking up into components too small for me to see; but at times I saw how these discarded bits of Constructor trekked hither and thither across the floor, again after the fashion of ants, to unknown destinations. In a similar fashion – I observed now – more clumps of the cilia emerged from the floor, clambered up the skirts of the Constructor, and merged into its substance, as if they had always been a part of it!

I remarked on this to Nebogipfel. 'It is astonishing,' I said, 'but it is not hard to surmise what is going on. The components of the Constructor attach and detach themselves. They squirm off over the floor – or even fly away through the air, for all I know, or can see. The discarded pieces must either die off, in some fashion, if they are defective – or else join the glistening carcass of some other unfortunate Constructor.

'Confound it,' I said, 'the planet must be covered with a thin slime of these detached cilia, squirming this way and that! And, in some interval of time – perhaps a century – there must be nothing left of the original body of this beast we see here. All its bits, its analogues of hair and teeth and eyes, have trekked off for a visit to its neighbours!'

'It is not a unique design,' Nebogipfel said. 'In your body – and mine – cells die and are replaced continually.'

'Perhaps, but even so – what does it mean to say that this Constructor, here, *is* – an individual? I mean: if I buy a brush – and then replace the handle, and then the head – do I have the same brush?'

The Morlock's red-grey eye turned back to the pyramid, and that tube of extruded metal sank into the hole in his face with a liquid noise.

'This Constructor is not a single machine, like a motor-car,' he retorted. 'It is a *composite*, made up of many millions of sub-machines – limbs, if you like. These are arranged in a hierarchical form, radiating out from a central trunk along branches and twigs, after the manner of a bush. The smallest limbs, at the periphery, are too small for you to see: they work at the molecular or atomic levels.'

'But what *use*,' I asked, 'are these insectile limbs? One may push atoms about, and molecules – but *why*? What a tedious and unproductive business.'

'On the contrary,' he said wearily. 'If you can do your engineering at the most fundamental level of matter – and if you have enough time, and sufficient patience – you can achieve anything.' He looked up at me. 'Why, without the Constructors' molecular engineering, you – and I – would not even have survived our first exposure to White Earth.'

'What do you mean?'

'The "surgery" performed on you,' Nebogipfel said, 'was at the level of the cell – the level where the frost damage occurred . . .'

Nebogipfel described, in some grisly detail, how, in the severe cold we had encountered, the walls of my very cells (and his) had been burst open by the freezing and expansion of their contents – and no surgery, of the type I was familiar with, could have saved my life.

Instead, the microscopic outer limbs of the Constructor had become detached from the parent body, and had travelled *through* my damaged system, effecting repairs of my frost-bitten cells at the molecular level. When they reached the other side – crudely speaking – they had emerged from my body and rejoined their parent.

I had been rebuilt, from the inside out, by an army of swarming metal ants – and so had Nebogipfel.

I shuddered at this, feeling colder than at any time since my rescue. I scratched at my arms, almost involuntarily, as if seeking to scrape out this technological infection. 'But such an invasion is monstrous,' I protested to Nebogipfel. 'The thought of those busy little workers, passing through the substance of my body . . .'

'I take it you would prefer the blunt, invasive scalpels of the surgeons of your own age.'

'Perhaps not, but –'

'I remind you that, by contrast, *you* could not even set a broken bone without rendering me lame.'

'But that was different. I'm no doctor!'

'Do you imagine this creature *is*? In any event, if you would prefer to have died, no doubt that could be arranged.'

'Of course not.' But I scratched at my skin, and I knew it would be a long time before I felt comfortable again in my own rebuilt body! I thought of a drop of comfort, though. 'At least,' I said, 'these limb-things of the Constructor are merely mechanical.'

'What do you mean?'

'They are not *alive*. If they had been –'

He pulled his face free of the Constructor and faced me, the hole in his face sparkling with metal cilia. 'No. You are wrong. These structures *are* alive.'

'What?'

'By any reasonable definition of the word. They can reproduce themselves. They can manipulate the external world, creating local conditions of increased order. They have internal states which can change independently of external inputs; they have memories which can be accessed at will . . . All these are characteristics of Life, and Mind. The Constructors are alive, *and* conscious – as conscious as you or I. More so, in fact.'

Now I was confused. 'But that's impossible.' I indicated the pyramid-device. 'This is a machine. It is manufactured.'

'I have encountered the limits of your imagination before,' he said severely. 'Why should a mechanical worker be built within the limitations of the human design? With machine life –'

'*Life?*'

'– one is free to explore other morphologies – other forms.'

I raised an eyebrow at the Constructor. 'The morphology of the privet hedge, for example!'

'And besides,' he said, '*it* could manufacture *you*. Does that make you less than alive?'

This was becoming far too metaphysical a debate for me! I paced around the Constructor. 'But if it is alive, and conscious – is this a person? Or several people? Does it have a name? A *soul?*'

Nebogipfel turned to the Constructor once more, and let the eye-scope nuzzle into his face. 'A *soul?*' he asked. 'This is your *descendant*. So am I, by a different History path. Do *I* have a soul? Do *you?*'

He turned away from me, and peered into the heart of the Constructor.

4

THE BILLIARDS ROOM

Later, Nebogipfel joined me in the chamber I had come to think of as the Billiards Room. He ate from a plate of cheese-like fare.

I sat, rather moodily, on the edge of the billiards table, flicking the single ball across the surface. The ball was wont to exhibit some peculiar behaviour. I was aiming for a pocket on the far side of the table, and more often than not I hit it, and would trot around to retrieve it from its little net cache beneath. But sometimes the ball's path would be disturbed. There would be a *rattling* in the middle of the empty table surface – the ball would jiggle about, oddly, too rapidly to follow – and then, usually, the ball would sail on to the destination I had intended. Sometimes, though, the ball would be diverted markedly from the path I had intended – and once it even returned, from that half-visible disturbance, to my hand!

'Nebogipfel, did you see that? It is most peculiar,' I said. 'There does not seem to be any obstruction in the middle of the table. And yet, half the time, the running of this ball is impeded.' I tried some more demonstrations for him, and he watched with an air of distraction.

I said, 'Well, I'm glad at any rate that I'm not playing a game here. I can think of one or two fellows who might come to blows over such discrepancies.' Tiring of my idle toying, I sat the ball square in the middle of the table and left it there. 'I wonder what the motive of the Constructors was in placing this table in here. I mean, it's our only substantial piece of furniture – unless you want to count our Constructor out there himself ... I wonder if this is intended as a snooker or a billiards table.'

Nebogipfel seemed bemused by the question. 'Is there a difference?'

'I'll say! Despite its popularity, snooker is just a potting game – a fine enough pastime for the bored Army Officers in India who devised it – but it has nothing like the *science* of billiards, to my mind ...'

And then – I was watching it as it happened – a second billiard ball popped out of one of the table's pockets, quite spontaneously, and began to roll, square on, towards my ball at rest at the centre of the table.

I bent closer to see. 'What the devil is happening here?' The ball was progressing quite slowly, and I was able to make out details of its surface. My ball was no longer smooth and white; after my various experiments, its surface had become scarred with a series of scratches, one quite distinctive. And this new ball was just as scarred.

The newcomer hit my stationary ball, with a solid clunk; the new ball was brought to rest by the impact, and my ball was knocked across the table.

'Do you know,' I said to Nebogipfel, 'if I didn't know better, I would swear this ball, that has just emerged from nowhere, is the same as the first.' He came a little closer, and I pointed out that distinctive long scratch. 'See that? I'd recognize this scar in the dark ... The balls are like identical twins.'

'Then,' the Morlock said calmly, 'perhaps they are the same ball.'

Now my ball, knocked aside, had collided with a

cushion on the far side of the table and had rebounded; such was the non-regular geometry of the table that it was now heading back in the direction of the pocket from which the second ball had emerged.

'But how can that be? I mean, I suppose a Time Machine could deliver two copies of the same object to the same place – think of myself and Moses! – but I see no time travel devices here. And what would be the purpose?'

The original ball had lost much momentum with these various impacts, and it was fairly creeping by the time it reached the pocket; but it slid into the pocket, and disappeared.

We were left with the copy of the ball which had emerged so mysteriously from the pocket. I picked it up and examined it. As far as I could tell it was an identical copy of our ball. And when I checked the cache beneath the pocket – it was empty! Our original ball had gone, as if it had never existed. 'Well!' I said to Nebogipfel. 'This table is trickier than I imagined. What do you suppose happened there? Is this the sort of thing which goes on, do you think, during the disturbed paths – all that rattling – which I've pointed out to you before?'

Nebogipfel did not reply immediately, but – after that – he took to devoting a substantial fraction of his time, with me, to the puzzles of that strange billiards table. As for me, I tried inspecting the table itself, hoping to find some concealed device, but I found nothing – no trickery, no concealed traps which could swallow and disgorge balls. Besides, even if there had been such crude illusion-machinery, I would still have to find an explanation for the apparent identity of 'old' and 'new' balls!

The thing which caught my mind – though I had no explanation for it at the time – was the odd, greenish glow of the pocket rims. For all the world, that glow reminded me of *Plattnerite*.

Nebogipfel told me of what he had learned of the Constructors.

Our silent friend in Nebogipfel's living room was, it seemed, one of a widespread species: the Constructors inhabited the earth, the transformed planets – and even the stars.

He told me, 'You must put aside your preconceptions and look at these creatures with an open mind. They are *not* like humans.'

'That much I can accept.'

'*No*,' he insisted, 'I do not think you can. To begin with, you must not imagine that these Constructors are individual personalities – after the fashion of you, or me. They are *not* men in cloaks of metal! They are something qualitatively different.'

'Why? Because they are composed of interchangeable parts?'

'Partly. Two Constructors could flow into one another – merging like two drops of liquid, forming one being – and then part as easily, forming two again. It would be all but impossible – and futile – to trace the origins of this component or that.'

Hearing that, I could understand how it was that I never saw the Constructors moving about the ice-coated landscape outside. There was no *need* for them to lug the weight of their great, clumsy bodies about (unless for a special need, as when Nebogipfel and I had been *repaired*). It would be enough for the Constructor to disassemble himself, into these molecular components Nebogipfel described. The components could wiggle across the ice, like so many worms!

Nebogipfel went on, 'But there is more to the Constructors' consciousness than that. The

490

Constructors live in a world we can barely imagine – they inhabit a *Sea*, if you like, a Sea of *Information*.'

Nebogipfel described how, by phonograph and other links, the Universal Constructors were linked to each other, and they used those links to chatter to each other constantly. Information – and awareness, and a deepening understanding – flowed out of the mechanical mind of each Constructor, and each received news and interpretation from every one of his brothers: even those on the most remote stars.

So rapid and all-encompassing was the Constructors' mode of communication, in fact, that it was not really analogous to human speech, said Nebogipfel.

'But *you've* spoken to them. *You've* managed to get Information out of them. How so?'

'By mimicking their own ways of interacting,' Nebogipfel said. He fingered his eye-socket, gingerly. 'I had to make this sacrifice.' His natural eye gleamed.

Nebogipfel had sought a way, as it were, to immerse his brain into the Information Sea of which he'd spoken. Through the eye-socket, he was able to absorb Information directly from the Sea – without its passing through the conventional medium of speech.

I found myself shuddering, at the thought of such an invasion of the comfortable darkness of my own skull! 'And do you think it was *worth* it?' I asked him. 'This sacrifice of an eye?'

'Oh, yes. And more . . .

'Look – can you see how it is for the Constructors?' he asked me. 'They are a different order of life – united, not just by this sharing at the gross physical level, but by this pooling of their experiences.

'Can you imagine how it is to exist in such a medium of Information as their Sea?'

I reflected. I thought of seminars at the Royal

Society – those rich discussions when some new idea has been tossed into the pool, and three dozen agile minds battled over it, reshaping and refining it as they go – or even some of my old Thursday night dinner parties, when, with the help of liberal quantities of wine, the rattle of ideas could come so thick and fast it was hard to tell where one man had stopped speaking and the next resumed.

'Yes,' Nebogipfel cut in when I related this last. 'Yes, that is exactly it. Do you see? But with these Universal Constructors, such conversations proceed continuously – *and at the speed of light,* with thoughts passing directly from the mind of one to another.

'And in such a miasma of communication, who can say where the consciousness of *one* finishes, and that of *another* begins? Is this *my* thought, *my* memory – or yours? Do you see? Do you follow the implications?'

On the earth – perhaps on each inhabited world – there must be immense central Minds, composed of millions of the Constructors, fused together into great, God-like entities, which maintained the awareness of the race. In a sense, Nebogipfel said, the race itself was conscious.

Again I had the feeling that we were straying too far into metaphysics. 'All of that is fascinating stuff,' I said, 'and it's all as may be; but perhaps we should return to the practicalities of our own situation. What does it all have to do with you and me?' I turned to our own patient Constructor, who sat there, shimmering, in the middle of the floor. 'What of this fellow?' I said. 'All of this stuff about consciousness and so forth is all very well – but what does *he* want? Why is he here? Why did he save our lives? And – what does he want with us now? Or is it a case of these mechanical men all working together – like bees in a hive, united by these common Minds you

492

speak of – so that we are faced with a *species* with common aims?'

Nebogipfel rubbed his face. He walked up to the Constructor, peered into his eye-scope, and was rewarded, within a few minutes, by the extrusion, *from within the Constructor's glistening body*, of a plate of that bland, cheese-like food of which I had seen so much in Nebogipfel's home century. I watched with disgust, as Nebogipfel took the plate and bit into his regurgitated food. It was no more horrible, truthfully, than the extrusion of materials from the Floor of the Morlocks' Sphere, but there was something about the Constructor's liquid mixture of Life and Machine which repelled me. I averted my thoughts, with determination, from speculations as to the source of my own food and water!

'We cannot talk of these Constructors as *united*,' Nebogipfel was saying. 'They are *linked*. But they do not share a common purpose – in the fashion, let us say, of the various components of your own personality.'

'But why not? That would seem eminently sensible. With perfect, continuous communication there need be no understanding – no conflict –'

'But it is not like that. The totality of the Constructors' mental universe is too big.' He referred to the Information Sea again, and described how structures of thought and speculation – complex, evolving, evanescent – came and went, emerging from the raw materials of that ocean of mentation. 'These structures are analogous to the scientific theories of your own day – constantly under stress, from new discoveries and the insights of new thinkers. The world of understanding does not stay still, you see . . .

'And besides, remember your friend Kurt Gödel, who taught us that no body of knowledge can be codified and made complete.

'The Information Sea is unstable. The hypotheses and intentions which emerge from it are complex and multi-faceted; there is rarely complete unanimity among the Constructors about any point. It is like a continuing, emerging debate; and within that debate, factions may emerge: groupings of quasi-individuals, coalescing around some scheme. One might say that the Constructors are united in their drive to advance the understanding of their species, but *not* so as regards the means by which this might be achieved. In fact, one might hypothesize in general, the more advanced the mentation, the more factions appear to emerge, because the more complex the world appears . . .

'And thus, the race progresses.'

I remembered what Barnes Wallis had told me of the new order of Parliamentary debate, in 1938, where Opposition had essentially been banned as a criminal activity – a divergence of energy from the one, self-evidently correct approach to things! – But if what Nebogipfel was saying was correct, there can be *no* universally correct answer to any given question: as these Constructors had learned, multifarious views are a necessary feature of the universe in which we find ourselves!

Nebogipfel chewed patiently on his cheese stuff; when he was done, he pushed the plate back into the substance of the Constructor, where it was absorbed – it was comforting for him, I thought, for it was a process so like the extruding Floor of his own home Sphere.

494

5

WHITE EARTH

I spent many hours alone, or with Nebogipfel, at the windows of our apartment.

I saw no evidence of animal or vegetable life on the surface of White Earth. As far as I could tell, we were isolated in our little bubble of light and warmth, atop that immense tower; and we never left that bubble, in all the time we were there.

At night the sky beyond our windows was generally clear, with only a light frosting of cirrus cloud high in the depleted, lethal atmosphere. But, despite this clarity – I still could not understand it – *there were no stars* – or rather, very few, a handful compared to the multitude which had once blazed down on the earth. I had made this observation on our first arrival here, but I think I had dismissed it as some artefact of the cold, or my disorientation. To have it confirmed, now that I was warm and clear-headed, was disturbing – perhaps the strangest single thing in this new world.

The moon – that patient companion planet – still turned about the earth, going through its phases with its immemorial regularity; but its ancient plains remained stained green. Moonlight was no longer a thing of cool silver, but washed the landscape of White Earth with the gentlest verdant glow, returning to the earth an echo of that greenness she had once enjoyed, and which was now locked under the unforgiving ice.

I saw again that gleam, as if of a captive star, that shone steadily at us from the moon's extreme easterly limb. My first speculation had been that I was seeing the reflection of the sun from some lunar lake, but the glare was so steady that eventually I decided that it must be purposeful. I imagined a *mirror* – an artificial construct – perhaps fixed to some lunar mountain-top, and designed so that its reflection always falls on the earth. As to the purpose of such a device, I speculated that it might date from a time when the degradation of atmospheric conditions, here on the Mother Planet, had not yet become so bad as to drive men off the earth, but, perhaps, were so severe that they had caused the collapse of whatever culture had survived.

I imagined moon-men: *Selenites*, as we might call them, themselves descended from Humanity. The Selenites must have watched the lethal progress of the great fires which broke across the crust of the oxygen-choked earth. The Selenites had known that men still lived on the earth – but they were men fallen from civilization, men living as savages, even as animals once more, sliding back into some pre-rational state. Perhaps the collapse of the earth impacted them too – for it may be that Selenite society could not survive without provision from Mother Earth.

The Selenites could grieve for their cousins on the Mother world, but could not reach them . . . and so they attempted to *signal*. They built their immense mirror – it must have been half a mile across, or more, to be visible across inter-planetary distances.

The Selenites may even have had some more ambitious aim in mind than simple inspiration from the sky. For example, they may have sent – by making the mirror flicker, using some equivalent of Morse –

instructions on crop-rearing, or engineering – the lost secrets of the steam engine, perhaps – something, at any rate, rather more useful than mere good-luck messages.

But in the end it was to no avail. In the end, the fist of Glaciation closed about the land. And the great lunar mirror was abandoned, as men disappeared from the earth.

Such, at any rate, was my speculation, as I stood gazing through the windows of my tower; I have no means of knowing if I was right – for Nebogipfel was unable to read this new History of Humanity in such detail – but in any event the gleam of that isolated mirror on the moon became, for me, a most eloquent symbol of the collapse of Humanity.

The most striking feature of our night sky was not the moon, however, nor even that absence of stars: it was the great, web-like disc, a dozen times Luna's width, that I had noticed on our first arrival. This structure was extraordinarily complex and alive with motion. Think of a spider-web, perhaps lit from behind, with drops of dew glistening and rolling over its surface; now envisage a hundred tiny spiders crawling over that surface, their motion slow but quite visible, evidently working to strengthen and extend the structure – and then cast your vision across many miles of inter-planetary space! – and you will have something of what I saw.

I made out the web-disc most clearly in the early hours of the morning – perhaps around three o'clock – and at such times I was able to make out ghostly threads of light – tenuous and thin – which reached up, from the far side of the earth, and out through the atmosphere towards the disc.

I discussed these features with Nebogipfel. 'It's quite extraordinary . . . it's as if those beams make up a kind of rigging of light, which attach the disc to the earth; so that the whole affair is like a sail, towing the earth through space on some spectral wind!'

'Your language is picturesque,' he said, 'but it captures something of the flavour of that enterprise.'

'What do you mean?'

'That it *is* a sail,' he said. 'But it is not towing the earth: rather, the earth is providing a base for the wind which drives the sail.'

Nebogipfel described this new type of space yacht. It would be constructed in space, he said, for it would be much too fragile to haul upwards from the earth. Its sail consisted, essentially, of a mirror; and the 'wind' which filled the sail was *light*: for particles of light falling on a mirrored surface deliver a pushing force, just as do the molecules of air which make up a breeze.

'The "wind" comes from beams of coherent light, generated by earthbound projectors as wide as a city,' he said. 'It is these beams which you have observed as "threads" joining planet to sail. The pressure of the light is small but insistent, and it is extraordinarily efficient in transferring momentum – especially as light speed is approached.'

He imagined that the Constructors would not sail upon such a ship as discrete entities, as had the passengers of the great ships of my day. Rather, the Constructors might have disassembled themselves, and allowed their components to run off and knit themselves into the ship. At the destination, they would reassemble as individual Constructors, in whatever form was most efficient for the worlds they found there.

'But where is the space-yacht's destination, do you think? The moon, or one of the planets – or –'

In his flat, undramatic Morlock way, Nebogipfel said: 'No. The *stars*.'

6

THE MULTIPLICITY GENERATOR

Nebogipfel continued his experiments with the billiards table. Repeatedly the ball would encounter that peculiar clattering I had observed about the middle of the table, and several times I thought I saw billiard balls – more *copies* of our original – appearing from nowhere and interfering with the trajectory of our ball. Sometimes the ball emerged from these collisions and continued along the path it might have followed regardless of the clattering-about; sometimes, though, it was knocked onto quite a different path, and – once or twice – we observed the type of incident I described earlier, in which a *stationary* ball was knocked out of its place, without my, or Nebogipfel's, intervention.

This all made for an entertaining game – and clearly something fishy was going on – but for the life of me *I* could not see it, despite that hint of Plattnerite glow about the pockets. My only observation was that the slower the ball travelled, the more likely it was to be diverted from its path.

The Morlock, though, grew gradually more excited about all this. He would immerse himself in the hide of the patient Constructor, delving once more into the Information Sea, and emerge with some new fragment of knowledge he'd fished up – he mumbled to himself in that obscure, liquid dialect of his kind – and then he would hurry straight to the billiards table, there to test his new understanding.

At last, he seemed ready to share his hypotheses with me; and he summoned me from my steam bath. I dried myself on my shirt and hurried after him to the Billiards Room; his small, narrow feet pattered on the hard floor as he half-ran back to the table. He was as excited as I could remember seeing him.

'I think I understand what this table is for,' he said, breathless.

'Yes?'

'It is – how can I express it? – it is only a demonstration, little more than a toy – but it is a *Multiplicity Generator*. Do you see?'

I held up my hands. 'I fear I don't see a thing.'

'You are familiar enough with the idea of the Multiplicity of Histories, by now . . .'

'I *should* be; it's the basis of your explanation of the divergent Histories we have visited.'

At every moment, in every event (I summarized), History bifurcates. A butterfly's shadow may fall *here* or *there*; the assassin's bullet may graze and pass on without harm, *or* lodge itself fatally in the heart of a King . . . To each possible outcome of each event, there corresponds a fresh version of History. 'And all of these Histories are *real*,' I said, 'and – if I understand it right – they lie side by side with each other, in some Fourth Dimension, like the pages of a book.'

'Very well. And you see, also, that the action of a Time Machine – including your first prototype – is to cause *wider* bifurcations, to generate new Histories . . . some of them impossible *without* the Machine's intervention – like this one!' He waved his hands about. 'Without your machine, which started off the whole series of events, humans could never have been transported back to the Palaeocene. We should not now be sitting on top of fifty million years of intelligent modification of the cosmos.'

500

'I see all that,' I said, my patience wearing. 'But what has it to do with this table?'

'Look.' He set the single ball rolling across the table. 'Here is our ball. We must imagine *many* Histories – a sheaf of them – fanning out around the ball at every moment. The most *likely* History, of course, is the one containing the classical trajectory – meaning a straightforward roll of the ball across the table. But other Histories – neighbouring, but some widely divergent – exist in parallel. It is even possible, though very unlikely, that in one of those Histories the thermal agitation of the ball's molecules will combine, and cause it to leap up in the air and hit you in the eye.'

'Very well.'

'Now –' he ran his finger around the rim of the nearest pocket. 'This green inlay is a clue.'

'It is Plattnerite.'

'Yes. The pockets act as miniature Time Machines – limited in scope and size, but quite effective. And, as we have seen from our own experience, when Time Machines operate – when objects travel into future or past to meet themselves – the chain of cause and effect can be disrupted, and Histories grow like weeds . . .'

He reminded me of the odd incident we had witnessed with the stationary ball. 'That was, perhaps, the clearest example of what I am describing. The ball sat at rest on the table – *our* ball, we will call it. Then a *copy* of our ball emerged from a pocket, and knocked our ball aside. Our ball travelled to the cushion, rebounded, and fell into the pocket, leaving the *copy* at rest on the table, in the precise position of the original.

'Then,' Nebogipfel said slowly, 'our ball travelled *back* through time – do you see? – and emerged from the pocket in the past . . .'

501

'And proceeded to knock *itself* out of the way, and took its *own* place.' I stared at the innocent-looking table. 'Confound it, Nebogipfel – I see it now! It *was* the same ball after all. It was resting quite happily on the table – but, because of the bizarre possibilities of time travel, it was able to loop through time and knock itself aside!'

'You have it,' the Morlock said.

'But what made the ball start moving in the first place? Neither of us gave it a shove towards the pocket.'

'A "shove" was not necessary,' Nebogipfel said. 'In the presence of Time Machines – and this is the point of the demonstration, really – you must abandon your old ideas of causality. Things are not so simple! The collision with the copy was just one possibility for the ball, which the table demonstrated for us. Do you see? In the presence of a Time Machine, causality is so damaged that even a stationary ball is surrounded by an infinite number of such bizarre possibilities. Your questions about "how it started" are without meaning, you see: it is a closed causal loop – there was *no* First Cause.'

'Maybe so,' I said, 'but look here: I still have an uneasy feeling about all this. Let's go back to the two balls on the table again – or rather, the one *real* ball and its copy. Suddenly, there is twice as much material present as there was before! Where has it all come from?'

He eyed me. 'You are worried about the violation of Conservation Laws – the appearance, or disappearance, of Mass.'

'Exactly.'

'I did not notice any such concern when you dived into time in search of your younger self. For that was just as much – more! – of a violation of any Conservation Principle.'

502

'Nevertheless,' I said, refusing to be goaded, 'the objection is valid – isn't it?'

'In a sense,' he said. 'But only in a narrow, single-History sort of way.

'The Universal Constructors have been studying these paradoxes of time travel for centuries now,' he said. 'Or rather, *apparent* paradoxes. And they have formulated a type of Conservation Law which works in the higher Dimension of the Multiplicity of Histories.

'Start with an object – like yourself. If, at any given moment, you *add* in a copy of yourself which may be *absent* because you have travelled away into past or future – and then *subtract* any copies *doubly present* because one of you has travelled to the past – then you will find that the sum, overall, stays constant – there is "really" only one of you – no matter how many times you travel up and down through time. So there *is* Conservation, of a sort – even though, at any moment in any given History, it may *seem* that Conservation Laws are broken, because there are suddenly two of you, or none of you.'

I saw it, on thinking it through. 'There is only a paradox if you restrict your thinking to a single History,' I observed. 'The paradox disappears, if you think in terms of Multiplicity.'

'Exactly. Just as problems of causality are resolved, within the greater frame of the Multiplicity.

'It is the power of this table, you see,' he told me, 'that it is able to demonstrate these extraordinary possibilities to us . . . It is able to use Time Machine technology to show us the possibility – no, the *existence* – of Multiple, divergent Histories at the macroscopic level. Indeed, it can pick out particular Histories of interest: it has a very subtle design.'

He told me more of the Constructors' Laws of the Multiplicity.

'One can imagine situations,' he said, 'in which the Multiplicity of Histories is *zero, one, or many*. It is *zero* if that History is impossible – if it is not self consistent. A Multiplicity of *one* is the situation imagined by your earlier philosophers – of Newton's generation, perhaps – in which a single course of events unfolds out of each point in time, consistent and immovable.'

I understood him to be describing my own original – and naive! – view of History, as a sort of immense Room, more or less fixed, through which my Time Machine would let me wander at will.

'A "dangerous" path for an object – like you, or our billiard ball – is one which can reach a Time Machine,' he said.

'Well, that's clear enough,' I said. 'It's been obvious that I've been splitting off new Histories right, left and centre since the moment the Time Machine was first switched on. Dangerous indeed!'

'Yes. And as the machine, and its successors, delve ever deeper into the past, so the Multiplicity generated tends towards *infinity*, and the divergence of the new copies of History grows wider.'

'But,' I said, a little frustrated, 'coming back to the matter at hand – what is the purpose of this table? Is it just a trick? – Why have the Constructors given it to us? What are they trying to tell us?'

'I do not know,' he said. 'Not yet. It is difficult . . . The Information Sea is wide, and there are many factions among the Constructors. Information is not offered freely to me – do you understand? – I have to pick up what I can, make the best understanding of it, and so build up an interpretation that way . . . I think there is a faction of them who have some scheme – an immense Project – whose outlines I can barely make out.'

'What is the nature of this Project?'

Nebogipfel said for answer, 'Look: we know that there are many – perhaps an infinite number – of Histories emerging from each event. Imagine yourself, in two such neighbouring Histories, separated by – let us say – the details of the rebound of your billiard ball. Now: could those two copies of you communicate with each other?'

I thought about that. 'We have discussed this before. I don't see how. A Time Machine would take me up and down a single History branch. If I'd gone back to change the rebound of the ball, then I would expect to travel forward and observe a difference, because, it seems, if the Machine causes a bifurcation, it then tends to follow the newly-generated History. No,' I said confidently. 'The two versions of me could not communicate.'

'Not even if I allow you any conceivable machine, or measuring device?'

'No. There would be two copies of any such device – each as disconnected from its twin as I was.'

'Very well. That is a reasonable, and defensible, position. It is based on an implicit assumption that twin Histories, after their split, do not affect each other in any way. Technically speaking, you are assuming that Quantum-Mechanical Operators are linear . . . *But*,' and now that note of excitement returned to his voice, 'it turns out there *may* be a way to talk to the other History – *if*, on some fundamental level, the universe and its twin do remain entangled. If there is the smallest amount of Nonlinearity in the Quantum Operators – almost too small to detect –'

'Then such communication would be possible?'

'*I have seen it done* . . . in the Sea, I mean . . . the Constructors have managed it, but only on the smallest of experimental scales.'

Nebogipfel described to me what he called an 'Everett phonograph' – 'after the twentieth-century

505

scientist, of *your* History, who first dreamed up the idea. Of course the Constructors have another label – but it is not easily rendered into English.'

The Nonlinearities of which Nebogipfel spoke worked at the most subtle of levels.

'You must imagine that you perform a measurement – perhaps of the spin of an atom.' He described a 'Nonlinear' interaction between an atom's spin and its magnetic field. 'The universe splits in two, of course, depending on the experiment's outcome. Then, *after* the experiment, you allow the atom to pass through your Nonlinear field. This is the anomalous Quantum Operator I mentioned. Then – it turns out – you can arrange affairs so that your action in one History depends on a decision taken in the *second* History . . .'

He went into a great deal of detail about this, involving the technicalities of what he called a 'Stern-Gerlach device', but I let this wash past me; my concern was to grasp the central point.

'So,' I interrupted him, 'is it possible? Are you telling me that the Constructors have invented such inter-History communication devices? Is our table one such?' I began to feel excitement at the thought. All this chatter of billiard balls and spinning atoms was all very well; but if I could talk, by some Everett phonograph, to my selves in other Histories – perhaps to my home in Richmond in 1891 . . .

But Nebogipfel was to disappoint me. 'No,' he said. 'Not yet. The table utilizes the Nonlinear effect, but only to – ah – to *highlight* particular Histories. At least some selection, some control, over the processes is displayed, but . . . The effects are so small, you see. And the Nonlinearities are suppressed by time evolution.'

'Yes,' I said with impatience, 'but what is your guess? By placing this table here, is our Constructor trying to tell us that all this stuff – Nonlinearity, and communication between Histories – that it's all important to us?'

'Perhaps,' Nebogipfel said. 'But it is certainly important to *him*.'

7

THE MECHANICAL HEIRS
OF MAN

Nebogipfel reconstructed something of the history of Humanity, across fifty million years. Much of this picture was tentative, he warned me – an edifice of speculation, founded on the few unambiguous facts he had been able to retrieve from the Information Sea.

There had probably been several waves of star colonization by man and his descendants, said Nebogipfel. During our journey through time in the car, we had seen the launch of one generation of such ships, from the Orbital City.

'It is not difficult to build an interstellar craft,' he said, 'if one is *patient*. I imagine your 1944 friends in the Palaeocene could have devised such a vessel a mere century or two after we left them. One would need a propulsion unit, of course – a chemical, ion or laser rocket; or perhaps a solar sail of the type we have observed. And there are strategies to use the resources of the solar system to escape from the sun. You could, for instance, swing past Jupiter, and use that planet's bulk to hurl your star-ship in towards the sun. With a boost at perihelion, you could very easily reach solar escape velocity.'

'And then one would be free of the solar system?'

'At the other end a reverse of the process, the exploitation of the gravity wells of stars and planets, would be necessary, to settle into the new system. It might take ten, a hundred *thousand* years to complete such a journey, so great are the gulfs between the stars . . .'

'A thousand centuries? But who could survive so long? What ship – the supply question alone –'

'You miss the point,' he said. 'One would not send *humans*. The ship would be an automaton. A *machine*, with manipulative skills, and intelligence at least equivalent to a human's. The task of the machine would be to exploit the resources of the destination stellar system – using planets, comets, asteroids, dust, whatever it could find – to construct a colony.'

'Your "automatons",' I remarked, 'sound rather like our friends, the Universal Constructors.'

He did not reply.

'I can see the use of sending a machine to gather information. But other than that – what is the point? What is the *meaning* of a colony without humans?'

'But such a machine could construct *anything*, given the resources and sufficient time,' the Morlock said. 'With cell synthesis and artificial womb technology, it could even construct humans, to inhabit the new colony. Do you see?'

I protested at this – for the prospect seemed unnatural and abhorrent to me – until I remembered, with reluctance, that I had once watched the 'construction' of a Morlock, in just such a fashion!

Nebogipfel went on, 'But the probe's most important task would be to construct *more copies of itself*. These would be fuelled up – for example, with gases mined from the stars – and sent on, to further star systems.

'And so, slow but steady, the colonization of the Galaxy would proceed.'

'But,' I protested, 'even so, it would take so much

509

time. Ten thousand years to reach the nearest star, which is some light years away –'

'Four.'

'And the Galaxy itself –'

'Is a hundred thousand light years across. It would be slow. The migration across the Galaxy would be like the expansion of gas molecules into a vacuum,' he said. 'At least at first. But then the colonies would begin to interact with each other. Do you see? Empires could form, straddling the stars. Other groups would oppose the empires. The diffusion would slow further . . . but it would proceed, inexorably. By such techniques as I have described, it would take tens of millions of years to complete the colonization of the Galaxy – *but it could be done.* And, since it would be impossible to recall or redirect the mechanical probes, once launched, it *would* be done. It *must* have been done by now, fifty million years after the founding of First London.'

He went on, 'The first few generations of Constructors were, I think, built with anthropocentric constraints incorporated into their awareness. They were built to serve man. But these Constructors were not simple mechanical devices – these were conscious entities. And when they went out into the Galaxy, exploring worlds undreamed of by man and redesigning themselves, they soon passed far beyond the understanding of Humanity, and broke the constraints of their authors . . . The machines broke free.'

'Great Scott,' I said. 'I can't imagine the military chaps of that remote Age taking to that idea very kindly.'

'Yes. There were wars . . . The data is fragmented. In any event, there could be only one victor in such a conflict.'

'And what of men? How did they take to all this?'

510

'Some well, some badly.' Nebogipfel twisted his face a little and swivelled his eyes. 'What do you think? Humans are a diverse species, with multiple and fragmented goals – even in your day; imagine how much more diverse things became when people were spread across a hundred, a thousand star systems. The Constructors, too, rapidly fragmented. They are more unified as a species than man has ever been, by reason of their physical nature, but – because of the much greater Information pool to which they have access – their goals are far more complex and varied.'

But, through all this conflict, Nebogipfel said, the slow Conquest of the stars had proceeded.

The launching of the first star-ships, Nebogipfel said, had marked the greatest deviation we had yet witnessed from my original, unperturbed History. 'Men – your friends, the New Humans – have changed everything about the world, even on a geological – a *cosmic* scale. I wonder if you can understand –'

'What?'

'I wonder if you understand, *really*, the meaning of a million years – or ten million – or fifty.'

'Well, I ought to. I've traversed through such intervals, with you, on the way to the Palaeocene and back.'

'But then we travelled through a History *free of intelligence*. Look – I have told you of interstellar migration. If Mind is given the chance to work on such scales –'

'I've seen what can be done to the earth.'

'More than that – more than a single planet! The patient, termite-burrowing of *Mind* can undermine even the fabric of the universe,' he whispered, 'if given enough time . . . Even *we* only had a half-million years since the plains of Africa, and *we* captured a sun . . .

'Look at the sky,' he said. '*Where are the stars*? There is hardly a naked star in the sky. This is 1891, or thereabouts, remember: here can be no cosmological reason for the extinction of the stars, as compared to the sky of your own Richmond.

'With my dark-evolved eyes, I can see a little more than you. And I tell you there is an array of dull-red pinpoints up there: it is infra-red radiation – heat.'

Then it struck me, with almost a physical force. 'It is true,' I said. '*It is true* . . . Your hypothesis of Galactic conquest. The proof of it is visible, in the sky itself! The stars must be cloaked about – almost all of them – by *artificial shells*, like your Morlock Sphere.' I stared out at the empty sky. 'Dear God, Nebogipfel; human beings – and their machines – have changed Heaven itself!'

'It was inevitable that it would come to this, once the first Constructor was launched – do you see?

I stared into that darkened sky, oppressed by awe. It was not so much the changed nature of the sky that astonished me so, but the notion that all this – *all* of it, to the furthest end of the Galaxy – had been brought about by my shattering of History with the Time Machine!

'I can see that men have gone from the earth,' I said. 'The climatic instability has done for us here. But somewhere –' I waved a hand '– somewhere out *there* must be men and women, in those scattered homes!'

'No,' he said. 'The Constructors see everywhere, remember; they know everything. And I have seen no evidence of men like you. Oh, here and there you may find biological creatures descended from man – but as diverse, in their way, from *your* form of human as I am. And would you count *me* a man? And the biological forms are, besides, mostly degenerated . . .'

'There are *no true men*?'

512

'There are descendants of man *everywhere*. But nowhere will you find a creature who is more closely related to you than – say – a whale or an elephant . . .'

I quoted to him what I remembered of Charles Darwin: '"Judging by the past, we may safely infer that not one living species will transmit its unaltered likeness to a distant futurity . . ."'

'Darwin was right,' Nebogipfel said gently.

That idea – that, of your type, you are alone in the Galaxy! – is hard to accept, and I fell silent, gazing up at the blanked-out stars. Was each of those great globes as densely populated as Nebogipfel's Sphere? My fertile mind began to inhabit those immense world-buildings with the descendants of true men – with fish-men, and bird-men, men of fire and ice – and I wondered what a tale might be brought back if some immortal Gulliver were able to travel from world to world, visiting all the diverse offspring of Humanity.

'Men may have become extinct,' Nebogipfel said. 'Any biological species will, on a long enough timescale, become extinct. But the *Constructors* cannot become extinct. Do you see that? With the Constructors, the essence of the race is not the form, biological or otherwise – it is the *Information* the race has gathered, and stored. And that is immortal. Once a race has committed itself to such Children, of Metal and Machines and Information, it *cannot* die out. Do you see that?'

I turned to the prospect of White Earth beyond our window. I saw it, all right – I saw it all, only too well!

Men had launched off these mechanical workers to the stars, to find new worlds, build colonies. I imagined that great argosy of light reaching out from an earth which had grown too small, going glittering up into the sky, smaller and smaller until the blue had swallowed them up . . . There were a million lost stories, I thought, of how men had come to know how to bear the strange gravitations, the attenuated and unfamiliar gases and all the stresses of space.

It was an epochal migration – it changed the nature of the cosmos – but its launch was, perhaps, a last effort, a spasm before the collapse of civilization on the Mother World. In the face of the disintegration of the atmosphere, men on earth weakened, dwindled – we had the evidence of the pathetic mirror on the moon to show us that – and, at last, *died.*

But then, much later, to the deserted earth, back came the colony machines man had sent out – or their descendants, the Universal Constructors, enormously sophisticated. The Constructors were descended from men, in a way – and yet they had gone far beyond the boundaries of what men could achieve; for they had discarded old Adam, and all the vestiges of brutes and reptiles that had lurked in his body and spirit.

I saw it all! The earth had been repopulated; and – not by man – but by the Mechanical Heirs of Man, who had returned, changed, from the stars.

And all of this – *all* of it – had propagated out of the little colony which had been founded in the Palaeocene. Hilary had foreseen something of this, I thought: the re-engineering of the cosmos had unfolded from that little, fragile huddle of twelve people, that unremarkable seed planted fifty million years deep.

8

A PROPOSITION

Time wore away slowly, in that bizarre, cocooned place.

For his part, Nebogipfel seemed quite content with our arrangements. He spent most of each day with his face pressed up against the glistening hide of the Universal Constructor, immersed in the Information Sea. He had little time, or patience, for me; it was clearly an effort – a loss – for him to break away from that rich vein of ancient wisdom, and to confront my ignorance – and even more so my primitive desire for company.

I took to mooching, aimlessly, about the apartment. I munched at my plates of food; I used the steam bath; I toyed with the Multiplicity table; I peered out of the windows at an earth which had become as inhospitable to me as the surface of Jupiter.

I had nothing to do! – and in this mood of futility, for I was now so remote from home and my own kind that I could not see how I might live, I began to plumb new depths of depression.

Then, one day, Nebogipfel came to see me, with what he called a *proposition*.

We were in the room in which our friendly Constructor sat, as squat and placid as ever. Nebogipfel, as usual, was connected to the Constructor by his tube of glistening cilia.

'You must understand the background to all this,' he said, and his natural eye rotated so he could watch me. 'To begin with, you must see that the goals of the Constructors are very different from those of your species – or from mine.'

'That's understandable,' I said. 'The physical differences alone –'

'It goes beyond that.'

Generally, when we got into this sort of debate – with myself cast in the role of the Ignoramus – Nebogipfel showed signs of impatience, of a salmon-like longing to return to the gleaming depths of his Information Sea. This time, though, his speech was patient and deliberate, and I realized that he was taking unusual care over what he had to say.

I began to feel uneasy. Clearly the Morlock felt he had to *convince* me of something!

He continued to discuss the goals of the Constructors. 'You see, a species cannot survive for long if it continues to carry around the freight of antique motivations that *you* bear. No offence.'

'None taken,' I said drily.

'I mean, of course, territoriality, aggression, the violent settlement of disputes . . . Imperialist designs and the like become unimaginable when technology advances past a certain point. With weapons of the power of *die Zeitmaschine*'s Carolinum Bomb – or worse – things must change. A man of your own age said that the invention of atomic weapons had changed everything – except Humanity's way of thinking.'

'I can't argue with your thesis,' I said, 'for it does seem that – as you say – the limits of Humanity, the vestiges of old Adam, were at last enough to bring us down . . . But what of the goals of your metal super-men, the Constructors?'

He hesitated. 'In a sense a species, taken as a

whole, does not *have* goals. Did men have goals in common, in your day, save to keep on breathing, eating, and reproducing?'

I grunted. 'Goals shared with the lowest bacillus.'

'But, despite this complexity, one can – I think – *classify* the goals of a species, depending on its state of advancement, and the resources it requires as a consequence.'

A Pre-Industrial civilization, Nebogipfel said – I thought of England in the Middle Ages – needs raw materials: for food, clothing, warmth and so forth.

But once Industry has developed, materials can be substituted for each other, to accommodate the shortage of a particular resource. And so the key requirements then are for capital and labour. Such a state would describe my own century, and I saw how one could indeed regard, in a generic sense, the activities of mankind in that benighted century as driven in the large by competition for those two key resources: labour and capital.

'But there is a stage beyond the Industrial,' Nebogipfel said. 'It is the *Post-Industrial*. My own species had entered this stage – we had been there for the best part of half a million years, on your arrival – but it is a stage without an end.'

'Tell me what it means. If capital and labour are no longer the determinants of social evolution . . .'

'They are not, because *Information* can compensate for their lack. Do you see? Thus, the transmutating Floor of the Sphere – by means of the knowledge invested in its structure – could compensate for any shortage of resource, beyond primal energy . . .'

'And so you are saying that these Constructors – given their fragmentation into a myriad complex factions – are, at base, driving for more knowledge?'

'Information – its gathering, interpretation and storage – is the ultimate goal of all intelligent life.' He

517

regarded me sombrely. 'We had understood that, and had begun to translate the resources of the solar system to that goal; you men of the nineteenth century had barely begun to grope your way to that realization.'

'Very well,' I said. 'So, we must ask, what is it that limits the gathering of Information?' I peered out at the enclosed stars. 'These Universal Constructors have already fenced off much of this Galaxy, it seems to me.'

'And there are more Galaxies beyond,' Nebogipfel said. 'A million million star systems, as large as this one.'

'Perhaps, then, even now, the Constructors' great sail-ships are drifting out, like dandelion seeds, to whatever lies beyond the Galaxy . . . Perhaps, in the end, the Constructors can conquer *all* of this material universe, and turn it over to the storage and classification of Information which you describe. It would be a universe become a great Library – the greatest imaginable, infinite in scope and depth –'

'It is a grand project indeed – and, yes, the bulk of the energy of the Constructors is devoted to that goal: to studies of how intelligence can survive into the far future – when Mind has encompassed the universe, and when all the stars have died, and the planets have drifted from their suns . . . and matter itself begins to decay.

'But you are wrong: the universe is *not* infinite. And as such, *it is not enough.* Not for some factions of the Constructors. Do you see? This universe is bounded in Space and Time; it began a fixed period in the past, and it must finish with the final decay of matter, at the ultimate end of time . . .

'Some of the Constructors – a faction – are not prepared to *accept* this finitude,' Nebogipfel said. 'They will not countenance *any* limits to knowledge.

518

A finite universe is not enough for them! – and they are preparing to do something about it.'

That sent a chill – of pure, unadulterated awe – prickling over my scalp. I looked out at the hidden stars. This was a species which was already Immortal, which had conquered a Galaxy, which would absorb a universe – how could their ambitions stretch further still?

And, I wondered grimly, how could it involve *us*?

Nebogipfel, still locked to his eye-scope, rubbed his face with the back of his hand, in the manner of a cat, removing fragments of food from the hair about his chin. 'I do not yet have a full understanding of this scheme of theirs,' he said. 'It is to do with time travel, and Plattnerite; and – I think – the concept of the Multiplicity of Histories. The data is complex – so *bright* . . .' I thought this was an extraordinary word to use; for the first time it occurred to me what courage and intellectual strength it must take for the Morlock to descend into the Constructors' Information Sea – to confront that ocean of blazing Ideas.

He said, 'A fleet of Ships is being constructed – huge Time Machines, far beyond the capabilities of your century or mine. With these, the Constructors intend – I *think* – to penetrate the past. The deep past.'

'How far back? Beyond the Palaeocene?'

He regarded me. 'Oh, *much* further than that.'

'Well. And what of us, Nebogipfel? What is this "proposition" you have?'

'Our patron – the Constructor here with us – is of this faction. He was able to detect our approach through time – I cannot give you details; they are very advanced – they were able to *sense our coming*, on our crude Time-Car, up from the Palaeocene. And so, he was here to greet us.'

Our Constructor had been able to follow our

progress, up towards the surface of time, as if we were timid deep-sea fish! 'Well, I'm grateful he was. After all, if he *hadn't* been on hand to meet us as he did, and treat us with his molecular surgery, we'd be dead as nails.'

'Indeed.'

'And now?'

He withdrew his face from the Constructor's eye-scope; it came loose with an obscene plop. 'I think,' he said slowly, 'that they understand *your* significance – the fact that *your* initial invention propagated the changes, the explosion in Multiplicity, which led to all *this*.'

'What do you mean?'

'*I think they know who you are.* And they want us to come with them. In their great Ships – to the Boundary at the Beginning of Time.'

9

OPTIONS AND INTROSPECTIONS

To travel to the Beginning of Time . . . My soul quailed at the prospect!

You may think me something of a coward for this reaction. Well, perhaps I was. But you must remember that I had already been granted a vision of one extremity of Time – its bitter End – in one of the Histories I had investigated: the very first, where I had watched the dying of the sun over that desolate beach. I remembered, too, my nausea, my sickness and confusion; and how it had only been a greater dread of lying helpless in that rayless obscurity which had impelled me to get aboard the Time Machine once more and haul myself back into the past.

I knew that the picture I should find at the dawn of things would be rather different – unimaginably so! – but it was the memory of that dread and weakness which made me hesitate.

I am a human – and proud of it! – but my extraordinary experiences, I dare say more unusual that any man of my generation, had led me to understand the limitations of the human soul – or, at any rate, of *my* soul. I could deal with the descendants of man, like the Morlocks, and I could make a fair fist of coping with your prehistoric monstrosities like *Pristichampus*. And, when it was a mere intellectual exercise – in the warmth of the lounge of the Linnaean – I could conceive of going much further: I could have debated for long hours the Finitude of Time, or von Helmholtz's views on the inevitability of the Heat Death of the universe.

. . . But, the truth is, I found the reality altogether more daunting.

The available alternative, however, was hardly attractive!

I have always been a man of action – I like to get hold of things! – but here I was, cushioned in the hands of metal creatures so advanced they could not conceive even of talking to me, any more than I should think of holding spiritual conversations with a flask of bacillus. There was nothing I could *do* here on White Earth – for the Universal Constructors had *done* it all.

Many times, I wished I had ignored Nebogipfel's invitation and stayed in the Palaeocene! There, I had been a part of a growing, developing society, and my skills and intellect – as well as my physical strength – could have played a major part in the survival and development of Humanity in that hospitable Age. I found my thoughts, inwardly directed as they were, turning also to Weena – to that world of A.D. 802,701 to which I had first travelled through time, and to which I had intended to return – only to be blown off my course by the first Bifurcation of History. If things had been different, I thought – if *I* had behaved differently, that first time, perhaps I could have retrieved Weena from the flames, even at the cost of my own health or life. Or, if I had survived *that*, perhaps I could have gone on to make a genuine difference in that unhappy History, by somehow leading Eloi and Morlock to confront their common degradation.

I had done none of that, of course; I had run for home, as soon as I retrieved my Time Machine again. And now I was forced to accept that, because of the endless calving-off of Histories, I could never return to 802,701 – or, indeed, to my own time.

It seemed that my nomadic trail had ended here, in these meaningless few rooms!

I would be kept alive by these Constructors, it seemed, as long as my body continued to function. Since I have always been robust, I supposed I could look forward to several decades more of life – and perhaps even longer; for if Nebogipfel was right about the sub-molecular capabilities of these Constructors, perhaps (so Nebogipfel speculated, to my astonishment) they would be able to halt, or reverse, even the ageing processes of my body!

But it seemed I would be deprived of companionship forever – save for my unequal relationship with a Morlock who, already being my intellectual superior, and with his continuing immersion in the Information Sea, would surely soon pass on to concerns far advanced beyond my understanding.

I faced a long and comfortable life, then – but it was the life of a zoo animal, caged up in these few rooms, with nothing meaningful to achieve. It was a future that had become a tunnel, closed and unending . . .

But, on the other hand, I knew that concurring with the Constructors' plan was a course of action quite capable of destroying my intellect.

I confided these doubts to Nebogipfel.

'I understand your fears, and I applaud your honesty in confronting your own weakness. You have grown in understanding of yourself, since our first meeting –'

'Spare me this kindness, Nebogipfel!'

'There is no need for a decision now.'

'What do you mean?'

Nebogipfel went on to describe the immense technical scope of the Constructors' project. To fuel the

523

Ships, vast amounts of Plattnerite would have to be prepared.

'The Constructors work on long time-scales,' the Morlock said. 'But, even so, this project is ambitious. The Constructors' own estimates of completion (and this is vague, because the Constructors do not *plan* in the sense that human builders do; rather they simply build, cooperative and incremental and utterly dedicated, in the manner of termites) are that another million years will pass before the Ships are made ready.'

'*A million years?* . . . The Constructors must be patient indeed, to devise schemes on such scales!'

My imagination was caught by the scale of all this, so startled was I by that number! To consider a project spanning geological ages, and designed to send ships to the Dawn of Time: I felt a certain awe settling over me, I told Nebogipfel: a sense, perhaps, of the numinous.

Nebogipfel favoured me with a sort of sceptical glare. 'Very well,' he said. 'But we must strive to be practical.' He said that he had negotiated to have the remains of our improvised Time-Car brought to us; as well as tools, raw materials, and a supply of fresh Plattnerite . . .

I understood his thinking immediately. 'You're suggesting we just hop on the Time-Car, and skip forward through a million-year interval, while our patient Constructors complete the Ships' development?'

'Why not? We have no other way to reach the launch of the Ships. The Constructors may be functionally immortal, but we are not.'

'Well – I don't know! – it just seems . . . I mean, can the Constructors be so *sure* of completing their building programme – on time, and as they have envisaged it – over such immense intervals? Why, in my day, the human species itself was only a tenth that age.'

'You must remember,' Nebogipfel said, '*the Constructors are not human.* They are, truly, an immortal species. Individual foci of awareness may form and dissolve back into the general Sea, but the continuity of Information-gathering, and their consistency of purpose, is unwavering . . .

'In any event,' he said, regarding me, 'what have you to lose? If we travel up through time and find that, after all, the Constructors gave up before completing their Ships – what of it?'

'Well, we could die, for one thing. What if no Constructor is available to greet us, and tend to our needs, at the distant end of your million years?'

'*What of it?*' the Morlock repeated. 'Can you look into your heart, now, and say that you are happy –' he waved a hand at our little apartment '- to live like *this* for the rest of your life?'

I did not answer; but I think he read my response in my face.

'And besides –' he went on.

'Yes?'

'Once it is built, it is possible we may choose to use the Time-Car to travel in a different direction.'

'What do you mean?'

'We will be given plenty of Plattnerite – we could even reach the Palaeocene again, if you would like.'

I glanced about furtively, feeling like some plotting criminal! 'Nebogipfel, what if the Constructors hear you saying such things?'

'What if they do? We are not *prisoners* here. The Constructors find us interesting – and they feel that *you* should accompany the Ships on their final quest, because of your historical and causal significance. But they would not force us, or keep us here if our distress was so deep that we could not survive.'

525

'And you?' I asked him carefully. 'What do *you* want to do?'

'I have made no decision,' he retorted. 'My main concern *now* is to open as many options to the future as I can.'

This was eminently sensible advice, and so – having done with introspection! – I concurred with Nebogipfel that we should make a start at rebuilding the Time-Car. We fell into a detailed discussion as to the requirements we would have for materials and tools.

10

PREPARATIONS

The Time-Car was brought in from the ice by the Constructor. To achieve this, the Constructor split himself into four small sub-pyramids, and positioned these child-machines beneath each corner of the car's battered frame. The child-machines moved with a kind of oily, flowing motion – think of the way a sand-dune advances, grain by grain, under the influence of a wind – and I saw how migrating threads of metal cilia connected the child-machines to each other as the strange procession continued.

When the remains of our car had been deposited in the middle of one room, the child-machines coalesced into their parent Constructor once more; they flowed upwards and into each other, as if melting. I found it a fascinating sight, if repulsive; but soon Nebogipfel was happily plugged into his eye-scope once more without a qualm.

The essential sub-structure of the Time-Car came from the skeleton of our 1938 Chronic Displacement Vehicle, but its super-structure – such as it was, merely a few panels for walls and floor – had been improvised, by Nebogipfel, from the wreckage of the Expeditionary Force's bombed-out Juggernauts and the Messerchmitt *Zeitmaschine*. The simple controls had been a similarly crude affair. Much of this, now, was depleted and wrecked. So, in addition to the replacement of the Plattnerite, it was pretty clear that we needed to perform some pretty extensive renovation work on the car.

I contributed much of the skilled manual work, under the direction of Nebogipfel. At first I resented this arrangement, but it was Nebogipfel who had the access to the Information Sea, and thereby the accumulated wisdom of the Constructors; and it was he who was able to specify to the Constructor the materials we needed: pipe of such-and-such a diameter, with a thread of this-or-that pitch; and so forth.

The Constructor produced the raw materials we needed in his usual novel fashion; he simply extruded the stuff from his hide. It cost him nothing, it seemed, save a material depletion; but that was soon made up by an increased flow into the apartment of the migrating cilia which sustained him.

I found it difficult to trust the results of this process. I had visited steel-works and the like during the manufacture of components of my own Time Machine, and earlier devices: I had watched molten iron run from the blast-furnaces into Bessemer converters, there to be oxidized and mixed with spiegel and carbon . . . And so on. By comparison, I found it hard to put my faith in something which had been disgorged by a shapeless, glistening heap!

The Morlock pointed out my folly at this prejudice, of course. 'The sub-atomic transmutation of which the Constructor is capable is a far more refined process than that mess of melting, mixing and hammering you describe – a process which sounds as if it had barely evolved since your departure from the caves.'

'Perhaps,' I said, 'but even so . . . It's the invisibility of all this!' I picked up a wrench; like all the tools we had specified, this had been disgorged by the Constructor within moments of Nebogipfel's request for it, and it was a smooth, seamless thing, without joints, screws or mould marks. 'When I pick up this thing, I half-expect it to feel *warm*, or to be dripping with stomach-acid, or to be covered with those dreadful iron cilia . . .'

Nebogipfel shook his head, his gesture a conscious mockery. 'You are so *intolerant* of ways of doing things other than your own!'

Despite my reservations, I was forced to allow to the Constructor providing us with more equipment and supplies. I reasoned that the journey should take thirty hours, if we retreated all the way to the Palaeocene – but no more than thirty minutes if we performed the limited hop to the future of the Time Ships. So, determined not to be unprepared *this* time, I stocked up our new car with enough food and water, to our varying requirements, to last us for some days; and I asked for thick, warm clothing to be provided for us both. Still, I was uneasy as I lifted the heavy coat the Constructor had made for me over the battered remains of my jungle-twill shirt; the coat was an affair of silvery, unidentifiable cloth, quite heavily quilted.

'It just doesn't seem natural,' I protested to Nebogipfel, 'to *wear* something which has been vomited up in such a fashion!'

'Your reservations are becoming tedious,' the Morlock replied. 'It is clear enough to me that you have a morbid fear of the body and its functions. This is evidenced not only by your irrational response to the Constructor's manufacturing capabilities, but also by your earlier reaction to Morlocks –'

'I don't know what you mean,' I retorted, startled.

'You have repeatedly described to me your encounters with those – cousins – of mine, using terms associated with the body: faecal analogies, fingers like worms, and so on.'

'So you're saying – wait a minute – you're saying

that, in fearing the Morlock, and the products of the Constructors, I fear my own *biology*?'

Without warning, he flashed his fingers in my face; the pallor of the naked flesh of his palm, the worm-like quality of his fingers – all of it was horrifying to me, of course, as it always was! – and I could not help but flinch away.

The Morlock evidently felt he had made his point; and I remembered, too, my earlier connection between my dread of the Morlocks' dark subterranean bases and my childhood fear of the ventilation shafts set in the grounds of my parents' home.

Needless to say I felt distinctly uncomfortable at this brusque diagnosis of Nebogipfel's: at the thought that my reactions to things were governed, not by the force of my intellect as I might have supposed, but by such odd, hidden facets of my nature! 'I think,' I concluded with all the dignity I could muster, 'that some things are best left unsaid!' – and I stopped the conversation.

The finished Time-Car was quite a crude design: just a box of metal, open at the top, unpainted and roughly finished. But the controls were by some distance advanced over the limited mechanisms Nebogipfel had been able to manufacture with the materials available in the Palaeocene – they even included simple chronometric dials, albeit hand-lettered – and we would have about as much freedom of movement in time as I had been afforded by my own first machine.

As I worked, and the day approached on which we had set ourselves to depart, my fear and uncertainty mounted. I knew that I could never return home – but if I went on from here, on with Nebogipfel into future and past, I might enter such strangeness that I might not survive, either in mind or body. I might, I knew, be approaching the end of my life; and a soft, human terror settled over me.

Finally it was done. Nebogipfel set himself on his saddle. He was done up in a heavy, quilted overall of the Constructor's silvery cloth; and new goggles were fixed over his small face. He looked a little like a small child bundled up against the winter – at least until one made out the hair cascading from his face, and the luminous quality of the eye behind the blue glasses he wore.

I sat down beside him, and made a last check over the contents of our car.

Now – as we sat there, in a startling second – the walls of our apartment melted, silently, to glass! All around us, visible now through the translucent walls of our room, the bleak plains of White Earth stretched off to the distance, gilded red by an advanced sunset. The Constructor's cilia – again to Nebogipfel's specification – had reworked the material of the walls of the chamber within which the Time-Car sat. We should continue to need some protection from the savage climate of White Earth; but we wished to have a view of the world as we progressed.

Although the temperature of the air was unchanged, I immediately felt much colder; I shivered, and pulled my coat closer around me.

'I think we are set,' Nebogipfel said.

'Set,' I agreed, 'save for one thing – our decision! Do we travel to the future of the completed Ships, or –?'

'I think the decision is yours,' he said. But he had – I like to think – some sympathy in his alien expression.

Still that soft fear quivered inside me, for, save for those first few desperate hours after I lost Moses, I have never been a man to welcome the prospect of death! – and yet I knew that my choice now might end my life. But still –

'I really don't think I have much choice,' I told Nebogipfel. 'We cannot stay here.'

'No,' he said. 'We are exiles, you and I,' he said. 'I think there is nothing for us to do but continue – on to the End.'

'Yes,' I said. 'To the Ends of Time itself, it seems . . . Well! So be it, Nebogipfel. So be it.'

Nebogipfel pressed forward the levers of the Time-Car – I felt my breathing accelerate, and blood pounded in my temples – and we fell into the grey clamour of time travel.

11

FORWARD IN TIME

Once more the sun rocketed across the sky, and the moon, still green, rolled through its phases, the months going by more quickly than heartbeats; soon, the velocities of both orbs had increased to the point where they had merged into those seamless, precessing bands of light I have described before, and the sky had taken on that steely greyness which was a compound of day and night. All around us, clearly visible from our elevated viewpoint, the ice-fields of White Earth swept away and over the horizon, all but unchanging as the meaningless years flapped past, displaying only a surface sheen smoothed over by the rapidity of our transition.

I should have liked to have seen those magnificent inter-stellar sail-craft soar off into space; but the rotation of the earth rendered those fragile ships impossible for me to make out, and as soon as we entered time travel the sail-ships became invisible to us.

Within seconds of our departure — as seen from our diluted point of view – our apartment was demolished. It vanished around us like dew, to leave our transparent blister sitting isolated on the flat roof of our tower. I thought of our bizarre, yet comfortable, set of chambers – with my steam-bath, that ludicrous flock wallpaper, the peculiar billiards table, and all the rest – *all* of it had been melted back, now, into general formlessness, and our apartment, no longer required, had been reduced to a dream: a Platonic memory, in the metal imagination of the Universal Constructors!

But we were not abandoned by our own, patient Constructor, however. From my accelerated point of view I saw how he seemed to rest *here*, a few yards from us – a squat pyramid, the writhing of his cilia smoothed over by our time passage – and then he would jump, abruptly, to *there*, to linger for a few seconds – and so on. Since a mere second for us lasted centuries in the world beyond the Time-Car, I could calculate that the Constructor was remaining close to our site, all but immobile, for as much as a thousand years at a time.

I pointed this out to Nebogipfel. 'Imagine that, if you can! To be Immortal is one thing, but to be so devoted to a single task ... He is like a solitary Knight guarding his Grail, while historical ages, and the mayfly concerns of ordinary men, flutter away.'

As I have described, the buildings which neighboured ours were towers, standing two to three miles apart, all across the Thames valley. In the several weeks we had spent in our apartment I had seen no evidence of change about these towers – not even the opening of a door. Now, though, with the benefit of my accelerated perceptions, I saw how slow evolutions crept over the buildings' surfaces. One cylindrical affair in Hammersmith had its mirror-smooth face swell up, as if raddled by some metallic disease, before settling into a new pattern of angular bumps and channels. Another tower, in the vicinity of Fulham, disappeared altogether! – One moment it was there, the next not, without even the shadow of foundations on the ground to show where it had been, for the ice closed over the exposed earth more rapidly than I could follow.

This sort of flowing evolution went on all the

534

time. The pace of change in this new London must be measured in centuries, I realized – rather than the *years* within which sections of my own London had been transformed – but change there was, nevertheless.

I pointed this out to Nebogipfel.

'We can only speculate as to the purpose of this rebuilding,' he said. 'Perhaps the change in outer appearance signifies a change in inner utilization. But the slow processes of decay are working even here. And perhaps there are, occasionally, more spectacular incidents, such as the fall of a meteorite.'

'Surely intelligences so vast as these Constructors could plan for such accidents as the fall of a meteor! – by tracking the falling rocks with their telescopes, perhaps using their ships with rockets and sails to knock the things away.'

'To some extent. But the solar system is a random and chaotic place,' Nebogipfel said. 'One could never be sure of eliminating *all* calamities, no matter what resources were available, and no matter what planning and watching was performed . . . And so, even the Constructors must sometimes rebuild – *even the tower we inhabit.*'

'What do you mean?'

'Think it out,' Nebogipfel said. 'Are you warm? Do you feel comfortable?'

As I have noted, my apparent exposure to the wastes of White Earth, sheltered only by this invisible dome of the Constructors, had left me feeling chilled; but I knew this could only be an internal reaction. 'I'm quite satisfactory.'

'Of course. So am I. And – since we have now been travelling perhaps a quarter-hour – we know that equable conditions have persisted in this building *for more than half a million years.*'

'But,' I said, following his thinking, 'this tower of

535

ours is just as prone to the predations of time as any other . . . therefore our Constructor must be repairing the place, continually, to allow it to continue to serve us.'

'Yes. Otherwise this dome which shelters us would surely have splintered and fallen away a long time ago.'

Nebogipfel was right, of course – it was another facet of the extraordinary steadiness of purpose of the Constructors – but it scarcely made me feel more comfortable! I glanced about, studying the floor beneath us; I felt as if the tower had become as insubstantial as a termite hill, being endlessly burrowed through and rebuilt by the Universal Constructors, and I was filled with vertigo!

Now I became aware of a change in the quality of light. The glaciated landscape stretched around us, apparently unchanged; but it seemed to me that the ice was rather more darkly lit than before.

The bands of sun and moon, rendered diffuse and indistinct by their precessional motions, still rocked through the sky; but – though the moon still seemed to be shining with the violent green of its transplanted vegetation – the sun appeared to be undergoing a cycle of change.

'It seems,' I observed, 'that the sun is *flickering* – varying in brightness, on a scale covering centuries or more.'

'I think you are right.'

It was this uncertainty of light, I was sure now, which was casting that odd, disorienting illusion of a shadow over the icy landscape. If you will stand by a window, hold your hand before your face with fingers outspread, and rattle your hand to and fro before your eyes – then, perhaps, you will get some impression of what I mean.

'Confound that flickering,' I protested, 'it has a way of getting under the surface of the eye – of disturbing the rhythms of the mind, perhaps . . .'

'But watch the light,' Nebogipfel said. 'Follow its quality. It is changing again.'

I stuck to my task, and presently I was rewarded by glimpses of a new aspect of the sun's peculiar behaviour. There was a *greenness* about it – only at odd moments, when I would see a sort of pale verdancy streak along the sun's celestial path – but real, nevertheless.

Now that I knew this green behaviour was present, I was able to detect an emerald flashing over the frozen hills and stark buildings of London. It was a poignant sight, like a memory of the life that had vanished from these hills.

Nebogipfel said, 'I suspect that the flickering and the green flashes are connected . . .' The sun, he pointed out, is the solar system's greatest source of energy and matter. His Morlocks had themselves had exploited this, to construct their Sphere about the sun. 'Now, I think,' he said, 'the Universal Constructors too are delving into that great body: they are mining the sun, for the raw materials they need . . .'

'Plattnerite,' I said, excitement growing within me. 'That's the meaning of the green flashes, isn't it? The Constructors are extracting Plattnerite from the sun.'

'Or using their alchemical skills to turn solar matter and energy into the substance of Plattnerite, which amounts to the same thing.'

For the glow of the Plattnerite to be visible to us, Nebogipfel argued, the Constructors must be building great shells of the stuff about the star. When completed, these shells would then be shipped off, in immense convoys, to construction sites elsewhere in the solar system; and the accretion of a fresh shell begun. The flickering we saw must represent the accelerated assembly and dismantling of these great Plattnerite dumps.

'It is extraordinary,' I breathed. 'The Constructors must be lifting the stuff out of the sun in batches that compare with the mass of the greatest of the planets! This overshadows even the building of your great Sphere, Nebogipfel.'

'We know that the Constructors are not without ambition.'

Now, it seemed to me, the flickering of the patient sun grew rather less marked, as if the Constructors were nearing the end of their mining. I could see more patches of Plattnerite's characteristic green about the sky, but these were separate from the sun-band: rather, they hurtled across the sky rather in the manner of false moons. These were Plattnerite structures, I realized – huge, space-spanning buildings of the stuff – which were settling into some slow orbit about the earth.

Shifting Plattnerite light glistened from the hide of our patient Constructor, who stood by us while the sky went through these extraordinary evolutions!

Nebogipfel consulted his chronometric gauges. 'We have travelled through nearly eight hundred thousand years . . . time enough, I think.' He hauled on his levers – and the Time-Car lurched, displaying that clumsiness so characteristic of time travel – and I had nausea to contend with in addition to my awe and fear.

Immediately our Constructor disappeared from my view. I cried out – I could not help it! – and gripped the bench of the Time-Car. I think I had never felt so lost and alone, as at that moment when our faithful companion of eight thousand centuries suddenly – or so it seemed – abandoned us to strangeness.

The precessional juddering of the sun-band slowed, smoothed out and disappeared; within seconds, I perceived that disconcerting rattling of light which marks the passage of night and day, and the sky lost its washed-over, luminous-grey quality.

And now the green light of Plattnerite filled the air about me; it was all around our dome, and obscured the impassive plains of White Earth with its milky flickering.

The flapping of day and night slowed, to a beat slower than my pulse. Just in that last instant, I caught a vision – no more than a flash – of a field of stars breaking through the surface of things, dazzling and close; and I caught shadowy glimpses of several wide skulls, and huge, human eyes. Then Nebogipfel pushed his levers to their furthest extreme – the car stopped – and we emerged into History, and the crowd of Watchers vanished; and we were immersed in a flood of green light.

We were embedded in a Ship of Plattnerite!

12

THE SHIP

Myself, the Morlock, the workings and apparel of our little Time-Car – *all* of it was bathed in the emerald glow of Plattnerite, which was all about us. I had no idea of the true size of the Ship; indeed, I had some difficulty in finding my orientation within its bulk. It was not like a craft of my century, for it lacked a well-defined substructure, with walls and panels to fence off internal sections, engine compartments, and the like. Instead, you must imagine a *net*: a thing of threads and nodes all glowing with that green Plattnerite tinge, thrown about us as if by some invisible fisherman, so that Nebogipfel and I were encased in an immense mesh of rods and curves of light.

This net did not extend inwards all the way to our Time-Car: it seemed to halt at about the distance at which our dome had been resting. I was still breathing easily, and felt no colder than before. The environmental protection of the dome must still be afforded us, by some means; and I thought that the dome itself was still present, for I saw the faintest of reflections in a surface above, but so uncertain and shifting was the Plattnerite light that I could not be sure.

Nor could I make out the floor beneath the Time-Car. The netting seemed to extend below us, on and deep into the fabric of the building I remembered. I could not see how that flimsy webbing could support a mass as great as our Time-Car's, however, and I felt a sudden, and unwelcome, stab of vertigo. I put such primitive reactions aside with determination. My situation was extraordinary, but I wished to behave well – especially if these were to be the last moments of my life! – and I did not care to waste any energy on salving the discomfiture of the frightened ape within me, who thought he might fall out of this green-glowing tree.

I studied the net around us. Its main threads appeared to be about as thick as my index finger, although they glowed so bright it was hard to be sure if that thickness was merely some artefact of my own optical sensitivity. These threads surrounded cells perhaps a foot across, of irregular shapes: as far as I could see, no two of these cells shared a similar form. Finer threads were cast across and between these main cells, forming a complex pattern of sub-cells; and these sub-cells were themselves divided by finer threads, and so forth, right to the limit of my vision. I was reminded of the branching cilia which coated the outer layer of a Constructor.

At the nodes where the primary threads joined, points of light glowed, as defiantly green as the rest; these lumps did not stay at rest, but would migrate across threads, or would explode, in tiny, soundless flashes. You must imagine these little motions going on, all throughout the extent of the net, so that the whole thing was illuminated by a gentle, shifting glow, and a continuous evolution of structure and light.

I had a sense of fragility – it was like being cocooned in layers of spider-silk – but the whole thing had an organic quality to it, and I had the impression that if I were to reach up, clumsily, and tear great holes in this complex structure, it should soon repair itself.

And about the whole Ship, you must imagine,

541

there was that odd, contingent quality induced by the Plattnerite: a sense that the Ship was not embedded solidly in the world of things, a sense that it was all insubstantial and temporary.

The fabric was open enough for me to be able to see through the filmy outer hull of 'our' craft and to the world beyond. The hills and anonymous buildings of the Constructors' London were still there, and the eternal ice showed no signs of disturbance. It was night-time, and the sky was clear; the moon, a silver crescent, sailed high amid the absence of stars . . .

And, sliding across the desolate sky of this abandoned earth, I saw more of the Plattnerite Ships. They were lenticular in form, immense, with the suggestion of the same net-structure exhibited by the one which encased me and Nebogipfel; smaller lights, like captive stars, gleamed and rustled through their complex interiors. The ice of White Earth was universally bathed with the glow of Plattnerite; the Ships were like immense, silent clouds, sailing unnaturally close to the land.

Nebogipfel studied me, the Plattnerite lending a rich green lustre to the hair coating his body. 'Are you well? You seem a little discomposed.'

I had to laugh at that. 'You've a talent for understating, Morlock. Discomposed? *I* should say so . . .' I twisted in my seat, reached behind me, and found a bowl filled with the unidentifiable nuts and fruit which the Constructor had supplied me. I buried my fingers in the food and stuffed it into my mouth; I found the simple, animal actions of eating a welcome distraction from the astonishing, barely comprehensible matters about me. I wondered, in fact, if this should be the last meal I should take – the last supper of earth! 'I think I expected our Constructor to be here to greet us.'

'But I think he *is* here,' Nebogipfel said. He raised his hand, and emerald light gleamed from his pale fingers. 'This Ship is clearly designed along the same architectural principles as the Constructors themselves. I think we could say that "our" Constructor is still here: but now his consciousness is represented by some set of those sliding points of light, within this net of Plattnerite. And the Ship is surely connected to the Information Sea – indeed, perhaps one could say this is a new Universal Constructor itself. *The Ship is alive* . . . as alive as the Constructors.

'And yet, since it is composed of Plattnerite, this craft must be so much *more*.' He studied me, his single eye deep and dark behind his goggles. 'Do you see? If this is life, it is a *new* sort of life – Plattnerite life – the first sort which is *not* bound, as the rest of us are, to the slow turning of History's cogs. And it was *constructed* here, with ourselves as its focus . . . The Ship is here for us – to carry us back – just as the Constructor promised. He *is* here, you see.'

Of course, Nebogipfel was right; and now I wondered, with a sort of nervous self-consciousness, how many of those other Ships, which prowled across the star-less skies of earth like huge animals, were also down here, in some way, because of our presence?

But now, gazing up into the Plattnerite-coated sky, another observation struck me. 'Nebogipfel – behold the moon!'

The Morlock turned; I saw how the green light which played over the hairs of his face was now overlaid with a delicate silver.

My observation was elementary: that the moon had lost its delicious greenness. The life-colour which had reached up from earth and coated it, for all those millions of years, had withered away, exposing the stark bone-white of the dusty mountains and

543

maria beneath. Now, the satellite was quite indistinguishable in its dead pallor from the moon of my own day, save perhaps for a more brilliant glow over its dark side: there was a vivid Old Moon cradled in the New Moon's arms – and I knew that this greater brightness must be due, solely, to the increased gleam of the ice-coated earth, which must blaze in those airless Lunar skies like a second sun.

'It might have been the enforced variation of the sun,' Nebogipfel speculated. 'The Constructors' Plattnerite project . . . That, perhaps, finally disrupted the balance of life.'

'You know,' I said with some bitterness, 'I think – even after all we've seen and heard – I had taken some comfort from the persistence of that patch of earth-green, up in the sky. The thought that somewhere – not so impossibly far away – a scrap of the earth I remembered might still persist: that there might be some improbable, low-gravity jungle, through which the sons of man might still walk . . . But now there can only be ruins and shallow footprints on that bleak surface – more of them, to match those littered across the carcass of the earth.'

And it was just at that moment, while I was in this maudlin mood, that there was a report uncommonly like a gunshot – and our protective dome fractured, like an eggshell!

I saw that a series of cracks – a complex delta of them – had spread out across the face of the dome. Even as I watched, a small piece of the dome, no bigger than my hand, fell loose and settled through the air, drifting like a snow-flake.

And beyond the shattering dome the threads of the Ship's Plattnerite web were extending – they were growing, *down towards me and Nebogipfel.*

'Nebogipfel – what is happening? Without the

dome, will we die?' I was in a febrile, electric state, in which my every nerve-end was live with suspicion and fear.

'You must try not to be afraid,' Nebogipfel said, and then with a simple, astonishing gesture, he took hold of my hand in his thin Morlock fingers, and held it as an adult might a child's. It was the first time I had felt the touch of his cold fingers since those dreadful moments when the Constructor had rebuilt me, and a distant echo of our companionship in the Palaeocene returned to warm me, here amid the ice of White Earth. I am afraid I cried out then, unhinged by my fear, and pressed myself deeper into my seat, longing only for escape; and Nebogipfel's weak fingers tightened around my own.

The dome cracked further, and I heard a soft rain of it patter down over the Time-Car. The threads of Plattnerite reached deeper into our splintering dome, with nodules of light squirting along their lengths.

Nebogipfel said, 'They mean to carry us with them – the Constructors – these beings of Plattnerite – back to the dawn of time, and perhaps beyond . . . But not like *this*.' He indicated his own fragile body. 'We could never survive it – not for a minute . . . Do you see?'

The Plattnerite tentacles brushed against my scalp, forehead and shoulders; I ducked, to avoid their cold grip. 'You mean,' I said, 'that we must become like *them*. Like the Constructors . . . we must submit to the touch of these Plattnerite cilia! Why did you not warn me of this?'

'Would it have helped? It is the only way. Your fear is natural; but you must contain it, just for a moment more, and then – then you will be free . . .'

I could feel the cool weight of Plattnerite coils settling over my legs and shoulders. I tried to hold myself still – and then I got the sense of one of those squirming cables moving across my forehead, and I could feel, quite clearly, the wriggling of cilia against my flesh, and I could not help but scream and struggle against that soft weight, but already I was unable to rise from my seat.

I was immersed in greenness now, and my view of the world beyond – of the moon, the earth's fields of ice, even of the greater structure of the Ship – was obscured. Those shifting, quasi-animate nodes of light passed over my body, glaring in my vision. My bowl of fruit slipped from my numbing fingers, and rattled against the floor of the car; but even that rattle subsided quickly, as my senses faded to dimness.

There was a final crumbling of the dome, a hail of fragments about me. On my forehead there was a touch of cold, the distant breath of winter, and then there was only the coolness of Nebogipfel's fingers about mine – it was all I could feel, save for that omnipresent, liquid fumbling of Plattnerite! I imagined cilia detaching and – as they had once before – squirming into the interstices of my body. So rapidly had this invasion of light progressed, I could no longer move so much as a finger, nor could I cry out – I was pinned as if by a strait-waistcoat – and now the tentacles forced themselves between my lips, like so many worms, and into my mouth, there to dissolve against my tongue; and I felt a cold pressure on the surface of my eyes –

I was lost, disembodied, immersed in emerald light.

BOOK SIX

The Time Ships

1

DEPARTURE

I was outside Time and Space.

It was not like sleep – for even in sleep, the brain is active, functioning, sorting through its freight of information and memories; even in sleep, I contend, one remains conscious, aware of one's self and of one's continued existence.

This interval, this timeless spell, was *not* like that. It was more as if the Plattnerite web had, subtle and silent, disassembled me. I was simply *not there*, and the fragments of my personality, my shards of memory, had been broken up and disseminated about that immense and invisible Information Sea of which Nebogipfel was so fond.

. . . And then – more mysterious by far! – I found myself *there* again – I cannot put it more plainly than that – it was less like a waking than a *switching-on*, as one operates an electric bulb. One moment – nothing; the next – a full, shuddering awareness.

I could *see* again. I had a clear view of the world – of the green-glowing hull of the Time Ship all around me, of the earth's bone-gleam beyond.

I was existent once again! – and a deep panic – a horror – of that interval of Absence pumped through my system. I have feared no Hell so much as non-existence – indeed, I had long resolved that I should welcome whatever agonies Lucifer reserves for the intelligent Non-Believer, if those pains served as proof that my consciousness still endured!

But I was not permitted to brood on my disquietude, for now came the most extraordinary sensation of being lifted. I realized a growing stress upon me, a feeling as though some huge magnet was drawing me upward. The stress grew – I seemed an atom for which monstrous forces were fighting – and then of a sudden, that tension was resolved. I flew up, feeling exactly as if I was a small child again, being picked up by the strong, safe hands of my father; I had that same lightness of being, the sensation of flying. The substance of the Time Ship arose with me, so that it was like being at the centre of an immense, open, green-glowing balloon, lifting from the ground.

I looked down – or at least I tried to; I could not feel my head or neck, but the sweep of my panoramic vision swivelled downwards. You must imagine that the Ship about me had something of the shape of a steam liner, but hugely blown up – its lenticular keel was miles long – and yet it floated above the landscape with the ease of a cloud. I could see through the open, web-like substance of the Ship to the land beyond, and now I was looking down at our Time-Car, from directly above. Although my view was obscured by the complex, evolving sparkle of the Ship, I thought I saw two bodies in the car, a man and a slighter figure, who slid to the car's floor, their motions already stiff from the invading cold.

My view had an odd sensation about it. It was without focus: or rather, it lacked a central point of observation. When you look at something, say a tea-cup, you see *it*, and that's pretty much the centre of your world, with everything else relegated to a sort of sideshow around the periphery of your vision. But now I found that my world *had* no centre, or periphery. I saw it all – ice, Ships, Time-Car – it was as if it were all central, or all peripheral, all at once! It was disorienting and very confusing.

My belly and head seemed to have been numbed, gone quite beyond feeling. I could see, all right; but I could *feel* nothing of my face, my neck, the posture of my body – nothing, in fact, save a light, almost ghostly touch: the fingers of Nebogipfel, still wrapped around my own. I took some comfort in that, for it was good to know that *he* was here with me at least!

I thought I was dead – but I recalled I had thought that before, when I had been absorbed and remade by the Universal Constructor. What would become of me *now* I could not tell.

The Ship began to rise again, and now much more rapidly. The Time-Car and the tower on which it sat were swept away from under me. I was raised a mile, two miles, ten miles above the surface; the whole sparse map of this remote London was laid out beneath me, visible through the sparkle of the Time Ship.

Still we rose – we must have been travelling faster than a cannon-ball – and yet I heard no rush of air, felt no wind on my face; I felt secure, with that child-like sense of lightness I have mentioned. The circle of scenery beneath me grew wider, and the details of the buildings and ice-fields grew hazy and pale and indistinct, and a sort of luminous grey mixed more and more with the cold white of the ice. As the veil of atmosphere between myself and outer space grew thinner, the night-time sky, which had been an iron grey in colour, grew deeper and richer in tone.

Now our height was so great that the curving away of the planet became apparent – it was as if London was the highest point of some immense hill – and I could make out the shape of poor Britain, locked within its frozen Sea of Ice.

I remained without hands or feet, without belly

551

or mouth. I seemed to have been cut loose of matter, quite suddenly, and I saw things with a sort of serenity.

And still we climbed – I knew we were already far beyond the atmosphere – and the frozen plains mutated from a landscape into the surface of a spherical world, which turned, white and serene – and quite dead – beneath me. Beyond the earth's gleaming limb there were more Time Ships – hundreds of them, I saw now, great, green-glowing, lenticular boats miles long; they made up a loose armada which sailed across the face of space, and their light reflected from the wrinkled ice which coated the earth.

I heard my name called: or rather, it was not *hearing*, but an awareness, by some means I would be loath to try to explain. I tried to turn, but I found my point of view twisting about.

Nebogipfel? Is that you?

Yes. I am here. Are you all right?

Nebogipfel . . . I can't see you.

Nor I you. But that does not matter. Can you feel my hand?

Yes.

Now the earth drifted off to one side, and our Ship moved into formation with its fellows. Soon the Time Ships were all about us, in an array that filled the inter-planetary void for many miles about; it was like being in the middle of a school of great, glowing whales. The light of Plattnerite was brilliant, and yet there was a surface of unreality about it, as if it was reflecting from some invisible plane; again I had that feeling of contingency about the Ships, as if they did not belong quite in this Reality, or any other.

Nebogipfel, what is happening to us? Where are we being taken?

Gently, he replied, *You know the answer to that. We*

are to travel back through time . . . back to its Boundary, to its deepest, hidden heart.

Will we start soon?

We have already started, he said. *Look at the stars.*

I turned – or felt as if I did – so that I looked away from White Earth, and I saw:

All over the sky, the stars were coming out.

2
_____

THE UNRAVELLING OF EARTH

As we drew back through time, the colonizing
fleets from earth were washing back to their
origin, in successive waves, and the changes men had
wrought to worlds and stars were dismantled. And as
that tide of civilization and cultivation receded from
the cosmos, the star-masking Spheres were broken
apart, one by one. I gazed about in wonder as the old
constellations assembled themselves like so many
candelabras. Sirius and Orion shone as splendid as
on any winter's night; the Pole Star was over my
head, and I could make out the familiar saucepan
profile of the Great Bear. Away below me, beyond the
curve of earth, were strange groupings of stars I had
never seen from England: I did not know the
antipodean constellations so well that I could recognize them all, but I could pick out the brutal knife-
shape of the Southern Cross, the soft-glowing
patches that were the Magellanic Clouds, and those
brilliant twins, Alpha and Beta Centauri.

And now, as we sank further into the past, the stars
began to slide across the sky. Within moments, it
seemed, the familiar constellations were obscured, as
the stars' proper motions – much too slow to be
perceptible within a human's firefly lifetime –
became visible to my cosmic gaze.

I pointed out this new phenomenon to Nebogipfel.

Yes. And, see the earth . . .

I looked. The mask of glaciation which had disfigured that dear, exhausted globe was already falling away. I saw how the white of it receded towards the Poles, in great pulses, exposing the brown and blue of land and sea beneath.

Abruptly the ice was gone – banished back to its fastnesses at the Poles – and the world turned slowly beneath us, its familiar continents restored. But the earth was wreathed about by clouds; and the clouds were stained with virulent, unnatural colours – browns, purples, oranges. The coasts were ringed with light, and great cities glowed at the heart of every continent. There were even huge, floating towns in the middle of the oceans, I saw. But the air was so foul that in those great cities – if anyone went about on the surface – masks or filters would surely have to be worn, to enable humans to breathe.

Evidently we are witnessing the final days of the modification of the earth by my New Men, I said. *We must be traversing millions of years with each minute . . .*

Yes.

Then, why do we not see the earth spin like a top on its axis, and hurtle around the sun?

It is not so simple . . . These Ships are not like your proto-type Time Machine.

Everything we see is a reconstruction, Nebogipfel went on. *It is a sort of projection, based on the observations which, as we travel, are entering the Information Sea: that part of the sea transported by the Ships, at any rate. Such phenomena as the rotation of the earth have been suppressed.*

Nebogipfel, what am I? Am I still a man?

You are still yourself, he said firmly. *The only difference now is that the machinery which sustains you is not made up of bone and flesh, but of constructs within the Information Sea . . . You have limbs, not of sinew and blood, but of Understanding.*

His voice seemed to float about in space, some-where around me; I had lost that comforting sensa-tion of his hand in mine, and I could no longer tell if he was near – but I had the feeling that 'nearness' was no longer a relevant idea, for I had no clear idea even where 'I' was. Whatever I had become, I knew that I was no longer a point of awareness, looking out from a cave of bone.

The air of earth cleared. All over the planet, with startling abruptness, the city-lights dimmed and winked out, and soon the hand of man made no mark on the earth.

There were flurries of vulcanism, great flashing spurts which threw up ash clouds that flickered over the world – or, rather, as we receded in time, the clouds drained away into those volcanic punctures – and it seemed to me that the continents were drifting away from their school-room map positions. Across the great plains of the northern hemisphere, there seemed to be a sort of struggle – slow, millennial – progressing between two classes of vegetation: on the one hand, the pale green-brown grasslands and deciduous forests which lined the continents at the rim of the ice-cap; and on the other, the virulent green of the tropical jungles. For a moment, the jungles won, and in a great flourish, they swept north from the Equator, until they coated the lands from the Tropics, all the way up through Europe and North America. Even Greenland became, briefly, verdant. Then, as fast as they had conquered the earth, the great jungles retreated to their equatorial fastnesses once more, and paler shades of green and brown chased across the faces of the northern conti-nents.

The sliding-about and spinning of the continents became more marked. And as the continents were brought into different climatic regions, their life-colours changed accordingly, so that great bands of green and brown swept across the hapless lands. Huge, devastating spasms of vulcanism punctuated these geological waltz-steps.

Now the continents slid together – it was like watching a jigsaw assemble – to form a single, immense land-mass which straddled half the globe. The interior of this great country immediately shrivelled to desert.

Nebogipfel said, *We have already descended three hundred million years into the past . . . There are no mammals, no birds, and even the reptiles are barely born.*

I replied, *I had no idea it was all so graceful, like some rocky ballet – the geologists of my day have so much to understand! It is as if the whole planet is alive, and evolving.*

Now the great continent split into three huge masses. I could no longer make out the familiar shapes of the lands of my own time, for the continents spun like dinner-plates on a polished table-top. As that immense central desert was broken up the climate became much more variegated; and I could see a series of shallow seas fringing the lands.

Nebogipfel said, *Now the amphibians are sliding back to the seas, their prototypical limbs melting away. But there are insects and other invertebrates still on the land: millipedes, mites, spiders and scorpions . . .*

Not a very hospitable place, I remarked.

There are giant dragonflies too, and other wonders – the world is not without beauty.

Now the land began to lose its greenness – a kind of bony brown poked through the receding tide of life – and I surmised that we were passing beyond the appearance of the first leafed plants on land. Soon, the surface of the earth had become a sort of featureless mask of brown and a muddy blue. I knew that life persisted in the seas, but it was simplifying there too, with whole phyla disappearing into History's womb:

first the fish, now the mollusca, now the sponges and jellyfish and worms . . . At last, I realized, only a thin, green algae – labouring to convert the beating sunlight into oxygen – must remain in the darkened seas. The land was barren and rocky, and the atmosphere had turned thick, stained yellow and brown by noxious gases. Great fires erupted over the earth, all at once. Thick clouds masked the globe, and the seas retreated like drying puddles. But the clouds did not persist for long. The atmosphere became thin, then quite wispy, until at last it vanished altogether. The exposed crust glowed a uniform, dull red, save where great orange scars opened and closed like mouths. There were no seas, no distinction between the ocean and the land: only this endless, battered crust, over which the Time Ships soared, observant and graceful.

And next the glowing of the crust grew brighter – intolerably bright – and, with an explosion of glowing fragments, the young earth shook on its axis, shuddered, and flew into bits!

It was as if some of those fragments had hurtled *through* me. The glowing rock battered its way through my awareness, and dwindling off into space.

And then it was done! Now there was only the sun . . . and a disc of rubble and gas, formless, eddying, which spun about the shining star.

A sort of ripple passed through our cloud of Time Ships, as if the reversed coalescence of the earth had sent a physical shock through that loose armada.

This is a strange Age, Nebogipfel, I said.

Look around you . . .

I did so, and saw that, from all around the sky, there were several stars – perhaps a dozen – which were growing in brightness. Now the stars had reached a sort of formation, an array scattered over the sky, though still so distant they showed only as points. Gas wisps seemed to be collecting into a cloud, scattered over the sky and wrapped about this collection of stars.

These are the sun's true companions, Nebogipfel said. *Its siblings, if you like: the stars which shared the sun's nursery-cloud. Once, they formed a cluster as bright and as close as the Pleiades . . . but gravity will not hold them together, and before the birth of life on earth they will drift apart.*

One of the young stars, directly over my head, flared. It expanded, soon becoming large enough to show a disc, but growing more red, and fainter . . . until at last it expired, and the glow of that part of the cloud died.

Now another star, almost diametrically opposed in position to the first, went through the same cycle: the flare, followed by the expansion into a brilliant crimson disc, and then extinction.

All of this magnificent drama, you must imagine, was played out against a background of utter silence.

We are witnessing the birth of stars, I said, *but in reverse.*

Yes. The embryonic stars light up their birthing gas cloud – such nebulae are a beautiful sight – but after the stellar ignition, the lighter gases are made to flee the heat, leaving only heavier rubble –

A rubble which condenses into worlds, I said.

Yes.

And now – so soon! – it was the turn of the sun. There was that uncertain flaring of yellow-white light, a glare that glinted from the Time Ships' Plattnerite prows – and the rapid swelling into an immense globe, which briefly swamped the armada of Time Ships in a cloud of crimson light . . . and then, at last, that final dispersal into the general void.

The Ships hung in the sudden darkness. The last of the sun's companions flared, ballooned out, and died; and we were left in a cloud of cold, inert hydrogen, which reflected our glow of Plattnerite green.

*

559

Only the remote stars marked the sky, and I saw how they too shimmered and flared, fading in their turn. Soon the skies grew darker, and I surmised that fewer and fewer stars yet existed.

Then, suddenly, a new breed of stars flared across the sky. There was a whole host, it seemed: dozens of them were close enough to show a disc, and the light of these new stars was, I was sure, bright enough to read a newspaper by – not that I was in a position to try such an experiment!

Confound it, Nebogipfel, what an astonishing sight! Astronomy should have been a little different under a sky like this – eh?

This is the very first generation of stars. These are the only lights, anywhere in the new cosmos . . . Each of these stars amass a hundred thousand times as much as our sun, but they burn their fuel prodigiously – their life-spans are counted in mere millions of years.

And indeed, even as he spoke, I saw that the stars were expanding, reddening, and dispersing, like great, overheated balloons.

Soon it was done; and the sky was left dark again – dark, save only for the green glow of the Time Ships, which forged, steady and determined, into the past

3

THE BOUNDARY OF SPACE
AND TIME

A new, uniform glow began to permeate space around me. I wondered if some earlier generation of stars was shining in this primeval age – a generation undreamt of by Nebogipfel and the Constructors with whom he communed. But I soon saw that the glow did not come from an array of point sources, like stars; rather, it was a light which appeared to shine, all about me, as if from the structure of space itself – although here and there the glow was mottled, as, I surmised, dense clumps of embryonic star-matter shone more brightly. This light was the deepest crimson at first – it reminded me of a sunset breaking through clouds – but it brightened, and escalated through the familiar spectrum colours, through orange, yellow, blue, towards violet.

I saw that the fleet of Time Ships had gathered more closely together; they were rafts of green wire, silhouetted against the dazzling emptiness, and clustering for comfort. Tentacles – ropes of Plattnerite – snaked out across the glowing void between the Ships, and were connected, their terminations assimilated into the Ships' complex structures. Soon, the whole armada about me was connected by a sort of web of cilia filament.

Even at this early stage, Nebogipfel told me, *the universe has structure. The nascent galaxies are present as pools of cold gas, gathered in gravitational wells . . . But the structure is imploding, contracting, as we travel back towards the Boundary.*

It is like an explosion in reverse, then, I suggested to Nebogipfel. *Cosmic shrapnel, collapsing to site of detonation. At last, all the matter in the universe will merge in a single point – at some arbitrary centre of things – and it will be as if a great Sun has been born, in the midst of infinite and empty space.*

No. It's rather more subtle than that . . .

He reminded me of the bending-about of the axes of Space and Time – the distortion which lay behind the principle of time travel. *That twisting of axes is going on now, all around us,* he said. *As we travel back through time, it is not that matter and energy are converging through a fixed volume, like a gathering of flies at the centre of an empty room . . . Rather, space itself is folding up – compressing – crumpling, like a deflated balloon, or like a piece of paper, crushed in the hand.*

I followed his description – but it filled me with awe, and dread, for I could not see how life or Mind could survive such a crumpling!

The universal light grew in intensity, and it climbed the spectral scale to a glaring violet with startling speed. Clumps and eddies in that sea of hydrogen swirled about, like flames within a furnace; the Time Ships, connected by their ropes, were barely visible as gaunt silhouettes against that uneven glow. At last the sky was so bright I had only an impression of whiteness; it was like staring into the sun.

There was a soundless concussion – I felt as if I had heard a clash of cymbals – the light rushed in towards me, like some encroaching liquid – and I fell into a sort of white blindness. I was immersed in the most brilliant light, a light which seemed to suffuse my being. I could no longer make out those mottled clumps, and nor could I see the Time Ships – not even my own!

I called to Nebogipfel. *I cannot see. The light –*

His voice was small and calm, in that clamour of illumination. *We have reached the Epoch of Last Scattering . . . Space is now everywhere as hot as the surface of the sun, and filled with electrically charged matter. The universe is no longer transparent, as it will be in our day . . .*

I could see why the Ships had been joined up by those ropes of Constructor-stuff, for surely no signal could propagate through this glare. The dazzle grew more intense, until I was sure that it must have passed far beyond the range of visibility of normal human eyes – not that a man could have lasted for a moment in that glowing cosmic furnace!

It was as if I hung, alone, in all that immensity. If the Constructors were there, I had no sense of them. My feeling for the passage of time loosened and fell away; I could not tell if I was witnessing events on the scale of centuries or seconds, or if I was watching the evolution of stars or atoms. Before entering this last soup of light I had retained a residual sense of place – I had kept a feeling of up and down – of near and far . . . The world around me had been structured like a great room, within which I was suspended. But now, in this Epoch of Last Scattering, all of that fell away from me. I was a mote of awareness, bobbing about on the surface of that great River which was winding back to its source all about me, and I could only allow that ultimate stream to carry me where it would.

The soup of radiation became hotter – it was unbearably intense – and I saw that the matter of the universe, the matter which would one day compose the stars, planets and my own abandoned body, was but a thin trace of solidity, a contaminant in that seething maelstrom of light and stars. At last – I seemed to be able to see it – even the cores of atoms fizzed apart, under the pressure of that unbearable light. Space was filled with a soup of still more elemental particles, which combined and recombined in a sort of complex, microscopic mêlée, all about me.

We are close to the Boundary, Nebogipfel whispered. *The beginning of time itself . . . and yet you must imagine that we are not alone: that our History – this young, glowing universe – is but one of an infinite number which has emerged from that Boundary; and that as we retreat all the members of that Multiplicity are converging towards this moment, this Boundary, like swooping birds . . .*

But still the contraction of it all continued – still the temperature climbed, still the density of matter and energy grew; and now even those final fragments of radiation and matter were absorbed back into the shearing carcase of Space and Time, their energies stored in the stress of that great Twisting.

Until, in the end . . .

The last, sparkling particles fell away from me softly, and the glare of radiation heightened to a sort of invisibility.

Now, only a grey-white light filled my awareness: but that is a metaphor, for I knew that what I was experiencing now was *not* the light of Physics, but that glow hypothesized by Plato, the light which underlies all awareness – the light against which matter, events and minds are mere shadows.

We have reached the Nucleation, whispered Nebogipfel. *Space and Time are so twisted over that they are indistinguishable. There is no Physics here . . . There is no Structure. One cannot point and say: that is there, such a distance away; and I am here. There is no Measurement – no Observation . . . It is all as One.*

And, just as our History has shrivelled to a single, searing point, so the Multiplicity of Histories has converged. The Boundary itself is melting away – can you understand

564

it? – lost in the infinite possibilities of the collapsed Multiplicity . . .

And then there was a single, very brilliant, pulse of light: of *Plattnerite green.*

4

THE NONLINEARITY ENGINES

The merged Multiplicity convulsed. I felt twisted about – stretched and battered – as if the great River of causality which bore me had grown turbulent and hostile.

Nebogipfel? . . .

His voice was joyful – exultant. *It is the Constructors! The Constructors . . .*

The buffeting faded. The green glow fell away, leaving me immersed again in the grey-white of that moment of Creation. Then a new, plain white light emerged, but that persisted for only a moment; and then I watched as energy and matter condensed like dew out of a new unravelling of Space and Time.

I was travelling forward in time once more, away from the Boundary. I had been pitched into a new History, unfolding out of the Nucleation. The universal glare remained brilliant, surely still many orders of magnitude brighter than the centre of the sun.

The Time Ships no longer accompanied me – perhaps their physical forms had been unable to survive that journey through the Nucleation – and the Plattnerite netting around me had gone. But I was not alone; all about me – like snowflakes caught in a flash-lamp's burst – were speckles of Plattnerite-green light, which bobbed and drifted about each other. These were the elemental consciousness of the Constructors, I knew, and I wondered if Nebogipfel was among this disembodied host, and indeed if I, too, appeared to the rest as a dancing point.

Had my journey through time been reversed? Was I to swim up the streams of History, to my own era once more?

. . . Nebogipfel? Can you still hear me?

I am here.

What is happening? Are we travelling through time again?

No, he said. Still he had that note of exultation – of triumph – in his disembodied voice.

Then what? What is happening to us?

Do you not see? Could you not understand? We passed beyond the Nucleation. We reached the Boundary. And –

Yes?

Think of the Multiplicity as a surface, he said. *The totality of the Multiplicity is smooth, closed, featureless – a globe. And Histories are like lines of longitude, drawn between the poles of the sphere . . .*

And, in the Time Ships, we reached one pole.

Yes. That point where all the longitude lines converge. And, in that precise instant of infinite possibility, the Constructors fired their Nonlinearity Engines . . .

The Constructors have travelled across the Histories, he said. *They – and we – have followed paths of Imaginary Time, paths scrawled sideways across the surface of the Multiplicity globe, until we have reached this new History . . .*

Now the cloud of Constructors – there were millions of them, I thought – drifted apart, like fragments of a child's firework. It was as if they were trying to fill up the infant vacuum with the light and awareness we had brought from a different cosmos. And as the new universe unravelled, the afterglow of Creation faded to an immense darkness.

It was the end-result – the logical conclusion – of my own dabbling with the properties of light, and the distortion of the frames of Space and Time that went with it. All of this, I realized, even the collapsing of the universe and this great progression across Histories – all of it had come about, growing inevitably, from *my* experiments, from my first, dear machine of brass and quartz . . .

It had led to this: the passage of mind between universes.

But where have we come to? What is this History? Is it like ours?

No, Nebogipfel said. *No, it is not like ours.*

Will we be able to live here?

I do not know . . . it was not chosen for us. Remember that the Constructors have sought, he said, *a universe – out of all the infinite sheaf of possibilities that is the Multiplicity – a universe which is optimal for them.*

Yes. But what can 'optimal' mean for a Constructor? I conjured up vague images of Heaven – of peace, security, beauty, light – but I knew these imaginings were hopelessly anthropomorphic.

Now I saw a new light emerging, from the darkness all around us. At first I thought it was the returned glow of that fireball at the beginning of time – but it was too gentle, too insistent, for that; it was more like *star-light . . .*

The Constructors are not men, the Morlock said. *But they are the Heirs of Humanity. And the audacity of what they have accomplished is astonishing.*

Nebogipfel said, *Among all the myriad possibilities, the Constructors have sought out that universe – the single one – which is Infinite in extent, and Eternal in age: where that Boundary at the Beginning of Time has been pushed into the infinite past.*

We have travelled beyond the Nucleation, to the Boundary of Time and Space themselves. And ape-fingers have reached out to the Singularity that lies there – and pushed it back!

Star-light, now, was erupting from beneath the darkness, all around me; the stars were igniting everywhere; and soon the sky blazed, as bright everywhere as the surface of the sun.

THE FINAL VISION

An infinite universe!
You might look out, through the smoky clouds of London, at the stars which mark out the sky's cathedral roof; it is all so immense, so unchanging, that it is easy to suppose that the cosmos is an unending thing, and that it has endured forever.

. . . But *it cannot be so*. And one only need ask a common-sense question – *why is the night sky dark?* – to see why.

If you had an infinite universe, with stars and galaxies spread out through an endless void, then whichever direction in the sky you looked, your eye must meet a ray of light coming from the surface of a star. The night sky would glow everywhere as brightly as the sun . . .

The Constructors had challenged the darkness of the sky itself.

My impressions had an adamantine hardness: there was no blurring softness, no atmosphere, nothing but that infinite brilliancy set with a myriad of acute points and specks of light. Here and there I thought I could make out patterns and distinguishing features – constellations of brighter stars against the general background – but the whole effect was so dazzling that I could never find a given pattern twice.

My companion sparks of Plattnerite light – the Constructors, with Nebogipfel among them –

receded from me, above and below, like green-glowing fragments of a dream. I was left isolated. I felt no fear, no discomfort. The buffeting I had experienced at the moment of Nonlinearity had faded, leaving me without a sense of place, time or duration . . .

But then – after an interval I could not measure – I perceived I was no longer alone.

The form before me coalesced against the star-light, as if a magic-lantern slide had been held up before me. It began as a mere shadow against that universal glare – at first I was not sure if there was anything there at all, save for the projections of my own desperate imagination – but at last it gained a sort of solidity.

It was a ball, apparently of flesh, dangling in space, as unsupported as I was. I judged it to be eight or ten feet from me (wherever, and whatever, *I* was) and perhaps four feet across. Tentacles dangled from its underside. I heard a soft, babbling sound. There was a fleshy beak, no sign of nostrils, and two huge eyelids which now wrinkled up like curtains, to reveal *eyes* – human eyes! – that fixed on me.

I recognized him, of course; he was one of the creatures which I had labelled *Watchers* – those enigmatic visions which had visited me during my trips through time.

The thing drifted closer to me. He held out his tentacles, and I saw those digits were articulated and gathered in two bunches, like distorted, elongated hands. The tentacles were not soft and boneless things, like a squid's, but multiply jointed, and seemed to terminate in nails or hoofs – they were more like fingers, in fact.

Now it was as if he gathered me up. None of this could be real – I thought desperately – for *I* was no longer real – was I? I was a point of awareness; there was nothing of me *to* pick up, in this way . . .

And yet I felt cradled by him – oddly safe.

The Watcher was immense before me. His flesh was smooth, and covered with fine, downy hairs; his eyes were immense – sky-blue – with all the beautiful complexity of human eyes – and I could even *smell* him now; he had a soft animal musk about him, a scent of milk, perhaps. I was struck by how *human* he was. This may seem odd to you, but there – so close to the beast, and suspended in all that unstructured immensity – his common points with the human form were more striking than his grosser differences. I grew convinced that this *was* human: distorted by tremendous sweeps of evolutionary time, perhaps, but somehow akin to me.

Soon the Watcher released me, and I felt myself float away from him.

His eyes blinked; I heard the slow rustle of his eyelids. Then his huge gaze tracked around the searing, featureless sky, as if seeking something. With the softest of sighs, he drifted away from me. He turned as he did so, and his tentacles dangled after him.

For a moment a stab of panic flooded me – for I had no wish to be stranded again with my own company, here in the desolate perfection of Optimality – but in a moment I drifted after the Watcher. I went without volition, like an autumn leaf swept along by the passage of a carriage's wheels.

I have mentioned those suggestions of constellations I had seen, shining against the background of light-drenched, infinite space. Presently it seemed to me that one group of stars, in the direction ahead of us, was scattering apart, like a flock of birds; while another, behind me (I was able to turn my point of view) was contracting.

Could it be so? I wondered. Could I be travelling with such enormous rapidity, that even the stars themselves moved across my field of view, like lamp-posts seen from a train?

Suddenly there came a flying multitude of particles of rock, glittering like dust-specks in a sunbeam; they swirled all about me, and vanished again in a twinkling, far behind. I saw nothing of planets, or other rocky objects, in my time in that Optimal History, save for that shoal of dust-motes; and I wondered if the great heat and intense radiation here would disrupt the coalescing of planets from the general debris.

Faster and faster the universe rushed by, a hurry of whirling motes against the general brilliancy. Stars grew brighter, to shine out, explode from points into globes that hurtled at me, only to vanish in moments behind me.

We soared upwards, and hovered over the plane of a galaxy; it was a great Catherine-wheel of stars whose variegated colours shone, pale and attenuated, against the general whiteness of the background. But soon even this immense system was dwindling below me, now to a whirling, luminous disc, and at last to a minute patch of hazy light, lost amid millions of others.

And, throughout all this astonishing flight – you must picture it – I had the vision of the dark, round shoulders of the Watcher, as he bobbed through that tide of light just ahead of me, quite unperturbed by the star-scapes through which we travelled.

I thought of the times I had witnessed this creature and his companions. There had been that faint hint of babbling during my first expeditions in time – and then my first clear view of a Watcher when, in the light of the dying sun of far futurity, I had watched that object hopping fitfully about on the distant shoal – a thing like a football, glistening with the water. I had thought it, then, a denizen of that doomed world

573

– *but it had not been,* any more than me. And, later, there had been those later visions – glimpsed through a glow of Plattnerite green – of the Watchers as they hovered about the machine, as I fled through time.

Throughout my brief, spectacular career as a Time Traveller, I saw now, I had been followed – studied – by the Watchers.

The Watchers must be able to follow at will the lines of Imaginary Time, crossing the infinite Histories of the Multiplicity with the ease of a steamship traversing an ocean's currents; the Watchers had taken the crude, explosive Nonlinearity Engines developed by the Constructors and developed them to a fine pitch.

Now we journeyed into an immense void – a Hole in Space – which was walled off by threads and planes, sheets of light composed of galaxies and clouds of loose stars. Even here, millions of light years from the nearest of those star nebulae, the general wash of radiation persisted, and the sky all around me was alive with light. And beyond the rough walls of this cavity I could make out a larger structure: I could see that 'my' void was but one of many in a greater field of star-systems. It was as if the universe was filled with a sort of foam, with bubbles blown into a froth of shining star-stuff.

Soon, I began to make out an odd sort of regularity about this foam. On one side, for instance, my void was marked off by a flat plane of galaxies. This plane, of matter gathered together so densely that it glowed significantly more brilliant than the general background, was so marked and clearly defined – so flat and extensive – that the thought popped into my fecund mind that it might be not be a *natural* arrangement.

Now I looked about more carefully. Over *here*, I

thought, I could see another plane – clean and well-defined – and *there* I made out a sort of lance of light, utterly rectilinear, which seemed to span space from side to side – and *there* again I saw a void, but in the shape of a cylinder, quite clearly delineated . . .

The Watcher was rolling about before me now, his tentacle-clumps bathed in star-light, and his eyes were wide and fixed on me.

Artificial. The word was inescapable – the conclusion so clear that I should have drawn it long before, I realized, had it not been for the monstrous *scale* of all this!

This Optimal History was engineered – and this artifice must be what the Watcher had brought me on this immense journey to understand.

I recalled old predictions that an infinite universe would be prone to disastrous gravitational collapse – it was another reason why our own cosmos could not, logically, be infinite. For, just as the earth and other planets had coalesced from knots in that turbulent cloud of debris around the infant sun, so there would be eddies in this greater cloud of galaxies which populated the Optimal History – eddies into which stars and galaxies should tumble, on an immense scale.

But the Watchers were evidently managing the evolution of their cosmos to avoid such catastrophes. I had learned how Space and Time are themselves dynamic, adjustable entities. The Watchers were manipulating the bending, collapsing, twisting and shearing of Space and Time themselves, in order to achieve their objective of a stable cosmos.

Of course there could be no *end* to this careful engineering, if this universe were to remain viable – and, I thought, if the universe was eternal, there could have been no *beginning* to it either. That reflection troubled me, briefly: for it was a paradox, a causal circle. Life would be required to exist, in order to engineer the conditions which were pre-requisite to the existence of Life here . . .

But I soon dismissed such confusions! I was, I realized, being much too parochial in my thinking: I was not allowing for the Infinitude of things. Since this universe was infinitely old – and Life had existed here for an infinitely long time – *there was no beginning* to the benign cycle of Life's maintenance of the conditions for its own survival. Life existed here *because* the universe was viable; and the universe was viable *because* Life existed here to manage it . . . and on, an infinite regression, without beginning – and without paradox!

I felt loftily amused at my own confusion. It was clearly going to take me some time to come to terms with the meaning of Infinity and Eternity!

576

6

THE TRIUMPH OF MIND

My Watcher halted and rotated in space like some fleshy balloon. Those huge eyes came towards me, dark, immense, the glare of the light-drenched sky reflected in pupils the size of saucers; at last, it seemed, my world was filled by that immense, compelling gaze, to the exclusion of all else – even the fiery sky . . .

But then the Watcher seemed to melt away. The scattering of distant constellations, the foamy galactic structure – even the glare of the burning sky – I saw them no more – or rather, I was aware of these things as an aspect of reality, but only as a surface. If you imagine focusing on a pane of glass before you – and then deliberately relaxing the muscles of your eye, to fix on a landscape beyond, so that the dust on that pane disappears from your awareness – then you will have something of the effect I am describing.

But, of course, my change in perception was caused by nothing so physical as a tug of eye muscles, and the shift in perspective I endured involved rather more than depth of focus.

I saw – I thought – into the structure of Nature.

I saw *atoms:* points of light, like little stars, filling space in a sort of array which stretched off around me, unending – I saw it all as clearly as a doctor might study a pattern of ribs beneath the skin of a chest. The atoms fizzed and sparkled; they spun on their little axes, and they were connected by a complex mesh of threads of light – or so it seemed to me; I realized that I must be seeing some graphical presentation of electrical, magnetic, gravitational and other forces. It was as if the universe was filled with a sort of atomic clockwork – and, I saw, the whole of it was dynamic, with the patterns of links and atoms constantly shifting.

The meaning of this bizarre vision was immediately clear to me, for I saw more of the regularity here which I had observed among the galaxies and stars. I could see – suffused in every wisp of gas, in every stray atom – *meaning and structure.* There was a purpose to the orientation of each atom, the direction of its spin, and the linkages between it and its neighbours. It was as if the universe, the whole of it, had become a sort of Library, to store the collective wisdom of this ancient variant of Humanity; every scrap of matter, down to the last stray wisp, was evidently catalogued and exploited . . . Just as Nebogipfel had predicted as the final goal of Intelligence!

But this arrangement was *more* than a Library – more than a passive collection of dusty data – for there was a sense of life, of urgency, all about me. It was as if consciousness was distributed across these vast assemblages of matter.

Mind filled this universe, seeping down into its very fabric! – I seemed to see thought and awareness wash across this universal array of fact in great waves. I was astonished by the scale of all this – I could not grasp its boundless nature – by comparison, my own species had been limited to the manipulation of the outer skin of an insignificant planet, the Morlocks to their Sphere; and even the Constructors had only had a Galaxy – a single star-system, out of millions . . .

Here, though, Mind had it all – an Infinitude.

Now, at last, I understood – I saw for myself – the meaning and purpose of infinite and eternal Life.

The universe was infinitely old, and infinite in extent; and Mind, too, was infinitely old. Mind had gained control of all Matter and Forces, and had stored an infinite amount of Information.

Mind here was omniscient, omnipotent, and omnipresent. The Constructors, by means of their bold challenge to the beginnings of time, had achieved their ideal. They had transcended the finite, and colonized the infinite.

The atoms and forces faded to the background of my immediate attention, and my eyes were filled once more with the unending light and star-patterns of this cosmos. My Watcher companion had gone now, and I was suspended alone, a sort of disembodied point of view, slowly rotating.

The star-light was all about me, deep, unending. I had a sense of the smallness of things, of myself, the irrelevance of my petty concerns. In an infinite and eternal universe, I saw, there is no Centre; there can be no Beginning, no End. Each event, each point, is rendered identical to every other by the endless setting within which it is placed . . . In an infinite universe, I had become infinitesimal.

I have never been much of a poetry buff, but I remembered a verse of Shelley's: on how *life, like a dome of many-coloured glass/ stains the white radiance of Eternity* . . . and so forth. Well, I was done with life now; the covering of the body, the shallow illusion of matter itself – all that had been torn from me, and I was immersed, perhaps forever, in that white radiance of which Shelley spoke.

For a while I felt a peculiar sort of peace. When I had first witnessed the impact of my Time Machine

on the unravelling of History, I had come to believe
that my invention was a device of unparalleled evil,
for its arbitrary destruction and distortion of
Histories: for the elimination of millions of unborn
human souls, with the barest flicker of my control
levers. But now, at last, I saw that the Time Machine
had *not* destroyed Histories: rather, it had created
them. All possible Histories exist in the greater
Multiplicity, lying against one another in an endless
catalogue of What-Can-Be. Every History which was
possible, with all its cargo of Mind, Love and Hope,
had an existence somewhere in the Multiplicity.

But it was not so much the reality of the
Multiplicity but what it signified for the destiny of
man which moved me now.

Man – it had always seemed to me since I first read
Darwin – had been caught in a conflict: between the
aspirations of his soul, which were lofty without limit,
and the baseness of his physical nature, which, in the
end, might floor him. I thought I had seen, in the
Eloi, how the dead hand of Evolution – the legacy of
the beast in us – would in the end destroy man's
dreams, and turn his tenure of the earth into nothing but a brief, glorious glow of intellect.

That conflict, implicit in the human form, had, I
think, worked itself into me as a conflict in my own
mind. If Nebogipfel had been right that I had a sort
of loathing for the Body – well, perhaps my over-
awareness of this million-year conflict was its root! I
had veered, in my views and arguments, between a
sort of bleak despair, a loathing of our minds' bestial
casings, and a fond, rather foolish Utopianism – a
dream that one day our heads would become clear,
as if from a mass delirium, and we would settle on a
society founded on principles of logic, self-evident
justice, and science.

But now, the discovery – or construction – and

colonization of this final History had changed all that. *Here*, man had at last overcome his origins and the degradation of Natural Selection; *here*, there would be no return to the oblivion of that primal, mindless sea from which we had emerged: rather, the future had become infinite, a climbing into an air of endless Histories.

I felt I had emerged, at last, from out of the Darkness of evolutionary despair, and into the Light of infinite wisdom.

7

EMERGENCE

But, you may not be surprised to read if you have followed me this far, this mood – it was a sort of elegiac acceptance – did not persist with me for long!

I took to peering about. I strained myself to hear, to see any detail, the slightest mottling in that shell of illumination that surrounded me; but – for a while – there was naught but infinite silence, intolerable brightness.

I had become a disembodied mote, presumably immortal, and embedded in this greatest of artifices: a universe whose forces and particles were entirely given over to Mind. It was magnificent – but it was terrible, inhuman, chilling – and a sort of crushing dismay fell on me.

Had I passed out of being, into something that was neither being nor not-being? Well, if I had – I was discovering – I did not yet have the *peace* of the Eternal. I still had the soul of a man, with all the freight of inquisitiveness and thirst for action which has always been part of human nature. There is too much of the Occidental about me, and soon I had had my fill of this interval of disembodied Contemplation!. . .

Then, after an unmeasured interval, I realized that the brilliancy of the sky was *not* absolute. There was a sort of hazing at the edge of my vision – the slightest darkening.

I watched for geological ages, it seemed to me, and through that long waiting the hazing grew more distinct: it was a sort of circle about my vision, as if I was peering out through the mouth of a cave. And then, in the middle of that spectral cave-mouth, I made out an irregular cloud, a mottling against the general glare; I saw a collection of rough rods and discs, all indistinct, arranged like phantoms over the stars. In one corner of this view there was a cylinder coloured pure green.

I felt a passionate impatience. What was this irruption of shadows into the interminable Noon of this Optimal History?

The surrounding cave-shape grew more clear; I wondered if this was some submerged memory of the Palaeocene. And as for that misty collection of rods and discs, I was struck by an impression that I had seen this arrangement before: it was as familiar as my own hand, I thought, and yet, in this transformed context, I could not recognize it . . .

And then the realization rushed upon me. *The rods and other components were my Time Machine* – the lines over there, obscuring that constellation, were the bars of brass which made up the fundamental frame of the device; and those discs, wreathed about with galaxies, must be my chronometric dials. It was my original machine, which I had thought lost, dismantled and finally destroyed in that German attack on London in 1938!

The coalescing of this vision proceeded apace. The brass rods glittered – I saw there was a sprinkling of dust over the faces of the chronometric dials, whose hands whirled about – and I recognized the green glow of Plattnerite which suffused the doped quartz of the infrastructure. I looked down and made out two wide, fat, darker cylinders – they were my own legs, clothed in jungle twill! – and those pale, hairy, complex objects must be my hands, resting on the machine's control levers.

And now, at last, I understood the meaning of that 'cave-mouth' around my vision. It was the frame of my eye-sockets, nose and cheeks about my field of view: once more I was looking out from that darkest of caves – my own skull.

I felt as if I was being lowered into my body. Fingers and legs attached themselves to my consciousness. I could feel the levers, cool and firm, in my hand, and there was a light prickling of sweat on my brow. It was a little, I suppose, like recovering from the oblivion of chloroform; slowly, subtly, I was coming into myself. And now I felt a swaying, and that plummeting sensation of time travel.

Beyond the Time Machine there was only dark – I could make out nothing of the world – but I could feel, from its decreasing lurching, that the machine was slowing. I looked around – I was rewarded with the weight of a laden skull on a stem of a neck; after my disembodied state it felt as if I were swivelling an artillery piece – but there were only the faintest traces of the Optimal History left in my view: here a wisp of galaxy clusters, there a fragment of star-light. In that last instant, before my intangible link was finally broken, I saw again the round, solemn visage of my Watcher, with his immense, thoughtful eyes.

Then it was gone – all of it – and I was fully in myself again; and I felt a surge of savage, primitive joy!

The Time Machine lurched to a halt. The thing went rolling over, and I was flung headlong through the air, into pitch darkness.

There was a crack of thunder in my ears. A hard, steady rain was pounding with a brute force against my scalp and jungle shirt. In a moment I was wet to

584

the skin: it was a fine welcome back to corporeality, I thought!

I had been deposited on a patch of sodden, soft turf in front of the overturned machine. It was quite dark. I seemed to be on a little lawn, surrounded by bushes whose leaves were dancing under the rain-drops. The rebounding drops hung in a little cloud about the machine. Close by I heard the bubble of a mass of water, and rain pattered into that greater mass of liquid.

I stood up and looked about. There was a building close by, visible only as a silhouette against the charcoal-grey sky. I noticed now that there was a faint green glow, coming from beneath the tipped-over machine. I saw that it came from a vial, a cylinder of glass perhaps six inches tall: it was a common eight-ounce graduated medicine bottle. This had evidently been lodged in the frame of the machine, but now it had fallen to the grass.

I reached to pick up the flask. The greenish glow came from a powder within: it was Plattnerite.

My name was called.

I turned, startled. The voice had been soft, almost masked by the hissing of the rain on the grass.

There was a figure standing not ten feet from me: short, almost childlike, but with scalp and back coated by long, lank hair that had been plastered flat by the rain against pale flesh. Huge eyes, grey-red, were fixed on me.

'Nebogipfel –?'

And then some circuit closed in my bewildered brain.

I turned, and inspected that building's blocky outline once more. There was the iron balcony, over there the dining-room kitchen with a small window ajar, and there was the blocky form of the laboratory . . .

585

It was my home; my machine had deposited me on the sloping lawn at the rear, between the house and the Thames. I had returned – after all this! – to Richmond.

8

A CIRCLE IS CLOSED

Once more – just as we had done before, so many cycles of History ago – Nebogipfel and I walked along the Petersham Road to my house. The rain hissed on the cobbles. It was almost completely dark – in fact, the only light came from the jar of Plattnerite, which glowed like a faint electric bulb, casting a murky glow over Nebogipfel's face.

I brushed my fingers over the familiar, delicate metalwork of the rail before the area. Here was a sight I had thought never to see again: this mock-elegant facade, the pillars of the porch, the darkened rectangles of my windows.

'You have both your eyes back,' I observed to Nebogipfel in a whisper.

He glanced down at his renewed body, spreading his palms so that the pale flesh gleamed in the light of the Plattnerite. 'I have no need for prosthesis,' he said. 'Not any more. Now that I have been rebuilt – as *you* have.'

I rested my hands against my chest. The shirt fabric was coarse, rough under my palm, and my own breast-bone was hard beneath. It all felt solid enough. And I still felt like *me* – I mean, I had a continuity of consciousness, a single, shining path of memory, which led back through all that tangling-up of Histories, back to the simpler days when I was a boy. But I could not be the same man – for I had been disassembled in that Optimal History, and remade here. I wondered how much of that shining universe remained in me. 'Nebogipfel, do you remember much of it all – after we broke through that Boundary at the start of time – the glowing sky, and so forth?'

'All of it.' His eyes were black. 'You do not?'

'I'm not sure,' I said. 'It all seems a sort of a dream, now – especially *here*, in this cold English rain.'

'But the Optimal History is the reality,' he whispered. 'All of this –' he waved his hands about at innocent Richmond '– these partial, sub-Optimal Histories – *this* is the dream.'

I hoisted the jar of Plattnerite in my hand. It was a commonplace medicine bottle, plugged with rubber; needless to say, I had no idea of where it had come from, nor how it had got in amongst the struts of my machine. 'Well, *this* is real enough,' I said. 'It's really quite a pretty solution, isn't it? Like the closing of a circle.' I stepped towards the door. 'I think you'd better get back – out of sight – before I ring.'

He stepped backwards, into the shadow of the porch, and soon he was quite invisible.

I tugged at the bell-pull.

From within the house, I heard the opening of a door, a soft shout – 'I'll go!' – and then a heavy, impatient tread on the stair. A key rattled in the lock, and the door creaked open.

A candle, sputtering in a brass holder, was thrust through the doorway at me; the face of a young man, broad and round, peered out, his eyes puffed up with sleep. He was twenty-three or twenty-four, and he wore a battered, thread-bare gown, thrown over a crumpled night-shirt; his hair, a mousy brown, stuck out from the sides of his odd, broad head. 'Yes?' he snapped. 'It's after three in the morning, you know . . .'

I'd not been sure what I had intended to say, but now that the moment was here, words fled from me altogether. Once again I suffered that queer, uncomfortable shock of recognition. I don't think a man of my century could *ever* have grown accustomed to meeting himself, no matter how many times he'd practised it – and now that whole raft of feeling was overlaid with an extra sort of poignancy. For this was no longer just a younger version of me: it was also a direct ancestor of Moses. It was like coming face to face with a younger brother I had thought lost.

He studied my face again, suspicious now. 'What the devil do you want? I make a point of having no truck with hawkers, you know – even if this *was* the appropriate time of day.'

'No,' I said gently. 'No, I know you don't.'

'Oh, you do, do you?' He began to push closed the door, but he had seen something in my face – I could see the look – some ghost of recognition. 'I think you'd better tell me what you want.'

Clumsily, I produced the medicine jar of Plattnerite from behind my back. 'I have *this* for you.'

His eyebrows went up at the bottle's odd green glow. 'What is it?'

'It's –' How could I explain? 'It's a sort of sample. For you.'

'A sample of what?'

'I don't know,' I lied. 'I'd like you to find out.'

He looked curious, but still hesitant; and now a certain stubbornness was settling over his features 'Find out what?'

I started to become irritated at these dull questions. 'Confound it, man – do you not have any initiative? Run some tests . . .'

'I'm not sure I like your tone,' he said stuffily. 'What sort of tests?'

'Oh!' I ran a hand through my soaked hair; such

pomposity did not sit well on such a young man, I thought. 'It's a new mineral – you can see that much!'

He frowned, his suspicion redoubled.

I bent and set the jar down on the step. 'I'll leave it here. You can look at it when you're ready – and I *know* you'll be ready – I don't want to waste your time.' I turned and began to make my way down the path, my footsteps on the gravel loud through the rainfall.

When I looked back I saw that he had picked up the jar, and its green glow softened the shadows of the candle on his face. He called: 'But your name –'

I had an impulse. 'It is Plattner,' I said.

'*Plattner?* Do I know you?'

'Plattner,' I repeated in some desperation, and I sought a more detailed lie in the dim recesses of my brain. '*Gottfried* Plattner . . .'

It was as if I had heard someone else say it – but as soon as the words were out of my mouth, I knew they had had a sort of inevitability.

It was done; the circle was closed!

He continued to call, but I walked resolutely, away from the gate and down the Hill.

Nebogipfel was waiting for me at the rear of the house, close to the Time Machine. 'It's done,' I told him. A first touch of dawn had filtered into the overcast sky, and I could see the Morlock as a grainy sort of silhouette: he had his hands clasped behind him, and his hair was plastered flat against his back. His eyes were huge, blood-red pools.

'You're a little the worse for wear,' I said kindly. 'This rain –'

'It hardly matters.'

'What will you do now?'

'What will *you* do?'

590

For answer, I bent over and hauled at the Time Machine. It twisted up, clattering like an old bed, and settled to the lawn with a heavy thump. I ran a hand along the battered frame of the machine; moss and bits of grass clung to the quartz rods and the saddle, and one rail was bent, quite out of shape.

'You can go home, you know,' he said. 'To 1891. We have clearly been brought back, by the Watchers, to your original History – to the Primal version of things. You need only travel forward through a few years.'

I considered that prospect. In some ways it would have been comfortable to return to that cosy Age, and to my shell of belongings, companions and achievements. And I should have enjoyed the company of some of those old chums of mine again – Filby and the rest. *But* . . .

'I had a friend, in 1891,' I said to Nebogipfel. (I was thinking of the Writer.) 'Only a young fellow. An odd chap in some ways – very intense – and yet with a way of looking at things . . .

'He seemed to see *beyond* the surface of it all – beyond the Here and Now which so obsesses us all – and to the quick of it: to the trends, the deeper currents which connect us to both past and future. He had a view of the littleness of Humanity, I think, against the great sweep of evolutionary time; and I think it made him impatient with the world he found himself stuck in, with the endless, slow processes of society – even with his own, sickly human nature.

'It was as if he was a stranger in his own time, you see,' I concluded. 'And, if I went back, that's how I should feel. *Out of time.* For, no matter how solid this world seems, *I* should always know that a thousand universes, different to a small or a great degree, lie all around it – just out of reach.

'I am become a monster, I suppose . . . My friends

591

will have to think me lost in time, and mourn me as they will.'

Even as we had been speaking my resolution had formed. 'I still have a vocation. I have not yet completed the task I set myself, when I returned into time after that first visit. A circle has been closed here – but another remains open, dangling like a fractured bone, far into futurity . . .'

'I understand,' the Morlock said.

I climbed into the saddle of the machine.

'But what of you, Nebogipfel? Will you come with me? I can imagine a role for you there – and I don't want to leave you stranded here.'

'Thank you – but no. I will not remain here for long.'

'Where will you go?'

He raised his face. The rain was slowing now, but a thin mist of drops still seeped out of the lightening sky and fell against the great corneas of his eyes. 'I, too, am aware of the closure of circles,' he said. 'But I remain curious as to what lies beyond the circles . . .'

'What do you mean?'

'If you had returned here and shot your younger self – well, there would be no causal contradiction: instead, you would create a *new* History, a fresh variant in the Multiplicity, in which you died young at the hand of a stranger.'

'That's all clear enough to me, now. There is no paradox possible within a single History, because of the existence of the Multiplicity.'

'But,' the Morlock went on calmly, 'the Watchers have brought you here, so that you could deliver the Plattnerite to yourself – so that you could initiate the sequence of events which led to the development of the first Time Machine, and the creation of the Multiplicity. So there is a greater closure – *of the Multiplicity on itself.*'

592

I saw what he was driving at. 'There *is* a sort of closed loop of causality, after all,' I said, 'a worm eating its own tail . . . The Multiplicity could not have been brought into existence, if not for the existence of the Multiplicity in the first place!'

Nebogipfel said that the Watchers believed that the resolution of this Final Paradox required the existence of *more* Multiplicities: a Multiplicity of Multiplicities! 'The higher order is logically necessary to resolve the causal loop,' Nebogipfel said, 'just as our Multiplicity was required to exist to resolve the paradoxes of a single History.'

'But – confound it, Nebogipfel! My mind is reeling at the thought. Parallel ensembles of universes – is it possible?'

'More than possible,' he said. 'And the Watchers intend to *travel* there.' He lowered his head from the sky. The dawn was growing quite bright now, and I could see the pasty flesh around his eyes wrinkle up in discomfort. 'And they will take me with them. I can think of no greater adventure . . . can you?'

Sitting there on the saddle of my machine, I took one last look around, at that plain, soggy dawn somewhere in the nineteenth century. The houses, full of sleeping people, were silhouetted, all the way along the Petersham Road; I smelled the moisture on the grass, and somewhere a door slammed, as some milkman or postman began his day.

I should never come this way again, I knew.

'Nebogipfel – when you reach this greater Multiplicity – what then?'

'There are many orders of Infinity,' Nebogipfel said calmly, the light rain trickling down the contours of his face. 'It is like a hierarchy: of universal structures – and of ambitions.' His voice retained that soft Morlock gurgle – its intonations quite alien – and yet it was suffused with wonder. 'The Constructors could

593

have owned a universe; but it was not enough. So they challenged Finitude, and touched the Boundary of Time, and reached through that, and enabled Mind to colonize and inhabit all the many universes of the Multiplicity. But, for the Watchers of the Optimal History, even *this* is not sufficient; and they are seeking ways of reaching beyond, to further Orders of Infinity . . .'

'And if they succeed? Will they rest?'

'There is no rest. No limit. No end to the *Beyond* – no Boundaries which Life, and Mind, cannot challenge, and breach.'

My hand tensed on the levers of my machine, and the whole, squat mass swayed like a branch in the wind. 'Nebogipfel, I –'

He held up his hand. '*Go*,' he said.

I drew a breath, gripped the starting lever with both hands, and went off with a thud.

BOOK SEVEN

Day 292,495,940

1

THE VALE OF THAMES

The hands of my chronometric dials whirled around. The sun became a streak of fire, then merged into a brilliant arch, with the moon a whirling, fluctuating band. Trees shivered through their seasons, almost too fast for me to follow. The sky assumed a wonderful deepness of blue, like a midsummer twilight, with the clouds rendered happily invisible.

The looming, translucent shape of my house soon fell away from me. The landscape grew vague, and once more the splendid architecture of the Age of Buildings washed over Richmond Hill like a tide. I saw nothing of the peculiarities which had characterized the construction of Nebogipfel's History: the stilling of the earth's rotation, the building of the Sphere about the sun, and so forth. Presently I watched that tide of deeper green flow up the hillside and remain there without the interruption of winter; and I knew I had reached that happier future age in which warmer climes have returned to Britain – it was once more like the Palaeocene, I thought with a stab of nostalgia.

I kept my eyes wide for any hint of the Watchers, but I could see nothing of them. The Watchers – those immense, unimaginable minds, outcroppings of the great reefs of intellect which inhabit the Optimal History – had done with me now, and my destiny was in my own hands. I felt a grim satisfaction at that, and – with the day-count on my dials passing Two Hundred and Fifty Thousand – I hauled carefully at the stopping-lever.

I caught a last glimpse of the moon as it spun through its phases, waning to darkness. I remembered that I had set off, with Weena, on that last jaunt to the Palace of Green Porcelain just before the time the little Eloi called the Dark Nights: that rayless obscurity during the dark of the moon, when the Morlocks emerged, and worked their will on the Eloi. How foolish I had been! I thought now; how impetuous, unthinking – how careless I had been of poor Weena – to have set off on such an expedition, at such a time of danger.

Well, I thought with a certain grimness, now I had returned; and I was determined to put right the mistakes of my past, or die in the attempt.

With a lurch, the machine dropped out of the grey tumult, and sunlight broke over me, heavy and warm and immediate. The chronometric dials rattled to a stop: it was Day 292,495,940 – the precise day, in the Year A.D. 802,701, on which I had lost Weena.

I sat on the familiar hill-side. The light of the sun was brilliant, and I had to shade my eyes. Because I had launched the machine from the garden at the rear of the house rather than the laboratory, I was perhaps twenty yards further down that little rhododendron lawn than when I had first arrived here. Behind me, a little higher up the Hill, I saw the familiar profile of the White Sphinx, with its inscrutable half-smile fixed forever. The bronze base remained thick with verdigris, although here and there I could see where the moulded inlays had been flattened by my futile attempts to break into the chamber within, and to retrieve the stolen Time Machine; and the grass was scarred and cut, showing where the Morlocks had dragged my machine off into the pedestal.

The stolen machine was in there now, I realized with a jolt. It was odd to think of that other machine sitting mere yards from me in the obscurity of that chamber, while I sat on this copy, perfect in every way, which glittered on the grass!

I detached and pocketed my control levers, and stepped onto the ground. From the angle of the sun, I judged it to be perhaps three in the afternoon, and the air was warm and moist.

To get a better view of things, I walked perhaps a half-mile to the south-east, to the brow of what had been Richmond Hill. In my day the Terrace had stood here, with its expensive frontage and wide views of the river and the country beyond to the west; now, a loose stand of trees had climbed over the Hill's crest – there was no sign of the Terrace, and I imagined that even the founds of the houses must have been obliterated by the action of tree-roots – but still, just as it had in 1891, the countryside fell away to the south and west, most attractively.

There was a bench set here, of that yellow metal I had seen before; it was corroded with a red rust, and its arm-rests were filed into the semblance of the creatures of some forgotten myth. A nettle, with large leaves tinted beautifully brown, had climbed over the chair, but I pulled this away – it was without stings – and I sat down, for I was already warm and perspiring.

The sun lay quite low in the sky, to the west, and its light glimmered from the scattered architecture and the bodies of water which punctuated the verdant landscape. The haze of heat lay everywhere on the land. Time, and the patient evolutions of geology, had metamorphosed this landscape from my day; but I could recognize several features, reshaped though they were, and there was still a dreamy beauty about the poet's 'matchless vale of Thames'. The silver ribbon of the river was some distance removed from me; as I have noted elsewhere, the Thames had cut through a bow in its course and now progressed direct from Hampton to Kew. And it had deepened its valley; thus Richmond was now set high on the side of a broad valley, perhaps a mile from the water. I thought I recognized what had been Glover's Island as a sort of wooded knoll in the centre of the old bed. Petersham Meadows retained much of its modern profile; but it was raised far above the level of the river now, and I imagined the area to be much less marshy than in my day.

The great buildings of this Age were dotted about, with their intricate parapets and tall columns, elegant and abandoned: they were spikes of architectural bone protruding from the hill-side's green-clad flank. Perhaps a mile from me I saw that large building, a mass of granite and aluminium, to which I had climbed on my first evening. Here and there huge figures, as beautiful and enigmatic as my Sphinx, lifted their heads from the general greenery, and everywhere I saw the cupolas and chimneys that were the signatures of the Morlocks. The huge flowers of this latter day were everywhere, with their gleaming white petals and shining leaves. Not for the first time, this landscape, with its extraordinary and beautiful blooms, its pagodas and cupolas nestling among the green, reminded me of the Royal Botanical Gardens at Kew in my day; but it was a Kew that had covered England, and had grown wild and neglected.

On the horizon there was a large building I had not noticed before. It was almost lost in the mists of the north-west, in the direction of modern Windsor; but it was too remote and faint for me to make out details. I promised myself that some day I should make the trek out to Windsor, for surely, if anything of my day had survived the evolution and neglect of the intervening millennia, it would be a relic of the massive Norman keep there.

I turned now and saw how the countryside fell away in the direction of modern Banstead, and I made out that pattern of copses and hills, with here and there the glint of water, which had become familiar to me during my earlier explorations. And it was in that direction – perhaps eighteen or twenty miles distant – that the Palace of Green Porcelain lay. Peering that way now I thought I could make out a hint of that structure's pinnacles; but my eyes were not what they were, and I was not sure.

I had hiked to that Palace, with Weena, in search of weapons and other provisions with which to take the fight to the Morlocks. Indeed, if I remembered correctly, I – my earlier self – must be rooting about within those polished green walls even now!

Perhaps ten miles away, a barrier interposed between myself and the Palace: a knot of dark forest. Even in the daylight it made a dark, sinister splash, at least a mile thick. Carrying Weena, I had made through that wood safely enough the first time, for we had waited for daylight to make the crossing; but the second time, on our return from the Palace (tonight!) I would let my impatience and fatigue get the better of me. Determined to return to the Sphinx as soon as possible, and to set to work retrieving my machine, I would push into that wood in the darkness – and fall asleep – and the Morlocks would descend on us, and take Weena.

I had been lucky to escape that folly with my life, I knew; and as for poor Weena . . .

But I put aside these feelings of shame, now, for I was here, I reminded myself, to make amends for all that.

It was early enough for me to reach that wood before the daylight faded. I was without weapons, of course, but my purpose here was not to fight the Morlocks – I had done with that – but simply to rescue Weena. And for that, I calculated, I should need no more powerful weapons than my intellect and my fists.

2

A WALK

The Time Machine itself looked very exposed, there on the hill-side with its brass and nickel glittering, and – although I had no intention to use it again – I decided to conceal it. There was a copse nearby, and I dragged the squat machine there and covered it with branches and leaves. This took me some effort – the machine was a bulky affair – and I was left perspiring, and the rails cut deep grooves in the turf where I had hauled it.

I rested for a few minutes, and then, with a will, I set off down the hill-side in the direction of Banstead.

I had travelled barely a hundred yards when I heard voices. For a moment I was startled, thinking – despite the daylight – that it might be Morlocks. But the voices were quite human, and speaking that peculiar, simple sing-song which is characteristic of the Eloi; and now a party, five or six, of those little people emerged from a copse onto a pathway leading up to my Sphinx. I was struck afresh at how slight and small they were – no larger than the children of my time, male and female alike – and clad in those simple purple tunics and sandals.

The similarities with my first arrival in this Age struck me immediately; for I had been chanced upon by a party of Eloi in just such a fashion. I remembered how they had approached me without fear – more with curiosity – and had laughed and spoken to me.

Now, though, they came up with circumspection: in fact, I thought they shied away. I opened my hands and smiled, intending to show that I meant no harm; but I knew well enough the cause of this changed perception: it was what they had seen already of the dangerous and erratic behaviour of my earlier self, especially during my unhinging after the theft of the Time Machine. These Eloi were entitled to their caution!

I did not press the case, and the Eloi went on around me, up the hill-side towards the rhododendron lawn; as soon as I was out of their sight their speech resumed in its bubbling rhythms.

I struck across the countryside towards the wood. Everywhere I saw those wells which led, I knew, to the subterranean world of the Morlocks – and from which emitted, if I drew close enough to hear, the implacable *thud-thud-thud* of their great machines. Sweat broke across my brow and chest – for the day remained hot, despite the dipping of the afternoon sun – and I felt my breath scratch in and out of my lungs.

With my immersion in this world, my emotions seemed to waken also. Weena, limited creature though she was, had shown me affection, the only creature in all this world of 802,701 to do so; and her loss had caused me the most intense wretchedness. But, when I had come to recount the tale to my companions by the familiar glow of my own fireside in 1891, that grief had been etiolated into a pale sketch of itself; Weena had become like the memory of a dream, quite unreal.

Well, now I was *here* once more, tramping across this familiar country, and all that primal grief came back to me – it was as if I had never left here – and it fuelled my every footstep.

As I walked on a great hunger fell on me. I realized that I could not remember the last time I had eaten – it must have been before Nebogipfel and I departed from the Age of White Earth – although, I speculated, it might be true to say that this body had *never* partaken of food, if it had been reconstructed by the Watchers as Nebogipfel had hinted! Well, whatever the philosophical niceties, my hunger was soon gnawing at my belly, and I began to feel a weariness from the heat. I came past an eating hall – a great, grey edifice of fretted stone – and I made a detour from my route.

I entered through a carved archway, with its decorations badly weather-worn and broken up. Within I found a single great chamber hung with brown, and the floor was set with blocks of that hard white metal I had observed before, worn into tracks by the soft feet of innumerable generations of Eloi. Slabs of polished stone formed tables, on which were heaped piles of fruit; and around the tables were gathered little clusters of Eloi, in their pretty tunics, eating and jabbering to each other like so many cage-birds.

I stood there in my dingy jungle twill – that relic of the Palaeocene was quite out of place in all that sunlit prettiness, and I mused that the Watchers might have outfitted me more elegantly! – and a group of the Eloi came to me and clustered around. I felt little hands on me, like soft tentacles, pulling at my shirt. Their faces had the small mouths, pointed chins and tiny ears characteristic of their race, but these seemed to be a different set of Eloi from those I had encountered near the Sphinx; and these little folk had no great memory, and therefore no fear, of me.

I had come here to rescue one of their kind, not to commit more of that graceless barbarism which had disfigured my previous visit; so I submitted to their inspection with good grace and open hands.

I made for the tables, followed everywhere by a

little gaggle of the Eloi. I found a cluster of hypertro-phied strawberries, and I crammed these into my mouth; and it was not long before I found several samples of that floury fruit in its three-sided husk which had proved my particular favourite before. I collected a haul I judged sufficient, found a darker, shaded corner, and settled down to eat, surrounded by a little wall of the curious Eloi.

I smiled at the Eloi, welcoming them, and tried to remember those scraps of their simple speech which I had learned before. As I spoke their little faces pressed around me, their eyes wide in the dark, their red lips parted like childrens'. I relaxed. I think it was the plainness of this encounter, the easy human-ity of it, which entranced me then; I had suffered too much inhuman strangeness recently! The Eloi were *not* human, I knew – in their way they were as alien to me as the Morlocks – but they were a good facsimile.

I seemed just to close my eyes.

I came to myself with a start. It had grown quite dark! There were fewer of the Eloi close to me, and their mild, unquestioning eyes seemed to shine at me in the gloom.

I got to my feet in a panic. Fruit husks and flowers fell from my person, where they had been arranged by the playful Eloi. I blundered across the main chamber. It was quite full of Eloi, now, and they slept in little clusters across the metal floor. I emerged at last through the doorway and into the daylight . . .

Or rather, what little there was left of the day! Peering about wildly, I saw how a last sliver of sun was barely visible – a mere fingernail of light, resting on the western horizon – and to the east, I saw a single bright planet – perhaps it was Venus.

I cried out and lifted my arms to the sky. After all my inner resolve that I should make amends for the impetuous foolishness of the past, here I had dozed through the afternoon, as indolent as you like!

I plunged back to the path I had followed and struck out for the wood. So much for my plans for arriving in the wood during daylight! As the twilight drew in around me, I caught glimpses of grey-white ghosts, barely visible at the edge of my vision. I whirled about at each such apparition, but they fled, staying beyond my reach.

The shapes were Morlocks, of course – the cunning, brutal Morlocks of this History – and they were tracking me with all the silent hunting skills they could command. My earlier resolve that I should not need a weapon for this expedition now began to seem a little foolish, and I told myself that as soon as I reached the wood I should find a fallen branch or some such, to serve me in the office of a club.

3

IN THE DARKNESS

I tripped on the unevenness of the ground several times, and would have twisted my ankles, I think, if it were not for the stiffness of my soldier's boots.

By the time I came upon the wood, it was full night.

I surveyed that expanse of dank, black forest. The futility of my quest came to me. I remembered how it had seemed to me that a great host of Morlocks had been gathered about me: how was I to find that malevolent handful which would bear away Weena?

I considered plunging into the forest – I remembered, roughly, the way I had gone the first time – and I might come upon my earlier self, with Weena. But the folly of that procedure struck me immediately. For one thing, I had got turned about in my struggles with the Morlocks, and had finished up stumbling about the forest more or less at random. And besides, I had no protection: in the dark enclosure of the forest I should be quite vulnerable. No doubt I should make a satisfying mess of some of them, before they brought me down – but bring me down they surely would; and in any event such a battle was not my intention.

So I retreated, through a quarter-mile or so, until I came upon a hillock which overlooked the wood.

The full darkness gathered about me, and the stars emerged in their glory. As I had done once before, I distracted myself by seeking out signs of the old constellations, but the gradual proper motion of the stars had quite distorted the familiar picture. Still, though, that planet I had noticed earlier shone down on me, as steady as a true companion.

The last time I had studied this altered sky, I remembered, I had had Weena at my side, wrapped up in my jacket for warmth, as we had rested the night while making for the Palace of Green Porcelain. I recalled my feelings then: I had reflected on the littleness of earthly life, compared to the millennial migrations of the stars, and I had been taken, briefly, by an elegiac remoteness – by a view of the grandeur of time, above the level of my earthly troubles.

But now, it seemed to me, I was done with all that. I had had enough of perspective, of Infinities and Eternities; I felt impatient and taut. I was, and always had been, no more than a man, and now I was fully immersed once more in the gritty concerns of Humanity, and only my own projects filled my consciousness.

I dropped my eyes from the remote, unfathomable stars, and down to the woods before me. And now, even as I watched, a gentle, roseate glow began to spread across the south-western horizon. I got to my feet, and did a sort of dance step, such was my sudden elation. Here was confirmation that, after all my adventures, I had finished up on the right day, of all the possible days, here in this remote century! For that glow was a fire in the forest – a fire started, with careless abandon, by *myself*.

I struggled to remember what had come next on that fateful night – the precise sequence . . .

The fire I had started had been a quite new and wonderful thing to Weena, and she had wanted to play with its red sheets and flickers; I had been forced to restrain her from

throwing herself into that liquid light. Then I picked her up
– she had struggled – and I had plunged on into that wood,
with the light of my fire illuminating my path.

Soon we had left the glow of those flames, and were
proceeding in blackness, broken only by patches of deep blue
sky beyond the trees' stems. It had not been long, in all that
oily darkness, before I had heard the pattering of narrow
feet, the soft cooing of voices, all around me; I remembered a
tug of my coat, and then at my sleeve.

I had put Weena down so that I could find my matches,
and there was a struggle about my knees, as those Morlocks,
like persistent insects, had fallen on her poor body. I got a
match lit – when its head flared I had seen a row of white
Morlock faces, illuminated as if by a flash lamp, all turned
up towards me with their red-grey eyes – and then, in a
second, they had fled.

I had determined to build a new fire and wait for the
morning. I had lit camphor and cast it on the ground. I
had dragged down dry branches from the trees above, and
built a choking fire of green wood . . .

I raised myself, now, onto the tips of my toes, and
cast about over the forest. You must imagine me in
all that inky darkness, under a sky without a moon,
and the only illumination coming from that spreading fire on the far side of the forest.

There – I had it! – a thread of smoke that curled up
into the air, forming a sort of narrow silhouette
against the greater blaze behind it. That must be the
site at which I had decided to make my stand. It was
some distance from me – perhaps two miles to the
east, and in the depths of the wood – and, without
allowing myself further contemplation, I plunged
into the forest.

For some distance I heard nothing but the cracking of twigs under my feet, and a remote, slumberous
roar that must have been the voice of the greater
fire. The darkness was broken only by the remote

glow of the fire, and by patches of deep blue sky over-head; and I could see the boles and roots about me only by silhouette, and I stumbled several times. Then I heard a pattering around me, as soft as rainfall, and I caught that queer, gurgling sound that is the voice of the Morlock. I felt a tug at my shirt-sleeve, a soft pull at my belt, fingers at my neck.

I swung my arms about. I connected with flesh and bone, and my assailants fell back; but I knew my reprieve should not be for long. And, sure enough, within a few seconds that pattering closed up around me again, and I was forced to push on through a sort of hail of touches, of cold pawing and bold, sharp nips, of huge red eyes all around me.

It was a return to my deepest nightmare, to that horrible dark I have dreaded all my life! – But I persisted, and they did not attack me – not outright, at any rate. Already I detected a certain agitation about them – the Morlocks ran about with increasing rapidity – as the glow of that remote blaze grew brighter.

And then, of a sudden, there was a new scent on the air: it was faint, nearly overpowered by the smoke . . .

It was camphor vapour.

I could be only yards from the place the Morlocks had fallen on me and Weena as we slept – the place where I had fought, and Weena had been lost!

I came upon a great host of Morlocks – a density of them, just visible through the next line of trees. They swarmed over each other like maggots, eager to join the fray or the feast, in a mass such as I did not remember seeing before. I saw a man struggling to rise in their midst. He was obscured by a great weight of Morlocks, and they caught at his neck, hair and arms, and down he went. But then I saw an arm emerge from the mêlée holding an iron bar – it had

611

been torn from a machine in the Palace of Green Porcelain, I remembered – and he laid about the Morlocks with a vigour. They fell away from him, briefly, and soon he had backed himself up against a tree. His hair stuck out from all around his broad scalp, and he wore, on his feet, only torn and blood-stained socks. The Morlocks, frenetic, came at him again, and he swung his iron bar, and I heard the soft, pulpy crushing of Morlock faces.

For a moment I thought of falling in with him; but I knew it was unnecessary. He would survive, to stumble out of this forest – alone, grieving for Weena – and recover his Time Machine from the plotting of the wily Morlocks. I remained in the shadows of the trees, and I am convinced he did not see me . . .

But Weena was already gone from here, I realized: by this point in the conflict, I had already lost her to the Morlocks!

I whirled about in desperation. Again I had allowed my concentration to lapse. Had I already failed? – had I lost her again?

By this time the panic among the Morlocks at the fire had taken a strong hold, and they fled in a stream away from the blaze, their hunched, hairy backs stained red. Then I saw a leash of Morlocks, four of them, stumbling through the trees, away from the direction of the fire. They were carrying something, I saw now: something still, pale, limp, with a hint of white and gold . . .

I roared, and I crashed forward through the undergrowth. The Morlocks' four heads snapped about until their huge, red-grey eyes were fixed on me; and then, my fists raised, I fell on them.

It was not much of a fight. The Morlocks dropped their precious bundle; they faced me, but they were distracted all the time by the growing glow behind them. One little brute got his teeth locked into my wrist, but I pounded at his face, feeling the grinding of bone, and in a few seconds he released me; and the four of them fled.

I bent and scooped up Weena from the ground – the poor mite was as light as a doll – and my heart could have broken at her condition. Her dress was torn and stained, her face and golden hair were smudged with soot and smoke, and I thought she had suffered a burn down one side of her cheek. I noticed, too, the small, pinprick imprints of Morlock teeth in the soft flesh of her neck and upper arms.

She was quite insensible, and I could not tell if she was breathing; I thought she might already be dead.

With Weena cradled in my arms, I ran through the forest.

In the smoky darkness, my vision was obscured; there was the fire which provided a yellow and red glow, but it turned the forest into a place of shadows, shifting and deceiving of the eye. Several times I blundered into trees, or tripped over some hummock; and I am afraid poor Weena got quite thrown about in the course of it.

We were in the midst of a stream of Morlocks, all fleeing the blaze with as much vigour as myself. Their hairy backs shone red in the flames, and their eyes were discs of palpable pain. They stumbled about the forest, clattering into trees and striking at each other with little fists; or else they crawled across the floor, moaning, seeking some illusory relief from the heat and light. When they collided with me, I punched and kicked at them to keep them off; but it was clear enough that, blinded as they were, they could offer me no threat, and after a time I found it was sufficient simply to push them away.

Now that I had grown used to the quiet dignity of

Nebogipfel, the bestial nature of these primal Morlocks, with their slack jaws, filthy and tangled hair, and hunched posture – some of them ran with their hands trailing on the ground – was distressing in the extreme.

We came on the edge of the forest abruptly. I stumbled out of the last line of trees, and found myself staggering across a meadow.

I hauled in great breaths of air, and turned to look back at the blazing wood. Smoke billowed up, forming a column which reached over the sky, obscuring the stars; and I saw, from the heart of the forest, huge flames – hundreds of feet tall – which stretched up like buildings. Morlocks continued to flee from the blaze, but in decreasing numbers; and those which emerged from the wood were dishevelled and wounded.

I turned, and walked on through long, wiry grass. At first the heat was strong on my back; but after perhaps a mile it had diminished, and the fire's crimson glare faded to a mere glow. We saw no more Morlocks after that.

I crossed over a hill, and in the valley beyond I came to a place I had visited before. There were acacias here, and a number of sleeping-houses, and a statue – incomplete and broken – which had reminded me of a Faun. I walked down the slope of this valley, and, cradled in its crook, I found a little river I remembered. Its surface, turbulent and broken, reflected the star-light. I settled beside the bank and laid Weena carefully on the ground. The water was cold and fast-running. I tore a strip off my shirt and dabbed it in the water; with this I bathed Weena's poor face, and trickled a little of the water into her mouth.

Thus, with Weena's head cradled in my lap, I sat out the rest of that Dark Night.

*

In the morning I saw him emerge from the burnt forest in a pitiable state. His face was ghastly pale, and he had half-healed cuts on his face, a coat that was dusty and dirty, and a limp worse than a footsore tramp's with only scorched grass bound up around his bloody feet. I felt a twinge of compassion – or perhaps of embarrassment – to see his wretchedness: had this really been *me*, I wondered? – had I presented such a spectacle to my friends, on my return, after that first adventure?

Again I had an impulse to offer help; but I knew that no assistance was necessary. My earlier self would sleep off his exhaustion through the brightness of the day, and then, as evening approached, he would return to the White Sphinx to retrieve his Time Machine.

Finally – after one last struggle against the Morlocks – he would be gone, in a whirl of attenuation.

So I stayed with Weena by the river, and nursed her while the sun climbed in the sky, and prayed that she might awaken.

Epilogue

My early days were the hardest, for I arrived here quite bereft of tools.

At first I was forced to live with the Eloi. I partook of the fruit brought to them by the Morlocks, and I shared the elaborate ruins they used as sleeping-halls.

When the moon waned, and the next sequence of Dark Nights came, I was struck by the boldness with which the Morlocks emerged from their caverns and assailed their human cattle! I set myself at the gate of a sleeping-house, with bits of iron and stone to serve as weapons, and in this way I was able to resist; but I could not keep them all out – the Morlocks swarm like vermin, rather than fight in the organized fashion of humans – and besides, I could defend only one sleeping-hall among hundreds dotted about the Thames Valley.

Those black hours, of fear and unparalleled misery for the defenceless Eloi, are as bleak as anything in my experience. And yet, with the coming of the day, that darkness was already banished from the little minds of the Eloi, and they were prepared to play and laugh as readily as if the Morlocks did not exist.

I was determined to make a change to this arrangement: for that – with the rescue of Weena – had, after all, been my intention in returning here.

I have further explored the countryside hereabouts. I must have made a fine sight as I tramped the hills, with my wild and spectacular beard, my sun-burnt scalp, and with my bulky frame draped in gaudy Eloi cloth! There is no transport, of course, and no beasts of burden to carry me, and only the remnants of my 1944 boots to protect my feet. But I have reached as far as Hounslow and Staines to the west, Barnet in the north, Epsom and Leatherhead to the south; and to the east, I have followed the Thames's new course as far as Woolwich.

Everywhere I have found a uniform picture: the verdant landscape with its scattering of ruins, the halls and houses of the Eloi – and, everywhere, the grisly punctuation of the Morlock shafts. It may be that in France or Scotland the picture is very different! – but I do not believe it. The whole of this country, and beyond, is infested by the Morlocks and their subterranean warrens.

So I have been forced to abandon my first, tentative plan, which was to take a party of the Eloi out of the reach of the Morlocks: for now I know that the Eloi cannot escape the Morlock – and nor *vice versa*, for the dependency of Morlock on Eloi, while less repellant to my mind, is just as degrading to the spirit of those nocturnal sub-men.

I have begun, quietly, to seek other ways to live.

I determined to take up a permanent residence in the Palace of Green Porcelain. This had been one of my plans in my previous visit here, for, although I had seen evidence of Morlock activity there, that ancient museum with its large halls and robust construction had commended itself to me as defensible a fastness as I had found against the cunning and climbing dexterity of the Morlocks, and I retained hopes that many of the artefacts and relics stored here might yet serve my purposes in the future. And besides, something about that derelict monument to the intellect, with its abandoned fossils and crumbled libraries, had caught at my imagination! It was like a great ship from the past, its keel broken on the reef of time; and I was a castaway of like origin, a Crusoe from out of antiquity.

I repeated and extended my exploration of the cavernous halls and chambers of the Palace. I settled, for my base, on that Hall of Mineralogy which I found on my first visit, with its well-preserved but useless samples of a wider array of minerals than I could name. This chamber is rather smaller than some of the others, and so more easily secured; and, when I had swept it of dust and built a fire, it came to seem almost homelike to me. Since then, by shoring up the broken valves of doors and fixing breaches in the ancient walls, I have extended my fastness into some adjoining halls. While investigating the Gallery of Palaeontology, with its huge and useless brontosaurus bones, I came across a collection of bones tumbled about and scattered on the floor, evidently by the playful Eloi, of which at first I could make no sense; but when I roughly assembled the skeletons, I thought that they were of a horse, a dog, an ox, and, I think, of a fox – in short, they were the last relics of the ordinary animals of my own, vanished England. But the bones were too scattered and broken, and my anatomical understanding too imprecise, for me to be sure of my identification.

I have also returned to that ill-lit and sloping gallery which contains the hulking corpses of great machines, for this has served me as a mine for improvised tools of all descriptions – and not just weapons, as was my first use of it. I spent some time on one machine which had the appearance of an electrical dynamo, for its condition was not too ruinous to look at, and I entertained fantasies of starting it up, and lighting such of the broken globes which hang from that chamber's ceiling as would take a current. I calculated that that blaze of electric light, and the noise of the dynamo, would send the Morlocks fleeing as nothing else! – but I have nothing in the way of fuel or lubricants, and besides the small parts of the hulk are seized up and corroded, and I have perforce abandoned that project.

In the course of my exploration of the Palace I came across a new exhibit which caught my fancy. This was close to the gallery with the model tin mine I had observed before, and it appeared to be a model of a city. This exhibit was finely detailed and so large it filled most of a chamber by itself, and the whole thing was protected by a sort of pyramid of glass, from which I had to wipe away centuries of dust to see. This city was evidently constructed far in my own future, but even the model was so ancient here in this sunset Age that its bright colours had faded at the dust-filtered touch of sunlight. I imagined this town might be a descendant of London, for I thought I saw the characteristic morphology of the Thames represented by a ribbon of glass which snaked through the exhibit's heart. But it was a London greatly transformed from the city of my day. It was dominated by seven or eight huge glass palaces – if you think of the Crystal Palace, vastly extended and several times twinned, you will have something of the effect – and these palaces had been joined over by a sort of skin of glass which carapaced the whole of the city. There was nothing of the sombreness of the London Dome of 1938, for this immense roof served to catch and amplify the sunlight, it seemed to me, and there were ribbons of electric lamps set about the city – though none of their pinpoint bulbs still functioned in my model. There was a forest of immense wind-mills set up over this roof – though the vanes no longer turned – and great platforms were set here and there about the roof, over which hovered toy versions of flying machines. These machines had something of the look of great dragon-flies, with huge tiers of sails hovering over them, and gondolas with rows of toy people sitting in them beneath.

Yes – *people!* – women and men, not unlike myself. For this city evidently came from a time not so impossibly removed from my own, that the blunt hand of evolution had not yet remade mankind.

Great roads looped off over the countryside, joining this future London to other cities about the country – or so I surmised. These roads were populated by vast mechanisms: monocycles which each bore a score of men, huge produce carts which seemed to have no driver and must therefore be directed mechanically; and so forth. There were no details to represent the countryside between the roads, however, just a bland, grey surface.

The whole design was so huge – it was like one enormous building – that I imagine it could have housed twenty or thirty millions, as opposed to the meagre four millions of the London of my day. Much of the model had its walls and floors cut away, and I was able to see little toy figures representing the populace, set about the many dozens of levels of the city. In the upper levels these inhabitants were dressed in variegated and gaudy designs, with capes of scarlet, hats as spectacular and impractical as a cock's comb, and so forth. Those upper layers seemed to me a place of great comfort and leisure, being a sort of multiply-levelled mosaic of shops, parks, libraries, sumptuous homes, and the like.

But at the base of the city – in its ground floor and basement, so to speak – things were rather different. There, great machines slouched, and ducts, pipes and cables ten or twenty feet across (in the full scale) snaked across the ceilings. Dolls were set here, but they were dressed uniformly in a sort of pale blue canvas, and their personal arrangements were restricted to great communal eating and sleeping halls; and it seemed to me that these lower workers must scarcely get a glimpse, in the general order of things, of the light which bathed the lives of the upper folk.

This model was aged and far from perfect – in one corner the pyramid-case had collapsed, and the model there had been smashed up out of recognition, and elsewhere the little dolls and machines had been tumbled over or broken by small disturbances down the ages; and in one place the blue-suited dolls had been set up in little circles and patterns, as if by the playful fingers of the Eloi – but still, the toy city has been a source of continuing fascination to me, for its people and gadgets are close enough to my sort to be intriguing, and I have spent long hours picking out new details about its construction.

It seems to me that this vision of the future might represent a sort of intermediate step in the development of the grisly order of things in which I have found myself. Here was a point in time at which the separation of mankind into Upper and Lower remained largely a social artefact, and had not yet begun to influence the evolution of the species itself. The city was a beautiful and magnificent structure, but – if it led to this world of Morlock and Eloi – it was a monument to the most colossal folly on the part of Humanity!

The Palace of Green Porcelain is set on a high, turfy down, but there are meadows nearby which are well-watered. I dismantled my Time Machine, and scoured the Palace for materials, and from these I devised simple hoes and rakes. I broke the soil in the meadows about my Palace, and planted seeds from the Morlock fruit.

I persuaded some of the Eloi to join me in this enterprise. At first they were willing enough – they thought it was some new game – but they lost enthusiasm when I had them keep at their repetitive tasks for long hours; and I had some qualms when I saw their delicate robes stained with soil, and those pretty oval faces running with tears of frustration. But I kept at it, and, when things got too monotonous, I jollied them along with games and dances, and clumsy renditions of 'The Land of the Leal', and what I could remember of the 'swing' music of 1944 – that is particularly popular with them – and gradually they have come about.

Growing cycles are not predictable, here in this Age which lacks seasons, and I had to wait no more than a few months before the first canes and plants bore fruit. When I presented these to the Eloi, my delight evoked only puzzlement in their little faces, for my poor first efforts could not compete for flavour and richness with the provisions of the Morlocks – but *I* could see the significance of these foodstuffs beyond their size and flavour: for with these first crops, I had begun the slow disentanglement of Eloi from Morlock.

I have found enough of the Eloi with an aptitude for the work to establish a number of little farms, up and down the valley of the Thames. So now, for the first time in uncounted millennia, there are groups of Eloi who can subsist quite independent of the Morlocks.

Sometimes I am wearied, and I feel what I am doing is less teaching than modifying the instinct of intelligent animals; but at least it is a start. And I am working with the more receptive of the Eloi to extend their vocabulary, to enrich their curiosity – you see, I mean to reawaken Minds!

*

But I know that to provoke and excite the Eloi in this way is not sufficient; for the Eloi are not alone, in this latter earth. And if my reforms among the Eloi continue, the equilibrium, however unhealthy, between Eloi and Morlock will be lost. And the Morlocks must inevitably react.

A new war between these post-human species would be disastrous, it seems to me, for I could not imagine that my precarious agricultural initiatives would survive much diligent assault by the Morlocks. And I must push out of my mind any antiquated notions of loyalty, to one side or the other! As a man of my time, my sympathies lie naturally with the Eloi, for they *appear* the more human, and my work with them has been pleasurable and productive. In fact it is an effort for me to remember these little folk are *not* human – I think if I saw a man of my own century now, I should be astonished by his height, bulk and clumsiness!

But neither Eloi nor Morlock are human – they are both *post*-human – regardless of my antique prejudices. And I cannot solve the equation of this degenerate History without addressing both its sides:

That is, I must face the Darkness.

I have determined to descend once more into the Morlocks' subterranean complex. I must find ways to negotiate with that subterranean race – to work with them, as I have the Eloi. I have no reason to believe this is impossible. I know that the Morlocks have a certain intelligence: I have seen their great underground machines, and I recall that, when it was in their captivity, they disassembled, cleaned and even *oiled* the Time Machine! It may be that beneath their surface ugliness the Morlocks have an instinct which is closer to the engineering enterprise of my own day than that of the passive, cattle-like Eloi.

I know well – Nebogipfel taught me! – that much

of my dread of the Morlocks is instinctive, and proceeds from a complex of experiences, nightmares and fears within my own soul, irrelevant to this place. I have had that dread of darkness and subterranean places since I was a boy; there is that fear of the body and its corruption which Nebogipfel diagnosed – a dread which I may share, I think, with many of my time – and, besides, I am honest enough to recognize that I am a man of my class, and as such have had little to do with the labouring folk of my own time, and in my ignorance I have developed, I fear, a certain disregard and fear. And all of these fragments of nightmare are amplified, a hundredfold, in my reactions to the Morlocks! – But such coarseness of soul is not worthy of me, or my people, or the memory of Nebogipfel. I am determined that I should put aside such inner dark, and think of these Morlocks not as monsters, but as potential Nebogipfels.

This is a rich world, and there is no need for the remnants of humanity to feed off each other in the ghastly fashion they have evolved. The light of intellect has dimmed, in this History: but it is not extinguished. The Eloi retain their fragments of human language, and the Morlocks their evident mechanical understanding.

I dream that, before I die, I might build a new fire of rationality out of these coals.

Yes! – it is a noble dream – and a fine legacy for me.

I found these scraps of paper when exploring a vault, deep under the Palace of Green Porcelain. The pages had been preserved by their storage in a tight package, from which the air had been excluded. It has not been difficult for me to improvise a nib of bits of metal, and an ink of vegetable dyes; and to do my writing, I have returned to my favoured seat of yellow metal set at the brow of Richmond Hill, not a half-mile from the site of my old home; and, as I write, I have the vale of Thames for company: that lovely land whose evolution I have watched across geological ages.

I have done with time travelling – I have long accepted that – indeed, as I have noted, I have broken up my machine, and pieces of it have served me as hoes, and other gadgets more useful than a Time Machine. (I have kept my two white control levers – they are beside me now, on the seat, as I write.) However, while I have been content enough with my projects here, my lack of opportunity to transmit to my contemporaries my discoveries and observations, and any account of my continuing adventures, has been an irritant for me. Perhaps it is just my vanity! But now, these pages have given me a chance to put that right.

To preserve these fragile pages from decay, I have chosen to seal them up in their original packet, and then I will place the whole within a container I have constructed from the Plattnerite-doped quartz of my Time Machine. I will then bury the container as deeply as I can.

I have no sure way of transmitting my account either to future or past – still less to any other History – and these words may moulder in the ground. But it seems to me that the cladding of Plattnerite will give my parcel its best chance of detection, by any new Traveller from across the Multiplicity; and it may be that, by some chance current of the Time Streams, my words may even find their way back to my own century.

At any rate, it is the best I can do! – and, now that I have set myself on this course, I have reached a certain contentment.

I will complete and seal up this account before my

departure into the Underworld, for I recognize that my Morlock expedition is not without peril – a trip from which I may not return. But it is an assignment I cannot forestall for much longer; I am already past my fiftieth year of age, and soon I should not be able to face all that climbing in the wells!

I will commit myself, here, to attaching as an Appendix to this monograph, on my return, a summary of my subterranean adventures.

It is later. I am prepared for my descent.

How does the poet say it? – 'If the doors of perception were cleansed, everything would appear to man as it is, infinite' – something on those lines, at any rate: you will forgive any misquote, for I have no references here. . . I have seen the Infinite, and the Eternal. I have never lost the vision of those neighbouring universes lying all about this sunlit landscape, closer than the leaves of a book; and nor have I forgotten the star-shine of the Optimal History, which I think will live in my soul forever.

But none of these grand visions count for half as much, for me, as those fleeting moments of tenderness which have illuminated the darkness of my solitary life. I have enjoyed the loyalty and patience of Nebogipfel, the friendship of Moses, and the human warmth of Hilary Bond; and none of my achievements or adventures – no visions of time, no infinite star-scapes – will live in my heart as long as the moment, on that first, bright morning after my return here, when I sat by the river and bathed Weena's diamond face, and her chest at last lifted and she coughed, and her pretty eyes fluttered open for the first time, and I saw that she was alive; and, as she recognized me, her lips parted in a smile of gladness.

**EDITOR'S NOTE: Here the account ends;
no further Appendix was found.**

Flux
Stephen Baxter

'A major new talent'
ARTHUR C. CLARKE

'Arthur C. Clarke, Isaac Asimov and Robert Heinlein succeeded in doing it, but very few others. Now Stephen Baxter joins their exclusive ranks – writing science fiction in which the science is right and the extrapolations a sheer pleasure to read, admire, enjoy. The reaction is that which C.S. Lewis referred to when he described science fiction as the only genuine consciousness-expanding drug. *Flux* is a highly imaginative and moving novel . . . It is a rare thing to find such a good read. Wonderful stuff!'

HARRY HARRISON, *New Scientist*

It should be impossible for human beings to live within the mantle of a star . . . but they do. The biology of these microscopic Star humans is bizarre, but their hopes and fears, and loves, are not. And the future of humans everywhere, on Earth and among the stars, depends on their courage in the face of attack by the mighty Xeelee, owners of the Universe . . .

'Stephen Baxter can work out superhard-sf environments with the best of them . . . he has a stunning talent'   *Locus*

'Baxter is destined to be one of the genre leaders for the Nineties'   *Starburst*

ISBN 0 00 647620 1